My Lost Sister

ALSO BY ELEONOR SAMUEL

The Nanny
The Cornish Diary
My Lost Sister

MY LOST
SISTER

ELEONOR SAMUEL

Joffe Books, London
www.joffebooks.com

First published in Great Britain in 2024

Cover art by Nick Castle

ISBN: 978-1-83526-752-3

For Mum,
who gave me the power of books and the love of stories.

And with special mention to Halyna and Natalia,
the bravest mothers I know.

PROLOGUE

Someone is screaming.

Screaming and screaming. Over and over again. I want to tell them to stop, because someone will hear, someone will come. I clamp my hands over my ears. She isn't making a sound, even though she's still awake — her eyes are open; the black circles in the middle are so wide that you can hardly see the green.

She's white. Sweating.

I did it.

I don't know what was supposed to happen. Not this. I didn't think she'd be awake, looking at me. Watching me scream — it's me, *I'm* screaming — a strange high sound that I didn't know I could make.

I did it.

I open my mouth again, and what I mean to say is, I hate you. *I hate you.* But I can't.

"I love you," I say instead.

She doesn't seem to hear.

"I love you," I say again, louder, the rage rising in my chest. "I love you, I love you, I love you and I hope you die. I hope you die!"

She's blinking fast. I go in. I walk past her and I take it. I take it from beside her, and I hold it against my chest. For a second she looks at me. Then I run, and I don't look back. The door bangs. I can hear feet on the stairs. Someone shouting. *Someone coming.*

I turn on the taps.

It won't wash away. It's sticky. Stained. My fingers aren't working. The water's too cold.

It slips from my hand. Hits the floor. A dull crack. The water has run up my arms; my sleeves are wet.

I crouch down to pick it up and the edge slices into my finger, making beads of blood jump out in a line and blur into the water.

I did it.

The tap's still running. I turn it off.

And then I lock the door.

CHAPTER 1

Rosalie

If I was du Maurier, I would tell you that last night I dreamt I went to Hailbury again. That it seemed to me I stood by the iron gate leading to the drive. But I don't have du Maurier's flair. Certainly not her artistry. And the simple truth is, I don't remember Hailbury. Despite all assurances, I'm not qualified to write its story, to annotate the chapters of its disaster. If I were to describe the rusted spokes of the gate, or the beeches or the shrubs, it would be like painting from someone else's photograph. To me, Hailbury is a name printed twenty years ago in the tabloids, little more.

My name was never one that went with it. When my parents bought it, it caused quite an uproar. Lara Lee Knight in the Lincolnshire Wolds? It didn't seem to occur to anyone that Louise Knight had lived the first decade of her life, before the stage name, just down the road. Twenty years ago, the village of Shellingsby St Mary had only just come to terms with its *OK!* magazine celebrity status when it found itself heading up the *BBC News at Ten*, Leonie's fourteen-year-old smile radiating out of every screen across the country.

I clamber back over the barbed wire, fighting my way through the hedge towards the road. The legs of my jeans are flecked wet from the undergrowth; it's a cold, steel-skied March day, without much reassurance that spring is around the corner. In Crouch End, the daffodils were blooming. They aren't here.

Most people I meet have no idea that Leonie Knight-Langton had a sister. Yet here I am, the poor substitute I always have been, regretting the coffee I bought at Watford Gap and scrambling into a lay-by at the side of the A16 in the absence of any further motorway services.

It was the run-up to the twenty-year anniversary that set everything in motion. My mother agreed to an interview, which led, naturally, to a biography. When they approached me to write it for her, I was surprised, on reflection, that no one had already done so. But who better to study Lara, and her life without Leonie, than me? Rosalie Knight-Langton: novelist, columnist, the un-parented child who grew up in the shadows of Hailbury and whatever secrets it has never given up. There still seems to me a certain irony in the fact that now it is my name that appears weekly in the newspaper. The reality that it goes unnoticed by the majority of the British population seems particularly fitting.

I disentangle myself from the brambles and get back into the car. I'd like to be nostalgic. To reminisce, as the roads get narrower, about childhood days in the long grass, or daytrips to the seaside. Unfortunately, I don't remember the scenery, either. And if there ever were daytrips, which I suppose there must have been, then nothing left an impression.

I've never talked about what I remember from before that day. The day that Leonie disappeared. Not with anyone. But that's going to have to change. Because to write about life without Leonie, I'm going to need to exhume life *with* Leonie. And so I'm going back to Hailbury.

I try to keep note as the miles tick down, to record the landmarks. The market town of Armsby is Shellingsby's nearest neighbour; I scrutinise buildings that ought to be familiar: a children's nursery in Fenland brick, ivy-covered townhouses, quaint shops and tearooms, the Queen Victoria grammar school. A manor house, covered with the skeletal fronds of last year's Virginia creeper — and it's this that strikes a chord: an out-of-tune and jangling note of recollection. I remember the red leaves on the gravel, like fluttering blood. Someone packing a car, the slam of doors. Winding the tough, woody stems around my fingers with Jessica poking out from the top of my bag. Jessica. She was the only toy that went with me, the day we drove away and left the house behind.

The town gives way to trees and hedgerows, undulating fields punctuated by bungalows and farms. It's a land of extremes; affluent country houses and rural poverty. A tiny petrol station is selling fuel at ten pence a litre more than the going rate. Shellingsby is eight miles from the coast. It's a village that values its reputation — not that being Lincolnshire's best-kept for three years running is ever going to blot out the mark that Leonie left on the map. The upper-middle-class centre houses a slightly different demographic to the edges. There was an influx of Eastern European immigrants around twenty-five years ago, drawn by the crop-picking, most of whom have moved on whilst a few have stayed, eking out a living from the inhospitable Brexit-voting local landscape like flowers clinging to a rockface.

My pulse quickens. I retraced this last part on Google Maps a dozen times. More bungalows, gaining in density, until the vista morphs into quaint red-brick cottages and then sizeable period houses. There are three roads in and out of Shellingsby St Mary. One has a huge floodlit riding arena, crisply new against the otherwise aged rural idyll. One nestles a tiny church in the crook of its ascent. And the last bears Hailbury House, or at least the opening of its drive. As per du Maurier, there are iron gates. Not rusty, though, it turns out.

I tap in the code and the gates open themselves. Beyond them is the nightmare world of dark and oversized shrubs that du Maurier described in *Rebecca*. Except, well hidden behind the monstrous plants and leafless trees, there is also razor wire along the walls, which is more than a little unsettling. The gravel, though, is clear and well maintained, pale Cotswold stone that is out of place in the rain and drear. A good half mile and the driveway widens to a sweeping circle with a fountain in a squared-off bed at its centre. It's easy to see that nothing but rainwater has cascaded over the sculpted limestone for years. But the bed is well tended, set with little clumps of snowdrops and other bulbs that are yet to bear more than determined sharp green tips.

I feel oddly reassured by them, these little spikes of life, as I turn off the engine and get out, leaving the key in the ignition.

Hailbury is built of red brick; two storeys plus modest attic windows above, peeping out nervously between the crenulations. There are four semi-circular steps to the front door and a heavy limestone-pillared porch. The Farrow & Ball on the door is fresh and crisp, the sash windows mirror-clean, their blinds half-lowered. I pause, more unnerved by the fact that it doesn't look abandoned and derelict than I am by the idea of being here at all.

There are birds singing. The wind is rushing through the branches of the trees. The place is alive, not dead and desolate as it has been in all my dreams. The steps are swept clean of leaves; I'm a little too afraid to set foot on them, so I open the car boot instead, and wrestle the smaller of my suitcases over the tailgate.

The clatter of the case wheels on the gravel bolsters me. I have to bump it up the steps, not quite strong enough to lift it in one go. I pause at the top and listen to the birdsong and the mundane sounds of a normal, rural day: the distant chunter of a tractor, the whinny of a horse.

I slide the key from my back pocket. A singular key. My father dropped it off three days ago. It was the first time he'd been to my flat in a year. We had an awkward coffee at the drop-leaf table, where he tried to persuade me for the hundredth time that I shouldn't travel to Hailbury, and I somehow managed to not tell him about Hamish, even though it was blatantly obvious that no one else had lived there for a long time. He didn't ask, I didn't lie. I also didn't mention that I've sublet for the next six months.

A key. I wonder whose it used to be. My mother's? My father's? The nanny's? Was there a nanny, back then? I presume there must have been. There's no name or face in my mind. I try to conjure one, but draw a blank.

I push the key into the lock. It rattles and I have to jiggle it into place. Even when it fits, it won't turn. I strain at it until my index finger blanches from the effort, wary of trying too hard and snapping it. Four hours of driving and I can't get in?

I jerk it free and try again. I can feel it catch, but it won't give. A door that doesn't want to be opened. I think about my therapist. The visualisation exercises. So many closed doors. I grit my teeth.

Minutes seem to pass, until I'm pretty sure it's on the verge of shearing off in the lock.

"Fuck you," I hiss. For all I know, it could even be the wrong key. I feel for my phone.

"Do you need help?"

I leap away from the door as if I've been caught trespassing. There's someone approaching across the gravel; he's got wood-stain on his trousers, and his sleeves are rolled above his elbows. Someone from the property management company? I know my father has been paying for years to make sure the shrubs are tamed and the doors are painted.

"Here." He reaches past me, pulls the door hard against its frame and turns the key. It clunks heavily in the lock, and admits him, instantly, to the expectant silence within. There's a second's pause, then the ominous countdown beep of an alarm. He punches in a code and turns back.

Perhaps it's because he surprised me, but I find myself glaring at him. His eyes are a serious grey, his face less furrowed by the elements than I expected. He can't be much older than me. It occurs to me that when it comes to first impressions, we're not doing well. The only words he has heard me utter so far were a profanity.

"I'm Rosalie." I keep my chin high. "Knight-Langton," I clarify, in case it wasn't obvious. Which it must have been. His steady gaze is impassive, even cool. In fact, between the unforgiving set of his lightly stubbled jaw and his now-folded arms, there's something of an edge to him.

"The lock's awkward. I'd offer to get it changed, but . . ." His eyebrows flicker, and I know that his silence is a direct reference to my father. "I can get a locksmith to look at it."

"Sure. Thanks." I look at the semi-darkness in the hall. I'm not quite ready to take the plunge. I turn back to face him. "Sorry. You are . . . ?"

"Kasper Miller." He jerks his head over his shoulder and, for the first time, I notice the opening at the far end of the drive, where the red-brick garden wall meets the dripping rhododendrons and a rectangle of privet screens a multitude of wheelie bins. The metallic charcoal of the pickup must have blended into the shadows before. Even now, all that really stands out is its silver-white signwriting: *KMM Ltd: Landscaping, Gardening and Property Management.*

"I'm here for sixteen hours a week. Until now I've done them ad hoc." His grey eyes assess me for a moment. "If you'd prefer set times, let me know."

"Oh. Uh . . ." I shake my head. "Whatever you usually do is fine."

He nods.

"Thank you," I add.

He pauses a moment. Then he descends the steps back into the drive. I see him swing himself onto the pickup and start hauling the bins onto the back.

I close my hand more tightly than is really necessary around the handle of my case and drag it inside.

The hallway is the one from the magazines, unchanged other than the chill that lies heavy in the air. The floor is marble, and the stairs are oak. The walls are papered in a navy-and-gold-leaf pattern that has gone out of fashion and come back in since I last walked between them. There's still a grand piano beside the stairs, without a single visible fleck of dust on its long-closed cover. There are even fresh flowers on the hall stand, ready for the day she strides back in, twenty years older and expecting things to be the same. Leonie is written on every pristine surface, her reflection gazes out of every polished mirror. In my father's mind, she's alive, and he just has to keep waiting.

In my mother's mind, she's dead, and she long has been. That was no secret from me, in my years of blossoming insufficiency. I was a poor substitute for the daughter she was bereaved of.

Leonie. Her name settles heavily on my heart as I listen to the sound of my own footsteps on the marble. I walk to the stairs and run a hand over the banister. Leonie and Rosalie. There's a painting of us over the stairs. She would have been seven. A cascade of glossy chocolate-brown hair, a beaming smile, an Alice band with a bow. I'm a crinkled newborn in a puff-sleeved romper that belonged firmly in the nineties. I gaze up at her beautiful green eyes.

They say that motor memory doesn't fade. It's why you never forget how to ride a bike. My feet remember their own path: left at the top, left again across the landing. I push the door.

The smell washes over me first. There aren't really words to describe it. I halt, floored by the sudden need to dig Jessica out of my case and clutch her to my chest, to climb onto my seat under the sash window and press my hands against the glass. I suck in a few deep breaths, taking it in: the perfectly lined-up books on the bookcase; the wooden dolls' house and its family still poised mid-meal; Nedward the rocking horse; the Sylvanians — a whole village of them: cottages, windmill, school, shops — frozen spotlessly in time by careful cleaners who for a good enough weekly sum honour Nathan Langton's insane instructions to the letter.

The pine four-poster bed is unmade, but someone has placed folded clean sheets at its foot; the fairy lights still dot the canopy and the white voile curtains hang at each corner in perfect arrangement, laundered regularly, no doubt, by my father's staff. I hadn't factored in the existence of cleaners and caretakers when I thought about coming here. In my head, I was going to be alone.

The window looks out across the striped lawn, immaculate even in the pre-spring gloom. There are trees in every direction, blocking out anything beyond the estate. I glance back around at the Sylvanians. On closer inspection, they are age-dulled and dated, and the plastic buildings have brittled with too many years of daylight.

I don't know when, if ever, I last felt sad about this place. About what happened to her, to me. To any of us. But the toys are sad. I realise I'm slightly nauseated, dizzied by the enormity of it. The family that stopped existing overnight. The home that has been waiting ever since.

I walk back out onto the landing. The radiators are on, battling valiantly against the pervasive chill. Window after window streams watered-down daylight onto the floor. I don't open many doors. The bathroom, a stack of fresh towels piled on the aged wicker chair beside the bath. My father's old study, leathered desk and vast CRT TV that brings to mind horse racing and washed-out cricket matches.

The last door is Leonie's.

I pause. I know, but I don't know. They took it all away in boxes. I've heard they brought it back; that he made them replace it exactly where they found it. Even the thought is creepy, now that my fingers rest on the unturned knob.

Get out of my stuff, Tiddler!

I draw a slow breath between my teeth, twist . . .

Then I let go of the handle. It recoils on its spring and I lower my hand.

A door that doesn't want to be opened. No amount of therapy is ever going to fix that.

I turn away and pretend to myself that I'm admiring the view from the windows. The sections of box hedges trimmed in squares around the carefully managed lavender, the sculptures along the pea-gravelled paths that must be greyer and more lichenified than they used to be, like ageing actresses. For some reason, I can't stop looking for the juniper.

It was the day before her fifteenth birthday. The first day after the Easter holiday. She'd been at school. It's only after that that things get hazy. She caught the number six bus back from the stop by the school gates in Armsby; there was a grainy greyscale video of her as it pulled up, distorted by the wide-angled lens. Three forty-five. She was wearing her riding clothes under her school blazer. At three fifty-three, Shellingsby was the first stop. There was no camera to catch her disembarking, but she wasn't on the bus by the next stop at the edge of Rollingford when the new driver took over. It was a ten-minute walk home, or a two-minute walk downhill to the old livery yard. All evidence suggests she did the latter. She had a mobile phone, but she didn't use it and they never found it. There was no signal in Shellingsby anyway.

By seven thirty, she wasn't home. At seven forty-five, when they went to check, there was no one at the yard, her horse Phoenix was stabled, and the manège was locked up. By eight, people were out looking in the dark with torches and Land Rovers. By nine, the police were at Hailbury. Another four days passed before they were 'seeking a man in connection with the disappearance'.

At the time, the nuances passed me by. The reality of what could have happened to a fourteen-year-old who resembled her famous mother. A fourteen-year-old who had recently discovered independence, who looked eighteen, and whose modelling debut had just appeared in high-end fashion magazines across the country. With her emerald eyes and glossy chocolate-brown hair, long legs and wide movie-star smile, Leonie was a mini Lara, but with my father's easy-tan skin to boot and a cute dusting of freckles over the bridge of her nose. She had just signed with an agency and become the new face of perfumier L'Église Rose. Deals were done, photos shot. And then she disappeared.

The vibration in my pocket jerks me from my reverie. I fumble to answer the phone.

"Darling, are you there?"

Shellingsby still doesn't have decent signal. My mother's voice fades in and out.

"At Hailbury, I mean? I asked you to call me."

"Sorry." I descend the stairs, half-hoping it will drop out altogether. "Bad signal. Hang on."

The hallway is as still as death. The front door is closed, and my second suitcase and squash racquet have appeared on the mat with my car keys. It's the first time she's physically picked up the phone and rung me in weeks. Usually, I get a poorly transcribed dictated text, or sometimes a WhatsApp voice recording from her car. I can't even recall when I last saw her. Christmas, probably.

"Yes, I'm here, Mum. Where are you?"

"I'm in Cannes, actually, for a few weeks, with Marie. I can't really chat."

I can hear car windscreen wipers down the line, and snatches of French conversation.

"Okay . . ."

"Rosalie, I had a word with my agent. Stefan will screen through things before you submit them. I've sent you his email and his number. Please copy him into everything."

Stefan; so that's why she's calling. Heaven forbid I paint her the wrong way. My father made that mistake when they divorced ten years ago. If she hadn't already been as rich as him, he would still be paying for it.

"Okay, Mum." I stare at the marble. Can I remember a time that was different? *Before.* I'd like just one mental image of it, other than the staged ones in the photos. A cuddle, a page of colouring. Because I don't remember her doing colouring or Play-Doh or baking cakes or building tepees, except when the photographer came. And it's been years since anyone cuddled me. Even Hamish couldn't really have been classed as affectionate.

"I don't think it will do you any good, you know." The windscreen wipers have upped a notch in Cannes. "I don't think it's a good idea you being there at all. Are you still seeing that counsellor . . . what was her name? I'm sure she'd agree."

"Joy." I tuck the phone under my chin. And no, the irony isn't lost on me. "Enjoy Cannes, Mum." One of us needs to end the conversation.

"Thanks, darling. Chat soon."

I hang up.

The only thing I have inherited from my mother is her porcelain skin. My introversion is torture to her, my lack of words insolence, my slight five-foot-two stature and untameable dark-copper hair a hard-to-stomach disappointment. I'm hypermetropic like my father, and needed glasses before I got my adult teeth. When I started in sixth form, contact lenses and a love of writing altered my fortunes forever. It turns out I come across far better on paper, where I'm a lot more charismatic than I am in person, and where my cup size and inside leg measurement are less important than Lara Lee Knight would have had me believe, growing up. I published my first, and only, novel in my second year of university. I've never repeated the success, but I enjoy the column and, combined with royalties and my freelance work, it makes me enough to get by without having to resort to an allowance from either of my parents.

I stand in the hallway, suffocated by the scent of the flowers. I need to unpack, and there's no food. I'm not sure there's a supermarket within ten miles.

Snatches of familiarity stab at me as I walk from one end of the house to the other. The expansive lounge is bitterly cold. Three Laura Ashley sofas are arranged around a hearthrug; there's an upholstery cleaning ticket from 2003 stuck behind the one of the cushions. It doesn't look like anyone has sat there since. I barely make a dent as I perch on the edge. Another monstrous TV, as deep as it is wide, and an array of surround-sound tech that now belongs in the Science Museum, is recessed beside the fireplace. There's even a VHS player. It's strange to try and superimpose what might have belonged here now. Maybe there would be graduation pictures on the walls, Leonie's debut shoots, her snaps from the red carpet displayed beside our mother's. There would be different photos on the sideboard, a spread of elegant wedding pictures, featured in *Vogue*. Perhaps even a new generation of newborn shots, crocheted swaddles and matching headbands. She would have been thirty-five this April.

My phone is ringing again.

"Rosy."

"Hi, Dad." It's a relief to let my imaginings evaporate. To look afresh at the dated room with its dew-heavy feeling of disuse.

"Did you get to Hailbury okay?"

"Yes. Thanks." I stand up. I'm beyond the eye-rolling stage. I've been having conversations in duplicate for the past decade. Most of Lara Lee Knight's and Nathan Langton's correspondence these days goes through a lawyer, but I occasionally get the pleasure of mediating.

"Is the . . . is the house in good shape?"

"Perfect." I look around at the pristine sash windows and half-shut Roman blinds. The complete absence of dust is at odds with the abandonment.

"Good. That's good."

Silence.

"Did you have any trouble getting in? Was the grounds-man there? Did you manage to unset the alarm?"

"Yeah." I mean, I couldn't open the door and I swore at the groundsman. What more is there to add?

"Excellent. Good. The cleaners are in twice weekly. I asked them to leave the heating on, so the place is warmed through."

"Right."

"You know, now you've been back, there's probably not much reason to stay. Take a couple of days to look around. But, don't feel you have to . . . You know?"

"Thanks, Dad. I'll stay for now, at least. Get my head round what I'm doing."

What am I doing?

I hear him sigh.

"Is it . . . ?" When he speaks again, he sounds uncertain. "The house, I mean. Is it . . . Do you think . . . Have you been in her room?"

Oh, Christ. I sit back down.

"It's exactly as I remember it." I lie on every level.

"Good. Okay." He's breathing heavily. "Good. Well, I'm actually between meetings, Rosy. I'll leave you to it. You can call me, if there's anything. Or the Miller chap, I'll send you his number. Let him know when you decide to come back. You can always leave the key with him."

"Thanks, Dad." The desertion of the lounge is getting to me. I head out to try and find the kitchen instead.

"Bye, Rosy . . . Bye." He trails off. "Bye."

He's gone. Three byes has to be a record, even for him.

I pause in the hallway. She's staring at me from over the banister. I look up into her perfectly green eyes — not the muddied blue-green North-Sea-on-a-good-day version that I was blessed with — and try to bring her to life. But she just stares back. Impassive. Silent.

"Where did you go?" I whisper to the oil on the canvas. "Where did you go?"

CHAPTER 2

Kacper
2003

There's a girl. Standing at the school gate, her face up against the close mesh weave of the fence, like a prison. She's small to be a prisoner, barely over a metre tall. Her elbows are bony in her blue cardigan, her hair braided tightly from each temple into two plaits that hang down her back. Her eyes, behind her pink-rimmed glasses, are red and swimming with tears. Tata takes me by the hand, and I strain my head around to keep looking as he leads me away. *Come on, kotek.*

I twist to look back. Mrs Churchman seems annoyed. She's shepherding the girl back into class R, muttering something about third time this week, and was it supposed to be Vesna today, or Mummy? And I wonder to myself whether it's better to have a mummy who forgets to pick you up or no mummy at all.

Come on, Tata repeats, and I squish his hand, deciding the last one is probably better, because Tata would never forget to pick me up, not in ten thousand years. We cross the green hand in hand, and I wait on the grass, watching a jet plane

16

above us as he unlocks the car. I climb in beside him, smelling the smell of farms, straw sticking to my trousers. I'd like to go in a jet. All I've ever been in is Tata's old car and a kind of boat called a ferry. Tata says one day, when I'm big.

I think I'd like to be big. Tata says now we are here, if I work hard, I can be anything I want to. And I think he's right. Maybe I'll be a jet plane pilot. Or a teacher.

There's buckwheat and chicken in the kitchen. Tata kisses my forehead and goes to do the locking up, and I sit with Jeanette at the table and listen to his car bump down the kerb and drive away. He's gone longer than usual. So long that by the time he gets back I've had my wash all by myself, and I'm waiting in my pyjamas while Jeanette hangs the wet laundry over the radiators. His skin is cold, and his clothes smell of fresh air. I start upstairs towards the back bedroom, and he stops to talk to Jeanette. *Have you heard* . . . I don't catch the end of his sentence, because a tractor goes by and the windows shudder, and a few moments later he finds me on the stairs and lifts me onto his shoulders. I have to duck my head to fit under the beams, and he drops me onto my bed so that I bounce right off again which makes me giggle.

I get under the covers, and Tata reads a page from the bedtime book in English. But all the while that he's reading, I can't help thinking about the girl at the gate and the way she wrapped her bony arms around herself when Mrs Churchman told her off. When I'm a teacher, I won't be cross with the girl from class R. I'll hold her hand and wipe the big fat tears from her face and put my arm around her little shoulders, and when she's stopped crying, I'll tell her it's okay, because one day she can be anything she wants to be, too. Whether or not her mummy remembers to pick her up. No one can stop her. She can be anything. Anything in the whole, wide world.

CHAPTER 3

Rosalie

Berries. I count them on the paper towel. Fourteen berries snuggled in my hand. They look a bit like blueberries. I let them fall out one at a time into the bowl, plud, plud, plud, until they roll tunefully around the melamine. Mary, Mary, quite contrary . . .

* * *

I drag my eyes away from the depleted racks of fruit and veg. Five to ten, and there's almost nothing left. There's no cashier at the till in the Co-op. She's sweeping up the spilled punnet from the fruit and veg aisle and mopping the squashed entrails off the floor as I tap my card at the automatic checkout.

I dump my shopping on the front seat of my car. I ought to know the way back to Hailbury intuitively, but I don't; the roads are dark and shadowed by trees, muddling the memory of my arrival. It's starting to sleet, bringing the wipers automatically to life as I plunge into the abyss beyond the last of Armsby's streetlights.

I shiver and grip the wheel with both hands. Even my car engine is too quiet to drown out the all-pervading silence. The road back to Shellingsby is undulating and deserted; there's a series of sharp bends, chevrons dimmed with mud, and a steep ascent through trees. I crawl my way around the corners. I can't remember ever having driven somewhere so dark; the branches seem to meet over the top of the car like reaching arms.

I change down a gear, making the shopping topple over in the passenger seat. I put out an arm to try and save it, and in the same instant something flashes in the periphery of my vision.

"Shit . . ."

I stand on the brakes.

"Shit, *shit*—"

Lights. Headlights. They're not on the road. I swing the wheel.

"No, no, *no.*"

I swerve to a halt on the verge.

A flush of panic beads my upper lip. The lights are shining from the ditch on the other side of the road. I fumble with the door handle.

The car is just beyond the next chevron, semi-upright, its headlights blazing into the ripped-off limbs of the bushes, its horn blaring. It's missed the sign by little less than a miracle. How long has it been there? I falter, lips numb. Not long. It wasn't there when I drove the other way.

"Fuck." I scramble out of my car, fumbling for my phone, and glance around, as if someone better qualified might be out here in the middle of nowhere to come to the rescue. My limbs are stiff with fear.

"Hello?" I dart a look both ways and stumble across the road. Sleet hits my face and runs down my neck. The tarmac is slick. No wonder they skidded.

"Shit. Jesus . . . *Hello?*" My boots struggle for purchase in the mud. I slither into the ditch. There's a collection of stickers in the rear screen. *Dogs die in hot cars. Give Blood.* A blue and yellow heart.

"Hello? Are you okay?"

Nothing. Nothing over the sickening drone of the horn. It must be stuck on. The whole car's at an angle. I lurch my way to the driver's door. The interior light is shining.

There's no one there.

"Hello?"

Nothing. The blare of the horn is unbearable. I fight the urge to clamp my hands over my ears.

"*Hello?*"

Nightmare images of ejected passengers flick across my mind. But all I can find is churned-up mud.

"Is there anybody there?"

There isn't. I gulp a few deep breaths. I didn't see anyone on the road. There can't have been anyone hurt; whoever was driving it is long gone.

I should call the police. A trickle of good sense is returning. I struggle to unlock my phone, but it has no signal. My hands are numb and my clothes are wet through; I'm standing up to my ankles in ice-cold water. I need to get out of the ditch.

"Okay," I gasp. "Okay."

I scramble onto the slippery tarmac, scanning the horizon for lights, for another good Samaritan, anything — even just someone with a level head. But there's nothing. Shivers overtake me. I blunder to my car, start the engine and turn up the heater. There's still no signal, not even enough for an emergency call. I'll have to call from Hailbury.

I'm shivering almost too hard to drive. It takes me two attempts to get the code in the gate, and more than three to turn the key in Hailbury's door. I huddle against the radiator in the hall and dial 101.

It takes a good fifteen minutes to get through and give my details, to flounder over the location and realise I never wrote down the number plate.

"It was in the ditch. I . . . I didn't . . . ."

"And there was no one in the vehicle?"

"No. No one. Not even nearby. But the lights were on, and the horn . . . I'd only just come that way, it couldn't have been there long . . ."

"And you didn't get the registration?"

"No . . ." I press myself harder against the radiator. "No, I'm sorry."

"Can you describe the vehicle?"

"A . . . uh, a car . . ."

"Make, model?"

"Oh." I grip the phone. "Small-ish. I . . . I don't know . . ."

A pause. I wet my lips.

"It was dark blue . . . or grey . . . I mean, I don't think it was black."

"Right." Another pause.

I can hear the frustration building in his silence at my utter lack of useful details. How can I not know? It was dark. I was panicking.

"Okay. Thanks for contacting us, Rosalie. We'll send an area car out to take a look."

"Okay." I let out my breath. "Thank you. Thanks. That's great."

"I can give you a reference number in case you need to call back."

"Sure." I don't have a pen. I try to memorise it, but the digits are gone before he's finished speaking. I hang up with the unsettling feeling that I'm being watched.

Leonie's green eyes are on me as I corner the bottom of the stairs to pick up the shopping and flinch my way to the kitchen in my wet socks. I fill the kettle and flick the switch.

There *was* a nanny. She was there earlier, a faint apparition standing by the Aga as I pushed open the kitchen door. She spoke broken English, made curd pancakes and cookies from sweet pastry, gave me medicine and ironed my school uniforms. I remember the smell of her cardigans. The rest of her is a blur, her name obscured by kindness.

I'm unsettled by the realisation. By the idea that there is more stored away than I let on to myself.

I make tea, even though I know it's not a good idea. Isn't that the great British response to a crisis — hot, sweet tea? I put away the shopping and lean against the table to drink, numb with exhaustion as the adrenaline rush fades. I should go to bed.

I pick up my phone. Joy has reproached me more times than is really necessary about screens and sleep. Even my intended doomscrolling isn't possible with Hailbury's patchy 3G. It takes most of five minutes for the first picture to appear on my feed. Someone has tagged me in the post: a blurry two-second animation of a suitcase landing in a car boot. I don't recognise the username.

The phone vibrates, and I almost drop it. It's ringing.

"Hello?"

"Hi, is that Rosalie Knight-Langton? It's Martin, calling back from Lincolnshire Police."

"Oh . . ." Did I miss something? Someone? Have they found someone? "Hi."

"Hi, Rosalie. I just wanted to let you know, the patrol's been out, and everything's fine. They couldn't find a car."

Couldn't find a car? I lower the phone and flick it to speaker, frowning.

"Really? Between Shellingsby St Mary and Armsby. On the bends . . . ?"

"That's right. My colleagues checked the whole length of the road between Armsby and Shellingsby, and they wanted me to reassure you there was no car, and no signs of a collision."

What?

"Oh." I lower myself into one of the kitchen chairs. "Okay. Thanks. Thanks for letting me know."

"No problem. Thank you for taking the time to call it in. Make sure you get some rest, now."

He doesn't sound very thankful. He sounds like he thinks I'm out of my mind.

"Bye," I whisper, and end the call.

I stare at my hands on the tabletop.

What was it that Joy said?

It doesn't matter what Joy said. I'm here. That's all that matters.

* * *

Daylight. It takes its time coming. It often does. I watch until the red hint of dawn bleeds over the horizon. *Get some rest*. Like that was happening. I knew the tea was a bad idea.

I unpack my yoga mat, throw my hair into a bun and wander through the house, looking for somewhere where I won't feel like Leonie is watching me. I settle on the garden room, even though my breath mists in front of my face. The glass doors don't do much to keep the morning chill outside, but watching the sun creep over the dewy grass as I work through the poses is somehow revitalising.

When I've finished, I make coffee, take my laptop and drive into Armsby. I try not to look too hard at the ditches and hedges. The driver was probably drunk and didn't want anyone to call the police. They must have got the car out and scarpered.

There's not much more to Armsby than was evident last night. A scattering of independent shops, the Co-op. There's a bistro, Room 42, on the edge of the cobbled marketplace; it's already open and advertising free Wi-Fi. I order a latte and sit on the leather couch in the window with my laptop, watching the foot traffic slowly increase outside whilst I try to book a broadband engineer for Hailbury. I've always liked observing. Taking little snapshots of strangers, building their characters, their imagined ordinary realities. Writing other people's stories.

However much of an idealistic mistake upping and moving here might turn out to be, I've got deadlines to meet. And a biography to write. Somehow, Leonie's unopened door and the accusatory looks of the abandoned toys have turned the lift of anticipation in my stomach into a tight twist of dread.

The café has Italian overtones; pictures of Venice and Florence on the bare-brick walls, leather sofas and trendy industrial-style tables one hundred percent out of keeping with the rest of the high street. The coffee smells and tastes authentic but nothing else is; the girl behind the bar is a few years older than me and has a confusing accent that seems to mash broad Yorkshire with the local Lincolnshire tones. She's tall and friendly, and seems genuinely interested, although that may be because I make up a third of her custom as I take back my cup and order another latte, eyeing the cakes on the countertop.

"Lemon drizzle's definitely t' best." She finishes steaming the milk.

"Did you make it?"

"No." She smiles. "But I can vouch for th' lady who did."

"Isn't it too early for cake?"

"Is it ever too early for cake?"

I smile, too. "I'll have some lemon drizzle, then."

She takes the most generous chunk out of the dome to go with my latte. Her eyes stray to my laptop.

"You found the Wi-Fi password okay?"

"Oh." I scald my lip on the coffee. "Yeah. Thanks. I . . . actually, I've only just moved here and I don't have internet yet. I've got a couple of deadlines."

"Sounds like I'll do well out of it, then. I'm Harriet, by t' way."

"Rosalie."

"Nice to meet you . . . Rosalie."

Perhaps she missed a beat. Perhaps it's in my mind. Either way, the uncertainty is enough reason to step safely back behind my computer screen. The caffeine finally begins to improve my focus, and I manage a good couple of hours and an emailed draft of my 'Millennial versus AI' article, the door opening and closing intermittently in the background.

When I next look up the bistro is full, and Harriet has been joined by a bearded man. I feel guilty taking up a table, so I close the laptop and venture out into the insipid spring sunshine.

The free car park has filled up, and the adjacent playground is full of parents and toddlers. I study it, trying to wring a memory from it, but the equipment and safety surfacing are all new. Did she bring us here? Swing us on the swings? Probably a stupid question. She might have swung Leonie on the swings. I give up and drive back to Hailbury.

The door opens on my fourth attempt. I must have forgotten to set the alarm, which comes as a relief. What day is it? Tuesday. I try to remember what my father said about cleaners. It doesn't sound like they're here.

I was seven. Seven years old, and in bed, when the search began. I woke, on the day my entire world flipped on its head, in a four-poster bed in a room filled with toys and fairy lights. There was no danger in the world I knew. Everyone thought it would be over; everyone expected the story to have a definite conclusion, a rolling end-credit, and yet here I am, twenty years on, still living out each protracted day of it. It's become increasingly clear that it will never end. That we will never know what happened to her.

What happened to her? I didn't come here to answer that question. Nevertheless, it *is* here. In every room, every picture, every cut peony. It's looking back at me from every mirror, wondering whether, when it *is* answered, there will be any reason to keep existing.

I wander, semi-consciously filling in a few more of the blanks. Through a door at the back of the hallway there's a utility room with a washing machine and a tumble dryer that looks so old, I'm not sure it's safe to turn on. Beyond the utility is the corridor to the orangery, its skylights dulled with moss. There was a pool in the orangery when I was a child — I've seen the pictures. I don't venture further than the utility door before I turn back. I can hear tyres on the gravel.

I know I ought to check if it's the cleaners, go and introduce myself. But my social courage has run out. I retreat to my room instead and close the door.

In the floor-length mirror my reflection looks tired and haunted. When I pull my hair out of its ponytail, it falls well below my shoulders. I search for the child that in my own eyes I still am, skinny and awkward and usually unnoticed behind her round glasses. But I can't see her anymore. For a disconcerting moment, it's easier to see Leonie, minus a few inches' height and without the dazzling smile. And then my gaze readjusts, and I realise that sleep deprivation and the imposition of societal norms have all but covered over the girl I'm looking for.

The lamp is on. I reach under the bed for my suitcase. Jessica is in the top pocket. Good old Jessica, whose fabric hair has never been out of place, even if it's now flatter than it used to be. Whose dress has been repaired more times than I can number, and whose long-lashed eyelids have been closed in a perpetual stitched arch of smiling bliss since the day that she was made. I lift her out and breathe her in. Her scent has almost gone, covered over, like childhood Rosalie, by all that has come since. I cradle her in my arms, like I know I used to, but can't remember when. The Sylvanians look up at me from their living death, and Nedward's baleful eyes fix upon me as I run a hand over the spines of the books: *Anne of Green Gables, Pollyanna, Matilda, The Secret Garden*. It's like they're still waiting for the child that never came back to play. I walk to the window. I don't need to climb onto the seat anymore. I lower myself to sit and pull my knees up to my chin, pressing one hand against the cold glass.

When I wake, Jessica has slipped from my grasp. I'm cold and nauseated, and it takes me a moment to figure out where I am. I slide to my feet. It's still daylight. The sun is muted, filtered through a scudding blanket of cloud.

If the cleaners have been, they must also have gone, and I can't even really tell the difference. The hallway marble is like ice underfoot. I pick up my trainers and walk to the garden room, flip the lock on the sliding doors and step outside, instantly immersed in the scent of wet lavender and rosemary. Everything is cool and damp. My breath mists in front of my face as I skirt the edge of the garden, traversing box hedges, borders and patio. There's something unsettling in the encroaching shrubs and trees. Even the sound is uneasy, the perpetual rush of wind through the branches, the absence of silence.

Eventually I reach the orangery. I wonder how many times, since I left, it has been repainted. The timbers around every pane of glass are immaculately preserved in spotless Wimborne White.

It's only as I draw closer, trying to superimpose flowers — wisteria perhaps? — onto the bare vines, that I notice the open door. I swallow a lurch of apprehension. Hidden at the back of the house, it's the perfect entrance for someone who doesn't want to be seen . . .

My teeth are chattering. What would anyone want with a derelict swimming pool?

Unless, of course, it's not the swimming pool they're trying to get into.

A shiver runs through me. I know full well there have been urban explorers. There's a whole host of pictures online; if you google Hailbury they're not hard to find. The ones I've seen were only of the living room, though, and the upstairs: *#leoniesroom*. It doesn't take much for an unsolved crime to become a modern legend.

I've broken a sweat. If razor wire isn't enough to keep people out, I don't know what is. But I do know that I'll probably never sleep again if I don't investigate.

I tiptoe to the open door and ease it open.

The shimmering light takes me utterly by surprise. Reflected sunshine, ripples on water. I take a step forward on the tiles and stop in disbelief. I'm surrounded by sun loungers, the muted echoes of brick and glass, the gentle lap and gurgle of tiny wavelets at the filters.

"There's water in it," I exclaim.

"It's a swimming pool."

I start, the shock of realising I'm not alone quickly cancelled out by recognition. Beyond the sun loungers another door is open, louvred wood with a key in the lock. Kasper Miller is clearly part-way through one of his sixteen hours. He appears, sleeves rolled. It must have been his pickup I heard.

"Really? I see that now." I narrow my eyes.

He regards me levelly. There's a hardness to his expression that makes it difficult to tell whether his comment was scathing or teasing.

"It just hadn't occurred to me that my father was crazy enough to pour his money down the drain maintaining it," I qualify.

And it hadn't occurred to me that *he* would be in the house. Or that his grey gaze would be quite so piercing. I avert my eyes quickly, crouch to touch the water instead and flinch straight out.

"*Christ*, that's cold."

"Unless he plans to fill it in, it's actually better not to drain it." Kasper moves past me to dip a test strip in the water. "It doesn't do the vinyl any good." He shrugs. "And he might be crazy enough to maintain it, but I'm not crazy enough to heat something no one's swum in for two decades. If you're planning on going in, you'll need to turn the thermostat up."

He straightens. He's taller than I'd realised. It occurs to me there's a hint of familiarity about him, but just like everything else, I can't place it. He shakes the strip off, slides it into the meter he's carrying, and moves to pull the cover back over the pool. I glance outside at the struggling sunshine. I know I should remember. Kasper isn't a common name.

"I didn't realise you were in. I apologise. I knocked, but you didn't answer."

"Oh." I look back. "It's okay. I mean, I didn't hear. But it's fine."

There's silence, other than the slow lick of the water at the steps. I catch myself staring at him. The meter beeps.

"We were at school together, I think." He's caught me looking, too. He turns away. I can't help noticing that he doesn't make eye contact.

"School." I nod.

He doesn't turn back. Eventually, I steel myself and walk past the cupboard, into the dim light of the corridor. I don't let out my breath until I'm safely in the utility.

School. There must be *something*. Joy says it's repressed trauma, the lack of recall. That it will all be accessible when I let myself open the doors. It feels like the more I focus, the more tightly it shuts down. I close my eyes for a moment, but all I can see is the green mesh weave of a fence.

I open them again. The only constant is her. I can remember her. I don't tell people that.

You look like an owl, Rosy. Twit-twoo, little owl.

Are you coming, Rosy? Faster than that! You're so slow. I'll be dead by the time you catch up.

I'm still catching up. Every single day. I'm still trying to catch up.

CHAPTER 4

There's a place. It's there, between asleep and awake, always waiting. Where your body thinks you've mis-stepped and fallen. Where you're locked in, paralysed and mute, even though you can hear the footsteps coming closer. Where you scream for help, and it's silent.

I can't sleep in the dark.

I feel like it's always been that way. Maybe there was a time when it wasn't — a time before monsters and kidnappers — I'm not sure. All I know is that it's a place I can't risk going. The dizzying rush between levels of unreal: believing, briefly, that I've woken, only to find myself back at the beginning, searching for a way out.

So, like DiCaprio in *Inception*, I keep a totem on the bed-side table. I need to be able to ground myself. I need the light to pull myself back.

Hamish couldn't bear it. After various expressions of exasperation, he resorted to wearing a blindfold. I tried not to mind. Hamish. Sometimes I think I miss his Etonian drawl and the mocking looks he would give me down his long nose. I used to think I loved that nose, despite its Roman grandeur. The floppy black hair that fell over his eyes, the way it would stand up backwards under his cycling headband when he took off his helmet. The way he tutted over the cooking, like a more decorous Gordon Ramsay.

My eyes burn with tiredness. Insomnia isn't a new friend. I wonder whether I was like this as a child, wandering the house while everyone else slept.

I keep saying that I don't remember. I don't remember anything.

But I do.

We were at school together, I think.

I tiptoe to the kitchen. It's half past four. Soon there will be no chance of getting back to sleep, and it will be the second night in a row that I've seen in the sunrise.

I open the fridge and stare at its meagre contents. Cheese, mostly. White wine. Milk. Hummus. Four thirty is morning, not night, so although I'm tempted, I pass over the wine and get myself a bowl of Coco Pops, listening to them sputter and succumb to the semi-skimmed.

In hindsight, my insomnia and Hamish's two-hundred-mile-a-week road-bike average were probably only contributory factors in our demise. We looked good on paper: we played racquet sports and took romantic walks in the park; he got on well with my father. But after an increasingly painful post-Covid year of working from home, it transpired that we couldn't actually stand each other's company. Hamish moved back in with his parents, and for the first time in my life I couldn't pay the bills.

It's still dark outside as I climb the stairs. I find myself paused, my eyes on her closed door. In the buzzing darkness, it's more forbidden than ever. For a fleeting moment, I imagine that she's sound asleep inside, her breathing slow and even, her chocolate hair spilled over the pillows. I picture her bed against the wall, draped with covers and throws and novelty cushions that have cascaded in a jumble onto the floor. It was never made. Only the tiny creases in her forehead and between her eyebrows now, the manicure of her adult hand resting on the covers, would belie the years that have passed since life rewrote itself for us all.

What dreams did she dream, that last night? Did she know? Did she know about the monsters, the kidnappers, the world that was waiting to swallow her up without a trace?

I go to my room and fall back on my bed. What if she *had* known? What if any of us had? If we could have changed it, altered our own trajectories, where would we be now? Would I still be here? Would the emptiness still ache open inside me? Is that space hers, even though she never really occupied it anyway?

There's no spectacular sunrise today. Just a spattering of rain, a gradual lightening of the sky. I give in at six and get out my laptop, doing what I can without internet until eight when I cave to the need for caffeine and go to make coffee, shivering on the tiles in my pyjamas. The stench of the flowers in the hall is overpowering. In a fit of rebellion, I pull them out of their vase and open the front door.

It's even colder in the drive and the gravel hurts my feet. I hobble a beeline for the wheelie bins and dump the bouquet into the first one. Then goosebumps ripple across my skin.

I lower the lid.

Kasper Miller is stood at the back of his truck. His steady gaze flickers to the bins, the resting place of the desecrated peonies, then back to my face. For the briefest moment, our eyes meet. He doesn't say a word. He turns and walks away, and I become abruptly aware of the morning breeze on my bare arms and the damp hems of my pyjama trousers.

I walk back to the open door. A petal has fallen from the peonies onto the marble, and I stoop to pick it up, my gaze drifting to the stairwell, to her scrutiny.

The crash behind me makes me jolt in shock; I spin, drop the petal, my back hitting the banister post with a thud. The front door has slammed. I scan the driveway beyond the windows, heart pounding. At the back of the house the lawn mower's drone is distant and unmistakable, and I'm alone; I must be. I wrap my arms across my chest.

I drive back to Armsby for nine and reclaim my table in the bistro. Perhaps I should ask Harriet if she offers a loyalty card. I open the laptop and click on my mother's notes. Sixty-eight pages. I've run out of ways to procrastinate — I'm up to date with the column, and have had nothing back on yesterday's draft — there's nothing left now except her.

Or her absence. *Life Without Leonie*. I'm not sure how long I sit and stare at the timeline on my screen, the mostly empty document burning itself onto my retinas.

I should write about the agonising wait for a ransom note that never came. About the press conferences and appeals for information, the days they spent combing the grounds at Hailbury, uniformed officers, forensic specialists. About police cordons. About how it must have felt, as the country's film and television actress of the decade, to be plunged from celebrity into interrogation rooms with detectives and lawyers. About the multi-millionaire husband who to all intents and purposes seemed to lose his mind, and has never really regained it.

But I'm not a detective, or a forensic specialist, or even a psychologist. I was there, but I wasn't. Now I'm here, but they're not.

My chair legs scrape on the floor as I go for more coffee. When I get to the counter, Harriet isn't there.

"Rosy?"

At first, it doesn't penetrate my sphere of awareness. No one here knows my name.

"Rosalie?"

"Huh?" I turn, startled.

There's a man approaching who I'm sure I've never seen before in my life. Maybe in his mid-thirties, his hair is styled to look careless in the same vein as the open-collared shirt that isn't quite properly tucked into his chinos, and the expensive wool blazer slung over his left arm.

"It *is* Rosalie, isn't it?" His right hand is held out in greeting. "Knight-Langton? You're . . ." Despite the assurance of his steps, it's hard to miss his hesitation. "Leonie's sister." The

33

softening of his voice on her name, the tiny flicker of emotion, is oddly reminiscent of my father.

"Yeah . . . Yes." After a beat, I take his hand. It's warm and strong. There's a momentary pause.

"I could tell." His small smile is poignant, somehow. Then he huffs a deep breath and releases me. "Sorry. It's nice to meet you. I heard you were coming back. I'm Joshua. Josh."

Josh. Externally, I smile back.

"Did you know her?" I ask. Of all the questions, it's probably the most pointless.

"Yeah." He nods, glances at my unattended laptop. "You're busy?"

"Oh . . . No." I move to close the screen. "I'm just about finished."

"May I?" He gestures at the second chair. I nod.

He knew my sister. My gaze travels over him again. Of course he did. He's handsome, rich, her age, or thereabouts. He went to Queen Victoria with her, judging by his BBC English with no twinge of Lincolnshire. And yet there's something polite and unassuming, almost apologetic, in the way he folds himself into the seat.

"I remember you, actually." Warmth crinkles around his eyes, and my distrust ebbs slightly. "Little Rosy. You were there, sometimes, when I came over."

"You came to Hailbury?"

"Once or twice. Usually she came out with us. There was a group of us. We used to get the bus back together from school."

I was right.

"We'd hang out, or whatever the kids call it now." He smiles, sheepish. "I don't even know what we found to do in Shellingsby. But Leonie was always the centre of everything. She could make sitting in a bus stop fun. I . . ." He pauses, smile gone. "I don't think I ever really believed it."

"Who did?" I shrug, give him a little shake of my head, as if this conversation is new to me and I'm not reading out the anticipated lines.

Who did? Me. I believed it. I believed it more and more as the days went by and my parents fell calamitously apart, as my once-ordered world packed itself piecemeal and relocated to a six-bedroomed townhouse in Muswell Hill and then to boarding school.

"Anyway, you were ordering coffee." He very evidently tries to lighten the tone. "I didn't mean to stop you."

"It's okay." I pick up my laptop and slide it into my bag. "I've been trying to break my caffeine addiction." The table-top stretches between us, scattered with artificial sweetener like granules of snow.

A trace of the smile returns to his eyes. "In that case I'm pleased to have helped."

There's a pause. Josh moves to rest his fingers on the tabletop.

"I heard a lot of rumours about you coming back. I hope it's not too hard for you."

Hard. I narrow my eyes, trying to work out what he means.

"I can't imagine the emotional courage it takes to bring her back into the spotlight. And to go back to that house. Is it true that Nathan's kept it exactly as it was?"

I nod, silent.

"It must be . . ." He pauses. "Never mind. It just strikes me no one has ever really talked about what *you* went through. Losing her when you were just a kid. You've come here to write about Lara, but . . ."

He trails off, and I realise I'm frowning.

"Shit." He rubs his forehead. "I'm sorry. I only meant to say hello, and here I am digging the most awful hole for us both."

"Don't worry about it." I force a smile. I know my actions are belying my words. I can feel how tightly I have hold of my bag.

"I will. Probably all night. Fuck." He rises to his feet as I do. "Really. At least let me get you the coffee. I was going to take mine to go, anyway."

I study him again. What was she, to him? At fourteen? A friend, not an acquaintance. More? He doesn't talk that way, and yet . . .

"Mr London." Harriet's arms are folded across her chest. "To what do we owe the pleasure?"

London. I feel my eyes dart back to his face. Joshua London?

"It's Wednesday, Harriet. Halfway to the weekend. Thank God." And at once he's all clumsy charm and flash smiles. I can't help noticing that Harriet's cheeks have turned pink.

James Edward London, or The Right Honourable Lord James Edward Armsby, is a hereditary peer, my godfather, and one of my father's closest acquaintances. Or was, back when Nathan Langton was a linchpin investment banker in the City. Lord London was a loud and influential voice in keeping Leonie in the headlines, in making sure no stone went unturned. For months, years, after the hype died down, his political reach stopped the case from going cold.

"Can I have a double Americano please? And whatever Rosalie was having. How are Sandeep and the boys?" He lolls against the counter, and I get a glimpse of the bratty kids they would have been, back then, *hanging out*. Entitled, without knowing the word. I wonder whether he grew into his humility because, despite his confidence, I can't help but quite like him. He hands me the latte and adds a gratuity before he taps his card.

"Enjoy your coffee, Rosalie." He shrugs into the blazer and picks up his cardboard cup. "And I *am* glad to have met you, even if I royally fucked it up. I hope you get on okay with everything."

"Thanks." I wrap my hands around the cup.

"I mean it. If there's anything I can do, even if it's just an offload or a chat, I'd like to help."

"Thank you." I nod. "And please don't worry. You didn't fuck anything up."

Is it my imagination, or is there a flare of relief in his parting smile? He touches a hand to his imaginary forelock.

"See you, Rosy."

I put down my bag and sip my latte, almost scalding my lip.

"*Rosy?*" Harriet's voice echoes his last word, bringing me back to reality with a jolt.

"Oh." I blink. "Uh, people used to call me that. A . . . childhood thing."

"You know Josh London?" She's trying to look casual as she wipes down the coffee machine and turns back.

"Not . . . not really." I'm suddenly reticent. "My sister did."

There's a pause. If she didn't miss a beat yesterday, she does now. Sharp eyes assess me: my answer; the familiarity, perhaps, that she sees in my face. The little glimpses of the girl the headlines never quite forgot.

"Leonie Knight-Langton," she observes at last. Maybe until now it had been lost on me. The fact that I'm recognisable here. "You're Rosalie Knight-Langton. Rachel mentioned that you were coming back."

"The rumour mill must make a killing round here." I don't meet her eyes.

"Hey." Harriet takes me by surprise, her hand brushing mine across the counter. "I think you should embrace it. I read your column. If anyone's going to tell her story, it should be you. And then the rumour mill can fuck right off, can't it?"

Her voice is refreshingly matter of fact. Her fingers rest a moment longer on the back of my hand. A gesture of reassurance, as if we already know each other. I swallow.

"Do people really remember?" I ask.

"They think they do."

"Do you?"

"Only from t' news. I wasn't local. I lived in Grimsby 'til I was fifteen. We used to visit my auntie in Shellingsby. It was still a big deal when we moved here, though. A teenage girl getting snatched dun't fade easily from people's minds."

"No." I toy with the Biscoff from my saucer. "No, I guess not."

Snatched. I close my eyes for a moment.

There was no evidence of a struggle. Snatched seems like the wrong word. Enticed, perhaps. Lured? As an adult looking back, the reality appears much bleaker than it did at the time.

There were press releases, appeals for information. And then came the breakthrough. A suspect. He worked at the livery yard; a witness thought they had seen her getting into his car. But when the police went to interview him, he was nowhere to be found. No one had seen him, or his car, since the day Leonie vanished. There was a nationwide search; the number plates of his dark red Fiesta became almost as famous as her face. But the trail wasn't just cold, it was non-existent. There was talk of leaving the country, Interpol. Overnight, he was deemed culpable for her fate, but no one ever found him to prove it.

I don't fancy the rest of the coffee. I take the Biscoff but don't eat it. It's wrong that everyone else remembers more than me. How can there be nothing? All that I know, I've been told: by my parents, by the media. Every fact I hold banked and ready to produce as a memory has come from other people. I'm a fake.

I pick up my bag as Harriet takes my cup and goes back to writing on the blackboard. Deep down, I know that Joy is right. I also know that I'm never going to open any doors unless I get over my fear of turning the handle.

I find myself double-checking Hailbury's drive as I pull to a halt on the gravel. I stand for a moment to admire the green shoots that have turned overnight into plants. They have more momentum than I do.

Turning the key in the lock makes me think of Kasper Miller, his parting words stuck like a taunt in my mind. Like he was daring me to remember.

I let myself into the silence. Someone has replaced the flowers: more peonies. Their perfection is unbearable. I have an almost uncontrollable urge to upturn the vase and run up the stairs. To shatter the stillness for good. A house like this was never meant to be still. It was never meant to be perfect. It wasn't meant to be empty.

I count my breaths instead of the steps, leaving the vase intact. I don't run. I focus on my movements. On forcing my muscles to relax, one group at a time, on feeling the floor under the balls of my feet. I don't look where I'm going, not until my muscle memory nudges me, because it knows what I know: that I'm there.

That it's time.

The handle turns smoothly. I almost expect it to be locked, except I know that it isn't, because of #leoniesroom and the pictures on the internet. Perhaps my brain anticipates falling headlong into an abyss; it certainly doesn't seem to expect my bare feet to sink into plush, aged carpet, or the waterfall of daylight through the sash window.

The covers and throws are folded, a little too neatly. Otherwise, the mess is everywhere: clothes, kirby grips, hairbrushes, body sprays. A steeplechase of Post-it notes, which must have been brightly coloured before the sun claimed their substance, are stuck around the perimeter of the Hollywood-style dressing-table mirror. There's a swing, an actual wooden swing with a cushioned seat, hanging from the high ceiling. Sheer voile curtains cover the window and disperse the light across the room in a dazzling fractionated radiance that almost hurts. Her posters are still on the walls. Who knows how many times the perished Blu Tack has been replaced? A pair of scissors lies beside the washstand with more fallen kirby grips. I have a morbid image of the policemen crawling around, laying them back out at Nathan Langton's orders, measuring with a ruler to get them exactly where they found them. They must be hard to hoover around. Maybe the cleaners have to do the same thing, twice a week.

I look at my hands, remembering the dream, and the blue stains on the paper towel. I always so badly wanted to swing on that swing.

I tiptoe across the floor, waiting for her voice to come. But it never does. I can feel their eyes on me — Alanis, No Doubt and Avril, all staring down in angsty disappointment.

She's gone. They all whisper the same thing. *She's long gone. It's a bit fucking late to be regretting it now.*

CHAPTER 5

Kacper
2003

To Tata,

My writing is wobbly. I do it in my best joined-up. I've
seen Jeanette write important letters; she doesn't have a computer, so she writes them on plain paper. She puts a sheet
underneath with lines on, so her writing doesn't wobble.

> *I ~~now~~ know you did'nt forget me. Jenet says it must be a very*
> *important thing you went away for. I wish you could come*
> *back. I miss you. I got good at football and I can run fastist*
> *in my class now since I gruw. Allso my trousers ~~don't~~ dont'*
> *fit and Jenet got me new ones. Theres a lot I wont to tell you.*
> *Dont' tell the other kids but I wont you to hug me and give*
> *me a shoulder carry too becose I miss that a lot. Pleas can you*
> *come back soon? Jenet makes me pack lunches but there not*
> *very nice and her cuddles are not the same and allso she ~~var~~*
> *can't pick me up becose she says I'm too big.*

"It's time to go! Come on, love!"

Jeanette's pen is hard to write with. My hand has made it all blotchy and smudged. My eyes hurt a bit and I rub them quickly on my way out onto the landing.

"Have you been doing some handwriting?" She's looking at my inky hands. I nod.

"Come on and get washed up. Have you done your teeth?"

I nod again.

"Let's get going then. We don't want to be late."

I frown. We get in the car. Jeanette's car isn't really a car. It's a van. She bought it when she sold the horse things. I ride in the front, on a booster seat. I hate the booster seat. The other kids don't have booster seats, but Jeanette said it's safer. She drops me off outside the gate and I walk in.

I like to be late. If I'm a bit late, then no one else is in the playground. If I'm the right amount of late, they're not in the cloakroom either and I can go straight into class five. I walk as slowly as I can. Mr Fennimore sent a letter to Jeanette. That's why she doesn't want me to be late. I did try to tell her why it's better, but she didn't really listen.

Today isn't the right amount of late. Everyone's still hanging up their bags and coats. I pretend to get a drink from the water fountain in the courtyard so I don't have to go in.

"Polack!"

Before I know what's happening, a hand hits the back of my head and my face smashes into the metal. Water blurs my eyes. I splutter. I think maybe my lip is bleeding or my tooth is broken. I don't let go of my bag. Last time they got it they put it in the girls' toilets and I couldn't get it all day. I stumble backwards, out of the water. Someone's laughing. The door bangs. Through the window I can see them in the cloakroom. I pull my sleeves over my hands and scrub my face. There's no blood. Water is dripping from the front of my hair. I stand still for a second, mostly to make sure I'm not going to cry, before I go in.

Mr Fennimore is cross. He tells me off for messing around in the water fountain, and makes me sit at the front.

I don't really mind because nothing bad can happen at the front. It's maths, and I think I make him crosser because I do the answers in my head without writing anything down, and they're right.

By break time my mouth hasn't stopped hurting. I want to check it in the mirror but I decided a while ago not to go into the toilets at school. There are no teachers in the toilets. If I don't drink during the day, I can usually make it until I get home. We're not allowed to stay in the classroom at break. I used to go to the courtyard where the girls did skipping, but I got teased worse for that. So I go to the big playground and kick a ball against the PE shed until Mrs Churchman comes and tells me not to.

After break it's topic time. Mr Fennimore counts us into pairs and I'm with Simon. I wait by my chair. I wish I could disappear into the floor. Simon has picked on me since class three when I started, when I didn't know any English. He used to push me over. Now I'm stronger, and he's cleverer, and it's sort of worse. He doesn't scare me as much as Zach Blakeman who lives in my road, though. No one scares me as much as Zach. Except maybe Marcus.

The thoughts seem to come in one giant flood, and I remember that even if I get through topic time, and lunchbreak, and PE, Tata isn't coming. And it hurts so much in my chest that I start to feel like I can't breathe or speak. And the more I wish that I could, that it would go away and not come now, the worse it gets, until I don't know what's going to happen. I grip my stomach with both hands and try to make it stop. Mr Fennimore is handing out templates at the front. I think I need to go outside in the cold. My head feels funny and I feel like I might be sick.

"Do you know where your dad is?"

I spin around. Simon has got the templates, and he's holding them out of reach. I don't really care about the templates. My mouth is hurting.

"I *said*, don't you know where your dad is yet?"

I stare at Simon. I can hear my breaths. They sound like when I've run around the school field. I ball my hands up in my pockets and let them go again. *Don't talk about Tata.* My eyes are stinging badly. I don't say anything.

"Your dad's in prison, didn't you know that?"

I shake my head.

"No, he's not."

"He is."

"No!" The funny feeling in my head explodes. I lash out with all my strength, taking Simon by surprise, and he tumbles backwards like a skittle, bashing into the table on the way down. Then, pandemonium breaks loose. Simon starts screaming, blood is coming from his ear; in two steps Mr Fennimore is across the room and picking him up, and kids are everywhere. The door to class six opens and Miss Wilson comes in, and the next thing I know she's marching me through the resource room to Mrs Honiton's office.

I've only been in Mrs Honiton's office once, and that was when I fell off the monkey bars and broke my arm and Tata had to come and take me to the hospital. I'm trembling from head to foot. I didn't mean to push Simon; I never meant to hurt him even if I hate him. I didn't know what I was doing. Jeanette will be so sad. And if Tata ever knew . . .

A deep hiccup pulls at my chest. The thought of what Tata would say makes the pounding behind my eyes get worse and worse. Mrs Honiton comes out from her desk and says something to Miss Wilson, but I don't really hear what because all I can think about is the *thump thump* in my head. Then she says something to me and sits down on one of the chairs, but I still don't hear; my ears are noisy and my legs feel wobbly. I take a deep breath, to say sorry, but instead sick comes up my throat and it's too late to stop it; it goes all over my school shoes that Jeanette polished this morning and splatters onto Mrs Honiton's carpet.

Miss Wilson runs back in, voices fly through the air, and I find a washing-up bowl in my hands. Someone brings me water in one of the school-dinner cups. But I still can't get any words to come; every time I open my mouth another big sob gets out instead, until I'm not sure if I'm ever going to be able to speak. And I just want Tata to come, more than anything. I just want Tata to come.

Eventually Jeanette arrives. She helps me get changed and puts my sicky clothes and shoes in a Tesco bag. We drive back super slowly, I think because she's worried I'll be sick again. When we get home, she runs me a bath and waits while I have a wash, then brings me my dressing gown and we go and sit on my bed.

The letter to Tata is on my desk, but what Simon said is going round and round in my brain. It makes the big sobs come back, and for a long while I can't tell Jeanette, and she sits worriedly and rubs my shoulders, asking every now and then if I need to be sick. How will I send my letter? What if he's not allowed to read it? I cry so much that I have to wipe the snot on the sleeve of my dressing gown, and Jeanette goes to get the tissues. When she comes back in, she picks me up onto her lap and strokes my hair, and I hide my face in her sweater.

"Is . . ." I can't make the hiccups stop. "Is Tata in prison?"

"*Absolutely* not." Jeanette's fierce voice makes me think of a lioness. I cling onto her sweater, feeling momentarily better. "Absolutely not," she whispers again. "He is absolutely not in prison, my darling. Don't let anybody tell you otherwise."

I sit up. She's still stroking my hair, like she's forgotten that she's doing it.

"Jeanette?" My voice is small.

"Mm?" She glances down at me.

"Is . . . is Tata . . . is Tata *dead*?" New tears, hotter and faster fall down my face and drip off my chin.

Jeanette stares at me. Her eyes are wide and her mouth is a little open, and her face is all screwed-up, like she's in pain.

"No," she says at last. "No. Tata's not dead."

And she takes hold of me and squeezes me so tightly that it actually hurts quite a bit, but I can't say anything, and the whole of her starts to judder as if she's crying too. And we sit like that for a long time, until the phone in the hall has rung at least twice, and someone has knocked on the door and given up again. At last she gets up, mopping her face with a big wad of tissues.

"I need to get you some lunch," she says, and I can tell she's trying to use her normal friendly Jeanette voice, but it's all shaky and croaky. "Do you think you could eat some pancakes?"

I nod. I don't really want pancakes. But I think that cooking pancakes might be good for Jeanette. I wait until she's gone, then slide down from the bed and find some clean jeans and a T-shirt. I climb up at my desk and sit on my heels.

When you get this, pleas can you call me, Jenet does'nt always pick up our phone but I'll listen for it, or come back even if it is only for a visit, I'll under stand. I think Jenet is worried about you. I promiss I'll be good it was an axident today. I just want you to come home. I miss you so much.

    Love,
    Kotek

CHAPTER 6

2004

Jeanette bought the greenhouses with the money from the stables. It used to be a nursery, for cut flowers. She said it was a little thing, to keep us going, but since she got the keys just after my tenth birthday we hardly seem to have stopped.

She's always loved plants. The garden at the cottage is one of my favourite places in the world, especially when we lock the gate and it's completely secluded. I like watching her make it come to life, as if she was born knowing what goes where and how it will look when it grows. Like painting an amazing picture without being able to see the shapes or colours until after it dries.

I curl my legs up to sit cross-legged, and balance my maths book on my knees. It's cold outside, but here on top of the stack of compost bags I'm warm and, I think, invisible. The sacks of feed have a distinct musky smell, and they're stacked so high I can completely disappear behind them.

Jeanette said plants aren't that good at making money, which was why she started out with the feed and the compost and, worst of all, the stinking bags of manure from Yarrops.

The final few weeks of last summer were horrible. I had to steer the sack barrow in and out, in and out, in the boiling-hot heat more times than I can actually bear to think about. I can probably tell the difference by smell now between the different brands of horse feed, between chick crumb and layers pellets and poultry corn.

It got a bit more exciting once she put together the long tables of plants and the hanging-basket displays. She's given it a name now — *Garden Gate* — and this summer, we're going to set out the patio between the greenhouses and the polytunnel with some shrubs and trees. In December, we stacked cut spruces out there and people came and paid loads of money to take them home as Christmas trees. She even let me do the till for a bit and count out the change.

I come here every day after school and do my homework on the compost bags, or sometimes, when the weather is nice, outside in my den in the blackcurrant bushes behind the polytunnel. It's better than getting the school bus home, anyway. I can walk here, then Jeanette takes me home after. The school bus to Shellingsby stops right outside the Blakemans' house, two doors along from us. When I started getting the bus at the beginning of year six, Zach was waiting every day. I even tried going the wrong way, away from our house down Cherrybrook and back up the snicket, but he still found me. I don't understand why he hates me so much. Jeanette says it's because of who his friends are, and that they don't know anything and not to take it to heart. It's easy for her to say that when it's not her getting punched. Sometimes Marcus is there too and I can see him behind their big gates, watching. Marcus is Zach's brother. He's nearly nineteen. Once, he came and held me still so that Zach could kick my kneecaps. He said if I told anyone, he'd break them next time, and I believe him. I think if it wasn't for Jeanette, they might actually kill me.

I also don't think she's telling the whole truth. I know it has something to do with Tata. I know lots of things that she doesn't think I know. I know Zach's best friend is Josh

London. Quite often he's at Zach's house, but he's never spoken to me except once when he told me to "get out of the way, scumbag". Josh's dad is rich and important. He owns a lot of Shellingsby and the land around it. Little Lord London, Jeanette calls Josh, even though he's sixteen, which makes me feel a bit better because I like it that he has a stupid nickname, too.

Something soft butts against my elbow, jerking my arm and spoiling the end of the sum I'm writing. Tabby Blair, the cat that came with the greenhouses, likes the compost bags. I make space for him and rub his matted under-chin. Jeanette has tried a few times to catch him with a brush, but he won't let anyone touch him except me. I can feel him purring. I scratch the top of his head and he bats at my pen. I like maths. I still don't like spelling, much.

"Jeannie, the place is looking great!"

Tabby Blair startles and runs away. Part of me wants to peep over the feed sacks to see who it is. I don't recognise the voice.

"Is he here?"

"He's about, somewhere." Jeanette's voice surprises me. She sounds cross, like she doesn't really want to answer.

"Did you see the news?"

"Can't say I've been following it closely." She sounds even crosser now. I shrink small on the faintly sweaty compost bags.

"They were talking about a lead in R—"

"I don't want to hear it, Carol. I'm not interested. It's all a lot of utter bullshit."

I sit up straight in shock. I've never heard Jeanette swear.

"Does—"

"I said I'm not interested, Carol. Now, can I help you with something?"

I slither to the floor. Whoever Carol is, for some reason I don't want her to see me. I slide between the feed sacks and out the back door. She was going to ask a question that Jeanette didn't want me to hear. Jeanette's not stupid. She doesn't know where I am, but she knows I'm here somewhere. I decide it would be better if I pretend to have been in the van. I'm pretty sure they were talking about Tata.

Jeanette never locks the door, so I get in and clamber through from the front seats to sit in the back. It's mostly dark, with only the square of sunlight that falls through the gap. I finish my homework lying on my belly with the maths book in the frame of light. I'd like to like school. If it wasn't for the other kids, I think I would. Jeanette says September will be a new start for me. Everyone will be new, and there'll be lots of kids that didn't go to Rollingford County Primary that I can make friends with. And Zach won't be there. I was scared he would, but Jeanette says he went to the other Armsby school, not North Wolds, and besides he's too old and he'll leave to go to sixth form this year anyway.

Jeanette closes up at five, just as the van is starting to get a bit too cold. She puts the heater on, and I climb through into the front beside her. She doesn't seem surprised. She asks a few questions about my day as we drive back to Shellingsby, and I don't answer much. It's getting too dark to ride my bike tonight. Jeanette bought me a mountain bike for Christmas. I nearly cried, a little bit, which felt stupid because I was happy. And whenever I cry, Jeanette cries, which is really awkward. So I try not to cry anymore.

Maybe I can ride tomorrow. It's Saturday tomorrow, and Jeanette will be at the greenhouses. If I get up early, Zach won't be up, and I'll be able to ride to the woods without anyone seeing. I've been borrowing Jeanette's fold-up spade to make some jumps. Jeanette doesn't think anyone will mind. She says it's common land, which means it's for anyone to use, and no one does use it so I might as well.

"You're going to get too big to fit through that little gap soon," she tells me.

I grin, realising she's right. I don't mention Carol.

"Aren't you frozen?"

I shake my head. "I'm okay."

She smiles, reaches over and messes up my hair. I'd hate it if anyone else did that. But it's Jeanette, and she's not the best at talking and neither am I, and the little Jeanette things she does make me feel better, like we both belong.

"You're the toughest not-so-little guy I know," she says.

We drive the rest of the way home without talking. The Blakemans' gates are shut. I don't ask about the woods. I play Nintendo in my room until tea is ready. We eat burnt sausages together at the kitchen table. Jeanette's a great gardener but she's not the best at cooking.

It takes me a long time to fall asleep. Since Tata left, I have bad dreams about waking up and finding that I'm all alone. Sometimes I creep to Jeanette's door to check she's still there.

I get up at half past seven. Jeanette wakes me up before she leaves for work. She asks if I want to go with her, and when I say no, thank you, she tells me to make sure I wear my helmet.

I make myself eggs for breakfast, in the microwave. Tata used to make me eggs every day in a saucepan but Jeanette doesn't let me light the gas. I wash up my bowl in the sink and get my bike from the outhouse. I hang my helmet from the handlebars and stuff the fold-up spade into my backpack.

It's uphill to the woods. I pedal as hard as I can, until I'm out of breath. When I first started I couldn't even get up the hill without stopping. I like it that I'm getting faster and fitter.

It's got warm by the time I get there. I take off my hoody and bike around in my T-shirt and jeans, enjoying the fresh air on my skin. The sun is shining through the leaves in moving patterns that make the ground look like water. I sprint the bike as fast as I can to the clearing where I made my ramps, and pretend for a while that I'm biking between islands, shifting my weight on my saddle to make the bike jump over the waves. I'd like to go and try out the big jumps in the skatepark, but Jeanette doesn't like the idea, and also there's always the risk in Armsby of Josh and Zach being there.

When I get tired I drop the bike in the bracken, and sit and eat an apple, looking at the jumps. I can't see why I couldn't make a bigger one. Jeanette did say this land belongs to everybody. I've got pretty strong, helping her move all the sacks around at the garden centre.

I draw out where I want to dig with a stick before I unfold the spade. I'm not sure how long it will take. Maybe all day. It doesn't matter if it does. Zach and Josh don't come up here. Not ever.

I get so hot and sweaty digging and compacting the earth that my T-shirt is wet. When I check my watch, it's lunchtime. I didn't bring any lunch, and my belly is growling. I sit down in the hollow at the bottom of the jump, wondering whether to go back.

And then I see it, something black and plasticky poking out of the scraped clay. I get up onto my knees to have a better look. It's not just broken rubbish, it's something whole. I use my fingers to gouge the soil from around it. It's the black top of a car key. My heart is beating loudly. The key is on a rusty ring, and stuck fast. I use the end of a stick, and sure enough there's another key on the ring too, clagged with mud. I dig until the whole thing comes away in a clump, and sit back on my heels. I poke the clod of mud out of the ring with the stick and scratch the dirt away with my fingernails.

There's a funny feeling in my stomach. Sort of like the feeling when Zach punched me and all the air went out of my body. I brush them carefully clean with my hands, and trace the logo with one finger. I know its shape. If I close my eyes, I can see it hanging from the ignition, or from Tata's hand. It makes me remember the smell of farms and straw.

I breathe in and out deeply, trying to hold onto the smell, because it feels like he's close by if I can smell the smell.

I look for a long time. I don't move or make a sound. Just look, at the old black plastic and the glinting metal, and the dirty oval badge.

He lost his car keys. I feel like I should tell Jeanette. But I don't want to. It would make her face scrunch up, like when she's hurt, or it might even make her cry. And I don't want her to take them away.

So instead, I wrap them in a tissue and push them deep into my pocket.

CHAPTER 7

Rosalie

Mary, Mary, quite contrary . . .

I woke up this morning to Hailbury's silence and the red dawn light with the words circling in my head. I can't get them out. My laptop case slips off my shoulder as I try to open the front door, pulling me off balance. I drop my bag of shopping with a curse so that I can use both hands. How did he do it? I tug the door hard against its frame and strain at the key.

How does your garden grow?

"Come *on*!" I drop the laptop, too, and fight the urge to smack a fist against the Farrow & Ball. I'm so late.

Six times out of ten, I can get straight in. But never when it matters. And never, it seems, when Kasper Miller's pickup is parked in the drive. In my pocket, my phone starts to buzz: the alarm I set to remind me not to miss the meeting with Tabitha, my agent, that I'm about to miss because I can't get into the house.

With silver bells and cockle shells . . .
And pretty maids all in a—

"Shut *up!*" I clamp my hands to my ears and sit down on the step. Maybe I could join the Zoom call from the porch? Except my laptop battery is flat. I fumble to silence the phone.

"Rosalie."

He has the gall to give me a polite nod as he ascends past me, pulls the door and turns the key first time.

"Thanks." I snatch up the laptop and shopping, and pause, realising I'm glaring. I try to soften my expression. "Sorry. I'm meant to be in a meeting. Thank you."

But Kasper has already gone. I watch for a moment as he turns his attention back to what he was doing, shouldering a sack of mulch and easing a barrow of plants off the gravel and onto the flagstone path at the corner of the house.

How does your garden grow?

The lounge is freezing. I plug in my laptop, check the Wi-Fi connection and wait for Zoom to load, wrapping a blanket around the bits of me that won't be visible on the webcam. I ventured into the attic yesterday. In case the Sylvanians aren't enough, there's an entire playroom up there, a tepee and a Wendy house, teddy bears, tea sets, dolls in prams, a *lot* of Lego. Through the playroom, the *attic proper* was a refreshing testimony to the time that has really passed, unfrequented by cleaners and thick with cobwebs, the boxes deep in dust. In contrast, my mother's old studio, complete with adjoining gym, is still preserved like a museum, the crenulations outside the window casting shadows on her framed movie posters. There were thousands of pounds' worth of clothes from the eighties and nineties stashed in her walk-in-wardrobes before the #*leonieshouse* images started to pop up online, but she sent a company to retrieve them a few years ago, and most of them were auctioned. All that was left was a stack of boxes that I can only presume the police never got round to unpacking. So, I unpacked them, one at a time, manhandling them down the stairs and unloading their contents over the lounge floor. It seemed like as good a place to start as any.

I gaze down at the pictures spread on the coffee table: the draft of Leonie's photo shoot, the one that would have got everyone's attention if her disappearance hadn't done the job instead.

"Rosalie?"

"Oh!" I look up at the screen. Tabitha and Stefan have started without me, their distorted, digitised voices feeding back through my unmuted microphone. One of them has let me in without me noticing. I can hear the familiar creak of Tabitha's computer chair. She's been unfailingly supportive over the last seven years, despite the dwindling royalties and lack of any material follow-up to my first — and at this rate, only — book.

"Oh, hi. Sorry I'm late." I angle the camera up. But my eyes are drawn, once more, to Leonie. To my sister. Fourteen years old. Was it really okay to be captured that way, at fourteen? With smoky-eyed make-up and waist-length hair, wide-legged jeans barely covering her protruding hipbones, a headband of flowers the only nod to what ought to have been innocence? *Mary, Mary, quite contrary*: the words are printed between the sepia shots, long legs crossed as she lounges across a wrought-iron bench, a grass stalk between her pouting lips. *How does your garden grow?* A carpet of flowers surrounding her, prone and propped up on her elbows, the perfume bottle cradled nonchalantly in her fingers. Contraire — by L'Église Rose. They're sultry and eye-catching and, it occurs to me, wrong on almost every level. Three months, three months after somebody took these photos, she was gone.

"How are you getting on?"

I swallow. Ten chapters of bullet points, that's how I'm getting on. Not even a single line of prose. I open them in the background. Is there anything more daunting than a blank page? Just line after line of emptiness, where there should be a story but there isn't, because it won't write itself — even though once it did, and now nobody can find an ending.

"Yeah, good . . . good. Thanks." I smile and pull the blanket tighter around my knees.

Leonie Olivia. I look back down into her sepia eyes, thinking of Christmas perfume adverts, of catwalks, of Cannes. She would have loved Cannes. There's a name printed at the corner of the spread. *PHOTOGRAPHY: Antonio DiPaci.* I wonder how he must have felt, watching his work get filed away in a police report. Whether she left a bloodstain that wouldn't quite wash off his career, just like she did to everybody else.

I avoid giving any more detail about my progress. Stefan seems to have a set agenda anyway, and we revert to that. I make notes against my bullet points, comments slowly filling the right-hand margin until, by the time we're finished, they highlight most of the pages in cyanotic purple, like the whole document is a mistake.

Outside the window, a shadow crosses the sun. I glance up at the silhouette of Kasper Miller's gilet, T-shirt and bare arms. Does he not feel the cold? I'm shivering. Stefan exits the call, and I'm momentarily glad of this post-pandemic world of virtual meetings and screens to hide behind. I've known Stefan, my mother's agent, since my teens, and we're definitely on strained air-kissing terms at social functions. Professionally speaking, I'm less sure. In fact, between my mother's sixty-eight pages of thinly veiled agenda and Stefan's comments, I'm not even entirely sure who's writing this book.

"Great to see you, Rosalie." Tabitha gives a jerky smile. Now Stefan has gone, she's picked up her mug. It makes me think of how things used to be, meeting her for lunch in Covent Garden, both of us bubbling over with excitement. "I hope you're keeping well? Sorry to have brought Stefan in, but we're going to have to make sure he's green-lighted everything before it goes to Alison, so it seemed best to appease him early on. I'd say probably just find your flow, and we'll work out the rest later."

Alison. My publisher. I nod and pull my cable-knit sleeves down over my hands. I'm craving another coffee. My head's starting to ache.

"That's okay." I smile. "Thanks, Tabitha."

"Is there anything else you wanted to chat about? What's it like being back in Shellingsby St Mary? I'm dying to hear about it."

"Oh, it's . . . different. But I'm getting to grips with it."

"Are you still speaking at that Rains College literary lunch? When is it? Perhaps we could pencil in dinner afterwards?"

"End of April, I think." Oh, God. I'd forgotten. "Yeah, that sounds good."

"Fab. Well, send me any bits you want. And let me know if you want to Zoom again, otherwise we can catch up then."

"Sure."

"Bye, Rosalie."

"Bye." There's still no way to wave on camera that doesn't seem awkward. I'm definitely not my mother's daughter.

And there's the problem. I stare at my butchered bullet points. I scroll to the top and type it in. *I'm not my mother's daughter.* Then I delete it, and shut the laptop.

I put away Leonie's pictures. Something about them is making me feel queasy. I pull the next unopened box across the floor towards me and rip off the tape.

The first few folders look like schoolwork. I put them to one side, and something drops out with a tinkle of metal on the floor. A brass key. I pick it up to look at it. It belongs to a jewellery box, perhaps, or a diary. I pocket it.

I pull out the next bundle of paper and card, completely unprepared for what's underneath. Instead of her, I come face to face with my six-year-old self. They're school photos, the ones that come in an extortionately overpriced pack. I look at my pink-rimmed glasses and tightly managed pigtails. Underneath the individual shots, there's a whole-school picture in a black cardboard frame. Rollingford County Primary wasn't big. I hold it up to look at it, something occurring to me.

It's summer, in the picture. The gingham dresses are startlingly familiar; if I sit very still, I can feel the insubstantial fabric against my skin. The boys are in blue polo shirts and knee-length shorts. I'm at the front, bony and awkward and small, the sun reflecting off the lenses of my glasses. I scan the forgotten faces of my class, disconcerted by the names that attach themselves. Laura, Rebecca Hill, Matthew, Rebecca Utherton, Nicholas. My heart is beating hard. Joy's right. The information is still there.

And so is he. It takes me a couple of minutes. He's not with my class; he's further back, at the end of the third row. Older than me, skinny, serious-eyed and pale: *Casper the ghost*. It comes at me from nowhere, the nickname, a flash of memory from the cloakroom doorway, my hands clutching the drawstring of my PE bag. The boy with grey eyes, standing in the corner as they unpack his lunchbox, holding up the contents like trophies while he watches, quiet and motionless. They're bigger than him, laughing at him, pocketing the best bits, banging the box shut, reaching over his head to hang it on the window-opener high above. He doesn't move. He waits in silence until they've gone. Then he climbs up expertly onto the coat pegs and hooks it down.

I rise to my feet, feeling unconsciously for the arm of the sofa. I'm dizzied by the clarity of the pictures, the smell of the floor cleaner. I see myself faltering, too frightened to go in, Vesna's soft voice echoing in my ears, bribing me not to cry with promises of kysil and cookies and stopping by the millpond to feed the ducks.

I grip the sofa to ground myself. Coffee. Bullet points. I mentally claw my way back into the cold sitting room. If this is recall, I'm not sure I want it. I replace the pictures in the box, head pounding.

I let out a slow breath. I should probably call Joy. Email her at the very least. This should be momentous. But I don't. I retrieve the laptop from amongst the archived remains of the turn of the millennium, and take it upstairs.

The new router in my father's study is an array of flashing lights. I find an extension lead and set the laptop up on the leather-topped desk, sitting in the high-backed chair and staring at the bullet points one last time before I close them and open a new document.

Not my mother's daughter.

And then I start to type.

The sun moves around the front of the house, and the heating clicks on. My stomach's growling when I look back up. The kitchen seems a long way away as I walk there and drop two toasting waffles into the toaster while I wait for the kettle to boil. By the time I get them back to the study, they're cold and crisp. I gulp back an ibuprofen with a sip of scalding tea and crunch my way through the waffles with my eyes on the screen and my fingers leaving sticky marks on the keyboard.

After a while my back starts to ache. I get up to stretch my legs, gaze out of the sash windows from the bathroom onto the drive. The pickup is gone, and a bird is pecking at the newly planted perennials in the bed around the fountain. Something nags at the periphery of my awareness. Something I feel like I should know, as I stare down at the freshly dug soil.

I back up my files before I turn off the laptop. It's late afternoon, and my brain has burnt itself out. I've left my phone somewhere; I feel my pockets, trying to remember. The sitting room, with pigtailed Rosalie and Casper the ghost, and L'Église Rose. I go downstairs, trying to fill the silence with my own footfalls, suppressing a shudder as I push open the door.

And for a split second, I'm not where I think I am.

I stumble, disorientated by the darkness, by the memory of fast irregular breaths and red, red lips. The heavy curtains are shut, the Roman blinds rattling against the window frames. A jolt of panic rises in my chest; I collide with a sofa arm and trip on the edge of the hearthrug. The door bangs closed behind me.

I gasp.

Someone's here.

Boxes, photographs, fluttering paper; I fumble amongst them for my phone and swipe on the torch, throwing the shadows large and looming across the walls, the tang of fear sharp in my mouth. I spin three-sixty, flashing the torch into the corners, feeling my way back towards the door. Someone's shut me in—

Then my sweating fingers find the old enamelled light switch and flick it on, and I realise with a rush of electric-lit clarity and relief that I'm actually going insane.

Why didn't I turn on the light to start with? I lower my trembling hand to kill the torch. I would have closed the curtains for the Zoom call. Wouldn't I?

Didn't I?

I walk to the garden room and sit down on my mat. I can't carry on like this. The sleep deprivation is killing me. I should register with a doctor. Although I won't risk taking sleeping tablets again; I made that mistake once to try and mollify Hamish and his blindfold. Unfortunately, it transpired that chemically induced nightmares were a lot worse than not being able to sleep at all.

I've been intending to find a yoga class or a squash club. Non-pharmacological treatments — exercise and meditation, cut the caffeine — Joy would be validated. I take out my phone to google. Armsby and the Wolds squash club has a club night every Tuesday: *mixed squash, no need to pre-book, just come down, sign up and have 20-minute matches with a range of players.* Today is Tuesday. I shelve the thought and flick through local yoga instructors before I force my own hand and block-book a Hatha class in Rollingford on spec.

A notification flashes up as I finish putting in my card details. I swipe through. I've barely been on social media since I arrived at Hailbury.

With good reason. I stare at the pictures, chilled, even though I knew they existed. Even though I knew they were there, somewhere, lingering in public view.

They're of Hailbury. Of the fountain and the perennials. Of the Farrow & Ball on the front door. Of the formal gardens, outside the window where my eyes rest now, immaculately impressive, *#leonieshouse*. I'm tagged. I hover over the need to block it from my feed, to obliterate it from the sphere of my knowledge. A shiver of unease runs down my spine.

Who knows?

What do they know?

These pictures are old. I remind myself of that as I screw my eyes closed. As I shove the phone into my back pocket. They pre-date the razor wire and the CCTV.

Of course they do . . .

Mary, Mary . . .

* * *

The photos tipped the balance; I had to get away from Hailbury. I found my squash racquet and left the house shivering, with a too-big hoody over my shorts. I'm trying not to think about my course of action if I can't unlock the front door when I get back.

The car park at the leisure centre is full. I take a membership pack and navigate the warren of corridors. The centre is small and there are only two squash courts, fluorescent-lit and smudged with ball marks. Nonetheless, it's busy. I walk up to the table where I can see sign-up sheets. A man who introduces himself as Paul takes my sub and writes down my name.

"Have you played before?" He's smiling, affable, perhaps not very perceptive given the state of my racquet case. I nod.

"Yeah, a bit."

"Nice one. Well, welcome, Rosalie. It's great to have new faces. We try and stick to twenty-minute matches, five minutes' changeover and warm-up."

"Sure." I glance around. The corridor is chilly. I can't imagine it will stay that way. There are already pairs warming up in each of the two courts.

"It's all mixed at the moment, I'm afraid. We used to run a ladies' club night but we got a bit short on numbers."

"Mixed is fine." I think, briefly, of Hamish. The first time we met, I envisaged him throwing down his racquet,

McEnroe style. In hindsight, it should probably have been a warning sign.

I don't go up to the balcony, daunted by the crowd. I stretch off in the corridor instead, then pick the right-hand court and half-watch the first match through the glass. I keep score in my head until it finishes. It's only as Paul taps my shoulder that I regain awareness of my surroundings.

"You're up, Rosalie. Court one."

"Oh, thanks." I flash him a smile and slip off my hoody. My opponent is already on court. I make myself relax and focus on the reassurance of the racquet grip in my hand. It certainly outlasted Hamish. I swing open the door and come to a dead stop.

For a moment, I can't make myself move. It literally never crossed my mind. Kasper Miller. I swallow my disbelief and re-adjust my hold on the racquet, trying to claw back the shreds of my composure. Wide-shouldered, lean and muscled, self-possessed: the antithesis of my limited memories, Casper the ghost and the stolen lunchbox. He doesn't miss a beat as the door closes behind me.

Nothing about him could ever be reminiscent of Hamish. I didn't notice before, but he has a circumferential tattoo on his right arm, some kind of elaborate woven pattern inked in black, accentuating the powerful bulk of his triceps and biceps. There's not an ounce of Eton in his genealogy; there's an edge to his expression, a quiet cynicism, as if he's been angry at the world for long enough that he's abandoned his rage and moved on from his expectations, and now nothing can surprise him.

"Rosalie." His gaze is calm, assessing.

"Hi." I meet it squarely.

"Paul really is full of surprises."

"You can say that again." I take my place on court, standing on one leg and then the other to stretch my Achilles. "I didn't know you played."

"Did you make your meeting?" His question is levelled at me lightly, but his brows are dark and his eyes are perceptive, and I can't interpret the undertone.

"Oh. Yes, thanks."

"Good. I didn't know you played either, although I should have figured from the racquet."

Should he? I remember the first afternoon at Hailbury. My cases in the hall.

"I never thanked you for that."

"You didn't need to. Do you want to take first serve?"

"No, we can spin." I frown, trying to work him out. He does as I say, and I take first serve anyway.

He returns easily, but not hard. I slice the next backhand, forcing him to move. He knocks it back. I narrow my eyes. He's not trying. I win the point. He takes the next one. We alternate politely to ten, like actors reading through a script for the first time, until I lose patience and smack the ball so hard that it takes him off guard. It finds its mark solidly just below his ribcage before he can get his racquet back far enough to intercept. He stumbles.

"Game," I murmur. He concedes with a lift of his brows. He hasn't broken a sweat.

"Your serve," I fire at him.

I watch. It's textbook, but without any real effort. It would have been another easy point. Instead, I let it bounce, step in and close my hand around the ball. Kasper lowers his racquet, something flickering across his expression. A smile? I glare at him.

"You're going easy on me."

"I wouldn't." He shakes his head.

"You are." I outstare him, and he holds up his hands.

"Okay. I won't."

"Sure?" I toss him the ball. He catches it left-handed.

"Sure." His voice is impossible to read. But I don't miss his fleeting sideways glance.

His real serve is formidable. He wins three points before I've adjusted, but it doesn't take long to get his measure. He hits hard, but I'm fast. There's a pattern to his game: he's never short and usually cross-court; his backswing and power are his mainstay, and he doesn't like drop shots. With some softly placed balls into the front corners, I find my stride. By the time he wins the second game, we're both gasping. I take a swig from my water bottle, trying not to watch him as he turns to do the same. Trying not to think about serious grey eyes and coat pegs.

"One all," he says.

I take my place in the service box.

"How long have you worked at Hailbury?" The swipe of my racquet cuts off the end of my question. He dives for the return.

"A few years."

"You've been in the house?" I volley it.

"Occasionally." He smacks it back. I lunge for the backhand and flinch as it hits the tin.

"Was it you that put up the razor wire?" I glance at him as he gets ready to serve.

"Yeah. He . . . your father . . . wanted it after the last lot of looters."

It's a body serve and it's fast. I leap backwards.

"Urban explorers." I flick the ball into the front corner. His eyebrow lifts as he concedes the point.

"Whatever they call themselves. His call, either way."

"You think he's out of his mind?"

"He pays well. I don't have to think anything." Kasper tosses me the ball.

"You've met him?"

"Only over the phone."

I pause in the service box, weigh up my strategy. Smash or lob.

I take a deep breath. "You think I'm out of mine?"

For a split second, he makes eye contact: impenetrable grey. I don't look away. The court has started to warm up, and I can feel the sweat on my face. Lob. The temperature's going to make the ball unpredictable. He has to volley high. I hit a straight drive back and we rally. He takes the point.

"Like I said." He's panting. "I don't have to think anything."

I wipe my upper lip. I don't have enough breath for more questions. We tie at ten all. I can tell he's trying to run me out, but I don't tire that easily. I played three times a week in Crouch End when I could still afford it. It's oddly satisfying, having an opponent who makes me work for it. We're both dripping sweat.

"Win by two," I gasp. "Your serve."

The tiniest shake of his head. I realise I'm distracted as he serves and goes a point ahead.

The next rally is brutal. Every one of his shots is offensive, aimed to end the game. My trainers squeak on the floor as I intercept his kill; he lunges for the return, I backstep—

And suddenly he's on top of me. He half falls over me; we both stumble into the wall. I put out an arm to save myself, and I can hear the labour of his breathing, feel the heat of his chest, the drop of his steel-grey gaze to my raging cheeks . . .

The wall is cool under my palm. I push off, pulse racing, and take my place in the service box. We play a let; I feel his sideways glance before he serves. But this time I've got him. I take the point on a backhand, and the next on a smashed serve. I realise as I hit the final point that Paul is at the door, and there are players waiting. Kasper lowers his racquet. He's breathing hard.

"*Are* you?" His gaze meets mine.

"Am I what?" I'm too breathless and tired to process it.

"Out of your mind."

I can't quite tell if he's serious. I look for a second too long at the shades of grey in his eyes.

"Yes," I whisper. "I'm beginning to think so."

He smiles outright this time. Then he holds open the door for me, and I duck outside into chaos and congratulation. I smile politely and field the comments, fighting the urge to look back. I hear the clap of a hand on his shoulder. A gale of laughter.

"I hope you like cold showers, Miller," somebody says.

And then I slip away through the unfamiliar faces, my heart beating a drumroll in my chest.

CHAPTER 8

Inside Leonie's room, the stillness is like held breath. A growing certainty. There's something here, something I'm missing. Like the turned earth in the bed around the fountain, closed curtains and rattling blinds. Something that I can't place.

Something that I can't escape.

I wrote two thousand words before breakfast this morning. I don't remember the last time they flowed so furiously. There's a liberation to it, excitement that I haven't felt in a long time. Or maybe it's the thrill of nerves. The soft close of a squash-court door. The uneasy feeling of impending disaster that seems resident in Hailbury's darker corners.

The tiny key is still in the back pocket of my jeans. One of the Post-its has fallen off Leonie's mirror; I stoop to pick it up and stick it back, and a chill ripples across my skin.

The bed is made. I wet my lips. One of the cleaners has deviated from instructions, that's all. I move to untuck the covers with morbid compulsion. Am I turning into my father? The lilac shade of the lamp on the bedside table is dustless, and the framed black-and-white *Breakfast at Tiffany's* print that stands beside it is immaculately polished. Behind the picture there's a doll propped against the wall, and I think for a moment of my sister holding Jessica hostage, dangling her from one hand: *If you want to see her again, you'll do what I say . . .*

I move the print aside. It's not Jessica; Jessica is safely back in the suitcase under my bed. It's much glossier than Jessica, with slim fabric limbs, a pink chiffon dress and real auburn hair that flows to its waist, a mockery of my own. It's wearing a child's necklace, gold with a locket. I click it open. A miniscule note: *love from your new baby sister.*

I replace the doll with a hand that's not quite steady. April rain is spitting against the window. The chime downstairs startles me so much that I almost knock over the print. The doorbell. I descend the stairs and jerk open the door.

"Hi," I exhale.

Kasper steps back, his gaze playing on my face. His shoulders are blocking out the brunt of the rain, but the damp air is chill against my leggings.

"Rosalie." His voice is polite, inscrutable. "How are you? Is now a good time for Carl to look at the lock?"

He glances over his shoulder, and I notice the van on the other side of the fountain, and the stocky man leaning against it, on his phone.

"Oh." I release the door. "Yes, by all means."

A pause. It hangs, waiting, a slow build of static.

"Seems you managed to get in okay last night," he says at last. The little non-committal smile is back. "I wasn't sure if I ought to shelve my injured pride and come and check the doorstep."

I bite back a smile, too.

"The concern's appreciated. I hope your pride's okay now?"

"It will be." He pushes his hands into the pockets of his gilet, and I find myself studying his face, the drizzle on his skin, the level scrutiny of his slightly narrowed grey eyes. There's the faintest flicker of his eyebrows. He's caught me looking, again. For a second, our eyes meet.

Kasper takes a step back. "I'm sorry. You must have been working. I'll ask Carl to find me when he finishes, so he doesn't have to interrupt you."

"Oh . . . no, it's fine." My glasses have slid down my nose. I need to find an optician. "Do you, er . . ." I look fleetingly at Carl, who is now approaching across the drive. "Can I get either of you a drink?"

"Tea, thanks." Carl touches his cap and deposits a hefty bag on the steps with a jangle. "Splash of milk, two sugars."

"I'm okay." Kasper shakes his head. "Thanks."

And then he's gone, boots crunching on the gravel.

I make Carl's tea and retreat upstairs. The occasional clatter and crash of tools and the echo of his cheerful whistling pervades Hailbury's usually sullen silence. I steel myself and go back into her room.

The key's too small to fit the dressing-table drawers and there's no lock on the wardrobe. I scan over the journals and notebooks on her desk. Reading them has been on my to-do list since I arrived. I move to the swing and lay a hand on the cushioned seat. The idea of opening them, just like sitting down and giving my weight in jubilant recalcitrance to the creaking ropes, makes my heart beat fast.

I know someone else has read them, probably lots of people. Along with everything else: the reams of MSN messages, the hard drive of her PC. They will all have been scanned, photocopied, stored away as evidence for a prosecution that never came. But those people weren't me. They weren't under explicit instructions not to touch.

I sit down in her chair. The top book has dates embossed in the spine: *2002–2003*. An academic diary. I open it to the front page. *If I plan to learn, I must learn to plan.* Hm. I flip through pages of homework assignments written in multi-coloured gel pens, doodles and scribbled notes: *SOS 2nite? Wot u wearing for NYE? Dunno. He fancies u. Whatevs. You like him? Only m8s. Yeh, rite.*

On it goes. *Biology pp 22–34. Qu 5–16. **Maths coursework FRIDAY** Does Iago cause the tragedy of Othello? 1500 words.*

I pull up my knees to sit cross-legged on the chair. I can picture her, here, fountain pen tucked in her left hand. Her CD player would be on, she'd be picking at bowls of fruit or yoghurt, long hair cascading over the back of the chair as she leant back at a dangerous angle to roll her eyes at me. *Go away, Rosy.*

There's not going to be anything new here. I fast-forward through the pages to February, March, 5 April: twenty years ago today.

Then, on 10 April:

u got a bf then?

No.

at the yard?

No.

Liar

I drink in a slow breath. Yes, this page will definitely be in the file. Along with the plates of the car, and his picture. Somehow, when they release photos of criminals and killers, they always look like criminals or killers. Which seems counter-intuitive, because who would ever have got into a car with someone so overtly terrifying? Krzysztof Woźniak was no exception. I've grown up with his face burn onto my subconscious — the man who stole my sister — like other children grow up with cautionary tales of monsters and wolves. Except this monster was real. And still is? A shudder runs along my spine.

There's one page left with writing on it. 28 April 2003. A Monday. *What does the behaviour of Shakespeare's Rosalind suggest about gender? 1500 words.* The last day. Someone has drawn balloons and fluorescent swirls around the twenty-ninth, but she never got there. *As You Like It* is on the desk, a battered school copy covered in pencil marks. I close the book. My appetite for the others has waned.

My phone buzzes in my pocket. I pull it out.

@RosalieK-L

I feel suddenly sick.

It's another series of pictures. Familiar pictures: prone and propped on her elbows, smoky eyes gazing beguilingly into mine. They're laid out on a coffee table . . .

I fumble to look for the time, the date. How? I half expect her head to appear around the door frame, her snidey voice. *April fool, Rosalie.* I can hear my own pulse. They're old. Someone else's copies. I'm breathing too fast. Someone else's coffee table . . . ?

The last picture isn't of a coffee table at all. It's of a door. A handle. A hand—

I ram the phone into my pocket and slam open the door onto the landing. There's no one there. Of course there's no one there. Carl's downstairs, tinkering with the lock, and Kasper Miller is outside mowing stripes in the immaculate lawn. I bang Leonie's bedroom door shut and bolt for my room. I pace to the window, trying to talk sense to myself. Drizzle is clinging to the box hedges and the lavender and marking out the spiderwebs in dewy intricacy.

I pick up one of the novels from the bookcase. The beady eyes of the Sylvanians are watching me. The illustrated animals on the wallpaper, a whole tiny menagerie with cartoon faces, are poised and waiting.

I hate wallpaper.

I close my eyes. When I open them again, the animals haven't moved, and the Sylvanians are lifeless.

"You're not here," I whisper to the silence. As though she might be listening. "You're not here anymore."

* * *

The hardware shop in Armsby has emulsion and paintbrushes. I choose a nondescript grey and juggle the purchases to my car in a cardboard box.

Carl has gone by the time I get back, and so has Kasper's pickup, and the key turns smoothly in Hailbury's lock. I don't check the coffee table. I haven't even been back into the sitting room to open the curtains. I take the paint to my room.

I have no idea how long it's going to take me to strip the wallpaper. Nonetheless, it's cathartic to sweep up the

Sylvanians and pile their once-perfect existence into the slightly damp cardboard box, to tip out the dolls' house into a bin bag and haul the whole lot outside the bedroom door. I move methodically through the room, stripping out almost everything. The only mementos I keep are the books.

In the soft glow of the table lamp, none of it looks so frightening. What's the point in preserving the house when the family is long since smashed to pieces? If we'd all stayed, and carried on in our perfectly ordered lives, we wouldn't have been frozen in time like the Sylvanians. We would have aged, moved on. Cleaned out our rooms and repainted them.

I sit down on the bed. We're human. Fallible. I reach underneath to pull out my suitcase. The box is shoved in behind it — it used to be called my treasure box — interring the fragments of my real childhood, and I'm not so sure that it was all as perfectly ordered as people like to think. A postcard written in my own seven-year-old cursive, to myself. A 7x5 studio portrait of dazzling-smiled Leonie with me, gap-toothed, the camera flash reflecting off my glasses. A smaller, older photo: my christening, my mother and father wound around each other like wisteria; my godparents — Lord James Edward Armsby and his wife, and a glamorous modelling colleague of my mother's. Underneath the photos there's Jessica's spare outfit, hand-stitched by someone once, a ribbon-edged blanket, a silver child's bracelet made all of tiny roses. The first edition of *Northanger Abbey and Persuasion* that my father bought me for my twenty-first birthday and my own novel in hardback.

I hold up the postcard. It's a seaside picture. I study the faded colours; greens gone turquoise, blues gone grey. There *is* a memory. One I've always had, even though I pretended to everyone, including myself, that I didn't. I study the gull perched on the concrete seawall, the brown sand, the washed-out colours of the beach huts. There's a bench, bright gaudy red — the only colour that hasn't bleached into the card — and I remember the feel of the enamelled metal. I remember climbing up beside her, huddling close, sobbing. Sorry. *I'm sorry* . . . The suck of the sea. It's the only time I ever remember her holding me. My big, beautiful, stolen sister.

The bench is empty on the postcard. I snap a photo of it with my phone, then put it back in the box.

There's something missing. Not just her. There's something that has never quite added up. I don't know what it is, but it's present, all the time. I can't repress it; I can't outrun it. It's becoming impossible to deny. Now that I'm here, it's in the periphery of my vision everywhere I look.

I push the box under the bed and slide to my feet. Wallpaper. Those tiny eyes watched my every moment as a child, judged my every action, invaded my every dream. Not anymore. They've got to go.

The cold and damp from around the window have done for the adhesive, and the first sheet comes away almost intact, folding around me like a shroud.

I pause.

Beyond the rustle of the settling paper, I'm sure I can hear something. A sound so familiar that it chills me to the bone. A creak of rope, a well-oiled carabiner. Leonie's swing is swinging. Back and forth, a steady pendulum of whispered motion.

It's not. I screw my eyes shut. I can't. I can't hear anything. Nothing except the heavy tick of the clock on the dressing table, the buzz of silence. I try to visualise instead: *repressed trauma*. Things that definitely are, written out over weeks and months in Joy's notebook. Things that definitely aren't.

I am Rosalie Knight-Langton. I am rational and capable. The house is locked. The door to Leonie's room is still shut. I am alone.

And the swing definitely isn't swinging.

CHAPTER 9

Kacper
2007

Jeanette was married before she knew Tata. He was called Geoff, and he died in an accident on a farm near Rollingford in 1998. It's weird, because Jeanette talks about him quite often, without being sad. And yet when she speaks about Tata, which is hardly ever, her eyes fill up with tears. Sometimes, lately, she'll squeeze my shoulder and tell me how nice it is "having a man around the place", especially when the deliveries arrive, or a customer needs something carrying to their car. I can carry a feed sack on my shoulders now. Since the end of year eight, I've got as tall as she is.

Garden Gate has got big, too. There's an indoors and an outdoors now; a proper building with a gift shop, a clothes section and a bit that sells expensive jam and boxes of posh sweets. There's a café, too; Geoff's sister, Lorraine, moved from Grimsby to help Jeanette set it up. She bakes amazing cakes and got Jeanette to order a fancy coffee machine that makes frothy milk. Lorraine's daughter is a bit older than me; she's just started at North Wolds in year ten. She sometimes

72

helps Lorraine in the café, or sometimes she comes to find me instead and we play canasta in the storeroom, perching on the warm compost sacks like I did when I was a kid.

The sun has crept around the end wall of the cottage while I've been working. It's Sunday morning, and Jeanette's at Garden Gate. The cottage always looks nice at this time of year with the clematis flowering deep purple against the white walls.

I sit back on my heels and look at the door. Jeanette asked me if I'd paint it for some extra pocket money. I would have painted it anyway, which I told her, and she laughed and said I need to be more cut-throat. I still don't really understand what she meant, but she said she'd pay me three pounds fifty an hour. Three pounds fifty didn't seem much when I thought it would only *take* an hour. But sanding it nearly killed me and now that I'm twenty minutes into my third coat, I'm starting to think I won't have to wait until Christmas for the new *Tomb Raider* game, even if Jeanette has to wait that long for the paint to dry enough to put the doorknocker back on.

Yesterday Mr Wilkinson from 31 Cherrybrook asked if I'd do his. I already cut his grass every other Saturday for a fiver. I said yes, for three pounds sixty an hour, and we shook on it like businessmen. That's what gave me the idea.

The blue gloss stinks. I'm covered in drips and smudges by the time I go inside, and I have to scrub my hands with white spirit. The smell hasn't faded from my hands even after a shower as I collect my rucksack and go to get my bike from the shed.

I start my venture on Cherrybrook, in case Mr Wilkinson has already put in a good word, flyering each letterbox with the adverts I printed out at Garden Gate. I work my way round the three main streets and then strike out for Rollingford, enjoying the wind through my hair even though I know Jeanette will kill me if she sees me on the road without a helmet. I do all of Wensley Close, Main Street and Thaxted Drive before I run out of flyers.

I set my watch to stopwatch before I start back, and cycle full pelt. It only takes me five and a half minutes to get to the sports ground, which is nearly halfway. I do football or rugby there most nights. I like sport. When I'm playing, I don't have to think about anything else. And I'm the best midfielder in the under fourteens.

I come into the outskirts of the village, past the place the stables used to be. I stand up on the pedals to get up the hill, and corner onto Back Lane. Going home along Cherrybrook is still the safest option by a long shot. I check over my shoulder and pull out round the row of parked cars.

I pass all but the last one, and it's as I power down on the right pedal that the car's rear door opens. There's no time to do anything. I hear the crunch, and the clatter of the bike on the tarmac, and all the breath leaves my lungs at once. Somehow, I rebound off the edge of the door, and then I'm lying in the road, lights flashing in front of my eyes.

"Sorry, Polack, mate, didn't see you there!"

There's an explosive snort of laughter from the driver's seat. The door swings wide then slams as the car revs and screeches away, and through the bursting stars and dazzling sunshine I can see Josh London in the front passenger seat with his feet on the dashboard and Zach's vulgar gesture out of the back windscreen.

Luckily the road isn't busy, because it takes me a moment to pick myself up. My elbows are scuffed and my head's pounding. I limp to the bike. I've bitten my lip and blood is running down my chin, and I can feel grazes on my face. I rub the blood away with one hand. Even the smallest breaths hurt my chest, and pushing the bike the 300 yards back to the cottage seems to take forever.

I put my bike in the shed. Jeanette is in the kitchen when I go in. I try to slink past her before she can turn around, and I bolt for the stairs.

"Hey, big lad . . ." She tails off. "Oh, good *God*. My darling . . ."

I jam my teeth together.

"What *happened*?" She abandons the cooking, even though one of the saucepans is bubbling hot foam over the top and onto the gas ring. "Good God." She snatches the kitchen roll from the table, ripping off a bit for me to press on my mouth. "Sit down." She steers me back to the table, her lips a hard, fierce line.

"If this was those—"

"I just fell off my bike," I mumble. It's hard to talk properly through the kitchen roll.

"Just!" She's lifting my arms one at a time to assess the damage. "Look at the state of you! Don't move. Did you hit your head? Were you on the road? Were you wearing your helmet?"

I'm no good at lying. I shake my head.

"Did you get up straight away? Do you remember falling? Do we need to go to the hospital?" She's dropped my arm to examine my face instead. "Oh, my silly, beautiful boy! What have I told you about helmets?"

"Yes . . . No. I remember." I squeeze the kitchen roll tighter to my mouth. "I remember falling off. I'm fine."

"Oh, love." She strokes my hair a moment, and I almost lose the fight not to cry. "Where else is hurt? Are your arms only grazed? Nothing's broken? Can you wiggle your fingers? Are you sure you didn't hit your head? Look at your face!"

"I'm fine," I whisper again. And I try hard to believe it. But part of me wonders how much worse it needs to get. I know what they think of me. I know why they hate me. Everyone knows. Even at football. Even at North Wolds, where she said people wouldn't.

"We need to get you cleaned up. Let me find the arnica."

I'm not sure that arnica works. I let her put it on anyway. It's hard to eat tea with my swollen lip, even though the potatoes are cooked so much they've almost turned to liquid. By the time I'm in bed, everywhere hurts. It takes me a long time to fall asleep.

I don't cycle to school in the morning. Jeanette drives me to Armsby before she goes to work, and when we get there she pushes a fistful of change into my hand and tells me to catch the number six home if I don't want to go on the school bus. Then she tells me she's thought about it, and she's getting me a phone, because if I'm big enough to be cycling around the countryside I should at least have a way of letting her know where I am. I've wanted one for ages, and it will help massively with people answering my next lot of adverts — not that I've told her about the adverts yet — which cheers me up for most of the morning, even though someone's graffitied on my locker and there's double English after morning break.

The stairs are busy when English finishes, with everyone heading for the canteen. I keep to one side, thinking about phones and whether Jeanette will let me choose or whether she'll get me a rubbish one. They cost a lot, but since Garden Gate expanded, Jeanette doesn't seem to worry about money so much anymore. I'm about halfway down, not really paying attention, when someone rams into me.

"Hey, dumbfuck!"

I swing around, just in time. Instead of the side of my head smacking into the wall, I take the shove to the centre of my chest. I'm sore everywhere from yesterday, and my blood is still bubbling hot with the memory of Zach looking out through the rear windscreen. I plant my feet, and I barely stagger. Then, before I can think about it, I shove back.

There's a crackle of excitement on the stairs. People have backed away. Someone is chanting, "*Fight, fight!*"; I grab hold of Eddie Watson's tie, partly to stop him falling down the stairs, and for a short moment I think of hitting him as hard as I can, so that it's his head that smacks into the wall, not mine. I could punch him like Zach Blakeman punches, with my fist curled tight and my thumb wrapped around my index finger.

Fight, fight . . .

I almost do it. But then I think of what will happen if I do, and what I promised. I yank on his tie instead, and then

76

let go and watch him stagger against the stair-rail, his eyes round with shock.

I turn without a word and go down the rest of the stairs, wary of taking a hit from behind, but Eddie doesn't come after me. He's still against the rail, rubbing his throat. And I know it's not over, but something has shifted. The other kids part to let me through. I kick open the door to the courtyard and walk out into the sunshine.

They don't know me. They don't know about Tata; they think they do, but they don't.

And one day, I'm going to prove it.

CHAPTER 10

Rosalie

Silver bells.

I suck my breath between my teeth. *Things that definitely are. Things that definitely aren't.*

I have to focus. Focus on the breath.

Cockle shells . . .

I make myself let go of the blind pull, even though the incursion of sunrise makes the truth impossible to ignore. I open the curtains the rest of the way instead and the movement of the air stirs the shreds of glossy paper on the coffee table, making them lift and settle as the nausea establishes itself in the pit of my stomach.

The pictures. *PHOTOGRAPHY*: *Antonio DiPaci.* I force the breath out again and move to examine them, even though I've already seen and there's no unseeing it, no matter how hard I want to. They're all destroyed. All of them, every page of the shoot, cut to shreds, jagged little pieces like murdered paper dolls or unrequited love letters. The scissors from Leonie's washstand are open on the tabletop. I close them and lay them back down. *Focus on the breath.* There's a tingling in my lips and my fingertips. I close my eyes and

78

try to force it away. There was no one in the house. Just the cleaners.

And me.

I open them again. The paper is still there. I scoop it together with trembling hands and take it to the recycling.

The cleaners. I clamp my teeth together and wrap my arms around my chest, shivering in my yoga kit. I should ask my father about the cleaners. I could confront them, demand an explanation. My eyes are burning with tiredness.

I don't want an explanation.

I walk to the garden room and lie down on the mat. *Deep breath in . . . and release.* The daylight bleeds red through my closed eyelids. Shavasana. I centre my mind on my points of contact, the back of my head and the dorsa of my hands; shoulders, elbows, sit-bones, calves. *Focus on the breath.*

I couldn't sleep again last night, too afraid of falling, in my exhaustion, into the place that's always waiting. I resorted to stripping wallpaper, damping it with an old sponge I found in the utility, digging at the edges with my fingernails until my hands hurt, with my earphones in my ears to drown out the curse of Hailbury's silence. I didn't even finish one wall.

I pull my knees to my chest, roll onto my side, and sit. The raw daylight through the aluminium-framed windows is dazzling. I don't even know what I'm doing anymore. Why I'm too stubborn just to give in. I don't have to stay here. It's like my father said; I've taken the time to look around. I could leave. Lock the door.

I stand for a moment at the top of the mat. Dust particles hover in a static ray of sun, glittering as they turn and meander, semi-committed to gravity.

I don't have anywhere else to go.

Under the mat, the tiled floor is chill. The wicker conservatory chairs have grown brittle with too many years and too much sun through the glass roof; the cushions have been plumped, but I can't imagine when someone last sat on one. An old briefcase of my father's still sags despondently between the brass legs of the glass coffee table.

Back bend. *Exhale*, forward fold. *Inhale*, right leg backward, lunge. *Retain the breath*, plank, knees–chest–chin, cobra . . .

My father. That's the only way I can ever remember him being referred to. *Your father and I have decided . . . Your father and I were thinking . . .*

I'm divorcing your father. The morning of my seventeenth birthday.

My thoughts have wandered. I push my weight into my heels and press my body down between my arms until they tremble with exertion. *Inhale*, right leg forward, lunge. *Exhale*.

I stand, letting my breath settle and my muscles loosen. The sweat is stinging the papercut on my thumb. I suck it away. I need to get on with my work.

I contemplate bringing the laptop to the garden room. I need to get away from Leonie's closed door and the darkness of the lounge, to banish the thoughts that have circled all night. I'm safe here, in the daylight. It's spring outside; the green spikes in the garden have become crocuses and an abundance of daffodils.

I walk to the kitchen and pour cereal into a bowl, watching the wholegrain pellets roll and circle, ringing against the fine china. For a moment I can't help but think of berries, round and plump. A blanket of Greek yoghurt, a spoon; I fetch one from the cutlery drawer and eat standing up, watching my reflection in the window, and beyond it the play of the sun on the kitchen garden. Across an abundance of herbs and rows of stiff, turned earth, beyond the blackcurrant bushes and raspberry canes, I can make out a shed with its door left open.

I rinse out the bowl, brew a coffee and go to fetch my laptop. It's hard to see the screen in the dazzling light. I trust my weight gingerly to one of the wicker chairs and stare at the backdrop, my fingers hovering over the trackpad. My phone has fallen behind the seat cushion. I retrieve it, ignoring the growing plethora of notifications, and swipe to my contacts. I hit call, before I can give it too much consideration.

"Hello?"

"Mum."

"Rosy? Darling, do you know what the time is?"

The time? It's nearly eight thirty on a Thursday morning. Most people are on their way to work with their second or third coffee. My mother, on the other hand, keeps the hours that she wouldn't allow me to as a teenager.

"Sorry." I'm not, really. "Are you still in Cannes?"

"Yes, for another month, at least. Why, is something wrong?"

Is something wrong? I swallow, trying not to think about scissors and glossy paper. In Cannes it's nine thirty.

"No, nothing's wrong." I arrange the phone under my chin and try to co-ordinate my laptop and my mug at the same time. "I just needed to ask a couple of things for the book, if it's a good time?"

"Mm. I haven't heard any updates from Stefan, darling. Have you sent him anything yet? You're not still at Hailbury are you?"

"No . . . erm . . . yes." If I'm vague enough I might get away with it. "I was wondering . . ."

"Was that no to Stefan, or to Hailbury, Rosalie?"

"Uhm . . ."

"For goodness' sake. It's been the best part of a fortnight. Surely you have what you need by now?"

"Actually," I croak, "I was wondering if you kept any of the press coverage."

It's a calculated question. Every part of her media history is archived, I know that: the good and the bad, although being Lara Lee Knight there was never any ugly. I carry on before she can shoot me down.

"Anything from around the time that . . . she disappeared . . ." I tail off. Another unspoken fact is that I can't say it. I can't say the name to her. It's like a sacred word that I'm not worthy to utter. Even though we've spent the last twenty years either talking, or not talking, about her.

I clear my throat.

"Stefan wanted me to go through it. He was very concerned about how we best . . . describe . . . that part. Where would I find it? Is it here?"

"At Hailbury? Don't be ridiculous. There's nothing of any use at Hailbury. Your father should have sold the wretched place years ago."

Of course. He bought her out. Anything that's still here, she doesn't consider hers. Perhaps she's forgotten the boxes, the school mementos, the childhoods. Or perhaps she just wants to. The thought reminds me. I put down the laptop and slide to my feet.

"I found a key. A tiny one. In one of the packing boxes from the attic. Do you know what it's for?"

"A key? Rosalie, please. This is getting out of hand. She's gone. Those things are finished with. Going through them was the detectives' job, not yours. For God's sake make sure it gets put back before you leave, or your father will be apoplectic."

"I'm not—"

"Listen to me, Rosalie. Darling, I wanted your name on this book because it will be authentic. That's *so* important. But Stefan should have made it very clear to you that the emphasis is to draw a relatable account of a family who have lost their child. Nothing more complicated than that."

I pause, half lower the phone, sucking my bottom lip against my teeth. A family? Yeah, right. Who lost their child? Shouldn't that be *one* of their children? At least Stefan made an attempt at empathy when he said it. There's a bitter taste in my mouth.

"Right." I nod. "Sure. Super clear."

"Good."

"Only, if I'm going to tell a . . . *relatable* story, then people will need to know her first. I need to draw a picture of *her*."

Silence.

"Perhaps we should . . . sit down together?" I grit my teeth. "Talk?"

82

"Like I said, darling, I won't be back in the UK for a month. You're welcome to fly out, but I've got a lot on. You've got my notes, that's really all you should need. And there was the interview in December. I can send you the transcript if you don't have it."

"Thanks." I pick up my coffee and examine its murky depths. Of course. How could I forget? It's not *my* book. It's *her* book. I'm just providing the medium to get it into print.

"Actually, on the subject of interviews, I was thinking you might interview Antonio. The photographer — we put together most of her portfolio with him. I believe he's local to you. Stefan, or Dell, my PA, should be able to dig out the details. You'll have come across his name if you've been going through those boxes. Antonio DiPaci. He goes by another name now, I think. If you want background, his input would be very pertinent. He worked a lot with Leonie at the start of that year — he actually shot the first shoot for L'Église — he really brought out the best in her."

Pertinent? Antonio DiPaci's photos? I screw my smarting finger inside my fist and frown at the travertine tiles.

"He didn't publish ever again. He would've been ever so famous, if it wasn't for what happened. He took himself out of modelling and film, out of public life completely." She huffs a deep sigh. "Anyway, I have to go, darling. I've got a brunch at ten thirty, and I need to get ready. Everything press-related is in the upstairs office at Palace Gardens. In the white wardrobes. Dell can get it out for you. I'll send you her number, just tell her the date range and she'll have it available for when you get back."

"I'm not—"

"Really, Rosalie. If you were in London, you would have easy access to all of this. Dell would be able to help you, and you could meet regularly with Stefan. Think about it."

"I—"

"If it's that you're struggling with bills," — I can almost hear the lift of her eyebrows — "you only need to say so."

"No, Mother." I lower the mug with all the self-control I can muster. "Thank you. I'm managing fine."

"Good. Well, it's good to hear your voice, darling. Let me know when you're home. We can catch up once I'm back from Cannes."

"Yeah," I exhale. "Looking forward to it. Bye, Mum."

I don't wait to hear her parting words. I put the phone down beside my mug and wait for it to go dead. A family. Relatable. I couldn't think of two words any further from my reality.

I'm not going back to London. I'm not. No matter what she insinuates. I'm not going to be scared away from my own past.

My coffee is stone cold. I take it back to the kitchen, empty out the percolator and brew a fresh one, gravitating to the window whilst it bubbles into life. The shed door is pushed to now, and Kasper Miller is spreading mulch around the raspberry canes. I find myself wondering what happens to the fruit when it comes. Do the birds eat it, or does he pick it? He seems too meticulous to leave it to rot. Perhaps he sells it or gives it away. Or maybe he leaves it in the house, overflowing bowls of #*leoniesraspberries*, and it rots there instead until it gets thrown back into the compost to fertilise next year's crop. The circle of death.

He straightens and notices me watching, and the sudden flutter in my abdomen takes me utterly by surprise. I gulp a deep breath and hold up my cup to try and disguise the rush of blood to my cheeks.

"Coffee?" I mouth.

I don't know what I expected. A courteous refusal, not the slightest softening at the corner of his lips, the tiny polite nod. I let out my breath. He drives his fork into the ground, and I flip the lock to open one of the glazed doors, the sun staining the tiles red, blue and green through the rows of coloured glass panes. I get out a second cup, trying to banish the thoughts of photos and papercuts. A minute or two later, he appears, tucking his gloves into the open pocket of his gilet.

"Thanks." His voice is softer than his three-day stubble and the set of his jaw. He comes to a halt on the step, not quite venturing inside. There's mulch on his boots and his work trousers are muddy, their multitude of pockets tattered at the edges from overuse.

"Milk? Sugar?" I lift the percolator off the Aga. He shakes his head. I pour both cups and take his to the door. Kasper accepts it in one hand and leans against the door frame.

"How's the book?" he asks.

I falter, coffee halfway to my lips.

"Harriet mentioned it." He shrugs.

"She did?" There's an odd feeling in my stomach. I lower my cup. He knows Harriet. I've never seen him in the bistro.

"She's family. Of sorts." He's perceptive. And as impervious to scalding liquid as he is to the cold. I watch him swallow his coffee.

"Oh." I nod. "Right." I'm suddenly tongue-tied. And it's not for my mother's taunts, or Leonie's lingering presence in the shadows.

"Yeah, the book. Well." I turn the cup in my hands. "Actually, it's um . . . it's a total disaster."

Kasper shakes his head. Amused?

I bite my lip.

"How're the uhm . . ." I gesture uselessly outside. Flowerbeds, wheelie bins? What am I even asking? "Plants?"

"You know much about plants?" His face is serious, but there's a glimmer at the corner of his lips; not quite the smile of the squash court. I take an overly big gulp of coffee.

"Nothing whatsoever." I smile despite myself and hear the breath of laughter that slips his guard. I cradle my cup.

"But you don't like flowers," he observes.

For a split second, our eyes lock. Peonies, the early morning breeze by the bins. My breath seems to have stuck in my throat.

"I like them in gardens," I clarify huskily.

Kasper nods. There's something conspiratorial in our silence. I find myself studying his profile, half in silhouette, and trying not to think about tie-breaks and laboured breathing. He finishes his coffee and reaches in to put the cup on the end of the granite countertop with a click.

"I know nothing whatsoever about books." His gaze rests on my face. "To me, a thousand words is an achievement. You write a column, too?"

I nod. "Pays the bills. Ish."

A frown flits across his forehead, quickly banished. His assumption is about as well hidden as my mother's low blow on the phone. It seems to be most people's expectation, that I'd live on their money in lieu of their love.

"But books are your . . . thing?"

"Yeah." I hesitate. "Yeah, I guess you could say so."

What's *his* thing? I glance back at his face. Competitive sports? Insidious questions? I want to ask him what he remembers, but I'm not brave enough.

"Harriet said you're here to research. So you're writing about your mother? Or your sister?"

There's something in the way he says the last word that snatches my attention.

"A bit of both." I release my breath. The laughter has faded from his face. We both seem to be paused. Caught, accidentally, on the name that neither of us has said. She's ever-present; she's worked her way in, like she always does, and always will. She's been gone for twenty years, and I still can't interact with anybody without her looking over my shoulder.

"There's a lot of her still here. More than I realised."

"Yeah." He half turns back towards the door, slipping the gloves from his pocket. "You must have a lot to do. Thanks for the coffee."

"Thanks for the company." I try for a smile, but in its place there only seems to be questions.

"It was a pleasure." Kasper's brows flicker. And his parting words leave me with a little rush of adrenaline that fades more slowly than his footprints in the dewy grass.

86

I don't let myself look back outside. I gulp the rest of my coffee and put the cups in the sink.

I don't want to confess that I don't want him to know about her, that I want to be exclusively Rosalie to him, not Leonie's sister. He wouldn't have known her, not personally; he's too young. He can't have been more than eight or nine in that school picture. She was at Queen Victoria by the time I started school. So what was he hiding in his silence? Something about this place. The house? The gardens . . . ?

The shredded paper on the coffee table?

My mother's right. I go to fetch my laptop, chilled despite the magnified sun through the garden-room roof. I shouldn't be here.

Dell has WhatsApped me. I take the laptop to the kitchen, flicking through the notifications on my phone as I walk, dwelling briefly on the possibility: *PHOTOGRAPHY: Antonio DiPaci.* A prickle runs down my spine.

I open the laptop on the kitchen table. Stare again at the backdrop, the one I set last night from the photograph that I sent myself — the off-colours of the sea wall, the sand, the beach huts.

Then I pick up my phone.

Mr DiPaci,

My fingers skate the touchscreen.

This is Rosalie Knight-Langton. My mother gave me your number. I didn't want to make an unsolicited call because I know you've moved on, but I was wondering . . .

I look back at the laptop. At the seagull and the gaudy red enamelled metal.

I was wondering if we could talk.

CHAPTER 11

"How long do you need? Ten? Twenty? Thirty? I'll count to thirty. One . . . two . . . "

Starting to run. I stumble, a lurch of fright in my belly.

"Three . . . four . . . "

Where, where? She never plays with me. I can't pick somewhere stupid, she'll laugh. The pampas grass — no, no I've hidden there before. She'll know. She remembers everything.

"Fifteen . . . sixteen . . . "

In the shed — too obvious. Under the bench? But the lawn is trim, she'll see right through the wrought iron.

I blunder back, leaping over the gravel. The juniper spreads wide, creeping low to the ground, an endless cloud of blue-green.

"Ready or not, here I come!"

* * *

No. I fight the urge to clamp my hands over my ears. No.

She's not there.

I feel my way along the panelling, palms slippery with sweat. It can't be her. But the noise has grown louder and louder in my ears, until it's all I can hear, until I've never been surer of anything. She hasn't swung on that swing for twenty years. I know that. I know . . .

"No." I clamp my teeth together. I don't know who I'm telling. Myself? Her? It isn't her . . . There's someone in the house, there must be; there were pictures, *#leoniesroom*, urban explorers. My phone is clammy in my hand. The police. I'll call the police. Now. Put an end to this—

Except . . .

Except they couldn't find a car.

I'm at the door. The darkness is pixellated in front of me. To and fro, to and fro, the creak of the ropes against the carabiners. I want to scream, but the sound dies in my throat.

And I shove the door.

And I fall—

Plush, aged carpet. I'm on my knees, looking up. Up at the moonlight through the voile, insipid and pale, and the empty cushioned seat drifting indolently to a stop. At the kirby grips and body sprays, gel pens, books. At the duvet, tangled at the foot of her bed, like someone's kicked back the covers, sweaty and agitated. One of the pillows is on the floor. My head is throbbing.

A dream. It was part of the dream. Ready or not. I grind my fingernails into the carpet. What if it still is? What if I haven't got out? Am I still there, trapped in another level of the same nightmare? There's no light on. Panic rises fresh; I lurch for the door and hit the switch and the blinding electric buzz sears my eyes.

The swing is motionless, and the moon is distant. There's a message illuminating the backlight of my phone.

Yes.

I wilt, confused, against the door frame. Dazed with tiredness, with sleep that I was convinced hadn't come. The covers are still thrown back, the pillow on the floor sagging under its own weight. The message is from Antonio DiPaci.

Yes.

* * *

One word. I let Room 42 cradle me in its low-key bustle. Antonio DiPaci — or, seemingly, now Tony Lawrence — sent me a one-word reply. By text. In the middle of the night.

So, tomorrow I'm going to Skegness. I'm going to meet the man who sold my sister's soul to the camera.

I've looked him up online: his studio, professional profile packages, family portraits, pets. Nothing more risqué than the odd wedding.

It's warm in the bistro. Safe, with a slow reassuring tick-over of custom, and enough background noise to help me concentrate. I've always struggled with sustained attention, although I've been off medication for years, now. Before I came back to Hailbury I'd got proficient at managing myself: an expert in circumventing my own impulsivity and ordering my errant thoughts. Perhaps trying to wean myself off the coffee was a bad move; Joy has pointed out more than once that caffeine is really just a means of self-medicating without appropriate professional oversight.

I know I need to work on the column; I've been blithely ignoring yesterday afternoon's missed deadline. But I haven't; I've spent the morning typing up questions. Questions for Antonio DiPaci, questions for myself. And now the opening of a book is staring back at me from my screen, daring me to answer them, to put the truth into words. Fifteen thousand words.

The problem is, I'm not sure I'm writing the right story. I haven't opened my mother's notes since the meeting with Tabitha.

"What is it, deadline day?"

I jump. Harriet slides onto the sofa opposite me and pushes a latte across the table. She probably has no idea just how right she is.

"Mm." I close down the Tony questions quickly.

"Isn't it meant to be a bank holiday?" Her smile is teasing. She has her own coffee in a mug that clearly doesn't belong to the café; there's a chip in the rim and the body bears a smudge of painted handprints. "It's nice t' have you back."

I return the smile. I can't tell her the truth. That there will soon be nowhere I can work at Hailbury that isn't getting distinctly too sinister for comfort. I push the computer screen to half-closed.

"I missed the cakes."

"I'll have to get Mum on with t'lemon drizzle."

"Your mum makes them?" I toy with the cup.

"Every day, usually." She nods, sinks back in the sofa. "She's been a bit busy this week. Easter holiday so she's had the boys."

"Your boys?" I close the laptop.

"Yeah. Rohan's seven, Rory's five. Here." She slips her phone from her pocket to show me a picture. "She has them a lot lately." She rolls her eyes. "Since Sandeep took t'partnership. He's a GP. I opened this place last year."

"I didn't realise you owned it. That's amazing."

"Sometimes I think so." Harriet laughs. "Other times, not so much. Especially with t'kids. It really does take a village. You know."

I don't, really. I nod.

"Rosalie, are you okay?"

Her question surprises me. I glance back.

"No offence meant, but you look like you've not slept inside of t'week."

"Oh." I chew my lip. I'm not the only one who's noticed, then. "Yeah." I cop out. "Deadline day. Literally today. Well, yesterday, but I missed it."

Harriet regards me steadily.

"But you're okay otherwise?"

"Yeah . . ." I make a deliberate effort not to look down at my hands, at my lacerated fingertip. "Yeah. I think so. Hailbury's just . . . isolated. Actually, kind of creepy." I flash her a sheepish smile in the hope that the redacted version will be enough to curb her curiosity.

"Have you managed to catch up with anyone you were kids with? People from school or t'like?"

"Oh." This time, I can't help but avert my gaze. "No. No, honestly I don't really remember anyone at all."

Except Kasper Miller. I remember Kasper Miller. But I'm not inclined to share that gem, especially not considering that she's family, "of sorts". What sort? I try not to look like I'm studying her. There's definitely no resemblance. "Of sorts" wouldn't mean a sibling, anyway.

Perhaps I *would* be able to remember people from my childhood, if I made an effort to meet them. The problem is, I don't really want to meet anyone. I don't know what I *do* want anymore. To carry on blindly in my confused solitude, somehow get my mother's book written, kickstart my career and move on with my life?

"I'm focussing on her at the moment, anyway. Leonie, I mean." I've got to get better at saying her name. "I'm meeting a photographer tomorrow who worked with her."

"Here?"

"Skegness. He has a studio there."

"Really?" Harriet's face is invaluable. "In Skeg? Not . . . Paris? Or Milan . . . ? *Skeg.*"

"Apparently."

"Have you ever been to Skeg?"

"I've been to Tesco."

She laughs out loud. "Next child-free night I've got, it's a date. You, me, Skeg Vegas." She eases herself out of the sofa and sweeps up the cups. "Girls' night out."

I don't know whether to smile or quail. "Night out", of any kind, hasn't really been a part of my vocabulary since university. In fact, probably since ever.

"Sounds good," I tell her. "I think . . . "

The door opens and clatters shut, admitting a new babble of conversation and a rush of cool air.

"Good luck with the photographer." Harriet starts back towards the bar.

"Thanks."

I open my laptop. I manage not to go back to the Tony questions. I close my draft and force myself to look at the column. It takes me an hour to turn out something more sarcastic than I intended and another two to trim it back into a suitable word count. I pack up my laptop. The bistro has filled for lunchtime. The door chimes as I fight my way through people queuing to get tables. Who knew that Armsby was a bank holiday destination? Good for Harriet.

"Rosy!"

"Oh—" I'm most of the way out, and I almost shut myself in the door.

"It's good to see you!" Josh London catches it and saves my laptop from almost certain crushing. "How are you?"

"I'm . . . good. Thanks." I'm wrong-footed, still half in and half out of the door. He moves to join me.

"Good! I'm glad to see you're still around."

"You are?" We're now completely blocking the doorway.

"Yeah. I need to stop arriving at places as you're leaving. I'd love to catch up."

He would? I'm off guard, exhausted, and overly conscious of the people trying to get by.

"Oh . . . okay. Sure."

"Is it going alright?"

"Uhm . . . yeah. Yeah."

"Good." He shifts his grip on the door. I waver, unsure whether to step inside or out. Out seems churlish, so I opt for in, and cause even greater confusion.

"Hey, you know what, take my number." He touches my elbow to draw me to one side. "Have you got your phone? I can see you're busy, but it would be awesome to chat. I promise not to get all emotional or nostalgic." There's sincerity in his eyes, a flash of apology in his smile.

I can feel Harriet's eyebrows raising by the inch behind the bar as I pass him my phone. He taps the number in with his thumbs and locks the screen before he passes it back.

"Drop me a line or a message when you get the chance."

I nod. "Thanks."

"No." He smiles. "It'll be my pleasure. See you soon, Rosy."

"See you."

I catch myself tossing back my hair as I push open the door.

I walk to the car park with burning cheeks, unlock my car and throw my laptop onto the passenger seat. Something cracks.

"Shit." I pick the laptop case out of the broken glass. A lightbulb. None of the aged spares in Hailbury's utility fitted my table lamp. I meant to try the hardware shop, but I forgot.

"Crap." I scrape together the jagged remnants. If I don't replace it, I won't sleep. And I'm not sure I can survive another night like last night.

It's only a two-minute walk back to the hardware shop. I find myself wondering if Kasper Miller is at Hailbury in my absence. Whether his eyes alighted on the kitchen window today, like mine scanned the shadows at the edge of the drive before I left.

By some miracle, the shop's not only open but it has the bulb. Sunshine squeezes its way between the red-brick buildings as I exit into the high street. The road is jam-packed with parked cars. I slip between the closest two to cross, and something on the other side catches my eye.

He's not at Hailbury. I come to a dead stop, the little leap of recognition lurching into something else entirely.

The pickup's parked at the end of the row. The back door on the far side is open. As I watch, it slams, and a second later Kasper appears by the front wing.

He's not alone.

There's a child beside him on the pavement, running a few steps to keep up. A boy, as tall as his elbow, with light-brown hair, and jeans that are turned up at the bottom. My eyes follow them as far as the bakery door. Then, before I can stop myself, I dart a look back at the pickup.

The woman in the front seat is tall and slim, with black hair in a sleek bob, and her sunglasses hide what little of her face I can make out past the reflections on the window.

How had it not occurred to me?

I flounder, under the pretence of looking for traffic, when really I can't drag my gaze away from the truck. Kasper

94

has disappeared inside the bakery. I exhale, a rush of breath, an unwelcome flash of half-smiles and squash-court doors. I didn't notice a ring.

Stupid.

I divert along a footpath at the side of the library, heart thumping. I somehow manage to find the car park, more by luck than judgement. I don't stop to organise myself before I drive away, pulling on my seat belt as I go with hands that are unjustifiably shaky. Suddenly, I want more than anything to be alone.

The problem is, I'm not sure I want to be alone at Hailbury.

Go away, Rosy. Is that what she's trying to tell me? That I shouldn't be here? Prying into her things, trying to capture her with my words the way that Antonio DiPaci did with his camera?

Except it's not her, is it? She's not at Hailbury. No one is. No one except me, an army of cleaners, and maybe Kasper Miller. There's an alarm, razor wire. CCTV recording 24/7; I found the box mounted in the utility cupboard when I was searching for the fuse box.

And I'm glad for him. Aren't I? Kasper Miller *and family.* Not that it's any business of mine, anyway.

I feel oddly bereft as I park. As I turn the key in the front door without difficulty. I can hear a hoover upstairs, a radio, the occasional exchange of voices. I heat up some day-old soup and sit at the kitchen table with my phone. Sure enough, there's a new number in my contact list. *Josh: Hey there! I am using WhatsApp.* I open a chat on impulse.

> *Hi, it's Rosalie. I thought I'd message you about that catch-up.*

I hesitate, my thumb skimming the letters. His status changes instantly from *last seen* to *online*. There's a lurch in my abdomen. I watch the row of dots flick up as he types.

> *Rosy, hi.*

A smiley face. Really? Is The Right Honourable Lord Joshua Armsby to be *really* the emoji sort? Text does bad things to people. Unless he's being ironic . . . I'm overthinking it; he's typing again.

So glad you messaged. When are you around? Tomorrow?

Tomorrow. Wow. I exhale. He's not being ironic.

Actually, this weekend's pretty busy.

Not a lie. After I meet Tony, I'm going to have to drive back to Palace Gardens to collect the boxes Dell has got out for me.

I have to travel back to Muswell Hill. Next week?

Next week's good.

Another flicker of dots. He's still typing.

You're meeting someone, back home?

No. Just got to collect some things from my mother's house.

Nice . . . I think.

Still typing.

I read your column but you don't give much away. Is there . . . anyone at home? Significant other/others . . . out of work commitments? Beyond the millennial strife?

Oh. I raise my eyebrows at the phone.

96

No, just me.

I scrape out the last of the soup and glance outside at the raspberry canes.

You know. Standard millennial strife.

I pause.

You?

I type it, then delete it. Retype it. I can't imagine there's anything standard about his existence.

Nope. Also just me. Still at Jericho.

Jericho?

My parents' house. Never moved out — standard millennial strife?

I know for a fact that Lord James London doesn't reside in Lincolnshire anymore. Which means Jericho is as good as inherited. I fight the urge to send him an ironic eyeroll.

Non-standard.

Are you writing? I'm not disturbing you, am I?

Nice attempt at a subject change. I get to my feet and go to rinse out my cup.

No. I probably should be, though.

I leave my laptop in the hall and go to my room. I have blisters on my right hand from the paint-scraper. I switch to the left, thinking of Leonie and her fountain pen. Something occurs to me.

You were friends with her.

The dots seem to flicker for a long time, this time. Especially considering it's a one-word answer.

Yes.

Yes, what? Yes and? Yes, but . . . ?

Tell me something about her.

For a moment, I think he's not going to reply. The message has been read, but he's not typing. I pick up the scraper, oddly nervous.

Like what?

The scraper bites into the next row of cartoon hedgehogs and googly-eyed foxes. I lift the phone and type one-handed.

Anything. I was seven. I

I send it without finishing it.

?

I don't remember her.

Not anything?

Not anything.

He's typing again. It occurs to me, for probably the millionth time, how much easier life would be if I could hold every interaction in writing.

She was stupidly clever. She talked French when she wanted to piss me off. She always won at cheat, and she could argue you round in a circle. Your writing reminded me of her, the first time I read it.

I lower the scraper.

I reminded you of her?

I'm nothing like her. I know, because I grew for twenty-seven years beside her yardstick and I've never once measured up. That has been made abundantly clear to me.

Yeah. Your style, I don't know. Your... fire. That sounds really cringey typed out, but I don't know how else to describe what I mean.

There's an unbidden flutter in my chest.

Column or book?

I can't quite help but ask. I lay the phone on top of the radiator, pick the scraper back up, and climb onto my stool to start at a new edge of the paper, daring myself not to look for a response.

Both.

I stoop to pick up the phone.

Because I'm her sister?

I balance precariously.

Not really. Because I was interested. Your family were like my family when we were kids. I sort of kept tabs.

On me? I attack the paper harder. I can't co-ordinate scraping left-handed. I shift the scraper to my right and curl my hand around the blisters, frowning at the scraps that litter the carpet like dated snow.

Fuck, now I sound super creepy. That's not what I mean. I mean, when your book came out I bought it because I remembered you and I was curious. Look, are you a lunch person or a dinner person? This would be way easier face to face.

I can't help smiling. My cheeks are pink, like Harriet's; maybe that's the effect he has on everyone. He's typing again.

If you need to work, just tell me and I'll stop bothering you. I don't want you to regret messaging me.

My palm is smarting. I glance around the room. I've barely managed a wall and a half. But my headache has receded, and the silence isn't too loud anymore.

I don't.

I try for left-handed typing instead, and it doesn't work. The phone tips from my hand and plummets, a clang of defiance as it disappears behind the radiator. I wait for it to drop out the other side. It doesn't.

I ease myself down. Sit on the stool and squint behind the radiator. It's an ancient cast-iron affair, with space to lose a whole limb behind. I kneel on the floor and reach in from one end. I can't even see the phone. I inch my arm into the space and my fingers contact something hard. I let out a hiss of triumph. But my relief is short-lived; I trace a semi-circular outline, a contour, a fractured edge. Whatever it is, it's firmly wedged.

There's more underneath. I work my hand downward. Two halves of a whole? The top one is stuck fast, but the bottom piece gives. With a gentle twist, I get it free and draw it out.

Suddenly my ears are ringing.

Mary, Mary . . .

I sit back on my heels. There's a buzzing in my brain, a swimming at the edges of my vision as I spell out the words printed on the rim of the bowl.

quite contrary, How does your garden grow? With silver bells

The fracture through the melamine is clean, still snowy-edged, even though the little printed flowers in the bottom of the dish have faded, and the girl's bonnet and dress are scratched and dull. My immediate urge is to drop it. To recoil. To let the berries spill and roll across the floor, to splatter the carpet with yoghurt.

Except it's empty. And it's been washed — no traces of yoghurt remain. Or berries, or guilt, other than the mere existence of it in its hiding place, forgotten even by the person who secreted it there. Until now.

I try not to hear the sound of my heartbeat against my ribs. Behind the radiator, my phone vibrates, reflecting blue-green light between the cast-iron columns. I lower the bowl to the carpet. Focus on the breath. Squeeze my eyes tight shut and reach back in, as though I might be plunging my hand into a nest of vipers.

and cockle shells, and pretty maids all in a row.

CHAPTER 12

"Ready or not, here I come!"

Not! I'm not. A flash of panic. I fall to all fours. Not ready. Underneath it's pitch black. I have to flatten myself to fit, my nose in the needly, scented earth. Quiet, I need to be quiet.

I can hear rain on the top of the juniper. After a while it starts to soak through, a drip at a time, thrumming into the soil. My breathing has slowed down and my hands have pins and needles. She can't laugh at me now. It's been ages. Maybe I should leap out. But she might shout at me. No, no . . . hold on. Stay quiet. She's stealthy, like a tiger. Usually I play alone, or with Vesna, who only ever plays in the house and just pretends not to be able to find me. But Vesna's got the flu. So someone told her to watch me — her, Leonie, my actual sister — and instead of yelling and slamming her door, the words came out of her mouth. Hide and seek, Rosy?

My hands are so cold they hurt. It's raining properly now. I struggle into a squat, the needles spiking through my hair. The plants look different from underneath. Dark and mysterious, like caves. I spend a long time staring at them, imagining who or what might live there, until my ankles hurt and I'm starting to need the toilet. Where is she? I shuffle to the edge, where a tangle of other plants is mixed up with the juniper. I look at the leaves, the dusky blue berries . . .

* * *

I hate running. But I have to get out of the house. I jog along the drive, out onto the road. It occurs to me, as the gates creep closed behind me, that I actually don't know the geography of Shellingsby St Mary. I jam my headphones into my ears and ramp up my music.

It's starting to spit with rain, and there are fresh tyre tracks in the mud. It's early. Barely light. I falter over which way to turn and, daunted by the idea of meeting people in the village, I opt for the road towards Armsby. Then I remember the car in the ditch. I turn off the music with a shiver.

The rain grows heavier, penetrating the trees a drip at a time, thrumming onto the tarmac. Without the music, my pulse is too loud. This was a stupid idea.

There's a public bridleway on my right that looks as though it might follow Hailbury's perimeter. I divert around the yellow way-marker onto the rutted mud, thinking briefly of Leonie and Phoenix.

Ready or not . . .

She never came. It must have been almost an hour. I crossed my legs and held my nerve in the cold, soaked to the skin. When I came out, she wasn't there. She wasn't in the garden at all. Desperate for the bathroom, I limped across the grass to the kitchen door, and it was locked. The door was locked, and I couldn't find anyone, so I hammered and banged. I went to every window, but Leonie didn't come. She wouldn't let me in. She was there, in the kitchen, on the phone. Even as I sobbed and clenched and danced from foot to foot, as I pleaded and kicked the door. She didn't let me in.

Who am I kidding? She never let me in. She never did, never would have, never will. I can't look back and wonder, if things had turned out differently, what she would have confided in me, because she wouldn't. She wouldn't have told me anything.

I seem to have lost sight of Hailbury's wall. The trees have thickened and the track has narrowed. I squint ahead for another way-marker but I can't see one. The path appears to have taken a completely different direction.

I slow. I should turn back. I'm not sure if I have the stamina for more than a couple of kilometres. I pluck the silent headphones from my ears, unmuting the rush of the trees.

And something else . . . Something closer?

I turn, uneasy.

There's no one there. Just the intermittent drum of droplets falling from the tree branches. A pounding heart.

I start to jog again.

Ready or not . . .

I stop dead. And for a second, I'm certain of it: the concealed crackle of footsteps in the trees behind me.

Here I come . . .

I break into a full-on run. The way is overgrown; I crash through brambles, jarring my ankles in the ruts, my pulse crescendoing in my ears.

Snatched?

I sprint until my lungs are burning, too afraid to look over my shoulder. Some instinct tells me I can't be far from the village. The trail bears left, but straight ahead the trees thin out.

I divert off the path at the last moment, stumbling over rocks and roots, almost losing my footing. Behind me, the footfalls change direction too, tearing the foliage, gaining speed . . .

Oh God. I rip blindly through the remaining brambles. *Oh God.*

I wrench myself free; my feet hit stone, tarmac . . .

There's a flash of light on glass, shiny black paint; the screech of tyres and the stench of rubber. My hands hit metal and I half-vault the car's bonnet, my weight carrying me over it and into the opposite kerb. I don't have time to save myself. Grit, concrete, a resounding thud that sends stars across my vision . . .

And then I'm scrambling to my feet, eyes locked on the trees . . .

"Are you okay?"

The car door has opened.

"Ohh." I'm gasping. "Oh God."

"Are you hurt? Are you hurt anywhere?" Hands are helping me onto the pavement. "Did I hit you? I didn't hit you? Are you okay?"

I blink away the stars. The car's in the middle of the road and concern is etched across the driver's face.

"I didn't think I was going to stop," he says; alarm still lingers in his voice. "What—"

"There was someone there." I can't tear my eyes from the trees. The brambles. The darkness that isn't so dark now that the sun has emerged to cast its glare across the damp tarmac.

"Oh God. Someone was . . . I was being . . . was being . . ."

Followed?

But there's no one there. Is there? I can see right through the branches, back to the path. To the distant glimpse of a red-brick wall. They couldn't have vanished into thin air. People don't vanish.

"What's your name?" He's scouring my face, dark, kind eyes, a serious frown creasing his forehead. His white collar is crisp, and there's a tie tucked through his shirt buttons. "We should get you checked over. You've hit your head."

I have? My teeth are jarred and my forehead is throbbing. I raise a hand to touch it. I have.

"Rosalie," I manage, and something flickers across his brows.

"I'm Sandeep."

"Oh," I exhale. "Oh."

Shit. From beneath the blur of panic, realisation is surfacing. Sandeep? I can hear the name on Harriet's lips: *t'partnership. How are Sandeep and the boys?*

I could curl up and die. Sandeep.

"I'm . . . I'm fine. I'm so sorry. I didn't mean to . . . Oh, gosh . . ."

"It's okay," he says. "But you should really get yourself checked, Rosalie. Can I drive you to the health centre? I have a Saturday surgery. I was on my way there."

"I'm okay," I gulp. "Thanks. I'm not far from home, I can . . . I'll just—"

"Really. I mean it. I'm one of the doctors."

"Actually, I'm meeting someone in an hour. I—"

"I nearly ran you down. I can't carry on without seeing that you're cleaned up and okay. Here." He gestures me to the car. "Humour me?"

I perch reluctantly on the front seat. Sandeep goes to the boot. He comes back with a pen torch and a handful of packets, and examines the now undeniable lump in my hairline.

"Look straight ahead."

I try not to blink at the torchlight.

"You've met my wife. At the café?" He swings the torch to my other eye and back, then turns it off. "Harriet?"

"Yeah," I concede.

"I thought so. She mentioned you. I think she's planning you a girls' night out in Skegness?"

I wince.

"Here." Sandeep rips open a packet and empties a sachet of saline into it. "I'll let you do it, it might sting."

I take the wet gauze, glad of the excuse to look away, and dab the grit from my abraded forearms. Sandeep waits until I'm finished.

"You're not registered at the surgery yet?"

"No." I make a careful second pass of the graze. "I haven't . . . quite . . . got to it."

"Why don't I put you on my list for eleven thirty on Tuesday, at the end of morning surgery? I'd feel a lot better knowing I hadn't given you a subdural."

"Sure." I don't quite look up. "Thank you."

"In the meantime, any vomiting or dizziness, humour me a second time and go to A&E?"

"I will."

"Do you want a lift back home?"

"No, really. I'm good. Thanks. I'd prefer to walk."

"Okay." Sandeep peels off his gloves, folding the bloodied gauze inside them. "I'll see you on Tuesday, then. Take care, Rosalie."

"Thank you," I whisper.

I wait until his car's out of sight before I start to walk. Now that the adrenaline has faded, I'm shivering helplessly.

There was no car in the ditch. There was no one on the swing. And there was no one following me. Sandeep is clearly sharp enough to see what I don't want to admit. I need to get help.

The sun is fully up by the time I drag myself along Hailbury's drive, sore and starting to ache. I haven't got long before I need to leave for Skegness; it doesn't look far on the map, but it took me almost an hour last time to get to Tesco along the coastal roads. My overnight bag is ready; once I've met Antonio, I'll drive straight to London.

I peel off my running clothes and shower, wincing as the hot water hits the grazes. My laptop is open in my room. I dress, gazing at the screen. Between the lack of sleep, the isolation and the googling, it's little wonder my mind is running away with me.

Krzysztof Woźniak has his own Wikipedia summary, under *Knight-Langton Abduction*. Even grainy and pixellated, I'm classically conditioned to be terrified of him. His black, unseeing eyes, his early-noughties buzzcut. Did she know him? Is that why she got in his car? What did he tell her, promise her, to lure her away? What could anyone have promised to the girl who had everything?

I take my holdall to the hall and go back for the bin bags of toys. I want them to be gone when I get back. I drag them downstairs and out the front door, and pause to contemplate how to get them over the gravel. I can't see my feet when I lift the box. I stagger down the steps.

"Um . . . Can I . . . ?"

I stop abruptly. Kasper's brows are raised a fraction, expression puzzled, as Nedward looks balefully up at him. He's here during a weekend? I shouldn't be surprised by anything anymore. His gaze travels over my grazed arms. He frowns.

"I'm good, thanks." The box is slipping. I resolutely avoid his eyes. "They need chucking. I was going to leave them by the bins."

"I can take it." He catches the box and lifts it with one arm. "Those too?" He jerks his head at the bags on the step. I confirm with a reluctant nod, and actively don't watch as he picks them up and slings them into the pickup.

"Thanks." I find myself staring at the tinted truck windows instead. "I've got to um . . . I'll see you later."

He nods. There's a pair of women's sunglasses on his dashboard. My phone buzzes a timely notification from Josh London and I bolt, snatching my holdall from the hall.

* * *

Lawrence Photography is not so much a studio as a terraced house in a semi-commercial street, three roads back from the Skegness seafront. There's a funeral parlour two doors down, and an overabundance of closed takeaways. The front bay window, behind its display of prints and frames, has blackout blinds. I knock.

The door opens. My mind has concocted a description — plump, short, balding — but he doesn't match it. His hair is thick and was dark until probably not long ago; now it's half grey and a little too long. He's tall and unshaven, and there are creases of tiredness around his once heart-throb dark-brown eyes; eyes that stare as he catches sight of me on the pavement. He steps back.

"You're Rosalie." I'd thought the DiPaci part an artistic guise, but the faintest hint of his accent suggests that Lawrence is the pseudonym. He ushers me in. I enter as instructed and pause on the mat.

The room is a chaos of the unexpected. Faux-fur rugs heaped to one side, a long, narrow desk with three high-spec computer monitors. Two apple crates, three different kinds of step stool, a Christmas tree, a stuffed bird. I take a step further inside, coming to a halt beside a fireside chair on wheels and a box of crocheted baby blankets. The walls are covered in canvases — family portraits; somebody's graduation — and there's a stack of glossy pricelists on the coffee table beside the chair. I pick one up. On the other side of the room are soft boxes and umbrellas and a white-paper backdrop with a single barstool set in front.

"Thanks for meeting me." I can't quite bring myself to offer my hand. Tony's — Antonio's? — eyes are uncomfortably piercing. I'm not sure which of us is more ill at ease.

"You're welcome." He picks up a remote from the desk. The blackouts lift, letting in a flood of sunshine. I blink. In the natural light, the room feels even more unnatural. It would have been a sitting room once; there's a door in the back right-hand corner, presumably leading to the rest of his house.

"Please, sit." He gestures, and I perch on the edge of the fireside chair. At a second glance, and in the harsher light, everything looks somewhat shabby. Even his clothes are worn and limp.

"I really appreciate your time," I start; one of us has to. Tony nods.

"I expected someone would want this interview, eventually." He sits heavily in the computer chair. "It is an interview? I heard Lara's releasing a biography."

"It . . . sort of." His question throws me. "More of a chat, maybe? I wasn't planning to record anything."

His shoulders seem to relax a fraction.

"A chat about Leonie." The name has a different quality on his lips, chic and continental. He doesn't flinch away from it, although I see his eyes flicker to the half-open door in the corner.

"She was fourteen." It leaves my mouth before I can filter it. Antonio DiPaci doesn't miss a beat. He nods.

"I was twenty-five. A nobody. And bang, I'm approached. Apparently, someone likes my exhibition. Maybe I was in the right place at the right time — or maybe it was the wrong place. Either way, I'm thinking, this will make my career. To work with Lara and her daughter.

"So I said yes. My photos, my art, went from nothing . . ." — he gestures in the air — "to everything, overnight. The exposure, the people, famous names — suddenly *my* name is alongside these people. They want *my* photos. And I'm made. I think, at twenty-five, *I am made.*"

"What was it like to work with her?" I try to focus my eyes internally, on the script I've memorised. The problem with scripting conversations before you have them is that the other person hasn't read the script.

"People will say stupid things, like the camera loves her, she's born to it. No one is born to it, but Leonie was . . . beautiful . . . No," — he holds up a finger at my soundless interjection — "not in any way to be scrutinised. She knew how to create beauty. It was easy to work with her because she knew how to make a picture beautiful."

"She was a child . . ." I start.

He shakes his head. "You don't have to tell me that. She was a child, yes. A smart, headstrong child, who knew what she liked, what she wanted, what would work for her."

I swallow. We've gone off script completely. I let my eyes travel over the room and its oddities. No flowers. No single hint of flowers.

"Why Skegness?" The words are out of my mouth before I can stop them.

Tony's gaze darts to my face.

"Cheap property. Sea views." His voice contains no conviction. Beyond the blackout blind, the view is of a car dealership and a boarded-up Methodist chapel.

"My mother was heavily involved?"

"Hm?"

"In the photo shoots."

"The first one or two, yes. For the agency portfolio, and then L'Église Rose. Yes. Though it was much easier to work when she wasn't."

"When it was just you and Leonie?"

"On professional terms, for shoots, there was always a chaperone. Sometimes a director. But the chaperone did not interfere with my work every six seconds."

I chew my lip. I'm not sure how to feel about Antonio DiPaci, or how much to trust what he's saying, but he certainly seems to have the measure of my mother.

"There were *un*professional terms?"

His mouth hardens. "Leonie did not want to be a model. Or an actress."

It comes out of nowhere. Whatever I was expecting, it wasn't that.

"So yes, sometimes I met her, *off* the record, or whatever you would call it. She brought her pictures to me."

"Pictures?" I'm lost.

"She would bring me films. I would develop them. Then the next time, I would look at them with her. Sometimes during work on the portfolio, or the shoots for L'Église. Sometimes she sent them by post, then later on, when she was in London, we would make an opportunity to meet. She liked to discuss ideas and ways to improve the composition, or the light. Like I said, she knew how to create beauty."

"She *took* photos? Of what?" My head is starting to ache again. "What did my mother think to that?"

"Lara?" It's his turn to raise his brows. "Lara didn't know."

No. My mouth feels unusually dry. No, she didn't. Never once in twenty years has she alluded to Leonie being on the other side of a lens. To a camera, or a hobby. In fact, I have no idea about Leonie's hobbies, other than Phoenix and the Pony Club. About what made her tick, her favourite song, colour, what she did on a rainy day.

"She brought films to you to develop. So what happened to all the pictures?"

He shrugs. "Why would I know? They were hers. You would have them, or your parents."

But we don't. Do we? They would have been raked through by the police; someone would have known about them. But nobody did. So what did she do with them? Did she destroy them? Or take them with her? *Where?*

"You, uhm . . ." I clear my throat and glance around the studio again, searching for a way to regain control of the conversation. "I . . . Do you still develop films?" My gaze falls on the range of computer screens. "Or is it all digital now?"

Tony laughs dryly. Clearly, I'm ignorant of his art.

"I develop the ones that matter," he says.

"Here?"

I slide to my feet and move to look at the set, the screen, the stool. Tony shifts in his chair.

"There's a darkroom downstairs. In the cellar. You want to know anything else about Leonie and her pictures? Or are we done?"

The door in the corner is ajar. Now that I'm closer, I can see through it. It's mostly dark, beyond, and my eyes are drawn to the shadowy shapes of more canvases on the walls. Everything is suddenly very still. The dead bird is staring, glass eye glittering. Antonio DiPaci has frozen in his seat.

And there, on the other side of the door, she's looking back at me. Once, twice, thrice over in bold, Audrey Hepburn-style, black and white. My sister.

CHAPTER 13

Tony gets up abruptly. Before I can breathe another word, he's shut the door.

"I . . ." There's a sick feeling in my stomach.

"You mentioned in your message that you have to drive to London?" He turns away, back towards the shabby props. "It's a long way. You probably need to get on the road."

"Uh . . ." I falter. I want to confront him, to see if he tries to deny what we both know I just saw. But the impulse to flee is more urgent, a prickling of unease that tells me in no uncertain terms to run for the safety of my car. *Why Skegness?*

"Yes. Thank you for your time." I manage to force out a polite middle-ground.

"I hope it was helpful." He's still looking the other way. I can't judge anything from his demeanour. "If you need to know anything else, you have my number."

"Yeah." I frown. And if I did? If I called him to ask what was behind that door, would he really answer?

He opens the front door for me, and I step out onto the pavement.

"Thanks," I breathe.

Tony pauses. There's a distant two-tone of sirens.

"If you're writing fiction," he says flatly, "I want no part in it."

My headache pounds behind my eyes.

"I'm not writing fiction."

"Then you will write a story without an ending." His expression is impossible to read. "Give Lara my regards."

The sirens blare nearer, shaking the bay windows. By the time they Doppler-effect into the distance, Tony has shut the door.

I walk to my car. There's a parking ticket on the windscreen. I pull it off and get in. My blouse is damp with sweat and my head is throbbing. There's next to nothing left in my water bottle, and I gag on two paracetamol as I try to swallow them with the dregs. Palace Gardens. I programme my mother's address into the satnav with shaking hands, and Bluetooth my phone. I have three WhatsApp notifications. Two from Dell, one from Josh London.

> *I've just googled how long it's going to take you to drive from here to Muswell Hill. I hope you have something good to listen to. Have a safe trip and a nice weekend.*

I sink back in my seat and turn up the heater. I'm cold, despite the sweat.

> *Thanks. I'd bring you back a souvenir, but . . .*

A non-ironic shrug.
He replies right away.

> *You could always send a postcard.*

> > *It would be quicker to bring it back and put it through your door.*

> *In person would be even better.*

Direct. Although it was me that messaged him about arranging to meet. I rub my forehead. My brain is hurting.

114

The satnav says three hours and forty minutes in current traffic. That's a long time to worry about smashed melamine and what was hanging in Antonio DiPaci's back room. I start the engine, try to think about something else. Coffee-shop doorways, smiles, ironic emojis. Not grey eyes, faded anger, sweat on skin. Not wallpaper. Definitely not the cushioned seat of a swing.

* * *

Three hours and fifty-five minutes later, there are no parking spaces in Palace Gardens. I have to park round the corner on an awkward gradient in Alexandra Rise. Quarter to eight. It's almost dark, although only London dark; there are lights in all the windows and a river of uninterrupted streetlight, dappled with the shadows of the cherry-blossom branches. The gutters are adrift with petals. My mother's double-fronted townhouse is ghostly, up-and-down lit with outdoor wall lights in a brilliant azure white that's reminiscent of Antonio DiPaci's computer monitors. I shoulder my holdall and stagger up the steep flight of Edwardian steps before I remember the key safe. I leave my bag at the top and descend to retrieve the key.

Inside is anything but Edwardian. Every trace of history has gone, obliterated by high-gloss minimalism and underfloor heating. I walk on the tiles in my socks, relishing the warmth.

The office is on the first floor, up two flights of stairs. Dell has left the boxes in the middle of the room, just in case I might have missed them and gone looking in places I shouldn't. What I've somehow neglected to tell Dell is that I'll be staying the night here — because I've sublet my flat and nobody knows — but she won't be in until midday tomorrow, so I don't see the need to trouble her with details.

The screen of my phone is cracked from its argument with the radiator, cutting Joshua London's face in half. I swipe open his message.

Hope you're there safely. Looking forward to my postcard.

*Shouldn't it be you sending me the postcard? You're
the one at the seaside.*

The postcard. It's still on the backdrop of my laptop. I
unpack it onto the desk and flip up the screen. A reminder
to keep remembering. I look down at the dates on the filing
boxes, suddenly not sure where to start or how much it will
hurt when I do.

The phone buzzes on the desk.

*Happy to get you a souvenir. When can you pick it
up? Next Saturday?*

Saturday. Why not? I steel myself.

Saturday's good.

I suddenly realise how hungry I am. I didn't eat before
I drove to Skegness. I order food online. The streetlights are
shining in stripes through the Venetian blinds as I take a deep
breath and lift the lid off the top box. *2003*. It stares up at me,
or she does. Those green eyes. That smile. So bright it's painful.

Gone. Actress's daughter fails to return home . . .

*The new face of L'Église Rose, fourteen-year-old Leonie
Knight-Langton has been missing since yesterday evening
. . .*

*Police appeal for information . . . concerned for her wel-
fare . . . Plea for witnesses . . .*

I lift out the stack — originals, photocopies — and sit
down on the floor with a bump. Will they take me back; will
I feel it this time, the loss of her? Or is it just too late? Will it
always be too late?

Man wanted in connection with Leonie disappearance

Stolen away — Leonie Knight-Langton sighted in suspect's car

Police release pictures of key suspect in Leonie case

His picture, again. For the second time in a day, I find myself looking at his sullen eyes. The defiantly clenched jaw. The buzzcut. And I think of a girl who didn't want to be a model. A smart and headstrong girl who spoke French to piss people off, who could argue you round in a circle, who knew what she wanted.

Her Own Free Will? — "just because someone's older than me doesn't mean I can't be in love" — final fateful words of Leonie Knight-Langton days before disappearance . . .

Was this what she wanted? For maybe the first time in my life, I ache at the realisation. Of what was taken, not from my parents. Not from me. From her.

Leonie Lead in Rzeszów . . .
    Almost twelve months after tragic teenager's dis-appearance, Scotland Yard releases statement following new information from Polish authorities . . .

The shrill of the doorbell startles me out of my reading. I thunder down the stairs to accept the sweating bundle of foiled paper, and sit cross-legged on the floor between the filing boxes to eat. I wonder whether my mother's set Dell to scanning all this stuff. If something happened, it could all just be gone. The thought somehow compels me to document it all, so I finish the fries and abandon the burger, and start to spread it out, a ream of paper in rows across the floor. I photograph it, sheet by sheet, headline by headline spelling out the story for me. The story they want me to tell: Stefan, my mother. But what about the story between the lines? I'm becoming increasingly aware that it's there, but I can't quite see it.

I don't notice how quickly the room cools down when the heating clicks off, how my eyes start to burn with tiredness. I swig Diet Coke from the can, lay out the pieces like a giant jigsaw puzzle, gathering up a few at a time and filing them back in the boxes as I finish with them. I conjure romanticised images of police dramas, CSI, cold cases. The fact remains, even Leonie is cold now. My father poured years and millions into prolonging the agony, into appeals and resurrections and private investigators. In fairness to him he never stopped, even when they dragged his name through the mud; implicated, then exonerated.

I've never dared to wonder how hard they would have looked if it had been their other daughter who disappeared. I catch myself clenching my teeth, and think of Joy. What did she say? Something about grief being normal. About survivor's guilt. I don't feel guilty. Do I?

Saturday.

Josh's message flashes up, saving me from myself.

Awesome.

Awesome? Is his aspiration to be a teenager forever? Did any of us ever actually say that? I imagine him typing it, an overgrown fifteen-year-old. I sit back on my heels.

Yeah. Looking forward to it.

Non-ironic smiley face, for his benefit, not mine. He's typing.

. . .

> *I'll put it out there. I actually asked because I've got a pre-paid reservation at Chez Marques Saturday evening. The person I bought it for is, without any shadow of a doubt, not going to come. It's a shame*

118

to waste it (I'd feel like a total twat going on my own).

I've never heard of Chez Marques. I feel like I shouldn't tell him that. I'll google it later.

I'd love to help you out of your predicament then.

I find you hard to read, Rosalie, but I'm honoured.

I chew my lip. There's a pleasant, self-conscious warmth in my cheeks. Hard to read? Honoured? He's still typing.

Anyway, are you ok? I didn't think you'd still be awake.

00:23. I wrap my arms around myself. No, neither did I. But sleep is as elusive as ever. Exhaustion seems to permeate my limbs. The night is young. I'll have my archiving finished by morning.

Time flies when you're having fun.

I feel like I'm detecting a hint of sarcasm. Must be a Knight-Langton trait.

Something like that.

So what are you doing at your mother's, alone, that's fun enough to keep you up all night?

My hips are aching. I ease myself to my feet. The landing carpet is velvet soft. The floorboards creak under my feet as I cross to the next flight of stairs.

I've been archiving some of the old press stuff about Leonie.

A pause. He types for a second, then stops. If we were sat in Harriet's, the silence would be aching. I pick up my holdall and climb the next, narrower, staircase. The room on the top left was nominally mine. Above the Velux windows, the sky is dark and textured with cloud. There are no stars, no moon, just raindrops on the glass. The wood floor is cool and smooth, the full-length mirror polished. It's the only room that hasn't been fully redecorated since last time I came. My teenage years should have accumulated here, like the layers of history compiled in *#leoniesroom*, the snapshot of who she was. I guess I didn't know who I was at fourteen. The dressing table is abutted by bookshelves on both sides, and a few ornaments, which have been picked out by someone with better taste than me, are the only thing to intersperse the eclectic collection of volumes. The low double bed isn't made. No one was expecting me. I click on the bedside light. Josh is typing again.

Well, if you want company, even just by text, I have no place to be. When I said I wanted to help, I meant it.

I pause, throat constricting. It's like he can see me. Alone, floundering in my sister's wake.

Thanks.

I swallow.

I mean that, too.

Good to clarify the sarcasm by text. I'm a simple soul.

I smile, despite it all. He's trying. I need to get over whatever he may or may not have been to her; Leonie's gone and she's not coming back. I can't spend the rest of my life hiding under juniper bushes, holding my breath. The reflections in the mirror have changed. The children in the painting are history.

120

I leave my holdall and go in search of bedsheets. The cupboard in the guest room now houses a well-concealed HD TV. The airing cupboard over the stairs is full of towels. I try Dell's office, the second guest room — nothing. My mother's room? It's the biggest in the house, with its walk-through wardrobes and en suite; there are probably enough cupboards to store everything I've ever owned. I pull open a few at random. Everything is meticulously organised. Perhaps Dell files the clothes, too.

It's behind the third or fourth door that something catches my eye. I've already shut it before it registers. I jerk it open again.

A wooden case. Identical to the treasure box under my bed. And it has a lock, just like mine. My heart jumps into my mouth. I search the pockets of my jeans for the key, fumble to try it, and then realise my own stupidity. The keyhole's purely decorative. Which I should know, because my box never had a key. Deflated, I lift it down. It's heavy. There's little room for doubt that it's Leonie's. There was nothing I had that she didn't. Apart from glasses.

Something occurs to me. I carry the box to the bed and sit down on the white comforter to flip open the lid.

There's a scarf folded in the top — cotton, printed with ponies — and the scent hidden within its folds stops me in my tracks. I hold it to my face and inhale, the image flickering in front of my closed eyes. She's wearing jodhpurs and a riding hat, high boots that accentuate her long legs. The scarf is around her neck, her silky chocolate hair splaying from its ponytail almost to her waist; she whirls around, eyes on fire, half-smile pert and rebellious.

I refold it. Put it to one side. Underneath is a sheet of newspaper doubled over on itself. 23 April 2003. I don't understand the relevance of the date. She didn't disappear until the twenty-eighth. I draw it out and freeze as something slips from between the pages and lands in my lap.

What?

The image whirls again, shiny hair swishing as she turns to go.

I drop the paper.

CHAPTER 14

Kacper
2013

I'm going. It hasn't quite sunk in. I don't think I believed I could do it, even though Jeanette did. She still knows a lot more than I do about business, and definitely about horticulture.

The bit that Jeanette didn't believe, I think, is that I'd leave once it was finished. Maybe she wouldn't have helped me so much if she had.

She was wrong. Why *wouldn't* I leave? I've worked more hours than there are in a day for the last three years. It hasn't got easier since I finished my BTEC. In fact, I've worked more since finishing, because it's been summer and I've been snowed under with jobs. I've bought a second-hand car and saved enough money to see me through my first year. I'm going to study business. Get a degree. I'm not sure how I feel about lectures and academics, but that's irrelevant. What matters is I'm going to leave this place forever. I'm never coming back.

It's not that I want to leave Jeanette. But the idea that today's the last day I'll walk past the Blakemans' God-forsaken driveway is everything I've dreamt of since I was a kid. It's a new beginning. And this time, I'm going to do it by myself.

I park in the overflow at Garden Gate and go in through the office, but Harriet's not there. I should probably be sad that I won't get a chance to say goodbye, but I'm not. If it wasn't for Jeanette, I'd have put the last things in my car and gone this evening straight from work without saying anything to anyone.

I cut through the warehouse and walk through the store, weaving my way between the patio furniture to the tills. Jeanette's on the end one, near the wall, chatting with a customer. I'm not sure which one of us has changed more since she bought the greenhouses all those years ago. Her hair has turned mostly grey, and she's started wearing it in a knot. She joked the other day that when I come back to visit, she'll have to get a blue rinse.

I wait until the customer pays, and then wander a couple of paces closer. I'm not planning to interrupt, but Jeanette sees me and waves me across.

"Hi, big lad." Her eyes crinkle with a smile.

The nickname is more apt these days. Jeanette only stands as tall as my chin.

"Great timing, my darling. Could you help Ruth out? Two sacks of Heygates."

"Sure." I shove my car keys into my pocket and go to fetch the feed. I arrange the sacks over one shoulder. The blonde lady, presumably Ruth, is waiting by the tills. She lays a hand on Jeanette's arm, and I watch them both laugh at something. And I realise that, until this moment, there was still a bit of me that felt bad about leaving. Ungrateful. Uncaring. I don't want her to think I don't care.

But it seems to me, as I look at them, that it's fine. Jeanette is fine. She lost Geoff, she lost Tata, and now after everything, she's here, laughing. She's already carved out *her* new beginning. It's not like she won't see me. Nottingham is only two hours away.

I wait for Ruth to say her goodbyes, and follow her outside. She points out a Volvo at the back corner of the car park, and I carry the sacks to the car and dump them over the tailgate.

"Thank you," she says as I turn to go.

"No worries."

"And good luck." Ruth holds out her hand, and I hesitate. She wants me to shake it? I grasp it awkwardly.

"Thanks."

I don't wait for her to get in her car before I go back inside. Thanks. How many times have I heard that word, over the years? But I've never done anything for thanks. I've done it for self-preservation, for survival.

And I've survived.

I walk back in through the *exit only* door. Jeanette is signing off the till. I wait for her in silence, looking around at everything familiar for the last time. It's history now.

Who needs history? I thought I might feel sad, but I don't. I'm glad for Jeanette, and the only feeling apart from that, deep in my gut, is anger. What is there to miss, here? The abuse, the names, the green school gates, where one day he didn't come back to pick me up? Fuck that.

"Ready?" Jeanette is pulling on her bodywarmer, even though it must be twenty degrees outside in the September sunshine.

"Yeah." I nod, puzzled. "Have you finished work?"

"Lorraine's going to close up later."

"Right." I frown.

"I'm not letting you leave without feeding you." Her voice is teasing but her face isn't. I've come to know Jeanette well enough that I can tell everything she's hiding behind her laughter. I groan and roll my eyes, even though I know she can see right through me, too.

"It's okay. I haven't cooked. I thought pizza. I've booked us a table at Quattro."

Quattro is on the market square in Armsby, and has been for as long as I can remember. The décor hasn't changed in a decade and I'm not sure the menu has either. Pizza was always my favourite as a kid. We celebrated my tenth birthday there: me, Jeanette and an empty chair. She gets into my car and sits in the passenger seat, which still seems weird. I drive, and she tuts at my engine braking and grabs the dashboard every time we go around a corner. We sit at the table in the window and order without looking at the menu.

"So, my darling." Jeanette leans forward on her arms. "Are you?"

I frown again.

"Ready?" She shakes her head, and this time her smile is real, and aching. Suddenly my chest hurts.

"Yeah." If we were both different people, I'd hold her hand across the table.

"I'm so proud of you. Going to say it now, before things get too soppy."

"I know." My voice sounds gruff. "Me too."

"Good." She sits back. The waiter brings our drinks, and I sip my Coke, feeling ten again.

"I'll . . . uh . . . I'll . . ." I clear my throat. "Please don't get a blue rinse."

She laughs softly. "Please don't smoke anything illegal or get your eyebrows pierced."

I laugh too. I can't help it.

"Apart from that, you never have to call, and you never have to come, but pick up that phone or walk through that door any time you want to. And for God's sake, wear a helmet on your bike."

I press my lips together and pretend to stifle a smile, when really, I'm uncomfortably concerned that I might cry. Thankfully, the pizza arrives. We eat mostly in silence. Not the uneasy kind. It's one of the things that's most comforting about Jeanette, the fact that she's never tried to make me talk; that we can just sit, or walk, or work — outside for hours on end in the garden at the cottage — without the need to say anything at all. It occurs to me that Jeanette has pretty much taught me everything I know. That she's spent the last ten years selflessly and patiently equipping me to abandon her at my first opportunity.

I offer to pay, but she shoos me away from the counter. When we get back to the cottage, she asks me if I want help with the last bits, or whether I want a minute. I surprise myself by saying a minute, and she nods sagely and retires to the kitchen table with Brown Gordon winding around her legs and miaowing for food.

There's a weird feeling in my chest as I climb the stairs. I run my hand over the banister, the smooth worn bit up the middle, feel the creak of the top step under my foot. My room's semi-dark; I didn't open the curtains before I went to work. The desk is bare, so are the shelves. I thought of stripping the bed so Jeanette wouldn't have to, but I wasn't sure if that would make her sadder, so I left it. The room's not empty; it's still my room: the pine furniture; the jet plane picture on the wall over the desk; the rows of football trophies and swimming certificates. But the substance is gone. There are only a couple of things left in the bedside table, things I didn't want to put in a box or a suitcase. I sit down on the bed and take out the small collection of photos. Only one is framed, and it belonged to Tata: a picture of my mother. I was fifteen months old when she died.

I pull across my rucksack from the foot of the bed and slide the photos into the top pocket. I feel inside the drawer, behind the New Testament and a couple of packs of Anadin, until I find what I'm looking for. The bundle of rolled-up tissues is lumpy, old and starting to disintegrate. I undo the brittle Sellotape to open it. A few flakes of rust come away with the tissue, and a dusting of fine powdery earth trickles onto the duvet cover. I frown at the keys before I push them into my pocket. The rush of déjà vu is unsettling. I pick up the rucksack and go downstairs.

Jeanette is still in the kitchen. Gordon jumps down from her knee and runs to trip me up instead as Jeanette gets to her feet. I lower the rucksack. I don't know what to say. I draw in a deep breath, but she holds up a finger.

"Don't say a word. I know. You need to leave. And don't you look back, love. They've given you hell enough. Now it's time you gave some back. Go, and enjoy every minute. Go on." She jerks her head at the door. "You're going to bloody nail it. Tomorrow's the start of forever, and all that."

I nod. We both stand still for a moment. Then, out of nowhere, she strides over to me and hugs me hard.

"Beautiful boy," she breathes.

I extract myself, jaw clenched. I have to say something, I know I do, but I don't know what it is. I think about lunchboxes and waterlogged football fields, school buses and the smell of arnica.

"You don't have to worry about me anymore," I whisper at last.

Jeanette reaches up to ruffle my hair.

"Don't be daft," she says.

CHAPTER 15

2016

Never say never. I didn't used to understand the phrase. The blur of weeks to months. I hated halls; the freshers' parties that bled into club culture. But lectures weren't taxing and I wasn't used to having so much time on my hands to study, and university came with its own perks: more sports than I could fit into a week — football, rugby, a squash league — and with them socials, which in reality turned out to mean an evolving alcohol tolerance and a startling turnaround in my fortunes when it came to attracting girls.

Not that I actually dated anyone. I made a point not to; I'd seen what happened when you let it matter, the years Jeanette spent hurting. Why would I leave myself open to that kind of risk? But I couldn't see a problem with capitalising on it as long as everyone was upfront about their expectations. For months, everything I did was an assertion. Life goes on, no matter what.

That was all before. Before the text one evening that changed it all. *You don't need to come back, but . . .*

But I did need to come back. Because it turned out the breast cancer was pretty aggressive. Things escalated fast. The last year has been full of words and phrases I never wanted to know existed. Triple negative. Metastasis. Lasting power of attorney.

So I'm back. Never say never. I didn't rent a room in Nottingham this year. I told Jeanette I didn't want to waste my money when I could write a dissertation from anywhere. I've been commuting back to Shellingsby every weekend for nearly a year now anyway, while she's been sick. She told me not to, but I said I could do with work to fund my final year, and there are people in Shellingsby and Rollingford who pay well for gardening and odd jobs. I couldn't bring myself to go back to Garden Gate.

The jobs have dried up. They were an excuse anyway. Jeanette's sicker, now.

Actually, she's dying.

People don't say that word. No one will bloody say it, not even her, but it's spelt out in beads of sweat across her face. Everyone's cagey when it comes to the details. How long will it be? How bad will it be? How long's a piece of fucking string.

I change gear, check in the rear-view as I slow into the junction, and get an unwelcome view of the Brexit signs plastered along the perimeter of Jericho's grounds. They're everywhere and they boil my blood. I drive the rest of the way with my teeth clenched, and pull up in the market square in Armsby. Jeanette wanted pineapple juice, and I don't care if she can't eat or drink anymore, if she wants it then what harm is it really going to do? Like I said, she's dying.

I've kept a low profile since I came back. There's no need to invite more misery. Although it was very obvious to me, the day I shoved my boxes of stuff back into my room at the cottage, that I'm not the same kid who left this place. I haven't seen Zach Blakeman, and his brother's deployed, although I'm willing to bet Little Lord London is still flexing his importance locally and was probably behind the Brexit posters.

I lock the car, trying not to notice Quattro's whitewashed windows. It closed down a few months ago. I buy three kinds of pineapple juice in the Co-op and drive back to Shellingsby.

When I get back, Jeanette is asleep. She doesn't want juice. The carers are just leaving. I draw the sitting-room curtains and switch on the desk lamp. We had to put the hospital bed in the sitting room because it was too big to go up the stairs. I sit down on the chair beside the bed and hold her hand. Her hair is damp from being washed; she's warm and she looks peaceful, which is a relief.

After a while I lay her hand back on the covers and go to fetch my laptop. I move the chair to the foot of the bed and sit where I can keep half an eye on her over the screen. There has been a flurry of last-minute emails since I went out. I rub my forehead. It's taken months to negotiate the buyout of Garden Gate. I feel less guilty now than I did. But it's eaten up so much of my time that I've barely scratched the surface of my dissertation.

The night carer is due at eight. These couple of interim hours always make me anxious. Once I've replied to the emails, I stick a meal in the microwave and sit back with her while it warms up. She starts to stir, and I fetch the pineapple juice so I can freshen up her dry mouth with one of the little sponges on a stick. She mutters a bit, mostly about pruning the lavender, and then about where she put the Ranunculus bulbs, and I reassure her three or four times that both are in hand before she falls back to sleep.

The lasagne is almost cold by the time I eat it, but I'm not sure it's safe to re-heat it a second time. Eating doesn't take away the hollow feeling anyway. I let the night carer in and go and say goodnight to Jeanette. Awake or asleep, it's a rhythm now. I have no way of knowing when it will be the last time.

When I let myself think about it, the realisation makes me want to throw up. Every now and then my phone rings when I'm out, or I wake up in the night with a lurch of dread. Eighteen months ago I was basically still a kid.

Now . . . ? Life goes on, no matter what.

Until it doesn't.

I take the computer upstairs and open my dissertation. I don't let myself look at the word count. There are only a few weeks left. At midnight, I go and get a coffee. The light's still on in the front room. I take the coffee upstairs.

I don't know what wakes me up, the ache in my back or the pins and needles in my hands. I'm lying on my desk and the computer clock says *02:50*. There's a sick feeling in my stomach like the one I used to get on the school bus, but stronger. I chug half a pint of water, undress and get into bed.

I don't dream. When I wake again someone's knocking at the door and for a second I think I've overslept. The adrenaline is so hard-wired that I'm out of bed before I've opened my eyes, kicking my legs out of the limp duvet, pulling on my jeans. *06:03*. I fumble with a T-shirt. The knock comes again, harder.

"Coming," I croak. My throat's like sandpaper.

"I'm sorry." Laurel — the carer's name is Laurel — is a millimetre outside the door. I almost collide with her. I grab the door frame to steady myself.

"I'm so sorry to wake you . . ."

She doesn't finish the sentence.

I follow her downstairs.

Something's changed. I stop in the doorway, suddenly too afraid to go in.

Jeanette's eyes are open, but something's happened to her cheeks. They're sucked in, and her mouth is a circle, and her breathing sounds like the day I was sick on Mrs Honiton's shoes, when we sat for an hour on my bed and Jeanette pretended not to cry.

"Do you want me to call anyone?" Laurel asks, and her words don't make sense to me. My brain's a blur. Why would I want to call anyone?

"Uh . . ." My hand is in my hair, I'm tugging it without thinking. I make myself let go. "Uh . . . I think . . ."

"Anyone you want to . . . be with her? With you?"

Laurel is young. Probably no older than me. She's calm. Really calm. Anyone I want with me. With me? With Jeanette. That's what she's saying, isn't it? She wants to call someone. Because . . .

"Uh . . ." I rub my forehead. "Harriet. Lorraine. I think . . ."

"I have Lorraine's number. Shall I call her?"

I nod dumbly. Walk to the bedside. Laurel disappears.

Jeanette doesn't move. I'm not even sure if she knows I'm here. I feel like I should sit down, but panic has frozen my limbs. What am I meant to do? Where did Laurel go?

She blinks. Her lips are parched. Pineapple juice. I glance desperately around the bed . . .

"Hey, big lad."

Her voice takes me by surprise. I sit down quickly and reach for her hand on the cover. Her body looks so small under the sheets. She's almost disappeared.

"Need to stop . . . burning candle . . . both ends . . ." She's looking at the bags under my eyes. Her fingers flicker. Once it would have been a poke in the ribs. I hold them tighter.

"You know me." I try to smile.

"How's . . . Nottingham?"

I pause. She doesn't remember.

"It's good." I nod. "Busy."

Her eyes smile, but her mouth sags wide again. Her breaths seem to be getting louder. And slower. Should I do something? I glance around, for Laurel, for a clue, but can't find either. The silence grows louder. I catch myself rubbing my forehead.

"Tired . . ." she whispers.

I jolt back.

"You . . ." Her hand twitches again, as if she's trying to lift it.

"I'm fine. Late night, that's all."

"Football?"

I nod. I can't quite make myself lie. I've always been shit at lying to her. Even when I can't tell her the truth, either. I feel her fingers relax. She seems content with the answer. For a while we're quiet and her eyes are distant. I find myself counting how long it is between her breaths. There's a pain in my head; I feel like I'm nine years old again, trying to think past the pounding. Five seconds, six. The next one's a little gasp, like she'd forgotten.

"Blue . . . car . . ."

I glance out of the window. I can't see a car. It seems too soon for Harriet or Lorraine to have got here. I rub her fingers.

"It's gone, I think." I don't really know what she's talking about. The searing in my head makes it hard to process anything. All I seem to be able to do is count. Eight seconds, nine. Another gasp. Another whisper.

"*Your tata . . .*"

I freeze.

"It's okay." I rub her fingers again. "You don't . . ."

"Tata . . . never . . ."

No. I suck in a breath through my teeth. Don't say it. I don't want her to say it. Damn, the pain, it's actually blinding. I have to screw up my eyes against it.

"Your tata . . . never . . ."

"I know." I'm gripping her fingers. "I know."

There's the tiniest movement of her head. I stand up, lean over and touch her forehead. Where her skin was warm and clean last night, it's cold and grey and damp. She relaxes again, turning her face against the pillow.

"You're tired, too." I don't move my hand. "You should get some sleep."

I don't want her to go to sleep. Not this time. I don't want her to go to sleep . . . I clench my other hand behind my back. Six . . . seven. The silence in between is the worst thing I've ever heard. Where the fuck is Laurel? I don't know what to do.

The creases in her forehead seem to lessen as I leave my hand there. Her cheeks have sucked in again.

"Sleep," I whisper. "It's okay. You don't . . . You don't have to worry about me anymore."

Jeanette's mouth crinkles up.

"Don't . . . daft . . ." she says. And I grit my teeth so hard that they hurt, too.

The door creaks. Harriet looks half-awake and her hair is in the kind of messy ponytail that I don't remember her having since she was sixteen. Lorraine comes over and puts her hand on my arm, and I try not to recoil from the touch. No one says anything. Eight, nine. Another breath. I start back at one. Raindrops patter against the window.

Ten, eleven. A tiny sigh. Jeanette's eyes are closed. Was it a breath? I start again.

One, two.

Lorraine's touch on my arm seems to be burning into my skin. I stand, motionless.

Twenty-four, twenty-five.

I'm holding my own breath to listen.

Fifty-seven, fifty-eight . . .

A hundred and nineteen.

A hundred and twenty.

I lay Jeanette's hand back on the duvet. Her fingernails are blue.

Lorraine lets out a shuddering sound. For a long time, nobody moves. Then Harriet steps out, tears sliding down and dripping off her nose, and I hear her voice and Laurel's in the hall, someone on the phone. I'm not sure how long it is before a car pulls up outside and the front door opens. Hours, maybe. Laurel appears in the doorway with a lady with a lanyard and a stethoscope. Lorraine lets out another shuddering noise and takes away her hand. Her eyes meet mine.

I don't move. She nods, and then the door creaks again, and it's just me and Jeanette and the doctor.

It's lunchtime by the time everyone leaves. I tell them I'm okay. That I'll make some calls.

I do. I call from the hallway phone. The one he never called back on. The one that used to ring and ring and Jeanette wouldn't hear it until the last minute and then she'd thunder down the stairs not quite in time. Her voice is still on the answerphone. I listen to it when the funeral director calls back, instead of picking up.

I feel like I shouldn't leave her alone, so I go and sit with her. Her eyes are closed. I tuck her in and screw the lid onto the pineapple juice. Then I sit in the chair, and stare at the rain on the window for a long time, until the funeral director's black van stops on the road outside.

Life goes on, no matter what. I don't know what I expected, but when the van pulls away the sitting room gapes empty, and I have to shut the door. With it closed I can pretend she's behind it, like I used to pretend that Tata would read my letters.

I go into the kitchen instead. My eyes are tired and dry. I make an instant coffee and sit at the table, and Brown Gordon ventures in, sniffing uncertainly at the chair legs as if he senses the change. I scratch the back of his head and let the cup go cold.

There are biro marks in the wood. Maths homework and handwritten essays. Unaddressed envelopes.

I miss you so much.
   Love,
   Kotek

CHAPTER 16

2023

In hindsight, Jeanette must have actively avoided Hailbury. Not once in my entire childhood did I see behind those walls. At the age of ten, I knew better than to ask questions. But after she died, everything was a question. And when I picked up my phone one day and Nathan Langton was on the other end, I was too stunned to turn him down.

It was like a morbid bet with myself. We discussed the terms by phone, and he's never even set eyes on me. I think he's only been to the house once in five years and I simply made sure that I wasn't there. He'd found me online, read good reviews. And like I said on the squash court, he pays well, so I don't have to think anything.

The eight thirty April sunshine is dazzling, an inch too low for my eyes to be shielded by the sun visor. I squint against it as I hit the indicator. Armsby doesn't really have a rush hour; nonetheless, the petrol station is busy. The queue for the far-end pump is three cars deep, but there's a recovery truck blocking the middle row. I kill the engine and drum my fingers on the wheel.

To start with, I found Hailbury perverse, preserved like it was. But then I somehow got sucked into Langton's obsession with it: with keeping it immaculate, with keeping people out. He was pretty clear in his brief — the job's a lot more than just gardening. The razor wire wasn't his idea. Wherever the secret is hidden, whoever was responsible, the macabre shrine to Leonie Knight-Langton hidden inside those walls is no joke.

So for five years I've tended his secret garden, like the one in the book Jeanette read to me as a kid. Except in this garden there's no redemption, no curing of the lame. And now, after all this time, the house is inhabited. I heard the rumour that she was coming back before I heard it from him: his other daughter, the younger one, writing some kind of memoir. That put the bet in a whole new light. I read her column, once, enough of it to get her measure. Witty, educated, entitled.

I glance ahead at the queue. No one is moving. It seems like maybe the driver from the car at the front is doing their weekly shop before they pay. Someone else honks their horn. I unplug my seat belt.

She didn't resemble the picture I'd created in my mind, or the snatches of auburn pigtails and pink-rimmed glasses in my memory. I think maybe I was expecting Leonie: glamour, presence. But there she was, pretty and apprehensive, dressed in jeans and a woollen jumper two sizes too big, struggling to manhandle her case over the tailgate of her car. I watched her for longer than I could justify; the toss of her dark-copper hair, the hint of uncertainty in her frown, the little turn-up at the end of her nose that could have been described as cute if it wasn't for her scowl and the glare of warning in her grey-green eyes. I decided on the spot to give Langton my notice.

And then I didn't do it.

I let it linger on too long, drawn in, pulled back to the doorstep, the quiet banter, the coffee. The quick-fire inquisition on the squash court, while she thrashed me in front of half the club. I can't get her out of my head. If the place sucked me in before, it was nothing compared to this. I know it's not worth the risk. Jeanette was right to keep her distance. I can't get involved. But since Rosalie Knight-Langton arrived, I can't keep away from Hailbury.

I jolt back at the flash of brake lights. There's a surge of movement as two pumps become free at once. The morning air's still fresh as I leap down and fill up, watching the traffic gain pace on the Radby road. I go inside to pay, digging in my pocket for my card as the guy in front orders cigarettes. Harriet has texted me. I start a reply, glance up—

I freeze.

The adrenaline rush is as unexpected as his face in the aisle of sweets and screen wash. Marcus Blakeman. He turns around, cigarettes halfway to his pocket.

Ten years.

He hasn't changed much. He folds the bulging arms of his sports top across his chest. Maybe he's gained a couple of stone. Maybe the marines have made him a better person . . . maybe not.

We regard each other in silence. Ten years. No, more — it must be. What's he waiting for — *Hi, how are you?* The cashier has already rung up my pump. I step around him to get to the counter. A second later I hear the buzzer on the door.

When I go outside, the forecourt has almost emptied.

"You want to watch it, Polack." Marcus is leant against the middle pump with a jerry can. He pushes himself to his feet as the door shuts behind me. I pause. For a split second, he eyes me up and down. He's not the only one who's filled out.

"I heard there's a nasty spate of people nicking those things." He jerks his head at my pickup. I don't let my face betray anything, even though the blood is roaring in my ears. If he thinks he's going to get a rise from me, he's wrong. I draw out my key and walk between the pumps without a word, get in the truck and start the engine. It's only as I pull away and see my white knuckles on the wheel that I realise I'm trembling with rage.

I drive to Hailbury. I punch the code into the gate with shaking hands and pull up for five minutes in the flickering shadows of the drive to let my anger disperse. I had no idea he was back in Armsby. The Blakemans' old house, Stapleford Lodge, has sold; I know because the new owner called me for a quote on the garden.

I park in my normal spot by the bins and go round the back. I catch myself scanning the kitchen windows as I pass. Rosalie isn't there. The orangery is warm as I let myself in, glancing up at the mostly obscured security camera above the door. I need to clear back more of the wisteria.

I do the pool checks quickly. I've just finished rolling out the cover when a crash echoes from the direction of the house. It's close by — too close — the corridor or utility. I pause, drying off my hand against my back pocket. Those skylights have always made me uneasy. The flat roof is low and not easily visible.

There's a soft clatter. A scrape. Then nothing.

I push open the door. The skylights are closed but the air is chill, and through the blown glazing in the next door, I can see something moving. I swear under my breath. An intruder? What did she call them? *Urban explorers.* My left hand skims my pocket for my phone, but my right fist is clenched tight. She must be in the house; she's probably upstairs, out of earshot, working. Completely unaware . . .

I jerk open the door without stopping to think.

She looks up. I stop dead.

Rosalie. Her bright hair is bundled into a scruffy topknot, and she's wearing leggings and a man's shirt that was once eye-wateringly expensive and is now covered in grey paint. The breast pocket is monogrammed with her father's initials.

"Hi," she breathes.

One of the utility cupboards is open. She's attempting to tape a paintbrush to a broom-handle with perished duct tape. She drops the roll and curses.

"Hi." I lift an eyebrow.

"Uhm, sorry, this isn't . . . *your* cupboard, is it? I kind of helped myself."

I retrieve the duct tape from the floor. It must be as old as her.

"No, not mine." I pass it back to her. There's a brief silence. She leans the broom against the dryer and wraps her hand around the brush.

"I decided to paint my room." There's something stubborn in the way she says it.

"Right."

This time the silence is tense. I guess suddenly from the waver in her expression that she hasn't consulted anyone.

"There's a ladder in the garage," I say at last.

"It was padlocked."

She's not wrong. I padlocked it. For the same reason as I worry about the skylights and the paucity of security cameras. The key's somewhere on my bunch in the pickup.

"Book's going well, then?" I make a point of looking at the brush and not at the flecks of paint on her face. She almost smiles.

"It turns out that watching paint dry is faster," she quips. I smile too, despite every scrap of my better judgement. She could have been born knowing the right thing to say. And not many people can carry off wearing that amount of emulsion with her kind of grace.

"Are you playing squash tonight?" I ask, before I can remonstrate with myself. I turn away before she answers because I know it shouldn't matter to me either way.

"I was planning to." Rosalie turns away too, back towards the rest of the house, the shirtsleeves scrunched tightly in her hands. "I guess it depends how quickly paint dries. Are you?"

"Probably." I open the door to the corridor, glad of the blast of cold air.

"See you later, then," she murmurs. Then she's gone.

It's the wrong time of year to cut back wisteria; I pruned it in February. I do it anyway.

I spend four hours in the grounds before I break for lunch. The nearest DIY store is in Skeg, and I'm not sure if I can get there and back in two hours. I can't be late — I told Iryna I'd take Yvan to football. I drive back to the cottage instead. The kitchen's pretty much finished apart from plumbing in the new towel rail and putting on the socket fronts. My stepladder is smaller and lighter than the ones at Hailbury. I'm done decorating now, anyway.

I sit down at the kitchen island. The agent valuations are still there, staring up at me. Since yesterday, there's been a For Sale board driven into the polyanthus beside the front door. The wrench is threatening to be more painful than selling Garden Gate; there's a bit of Jeanette everywhere I look. But there are also lots of unwelcome memories, things I haven't quite been able to get rid of. Sneaking through the kitchen with a bloodied nose. The odd image of Tata: putting in the banister rail, building the understairs cupboards. The inescapable glimpse every morning of the Blakemans' old drive as I turn the key in the door.

I've renovated every room since she died. It's taken years. I renovated her mother's bungalow in Summercliffe first, because it was empty and I realised that if I invested some of the Garden Gate money in getting it finished and let, I'd have an income.

Eventually the business took over. Odd jobs and gardening quickly became a full week of clients. By the start of the pandemic, I'd saved up enough to put down a deposit on a second bungalow in Summercliffe.

The reality is, I don't need a character cottage in Shellingsby, where property is practically gold-plated. Its modest two and a half bedrooms have been valued at a ludicrous price, when Jeanette bought it for less than thirty grand in 1995.

I get up and find a screwdriver for the socket fronts. The radiator will have to wait; I need to leave for Yvan at three. Once I'm done, I go upstairs to the back bedroom where I've been sorting through the last of Jeanette's things. I offloaded a lot of it to Lorraine, years ago. What's left is mostly just the stuff she kept under her bed in the master room: things no one knew were there, not even me. Her wedding dress, from when she married Geoff. Some foolscap files full of papers: birth certificates, death certificates — I have no idea what I'm meant to do with those.

And there's a suitcase. The one that came with us in the back of the old car across the English Channel. *You can be anything.* Inside it are Tata's shirts and trousers, the smell of farms and straw. A duffel coat. A wallet with a picture of me at Yvan's age in it. Cards, documents, a visa.

And his passport.

Inside it is my father's passport.

CHAPTER 17

Rosalie

The water is cold. It makes the joints of my fingers ache, bone deep. I scrub like a surgeon might, up to my elbows, scratching at my skin with my fingernails until it's raw. Washing my guilt with the suds down the gurgling drain.

The paint streaks the basin, even as I run the tap to flush the last of it away. On Wednesday morning, when I went to put my squash kit in the washing machine, there was a lightweight stepladder and a set of rollers leaning against the utility-room cupboards.

I haven't spoken to either of my parents, even though it's blatantly obvious that I need to. Tuesday morning's appointment with Sandeep was even worse than I anticipated. Having established that I wasn't still concussed, he listened astutely as I rambled apologies about sleep and stimulants, then asked a few probing questions about my mood and whether I thought I felt more anxious than usual. I couldn't help noticing the way his eyes flicked every now and then to the computer screen.

Since then, apart from squash, I've stayed at Hailbury. Washed walls, painted, repeated. Once or twice, I've walked in the grounds, my thoughts consumed by what I discovered in my mother's wardrobe.

Hair.

It was folded in the newspaper. A braid of hair, tied up with emerald ribbons. Glossy, chocolate hair. But Leonie never had her hair cut. She was a fiery-eyed Disney princess, a Rapunzel; it was practically her trademark.

I flick the water out of the brush and dry my hands. I went back through the archive boxes to check. In every single photo, every single headline, my sister had long hair. So how is her braid folded in a newspaper from five days before she disappeared? There didn't seem to be anything pertinent in its content: an article about the rebranded London Mardi Gras and a letter about mobile phone masts on schools. But newspaper. Not silk, or tissue, or craft paper . . .

No matter how I try and frame it, I still feel faintly sick. Was it a keepsake? Did the police know? When they were searching, were they searching for short-haired Leonie? Or was it something much worse — a threat through the letterbox, a kidnapping. A ransom? What else did my parents keep secret?

And why?

I haven't got the first idea how to confront my mother. I should have driven to my father's flat. Woken him on Easter Sunday with the whole lot gripped grimly in my arms, and demanded an explanation.

But I didn't. I shoved it back in the cupboard and sat, shivering and sleepless, in my old bed until morning light crept around the blinds, and then I drove back to Hailbury and tried to pretend none of it had happened, like I could repress the memory as efficiently as I blocked out my childhood. It hasn't worked. I can't keep ignoring it. I can't even write, only stare, preoccupied, at the image of her face. I stopped by the juniper yesterday and sat for a while on the cold, needly earth. But nothing makes sense.

I type a text and delete it at least three times before I send it.

Hi Mum — too casual.

Mum — too accusatory.

Can you call me — I really don't want her to call me.

I need to ask a question, when you have a minute.

Which, realistically, might not be in the next week. I do realise that. I sit cross-legged in the wicker chair and look out at the gardens, greener overnight after the April rain and rising temperatures. I can't see any reason for them not disclosing a ransom demand, even if they paid it. Begging the next question: what did Krzysztof Woźniak do with hundreds of thousands — even millions — of pounds, *and* my sister? Unless she was dead.

Unless it wasn't a ransom at all.

I grit my teeth. I really have to stop constructing conspiracy theories. There are enough of those on the internet. Like I told Antonio DiPaci, I'm not writing fiction.

I open the list of notifications on my phone. I haven't been able to make myself look at any social media for days, not since the last round of #*leonieshouse* photos. @RosalieK-L: *Rosalieiswriting.* Except she isn't. I scroll through the unread likes and comments, a recent discourse from Tabitha, a smattering of new followers. One DM.

WHICH SISTER @*Leoniesangel*
5 April 2023
Are you in Leonie's room?

I falter. 5 April. Last Thursday. The pictures on the coffee table, the homework diary . . .

I was. I *was* in Leonie's room. But how could anyone know that, apart from me?

They couldn't. No one can know that. I wipe my sweating palms on my leggings. Unless . . .

I delete the message. Tiptoe across the dustsheets that cover my bedroom carpet and put the bowl out of sight in a drawer.

I retreat to Harriet's under the pretence of needing to go to the Co-op, actively avoiding the stacks of blueberry muffins and ordering from Mr Hipster-Beard at the other end of the counter. I stand and wait whilst he steams the milk, thinking about Skeg Vegas and Antonio DiPaci. Someone else who isn't telling the truth. I'm not completely sure that anyone is telling the truth. Not the whole truth and nothing but the truth.

Except maybe Josh London, whose heart is apparently nailed to his sleeve. I tap my card and sit on one of the bar-stools to nurse my latte, remembering that I was going to google Chez Marques. We're meeting in the leisure centre car park at ten to eight. I type it into the search bar.

"Chez Marques?"

I jump. Harriet is behind my shoulder, balancing three plates on one arm.

"Going upmarket, Rosalie?" Her voice is teasing. "I hope you've got t'mortgage agreed."

"Mortgage . . ." I don't catch onto the joke until I look back at the screen. Chez Marques at the Old Almonry, Armsby. *How* many Michelin stars? My eyes almost pop out of my head. In *Armsby*? We're not in Mayfair.

"Uh . . ." Shit. What in God's name am I going to wear? Why didn't I look this up sooner? "Er . . . I . . . I'm meeting someone."

Harriet's eyebrows part company with her eyes.

"I'll be back in a minute," she tells me.

She isn't lying. She takes the plates and reappears almost instantly.

"Who's someone, then?" Her eyes demand details. Her voice already knows. "Not t'same someone you ran into in here last week?"

"Yeah." My eyes are glued to the screen. Tasting menu. Restaurant. Kitchen table. A pre-paid reservation.

"You're having dinner with Josh London. At Chez Marques."

146

"He had someone cancel on him," I mumble. "Pre-paid reservation."

"That's what he said?"

"Ye . . . es?"

"Mm-hm." Harriet's eyebrows haven't come back to a normal height. "As you do, I s'pose."

"His parents are my godparents."

"Mm." Her expression hasn't changed. "And he's like, Britain's most eligible bachelor since his girlfriend left him just before Christmas. Fiancée, actually."

"She left him?"

"Heartbroken, apparently." There's the tiniest smirk at the corner of her mouth.

Well, that explains the reservation. Maybe. My phone pings. A text. I glance down. My mother.

I'm on set, is it important?

I feel the colour drain from my cheeks.

Yes, it's important.

"Sorry." I snatch up the phone. "I've got to make a call." I have an inexplicable urge to run. I stop outside the door to type.

Did Leonie get her hair cut?

I cradle the phone like an unexploded bomb as far as my car and slump in the driver's seat, waiting for the reply.

Why do you want to know?

I can read her anger. I press a suddenly shaky finger to my lips. Not the response I was hoping for.

Her braid is in your wardrobe.

I close my eyes, willing it not to ring. What am I even asking?

She cut it off.

The reply comes a lot sooner than I was expecting it. What?

She cut her own hair??

No answer.

I think about the scissors on the washstand. I'm not sure that I feel any better.

I almost get a speeding ticket to go with my parking fine on the way out of Armsby, and as I arrive back at Hailbury I realise I never got as far as the Co-op. I let myself in. This morning's coat of paint is dry, and the dust sheets are folded over the ottoman. The cleaners have been again, and so far I've not had any enraged phone calls from my father. I cross the landing.

Leonie's door opens silently, the voile curtains floating in the draught. The swing is static. There are still kirby grips on the carpet. Half of the Post-it notes have fallen off the mirror, lifting and blowing around the desk as I close the door.

I release a slow breath, letting my lungs deflate. The bed is exactly how it's supposed to be. Covers, throws, novelty cushions: a jumble of teenage insouciance perfected by twenty years of carefully practised arrangement. I rub my forehead. The scissors are back beside the sink. There isn't any hair. But, I suppose, once hoovered up it wouldn't have been replaceable.

I can picture her clearly. Standing in front of the mirror, the long brush strokes fluid and slow, the cascade of it like a waterfall down her back, blunt-cut level with her hips.

There's still no answer to my text. There isn't going to be.

Her cupboards are full of clothes. I flick through them, struck by the unnerving realisation that most of them would fit me. At the right-hand end they all still have labels; unworn — some of them even have price tags.

I know I shouldn't do it. But a voice has woken in my mind, daring me. Persuading me to find out, to see what happens if I do . . . whether Hailbury's walls will come crashing down, whether she'll materialise from the shadows after all this time to veer around and swipe her belongings from my all-too-willing hands. Leonie could have dined at Chez Marques, sultry and smoky-eyed. She could have had anything she wanted. Couldn't she?

I let the black fabric flow through my fingers. I shut the wardrobe door, and the slightest movement of the air lifts the voile curtains, revealing for a split second what's at the foot of the window. A flower, a single artificial flower — in colour, not sepia. One, just one; all that remains of a carpet of petals and blooms. Left behind.

Or placed, where it wasn't before, where it has no business being?

But my memory isn't reliable. I try desperately to remind myself of that, as I fold her dress in my arms and steal away, back to the present and the places I don't belong. As I slip it on in front of the bathroom mirror. I put on my make-up, doggedly avoiding smokiness and nonchalance, and brush out my hair with long, slow strokes, her face looking back at me from the glass.

I slow to a halt. Beside my reflection there's a flash of movement. A glint of light.

I spin.

Outside, the driveway is empty. But between the trees, for a fleeting fraction of a second, I think I see a mane of dark hair fan out and disappear.

I put down the brush.

* * *

It's dark by the time I park at the leisure centre. There's a gleaming new Tesla in the far corner with personalised plates, JL01DON. Josh is leaning against the bonnet, scrolling on his phone. He looks up as I open my car door, and his face creases in a smile.

"Rosy." He springs to greet me in a few long strides. I brace myself for North London air kisses, but thankfully there aren't any. Maybe he's more Lincolnshire than his accent lets on. His shirt's tucked in properly today, under a tailored blue blazer.

"You look beautiful. Here." He gestures for me to go first and I move at his direction. I couldn't find the restaurant on Google Street View. It's not the kind of place that has to advertise itself. On the far side of the car park, along a cobbled path, a church is set back behind a row of trees and an ancient red-brick wall with an arch in one corner. I thank the poor organisation that left all of my high-heeled shoes in storage as I navigate the cobbles in my ballet flats. Josh seems to be in no hurry, despite the fact I was late. We plunge through the arch into a sensory garden of pools, falling water, dwarf trees. The restaurant is at the top of the slope, an unlikely juxtaposition of ancient and modern. We go inside.

Josh hangs his jacket on the back of his chair whilst I sit up straighter than anyone else in the restaurant with the zipper of Leonie's cocktail dress digging into my ribs. Fine dining is wasted on me. As my mother has more than once pointed out, my tastes aren't very sophisticated.

"I brought you a souvenir." Josh grins apologetically and pushes a paper gift bag across the table. It takes me a second to remember.

"Oh . . ." I open it. It's a stick of rock candy, with *SOS* printed through it in scarlet. *SOS?*

I look around the room. There aren't many other tables. Maybe 2003 is long enough ago that the cocktail dress can be classed as vintage rather than unfashionable. I decline his offer to choose the wine, and nod knowledgeably as he discusses pairings with the sommelier. The food seems to come a fragment at a time, which in some ways is a relief.

"Was your trip home successful?"

Home? I chew my mouthful whilst I consider an answer.

"Mm." I nod. "Yes, I think so. I went through a lot of stuff . . . media reports . . . that sort of thing. It'll be much easier to have it on my laptop."

"I can't believe you write books." He shakes his head. "*Little Rosy.* I bet you hated everyone calling you that."

I pull a face. How to explain that when your big sister vanishes off the face of the earth, suddenly no one wants to emphasise the fact that you're the younger one? Little Rosy became Rosalie very quickly, and shortly afterwards left for boarding school, where her nicknames were often less flattering. I sit back as another course is swapped in for our empty plates. I let him steer the conversation on, and away. Back to Queen Victoria, the time he, Leonie and Zachary got a week's suspension for accidentally setting fire to a bin in Latin. The exploits in Shellingsby. The party where they stole a case of Babycham and Leonie vomited in his mother's Louis Vuitton handbag. The day they crashed the Land Rover into the ditch in the grounds at Jericho.

"Do you remember Jericho?" He leans forward on his elbows to study me across the table. The seriousness of his animation is captivating. There's something endearing in the contrast of his slightly unkempt hair with the fact that someone professional clearly irons his shirt collars. What did Harriet call him? The world's most eligible bachelor? But there's no pity in his attention. It's like we're old friends. Part of me can't help wondering how much I remind him of Land Rovers in ditches, school proms. Whether the broken heart happened a long time ago, before the fiancée that left.

"I don't think so." I shake my head and take another miniscule forkful of food.

"I was trying to remember how old you would have been the last time you came. My parents had New Year's parties every year. You definitely would have been there. You were a little kid, though, probably." His eyes dance. "Too young for the Babycham."

"I was seven when . . ." I alter the trajectory of my sentence. "We moved."

There are blueberries on the flatbreads. I try not to look at them. Neither of us is going to say the words: "when she disappeared". I don't miss his fleeting downward glance. Something shifts, almost imperceptibly, from affable older brother to a lingering awareness of his eyes on my reflection in the glass. There's a momentary pause. He swallows.

"You should come and look around sometime." He tops up both our glasses again. "I bet you'd remember it if you came. Although, I'm sort of glad that you don't. I was a total arse at fifteen."

And what was I? I can't quite pull my gaze away from the blueberries.

"Rosy, are you okay?"

Darkness seems to swirl at the edges of my vision. I think about the braid.

"Rosy?"

"Oh." I look up. I flash him a dazzling smile and take a big sip of wine. "Yes, I'm fine. Do you know where the bathroom is?"

I don't know how much wine I've had, but it's too much. The toilets are in the basement, down a set of stairs that are harder to navigate than they ought to be. I shut myself in one of the stalls and sit down, trying to claw back control. I don't remember. Do I? I don't . . .

My head is starting to throb. I root through my bag for painkillers, but there aren't any, just an empty cardboard box. Something flutters out with it, a little square of once-neon paper.

A Post-it note. Like the ones on her mirror. My eyes seem to take a moment to catch up. It's got writing on it. My sister's writing.

Talk not to me; I will go sit and weep,
Till I can find occasion of revenge.

I screw my eyes tight shut, then open them again. But it's still there. How? I didn't take it. I wouldn't have . . .

I blunder out of the cubicle. Run the cold tap over my wrists, trying to cool down, to slow my breathing. To focus.

It's a relief to make it safely back to the table. I've definitely had too much to drink. Josh is waiting, his knife and fork laid across his plate. I sit down, hoping I'm not as pale as I feel, and wonder to myself what my plan was to get home. Neither of us is going to be in a fit state to drive.

"Is she coming back to you?"

"Hm?" I look up sharply.

"Leonie." There it is again. The way his eyes soften on the name. "You said you didn't remember her. Is being back helping at all?"

"I . . ." I hesitate. "Yes, actually. More than I thought it would."

"Is it . . . ?" He seems oddly hesitant, too. "Is it helpful . . . to talk about her?"

I'm not sure that's the question he's meaning to ask. It sounds more like he wants to know if it's okay. Is it okay to talk about her? To me, with me, when he doesn't know me, and yet . . .

"You were in love with her." The alcohol makes me bold. I sense him pull up short.

"You mean . . ."

"Leonie. You were in love with my sister."

"I . . . Wow." He raises a hand to rub his forehead. "I . . . I'm not even sure that's what you call it at fifteen. We were friends. It was never . . . anything, really. She was dating someone else, anyway. Someone from the stables. But I . . . I guess I . . . And when she . . ." He exhales heavily. "Christ. What a question, Rosalie. I . . . I missed her. She left a hole that I couldn't fill. I . . . Yeah. I guess maybe I'd always . . . hoped . . ."

"You don't have to justify it." I crush a blueberry under my fork. "Everyone loved her."

"Including you." His voice is very soft. The pause is painful, the silence pounding behind my eyes. If only he knew. If he could see inside my head.

He reaches out, and the warmth of his hand on mine takes me by surprise. My breath catches.

"You look a lot like her, you know."

I frown at my plate.

"When I saw you in Harriet's, I thought for a second . . ." He shakes his head. "Even though I'd heard you were coming back."

I'm nothing like her. It's obvious. I look at our reflections in the window. Isn't it?

But everything is more blurred than it should be. The distinctions. The truths. And in outline the shapes of his fingers around mine are an unnervingly good fit.

When the last course is cleared, he orders a taxi on an app on his phone and watches me drink my coffee. I'm not sure either of us has appreciated the couple of hundred pounds' worth of food; the questions in his eyes don't pertain to the dining experience. There are white fairy lights in the trees, illuminating our path, and a chill in the evening air. He offers me his blazer as we descend back towards the car park, taking our time between the pools and fountains. Every now and then from the folds of fabric I catch a hint of something expensive and unfamiliar.

"The car shouldn't be long." He's carefully close, painfully polite. "I've paid for it to Jericho, but I'll ask the driver to call at Hailbury first. Unless . . ."

There's a degree of uncertainty in his voice.

"Unless you want to come back to Jericho?" Josh clears his throat. "I have some half-decent wine, and more than a respectable number of guest rooms. And it's a good bet I could find some pretty incriminating footage from the Babycham days . . ."

I waver. The white noise of the running water confuses my senses. I don't want to go back to Hailbury. Right now, I'd take anything over Hailbury.

"Uhm . . ." I teeter, uncertain, on the brink of recklessness. His hands rest lightly on my waist, under the guise of steering me through the arch. Jericho. It wouldn't be so wrong, to go to Jericho. Even if it's not me he's angling to take home. Even if it's Leonie he sees, in her sleek black dress, as we start down the cobbles towards the car park.

The taxi hasn't arrived. The small car park is practically empty. Beside my car and the Tesla, there's only one other vehicle and it's definitely not a taxi. I come to a dead stop.

Kasper's keys are still dangling from his raised hand, the pickup door rebounding with his mid-slam loss of momentum. He lowers them as I watch, not even as far as his pocket. His fist closes around them, and something colder than ice rushes through my veins. His eyes are on me, on Joshua London's hands. I see his shoulders draw back as he sucks in a slow breath, and his brows flick upwards before they pull darkly together, the bitter scowl of the boy from the cloakroom. He raises his hand to slam the door again.

Josh lets go of my waist. Kasper's fists tighten. He's not looking at me anymore. And for a confused, dizzying second, I actually think one of them might throw a punch.

Then a flash of headlights illuminates the puddles. Tyres, tarmac, licence plates. There's a car between them, earthing the static with a jolt. Josh steps forward to open the door for me. I climb in and shrug out of the blazer. Outside the opposite window, Kasper hasn't moved.

"Jericho, Sheepfold Lane?" The driver speaks over his shoulder.

I falter. An uncomprehending split second, but it's enough.

"No . . . actually." I curl my fingernails into my palms. "Hailbury House, Shellingsby St Mary. Please."

"Amazing to catch up, Rosy." Josh accepts the blazer. He still has hold of the door. He doesn't get in. Instead, he takes a discreet step back onto the kerb. "We should do it again."

"Yeah," I breathe. "Thanks for dinner. I've literally never had anything like it."

"Always a pleasure." He touches his forelock, throws me a wistful smile. Closes the door.

And out of the corner of my eye, I see Kasper Miller hold up his key and lock his pickup with a flash of orange lights, splintering through the darkness like sparks from a fire that fade as they fall, before he turns and walks away.

CHAPTER 18

"Hey, accident. You were an accident, did you know that? They didn't mean to have you. They only wanted me."

I'm on the doorstep, shivering, wet. My tights are soiled. I couldn't hold on. I tried to run to the bushes by the bins, but I was crying too much.

"Have you had an accident, accident?"

Her nose wrinkles up in disgust. I can't get in the door for crying; great, shuddering sobs of anger and shame. I want to hit her. To hit her again and again and scream and scream, but all I can do is cry . . .

* * *

The sun is rising. The sky is red at the edges, like blood diluting in water. Juice in yoghurt, curdling. I cradle the two halves of the bowl in my hands. The broken edges are sharp. Josh London is collecting me this afternoon so I can go and get my car from the leisure centre. It's Sunday morning, and in a few hours the church bells will start pounding through my delicate head. If I'd slept, I would have woken with a hangover. As it is, I've simply become slowly less intoxicated as the night has passed. Sat, listening to the beat of the clock hands. The truth. The whole truth. Nothing but the truth.

The truth is, I hated my sister. I hated Leonie, and I wished to God that she didn't exist.

And then one day . . . she didn't.

My eyes are burning. I rest my fingers on my pulse. It's light now. I could lie down, let them close. Let sleep come.

The tiredness hurts, raw in the base of my lungs, an ache that penetrates every part of me. I slide my head back in the pillows, stare at the empty canopy of the bed, the fairy lights wound haphazardly around the pine rail, the newly painted ceiling.

It doesn't. It doesn't come. All that comes is the flash of orange lights, reflecting off a red-brick wall. The chink of glasses. Clenched fists. A sleek black dress, undone and gliding to the floor.

I try to focus on my breath. In, out. On my points of contact, shoulders, knuckles, pelvis, heels. But I can't. Because with every breath in I imagine a movement beside me, with every millimetre of awareness I feel hands on my skin, making my heart beat harder until I open my eyes again to Hailbury's emptiness.

It's not until the church bells start to ring that I drift into fitful dreams. Dreams of artificial flowers, car chases through Florentine streets, a splintering windscreen, the crunch of metal. I'm standing in front of a camera, and I have no idea what I'm doing, and the dress zipper is digging into my ribs. And all the while they're coming; I can hear them hammering at the doors. My phone starts to ring, but I don't know where it is. The dress has no pockets . . .

I start upright. The sheets are damp with sweat. The church bells have stopped. The phone starts to ring again.

"Hello?" I snatch it from beside my pillow, trying to disentangle myself from the sheets. My hair is sticking to my forehead.

"Rosy. It's Josh. I'm in the drive."

Josh. *Josh?* Shit. It's half past three; there's wan daylight filtering through the trees.

"Josh, hi!" I trip over my jeans in my effort to pull them on. "Two seconds. I'm just tied up in something. I'm so sorry. I hadn't realised the time."

"Don't rush. It's fine."

"O . . . okay. I'll be down in a moment."

I throw on the rest of my clothes and pull my hair into a distinctly lumpy ponytail. I pick up Leonie's dress and something scatters over my feet.

Glass.

What?

Glistening shards of glass. For a moment I'm frozen, barefoot, too afraid to move. I was drunk. Not that drunk. I tiptoe backwards, trying to breathe away the nausea.

I have to grip the banister tightly as I descend the stairs, deliberately not looking up at her face. I open the front door to find Josh lingering beside the porch, hands buried in the pockets of his chinos.

"Sorry." I shove my feet into my boots. "Were you knocking? I didn't hear you."

"It's fine." He smiles at my clumsiness. The car doors open. "I didn't realise you'd be working. You need to cut yourself some slack sometimes, Rosy. You're going to burn out."

I nod, speechless. I'm not in a hurry to correct his assumption.

"You know, it was bloody weird coming down that drive after so long." He glances over his shoulder before he pulls away. The Tesla moves silently; even the crunch of the gravel seems muted.

"Rosy." He turns to me as we reach the gates, suddenly serious. "It's none of my business, but I really think your father ought to change the gate code. It's been the same for twenty-five years."

Oh. I look at his hands on the steering wheel. At the residue of a winter tan from some recent holiday. It hadn't occurred to me that he must have known the code to get in.

"Yeah." I say it with more bitterness than I intend. "The whole place has been the same for twenty-five years, remember?"

Because my father still believes she will come back. He's kept the locks unchanged and all the codes the same for twenty-five years so that when she does, she'll be able to get in.

Josh rubs his chin. "It worries me a little bit. Not going to lie."

"I don't think you need to worry." I fiddle with my ponytail, aware of my hypocrisy. "It's like my mother said, there's not really anything of any value there."

"*You're* there." He's still looking at me. We have to swerve sharply as a car comes the other way along the narrow lane. I can't frame a reply.

"They never caught Woźniak," he mutters. The tone of his voice is uncharacteristically grim. My stomach lurches as the Tesla swoops down and up the next gradient at speed. I chew my lip, trying desperately not to think about broken glass.

"Anyway." He huffs out a deep breath, changes the subject. "How's your mum these days? Is she still crazy busy? I still see her crop up in things from time to time. I watched her interview on *Breakfast England*, back in December."

"Crazy, yes." I screw up my face. "Busy, variably."

He laughs, or at least forces one to try and lighten the air.

"And your dad?"

"Still in the City. Also crazy. Still golfing."

"Yeah." He grins. "Dad tried to get me on their last weekend in St Andrews."

"You play golf?"

He assesses me for a moment.

"I'm not going to answer that in case I make myself look old and boring."

I snort.

"I pass no judgements," I tell him.

"That's a relief." We're on the edge of Armsby now. He steers with one hand around a ninety-degree bend and I grip the edges of my seat. We edge our way through the town centre and pull up in the car park, and I try not to look at the red-brick walls and the reflection of an indicator in the puddles. I undo my seat belt and root in my bag for my car key.

"So . . ." Josh leans back in his seat. His voice is casual. "Have you got plans tonight?"

"I . . ." I flounder, awkwardly unprepared. "I've got a yoga class, actually. In Rollingford." In my head, Harriet is gesticulating at me in despair. "I'm sorry. I . . . I don't want to give you the wrong idea. Last night was . . . was wonderful. But I . . ."

"Rosy, stop." Josh rests a gentle hand on my arm. "Please. Don't apologise to me. *I'm* sorry. You were right . . . What you said, about how I felt about her. You were right."

He pauses. There's something painful in it.

"I did. I loved her. More than I ever admitted. And I shouldn't have . . . shouldn't project that onto you. It wouldn't be fair on either of us."

Relief trickles through my hungover gut. Josh lets go of my arm.

"I had an amazing evening. I'm glad you did too. Let's not make it the last one."

"I'd like it if we can be friends." I can hear the cliché rolling off my tongue.

"I'd like that, too." He smiles. He taps a button to open my door. "If you're at Harriet's on Tuesday, I thought I might take a working lunch. I'll maybe see you there?"

"Yeah." I nod. "Yeah, that sounds good."

It's cold and dusty in my car. I wait for him to leave before I pull away, responding to the parting flash of his headlights with an awkward wave. I drive back to Hailbury.

Upstairs, the trail of glass leads towards her door, glittering crumbs that catch the light.

Except her door's still closed.

The bathroom door is open. The glass winks up at me from the tiles. I pull up short.

The mirror is smashed, obliterating her face — *smoki-ness, nonchalance* — a spray of debris across the floor. My shoes are underneath it, adorned with iridescent splinters, like dia-monds, and my make-up is still on the counter, strewn care-lessly over the words that are scrawled there in bold black eyeliner.

Did you love her?

Oh, God. I wrap my arms around my chest. *Oh, God.*

How could anyone know? The things inside my head? The things I don't remember?

I've got to get out. I stumble backwards, for the door.

But where will I go? How will Palace Gardens be any bet-ter than here, when she's there, too, woven through a glossy chocolate braid, present in her absence?

I go downstairs in search of a brush to sweep up the glass, scooping it in dustpan-loads into a bin bag. There's no one in the drive. No *KMM Ltd* to witness my quiet disposal of the evidence in the wheelie bins.

I retreat to the garden room, where I can hide from the silence. I should have gone with Josh, back to Jericho and the incriminating Babycham videos. Not here. Anywhere but here.

I kneel to roll up my yoga mat. The class is at seven. Not long, but too long. I grip the foam tightly in my hands.

I don't know why I suddenly notice the briefcase. There, under the table. I must have looked at the sagging leather every day through my trembling arms. But I've never looked at the lock. A tiny, scratched brass lock . . .

I already know, before I fetch the key from my room, that it's going to fit. The lock is stiff. I open the flap. Ease out the contents with tremulous fingers.

A phone?

No. I turn it over. There are still white earbuds connected to it. An iPod. I remember kids at school having similar ones when I moved to Muswell Hill. It's heavy, with a scroll wheel on the front and a piece of embossed plastic tape on the back, coming away at one corner. Leonie K-L. *Her* iPod. And there's more. A charger. Two, three black plastic cylinders with snap-on lids. Film canisters. Hidden here in plain sight since the day she disappeared.

I take the iPod through to the kitchen, trembling from head to foot at the realisation.

I don't know if the charger will work. I plug it in and pace the floor. It doesn't turn on. The battery must be completely dead. I try to distract myself with cooking, eating. Still nothing. I tidy the kitchen, fetch the yoga mat and change into my leggings, rubbing my legs compulsively through the lustrous Lycra to try and get warm.

It's still charging by the time I have to leave. There's a good chance it won't turn on at all, and even I can work out it's not healthy to stay and stare at it.

The yoga class is in the church hall. It took me several passes last week to spot the entrance into the shabby little car park. I park on the broken-up tarmac and tiptoe inside between the scattering of fake tea lights to the end of the row, lying in Shavasana as the room fills up. The hum of chatter swells then dies as Rollingford's church bells strike seven.

"We'll start with our three deep breaths in . . ."

I close my eyes.

"And release. Let's start to focus in on the breath . . ."

Focus on the breath. It used to work. A car races along the main street, bringing back my dream with a jolt. I open my eyes again and fix my gaze on the ceiling tiles.

"And when you're ready, rolling onto your side and coming up . . ."

Films. But no camera. There are films but no camera. There has never been a camera. So where did it go?

"And remember, when you find your thoughts wandering, bring them back to the breath. Give your mind permission to let them go . . ."

Open or closed, it makes no odds. I can see her face. Emerald eyes narrowed, brow creased.

You wore my dress.
You *never did.*
It's not the point, Rosalie. Why won't you leave me alone?
I can't.

I can't. I work through the poses on autopilot, and as everyone around me wobbles out of their balances, I'm the only one who is motionless. When the class finishes, it's all I can do not to run out of the hall.

I get into my car to discover my phone has lit up on the front seat. I'd got quite good at ignoring it. But I'm in the wrong frame of mind; the adrenaline is racing fast in my blood and the logo burns itself onto my retinas. I swipe it open.

WHICH SISTER @*Leoniesangel*
#leonie #leonieknightlangton #thetruth
16 April 2023
Come on.

WHICH SISTER @*Leoniesangel*
#leonie #leonieknightlangton #thetruth
16 April 2023
What are you afraid of @RosalieK-L?

I shouldn't have looked. I stare at the messages until the car park has emptied around me. The resounding silence as the last car swings out of the narrow gateway brings me back to my senses. I shove the phone into my pocket and start the car. A warning light pings on the dashboard. *Check tyre pressure.* I frown. Really? It was fine on the way.

I turn the engine off and back on again in the vague hope it will go away. It doesn't.

"No . . ." I groan. "Fuck's sake."

The sun is rapidly slipping over the horizon. I climb out to look. It doesn't take a pressure gauge to see the tyre is flat. I gaze at it for a moment in despair before I dig out the flimsy-looking jack and tyre iron from under the carpet of the boot. I've never done this before, but I watched Hamish do it once. From the amount of melodrama, he could have been repairing a nuclear submarine. How hard can it be?

Too hard. After a prolonged struggle, kicking and stamping on the tyre iron, I fail to undo even one wheel nut. Now what? My shoulders droop, dread beating a drumroll in my chest. It's a two-mile walk back to Shellingsby. What if . . . ?

No. I let out my breath. It will be fine. Half an hour, forty-five minutes, in plain sight on the road. It's nothing. My phone has a torch. I seize my belongings from the car and set out into the street. The streetlights are already flickering on in the dusk, reluctantly, one at a time.

Five minutes and I'm out of the village, leaving the last of the streetlights behind. I lengthen my strides, determined not to let haste become panic. Whatever the truth about Hailbury, there's nobody here. It's a peaceful Sunday evening on a picturesque country road. I try to focus on the scenery, the emerging wildflowers in the high verge, the rolling hills beyond the hedges. Not on the ceaseless movement of the leaves, the whispering in the grass.

There isn't. Anybody. There.

I grit my teeth. I'd be able to see if there were; there's nowhere for anyone to hide.

To hide . . . falling to all fours, scrambling into darkness . . .

No. I wrap my hand around my water bottle.

What are you afraid of . . . ?

I fight the urge to run. The road falls sharply downhill, into the cover of a remote patch of trees. London makes you forget that when it gets dark, it gets dark; the dusk is buzzing in front of my eyes, making everything look grainy. Making all the shadows bigger. If someone was waiting . . .

No. I flick on the torch on my phone and shine it at the trees to prove it to myself. Nothing. There's nothing there. Sandeep was on point with his probing questions; Hailbury is making me lose my mind. I lower the torch to my feet so that

I don't blind myself. There doesn't seem to be much traffic. I haven't seen a single vehicle since I left Rollingford.

Nonetheless, I clamber onto the verge, wary of a car coming fast around the bends. I'm shivering. It's everything I can do to stop my teeth chattering.

I sense before I see the glare of lights behind me. It's like I already know. I keep walking. I just have to keep walking. Slow motion; they throw my shadow long in the verge; the sound of the engine changes . . .

Slowing down. They're slowing down.

Of course they're slowing down. There's a pedestrian in the road. I grip my water bottle tightly. Running won't achieve anything. They'll go past. Any second, and they'll be accelerating away . . .

But they don't.

In a flash of headlights, and tail lights that become brake lights, the car swings across in front of me. It stops in the verge, blocking my path, and I hear the breath choked off in my throat.

Then the brake lights go out, and my eyes adjust well enough to discern that it's not a car, it's a pickup, and someone is opening the door.

He jumps down. The rap of his boots on the gritty tarmac is sudden and surprisingly loud.

Kasper Miller's gaze snaps quickly from my yoga leggings to my face. The relief is like cold, fresh air. I gulp it in lungfuls.

"Rosy . . . Rosalie," he corrects himself. Not before I've noticed the slip. The softening in the formality. Since when does he call me that?

"Why are . . . Is everything okay? What are you doing?"

His open driver's door is blocking the verge. He's unhappy. Perplexed; I see him run his hand back through his hair.

"I'm fine. Thanks." I'm determined not to falter, despite the damp chill of sweat inside my clothes. "Everything's fine, I just . . . Flat tyre. After my yoga class." I shrug. He looks at me askance, and I cut back in quickly.

"I'm perfectly capable of changing a tyre, actually. But I couldn't undo the wheel nuts."

There's a brief pause.

"And you didn't think to . . . call the AA?"

"I didn't want to wait there all night. It's only a couple of miles."

"You have my number. You could have called me."

I *could* have phoned Joshua London. But I didn't. My hands are shaking.

"What, you cover breakdowns now, too?"

Kasper glowers at me. Then he walks round the pickup and jerks open the passenger door, making adrenaline lurch in my gut.

"Please, get in."

"I'm fine." I try to sound assuring. He doesn't move an inch.

"Please." His voice is level now. His stare is very intense. "Just get in. I'll drop you at Hailbury. We can sort your car in the morning."

He's standing, waiting. I can see him in profile, half-silhouetted against the backdrop of the headlights. I want to refuse, to maintain my bravado. But I can't. My mouth is dry and my palms are sweating. Maybe it's the residual fear. But I'm suddenly not sure.

I swallow, climb into the passenger seat, and he waits for me to fasten my seat belt before he pulls away. I stare out of the windscreen, my pulse loud in my ears. Crashing relief has become something else entirely. I don't look at him. It's hard to reconcile him — the tight fit of his T-shirt sleeves, the fierce chiselled outline of his jaw — with the skinny serious boy they used to tease in the playground.

"Next time, call. I'm serious."

I blush, then scowl at the dashboard, furious at my own reaction. In the back of the cabin, right behind me, there's a child's car seat and a sticky handprint on the tinted window, and I can't let my thoughts travel in that direction. Not even for a second.

"I wasn't planning on there being a next time," I say.

"What were you thinking?" He isn't looking at me anymore. His gaze is fixed out of the windscreen too. At the flash of a deer in the verge.

"I—"

"You're not about to try and tell me that you were perfectly safe? That nothing would ever happen out here? I don't think you need me to tell you how ridiculous that would be coming from *you*, of all people. Especially given what you're doing here."

His sudden tirade takes me aback. The confusion is a knot in my chest; fright, relief, a fluttering of schoolgirl butterflies that have no place here, in his car, in the settling darkness.

"What do *you* know about why I'm here?" I try for a smart answer, but my voice sounds less sure than I'd hoped.

"Fuck all, I imagine." His fleeting glance is perceptive. "Apparently something about writing that book." He shrugs. "It's not up to me to speculate."

I pick at the upholstery, trying not to scour it for other reminders, sleek black hairs, a linger of perfume. I grit my teeth so hard that by the time he opens the window to put the gate code in, my head is starting to throb.

"You can leave me here." I start to undo my seat belt. "I'll—"

This time he doesn't even speak. The sideways look is enough to silence me. The gravel rumbles under the pickup wheels. The drive is uncomfortably long, my fingers clammy on the seat-belt buckle until he pulls up by the steps.

"I can get here for eight. Unless that's too early?"

"Oh," I falter. "Um no, eight's fine. If it suits you."

For a moment his eyes rest on my face.

"Thank you." I know my cheeks are flaming. If I could think of a single, feasible alternative to repeating this journey in reverse in the morning, I would take it. Perhaps I could walk to Rollingford, and call the AA like he suggested? Except I was too low on funds to renew my breakdown cover when it expired in November. And I'm too afraid to think about setting out across the lonely rural roads alone. I'm also less than convinced that he would accept the suggestion, anyway. I open the door and swing myself down. Kasper reaches across to pass me my water bottle.

"Goodnight, Rosalie."

The burning, split-second contact of our fingers on the scratched plastic is beyond my breaking point. I almost snatch the bottle.

"Night," I breathe. And I shut the door, before I can think another thought.

CHAPTER 19

Her music. Some of it's familiar, some of it's not; edgy pop-punk and angst, a smattering of which became iconic, the rest that's long since disappeared into the archives of MTV, never to be heard again.

I contemplated jogging to Rollingford and calling the garage. But I wasn't brave enough. I couldn't banish the idea of footsteps on the road behind me. Instead, I've paced Hailbury's corridors since it got light, listening to my sister's playlist through my earbuds and keeping a wary watch over the drive.

The bathroom has been added to the list of places to avoid, so at seven thirty I turn off the music and go to my parents' old en suite to shower. It's only as I leave their room, towel clutched around me, that I notice Leonie's door drifting on its hinges.

You're creepy, Rosalie.

I tiptoe closer.

She's there, by the window. Doing something to the windowsill, jiggling it out of place.

"What are you doing?"

She jumps so much that she drops all the things from her hand, paper mostly, and the windowsill falls down on her fingers.

"Fuck!" *Her green eyes are hot, burning my face. I can see the blood in her lips, bright bright red.*

170

"Fuck! You freak! Get out! You . . . you creepy . . . creepy little freak! Why do you have to be so creepy?"

The paper has all fallen on the floor. She drops to her knees to pick it up, crumpling it against her T-shirt. Her face is all blotchy, like she's been crying.

"Just fuck off! Right now!"

Right now. I grip the door frame. She's gone. The curtains are back in place, obscuring the cast-off flower. In the driveway outside, the struggling sun reflects off the dusty metallic charcoal of the pickup.

I fall over my feet. The pickup. But it's only quarter to eight? I snatch the towel around myself and dart for my room. This is the wrong kind of déjà vu.

He doesn't knock until eight. I manage to blow-dry my hair and scrape together something resembling poise by the time I step out into the spring sunshine. Inside, the pickup smells of pine and shower gel, faintly of woodsmoke. Kasper's gilet is hung on the back of his seat and his T-shirt is slightly damp across the shoulders. He turns to look at me.

"Where in Rollingford?"

"Oh." The directness of his stare has unnerved me. "The church hall."

He nods. I cross my legs tightly and train my mind on the idea of the family, in the park, walking on the beach. Kasper on the school run, strolling suspicious-eyed and silent through the babble of other parents to take his son by the hand. By the time we get to Rollingford, the sky has clouded over and the sun is gone.

The pickup barely fits through the narrow gateway. If I was driving, I wouldn't have dared to try. It's certainly too big for any of the parking spaces, but there's no one else there, so he parks it across three and jumps down, reappearing with a plank of wood, a rag and a much more sizeable wrench.

"Have you got a jack?" He jerks his head at my car. "I lent mine to Sandeep."

I nod. "I'll get it."

It's in the front seat with my yoga mat. I fetch it. Kasper has opened my car boot and dug out the flimsy-looking spare.

"Thanks." I hand him the jack.

"No worries." He reaches into the pocket of his jeans for his phone and keys and dumps them on the tarmac. He's not wearing his usual work trousers. The denim is crisp from washing but loose with age, frayed at the hems and around the pockets. There's an oil stain on one knee that hasn't washed out. I'm staring, again.

He raises the car and sets to work taking off the wheel. I try not to watch him, the snugness of his T-shirt across his shoulders, the way he scuffs the dirt off his hands against the rag he brought from the pickup. Thankfully the whole thing takes less than a minute. He drops the flat onto the tarmac.

"You're going to need a new tyre."

"I am?"

"This is fucked." He tips it up to show me. There's a two-inch long gash in the sidewall. I don't miss the fleeting furrow of his frown. He pushes the wheel aside and picks up the space saver tyre, testing it on the ground.

"And this is flat."

A gust of wind blows my hair across my eyes. So much for poise. I can feel the last shreds of my bravado from yesterday evening making their escape.

"We can't leave the car jacked up. I'll have to put it on." He checks his watch. "Tippingales in Armsby opens at nine, we can just take the wheel across."

"Shit. I'm sorry." The words don't quite seem to do it justice.

"It's not a problem." His voice gives nothing away. It never does. I can't tell if he means it, or whether he's about to be spectacularly late to work, wherever he's supposed to be. I watch in silence as he puts the spare on and lowers the car. He slings the ruined tyre into the back of the pickup and cleans his hands off on the rag.

"Come on." He throws the jack in the boot of my car and heads for the pickup. I grab my yoga mat and follow.

At the garage, the mechanic barely spares me a second glance. I sink low in my seat and google AA membership whilst Kasper manhandles the wheel out of the pickup and goes inside.

"They don't have one in." His voice makes me jump. I hadn't noticed him come back.

"We'll have to leave it here. They can get one by this afternoon. Or there's a Kwik Fit in Skeg. What would you rather do?"

"Don't waste any more of your day." I shake my head. "Leave it here. Did you give them my number? I'll hang around and wait. You must have things to do."

"It's fine." He regards me steadily. "I can take it out of my sixteen hours."

"Why don't you drop me at Harriet's? I can message you when I hear from the garage."

He nods. "Sure."

I fasten my seat belt in silence and make myself check in with the reflection of the child seat in the vanity mirror. He pulls up at the edge of the square but doesn't stop the engine.

"Thanks . . ." I start. But Kasper is looking past me through the shop window at the stacked chairs.

"It's Monday." He drums his fingers on the wheel.

Monday. Harriet doesn't open on Mondays. In fact, none of the tea rooms in Armsby, or even the bakery, opens on a Monday. I want to sink into the footwell with my yoga mat.

"There's a coffee van." He shrugs. "By the rec. I think I could do with one."

We park by the empty playground, its swings swaying forlornly in the breeze. It's starting to drizzle as I insist on getting the coffee, and we retreat under the bandstand in the middle of the park. I pull my cardigan around me, wishing I'd brought a coat. Kasper, as ever, appears immune to the cold. Drizzle clings to the hairs of his bare forearms. He sips his coffee.

"You remember primary school?"

His question takes me by surprise. I half turn, thrown by the fact he's asking. More thrown by the fact that, for some reason, I can't lie.

"A few odd things." I tighten my grip on the cup.

"You used to have a nanny. She forgot to pick you up."

I freeze. He remembers that?

"That would have been my mother, actually. The au pair never forgot me."

The tiniest hint of a smile plays at the corner of his lips.

"I don't have the happiest memories," I confess.

"No." He takes another sip of coffee. "Neither do I."

"You weren't in my class." I shoot a sideways look to judge his reaction.

"No." He shakes his head.

Casper the ghost. The memory is too uncomfortable to share. Does he know?

"I remember your lunchbox," I say at last.

Silence. It's hit the mark, and I wish almost straight away that I hadn't said it.

"That figures," he says under his breath.

Suddenly, my pulse is racing.

"Anything else?" His voice is soft. And this time, it's him that turns and looks. Those serious grey eyes. I want to stare into them, search for the boy I think I remember, the one that climbed the coat pegs, silent and stoic. I want to read the flecks of colour in the grey. To see what else is guarded beneath. But I can't. My cheeks are on fire. I cling to my cup.

"Not really." I shake my head. But he's too astute. I have to give him something, because he's already seen. "I remember you climbing the coat pegs, once, in the cloakroom. To get it back. They took your KitKat."

His expression is impossible to interpret. "I hated that cloakroom."

"How about you?" I turn it back on him.

"I remember the water fountain quite clearly."

The water fountain. I frown. What am I meant to do with that? I resort to a change of angle.

"Did you always stay here? Shellingsby, Armsby? Or did you leave and come back? Are your parents still local?"

His pause is loaded. He seems to assess me for a moment.

"I went to university for a couple of years. I came back because my stepmother had cancer. I grew up with her. She died a few months later."

"Oh," I exhale. "Oh, I'm so sorry."

He shrugs.

"You and your parents moved away after Leonie went missing," he says. It's a statement, not a question. Everyone knows my backstory.

"Mm. North London. I went to boarding school. They divorced."

"And you never came back, until now?"

"No." I shake my head.

"Even though the house was still . . ."

"Yeah." I screw up my face.

"Didn't you ever want to?"

I hesitate. I'm not sure where this is going. Twenty years of therapy, and I've never talked to anyone about this. How have we gone from a flat tyre to this flood of unspoken history? The blur of intermediary years that defined who I am, and destroyed who I was? But I can't help myself.

"To Hailbury, no. The truth is, I couldn't even remember it. My mind must have . . . wiped it out. Most of it, before . . . what happened."

Except I can now, can't I? I can remember.

"There was one place, though." I can't quite believe that I'm saying it. A lifetime of psychiatrists, therapists and I've never told anyone about the picture. "I went there with her. I have a postcard. I've always wanted to figure out where it was from."

For a moment, there's silence.

"You really don't remember Hailbury . . . Leonie? Or do you just tell yourself that you don't?" Kasper's eyes haven't left my face. I feel like he must be able to see right through me, like the stained glass in the kitchen doors, tinted with the colours I mean the world to see but too transparent.

"I . . . what do you mean?"

"To protect yourself? What you don't remember can't hurt you?"

"Actually," — I fiddle with my phone — "I don't think I believe that anymore."

I draw it out of my pocket, before I can think about it too much, and swipe through to the picture. "Do you know where this is?"

He takes it, flips it ninety degrees to make the picture fill the screen.

"Yeah." He hands it back to me. "You don't?"

I shake my head.

"It's ten minutes from here. You want to go?"

"Uhh . . ." Suddenly, my mouth is dry. Ten minutes away? All this time?

"It's Summercliffe." He shrugs. "I'm not sure exactly where on the promenade. They might have replaced the benches."

"I . . . Really? I . . . I mean . . . You don't—"

"It's fine." His gaze is level. "I have a property there. The new tenants recently moved in, so I need to drop by anyway, if you don't mind calling at theirs first."

"Of course not. You let houses?" It turns out I don't really know anything about him.

"Just two." He pushes himself to his feet and tosses his coffee cup into the overflowing bin. It rolls out. "Probably the only silver lining to inheriting at twenty-two."

Twenty-two. I find myself staring at the back of his gilet as he goes to retrieve the cup. Alone in the world at twenty-two? I've often felt I might be, but I'm not. My relationship with my parents may not be functional, but at least it's existent. Although he said Harriet is family. And maybe he was married by then, anyway. A sharp voice at the back of my mind is quick to point out that the child I saw must be at least six or seven years old.

I follow him to the bin and slot my cup in the top without a word. He's not exaggerating; the drive to Summercliffe-on-Sea only takes a few minutes. I scour the opening vista for familiar landmarks amongst the closed shops and empty restaurants. It's a town, but barely, mostly retirement properties and intermittently used second homes. There's one dated hotel, a plethora of charity shops, a mobility-scooter showroom and a frigid-year-round children's paddling pool. A beachfront café is selling chips and candy floss and the slipway is faced with stagnant, green water features. A once-colourful playground is sea-bleached and graffitied and missing its seats, and an anti-climb fence jangles over the rubble of a redevelopment that's never happened. The only continuity is the seawall — endless miles of grey.

We turn right, into a cul-de-sac overshadowed by the sea defences. The bungalows are all variations on a theme from the seventies or eighties. Two in three are uninhabited, lit by time-switches and waiting for the long-weekenders to return. The one we stop at is semi-detached, set behind a patch of spiky grass with a row of plant pots full of shells. Kasper undoes his seat belt.

"You can come in, if you want. I just need to check they're okay. They're . . ." He hesitates. "Actually, they're not tenants exactly." He opens his car door. "They're refugees. From Ukraine. The lady's called Iryna, she's here with her grandson. His father was killed in the early fighting and his mother's still in Donetsk. They got here at the start of March. They don't speak any English."

For a second, I have no idea what to say. Kasper jumps down, slams the door. I hover at an awkward distance as he knocks. The front door opens, and I catch little more than a glimpse of dark hair and the flash of a reflection. I follow him inside, onto a sandy doormat and into an oddly empty sitting room. There's a child kneeling on the rug, playing with some toys on the tiled coffee table: Sylvanians. My brain doesn't seem to be able to synapse fast enough. A little boy in a T-shirt and turned-up jeans, with ruffled light-brown hair.

Kasper turns back.

"Rosalie, this is Iryna. Iryna, Rosalie."

I'm staring, openly, at the woman's sleek black bob and turtleneck sweater. She smiles and the deep creases around her eyes are astute and kind and tired, all at once.

"And Yvan." Kasper nods in the direction of the coffee table. Iryna turns and says something, and the boy jumps to his feet.

"Hi." I manage. "It's nice to meet you."

I look down as Yvan approaches, his eyes wary, to reach for Kasper's hand.

"Hi, Yvan," I whisper.

The silence is so intense it hurts. I remember what Kasper said. That they've only been here since March, don't speak English, that Yvan's father is dead. Suddenly my throat feels tight. I think about the car seat and the sunglasses, and what I saw outside the hardware store, and a yawning, cavernous hole of realisation seems to open up in my abdomen. Kasper takes something from his pocket and stoops down. I see Yvan's eyes light up.

"Hey, Yvan," he says.

And then he says something else. Something indecipherable, soft and fluent. The child grins broadly, replies: a bubbling of excited intonation and unfamiliar words. Iryna laughs under her breath at the exchange. Kasper straightens.

I'm dead in my tracks. Gaping at him, incapable of logical thought.

"You . . ." I trail off. "You speak Ukrainian?"

He doesn't reply. But I think I see the wry hint of a smile before he turns away, a brief, painful twist of his lips. It occurs to me suddenly that pretty much everything I thought I knew about him has proved itself untrue within the last five minutes. He disappears into the kitchen with Yvan hanging from his arm and I'm left with Iryna.

I feel I ought to say something, but I don't know what or how. I glance around at the sparse furniture and scattering of toys. Under the window is the rest of the Sylvanian village;

Nedward the horse is enjoying a new position of prominence beside the TV. The tightness in my throat has become an ache. They're not waiting, anymore, for the child that never came back. This is where they belong.

"There are more," I blurt, before I remember that Iryna has no idea what I'm saying. "Toys. There are loads in the attic at Hailbury. Lego. Lots of Lego. Other stuff too. Yvan can have any of it he wants."

She glances up sharply. Our eyes meet. Then she touches a hand to her brow, shakes her head.

"I'm sorry." I shake mine too. "You don't understand."

She pulls out a phone, swipes and taps, holds it out for me to look.

I am sorry I am not able to talk to you. I try to learn English)) *it is very difficult.*

"It's okay." I smile. "My Ukrainian's not great either."

She takes the phone and types again, reverses the translation to check it before she hands it to me.

Your man has a very good heart, great kindness.

"Oh." I exhale a little breath. I guess I'm not the only one leaping to the wrong conclusions. "He's not . . . I mean, we're not . . ."

It's pointless. Her smile is knowing. She touches the back of my hand, and ushers me towards the kitchen. Yvan and Kasper are at the table, a whole collection of colourful cards spread out in front of them. Yvan drops to his feet as we come in and gathers them into a heap. Kasper stands too. Iryna asks him something, and he replies softly, a little shake of his head, a nod in the direction of the road.

"Have you heard anything from the garage?" He turns back to me.

The garage?

"Oh!" The tyre. The actual reason we're here. I check my phone. "No, nothing."

"Shall we go and find your bench?"

I bite my lip. I'm suddenly not sure.

"Don't you have things to do? Honestly, if you need to get back—"

His grey gaze holds mine, impossible to read. "I have the day off."

Outside, the cloud has broken and the blistering wind has already dried the drizzle from the pavements. We corner across a green and over a road. A set of crazy-paved steps ascend to the promenade, a coastal vista of windswept dunes and marram grass, brown sand and the browner North Sea. Concrete and asbestos beach huts with ridged roofs and barred windows, long past their heyday, are interspersed with occasional stretches of beautifully painted ones, with colourful shutters and imaginative names.

I find myself drawn to the sand. I climb up onto the seawall and the wind snatches at me, trying to change my mind. My hair is blowing in wild disarray across my eyes as I drink in a few deep breaths of the sweet, salty air.

I'm not sure what makes me turn back. A sudden return of awareness. Kasper's eyes linger on me for a second or two. Long enough that there's a childlike skip in my pulse, a breathless feeling that I can't quite attribute to the wind. He swings himself up a few feet further along.

"I think we have to head out of town." He jerks his head to our right, where the beach huts stretch on, huddled in a line along the dwindling promenade.

"Okay."

I look at the damp drifts of sand. There's a band of shells midway down the beach, glistening like treasure. I jump down and cross the sand, savouring the give of it under my boots. The shells are the tiniest I've ever seen, smaller than my littlest fingernail, a pure white that shines against the earthy brown shingle like stars in the night sky. I catch myself picking them up, pocketing them like a child might, my fingers numb with cold. I straighten at the crunch of Kasper's boots.

"That way?" I point.

A faint smile plays on his lips, and this time it's neither wry nor hidden.

"Only when you're ready." He pushes his hands into the pockets of his gilet.

I start to walk, watching the way the water claims my footprints. Kasper pauses a moment, then falls into step behind me.

We walk largely in silence, broken only by the gently rolling waves and the intermittent squabble of the gulls. After a while the sand becomes boggy, and our path is cut off by a family of little rivulets tracking their way seaward. We cut up the beach to the wall and ascend the next set of steps onto the promenade; I sit at the bottom to tip the worst of the sand out of my shoes, and Kasper zips up his gilet against a fresh assault of the wind. There's something uniquely beautiful about the wilderness of waving grasses and the soft ceaseless whisper of the low waves. Something forgotten, far removed from tourists and photoshopped sunshine.

"What I don't understand is why you chose to stay."

"Hm?" I look up, boot half fastened.

"At Hailbury." His voice is soft. As I get to my feet, his hand moves dangerously close to mine. And for a split second, I can't help wondering how it would feel to touch it.

"Sure, you needed to do your research. But you could have taken pictures and gone back to London, or wherever is home these days."

"I sublet my flat." He's the first person I've told, apart from the estate agent. "For six months. I thought it would be long enough to write the first draft. I'm not sure now."

"It's not going well?"

"Uhm." I look down at the stray sand on the concrete, then back up. "No. I mean, it is, it's not the writing . . ." Except it sort of is. "It's just . . . I thought she was gone, but she's not, she's everywhere."

"It must be hard." He's turned away. "Not knowing what happened to her."

I swallow. He's plunged his hands back into his pockets, out of sight, out of reach.

"I thought it wasn't," I admit. "I didn't think I felt anything about her. I was little. I didn't really know her. It was just a fact I grew up with."

"You weren't *that* little." He turns back suddenly, and the conviction in his voice surprises me.

"No." I don't flinch from his stare. There *are* flecks of colour in the grey, more colours than I can describe. I have no desire to look away.

"No." I release my breath. "And I did know her. I knew her . . . like other people didn't."

His eyebrows flicker. I think, fleetingly, that he's going to ask me what I mean, and I think, for a dizzying second, that I'd tell him. All of it. But he doesn't. He nods, instead.

We start to walk again. Salt spray, and silence that neither of us breaks. The promenade has grown quiet. For a clear, sharp spring day, there are remarkably few people around. A mile further along, and the place is deserted; we could be the only two people left on earth. The eerie faces of the longer-forgotten huts are boarded-up, barred and padlocked against the North Sea spray like some kind of post-apocalypse. I can't believe that we'll find the colours from the postcard here. For all I know, he could be leading us in completely the wrong direction.

I glance back at him and our eyes lock. I'm not sure who caught who looking. The wind in the dunes makes a haunting sound, and our shadows are almost touching. I finger the shells in my pocket.

"Did you finish painting your room?" he asks at last.

"Yeah. Thanks for the ladder."

Kasper smiles. "Any time." His eyes hold mine for a second more, before he glances out to sea. There's a ship of some kind on the horizon. "Your father doesn't know?"

"Not unless you've told him." I chew my lip.

"You aren't what I thought you'd be like." His voice is inscrutable. He's still watching the ship and its millimetres of progress across the horizon.

"You . . . huh?" I feel the mutinous rush of blood to my cheeks. "What did you think I'd be like?"

Her? Did he think I'd be like her?

"I don't know." He stops, suddenly, and his eyes are bright. Playful? I can't put it together with the solemn set of his mouth and jaw. "Less . . . single-minded."

Single-minded.

"Here's your bench."

"Oh . . ." For some reason, I don't want him to change the subject.

But he's right. It's there. Set away from the seawall, back by the beach huts. They're not so much washed-out now as just brown, like the sand; most of the paint has flaked away and the padlocks on the windows and doors are rusty.

The bench, in contrast, is still red. It looks like a railway bench, the kind you'd find on stations with initials scratched into the enamel. I'm not sure how it's withstood the salt when nothing else has, but there it is. The back rail is rusty underneath. The rest of it is apparently unchanged. I walk to it and run my hand over the metal, waiting for the memory to come. She held me, on this bench. She held me.

I sit down on the seat. It's cold, and I feel oddly bereft. There's an ache in my chest that wasn't there before; the depth of it is unfamiliar. I pull up my knees and hug them to me tightly.

Why would I have been sorry?

It's been a long time since someone held me. A really, really long time. I pull my knees harder against me and try to remember how to breathe.

"Are you okay?"

I'd almost forgotten he was there. I nod. He sits down carefully on the other end of the bench. He doesn't speak. Neither do I. I grip my shins and Kasper gazes out over the seawall at the still miniscule shape of the ship. When he does speak, it startles me.

"Ferries. They sail out of Hull. Do you need a minute?"

I shake my head. "I'm okay."

"I could go. If you want me to wait somewhere else—"

"No," I whisper. "Don't."

He nods. After a beat, he leans forwards and rests his elbows on his knees. I don't know how long we sit that way. Contemplating the ship, the suck of the sea, the silence. Long enough that the ferry disappears into the glare. Eventually Kasper slides to his feet.

"I think your phone rang."

I ease it out of my pocket. It's on vibrate. How would he have heard it when I didn't?

"Is it Tippingales?" He holds out his hand. "I'll call them back, if you want?"

"Thanks." I unlock it for him.

He takes the phone down to the beach, leaving me for a moment to gather my sensibilities. I don't know why some part of me thought there would be answers here. Just like at Hailbury, there are only questions. More and more questions. I'm starting to shiver.

"Your wheel's ready." He's back.

He hands me the phone, shooting a sideways glance at my chattering teeth. We walk the first stretch in silence. After a while he directs us a different way, through a gate and down from the promenade, out of the wind, and my shivering finally abates.

"You have no idea the amount of grief I got when I turned up for club night on Tuesday." Another sideways glance. "It seems word gets around. Do you think next time we get drawn for a match, you could at least make it *look* hard?"

I reach to tuck back my hair. It's windswept and tangled.

"I beat . . . what was his name . . . ?"

"Giles."

"I beat Giles, too, this week. Last week. Whenever it was. If it's any consolation."

The smile, *that* smile, less faint each time, is back at the corner of his lips.

"It's not, really."

"Sorry."

He laughs, softly. "This way."

We divert along a footpath between houses and out onto a road. The bungalows are familiar. I remember Iryna and Yvan with a jolt.

"Next time you're at Hailbury, will you take some toys for Yvan?" I drop my gaze to the unkempt tarmac, suddenly very aware of my assumptions and how wrong they turned out to be. Very aware of how narrow the pavement is, and the fact that this time he hasn't dropped in behind me. I can see his legs in the periphery of my vision, long and strong, his hands buried in his pockets.

"Yeah. Thanks. He'd really appreciate that. To . . . to lose a parent, and then leave everything behind. It's tough."

"It's unimaginable." I glance up in time to see him look away. He unlocks the pickup, a flash of orange light that flares and fades.

* * *

The drive back to Tippingales is over before it's even really begun. I pay as he loads the wheel into the truck. A scattering of surly raindrops strikes the windscreen as we arrive in Rollingford. By the time he's assembled the jack, the scattering is a downpour, and I turn out my glovebox to find a compact umbrella that does very little to keep either of us dry. Kasper's T-shirt is soaked, and I can see him blinking the rain out of his eyes as he tightens the wheel nuts. The wrench slips suddenly in his hand.

"Shit." He drops it, breathing the curse aloud. The rain is pouring over his skin, running in rivulets with the blood from his split knuckle. He stands up, shakes his hand, and before it even occurs to me what I'm doing, I catch hold of it to look. His skin is calloused, rough. The pause is tangible. An intake of breath that's sharp enough to hurt.

I let go.

"I've . . . um . . . got tissue . . . a plaster . . ." I turn, as if to go in search. As if the reality isn't blinding both of us.

"It's fine." He curls his hand into a fist, making blood drip onto the broken tarmac. "It's nothing."

"At least it's not your squash hand?" I try to sound light. To disguise the odd feeling in my throat.

He raises his eyebrows at me. "No. I don't need a handicap against you."

The plaster is futile. It falls off before he's even finished the last nut. He throws his wrench back into his truck. I go to pick up the space saver and stagger. It's heavier than I anticipated. He catches it with his good hand.

"You need to get this properly inflated." He pops the boot to put it in. "I'll bring a compressor to Hailbury in the morning."

"Thanks," I whisper.

"I'll see you tomorrow, Rosalie." His voice is very soft.

Tomorrow. It almost sounds like a promise, as I get in my car. As I watch him turn away and press his bleeding knuckle to his jeans.

At Hailbury the alarm is still armed, and the house is in silence. I cook a bowl of pasta and carry it up to the attic. I fold the tepee into its canvas bag, thinking about what he said — "to lose a parent, leave everything behind" — something about the phrasing of it nags at me.

There's an aged Nintendo and a basket of games, a train set that never even came out of its packaging. I pull out the crates of Lego. As I tip the bricks onto the floor, as I sort through the tiny people and re-assemble the sets — spaceships, pirates, jet planes — the image of the small boy in my head is no longer quite clear. His T-shirt blends, somehow, into a blue school sweater, and his watching eyes are serious and grey.

It takes a long time to piece them back together, the dismembered vehicles and broken homes. I search for missing pieces through landslides of tiny bricks, until my hands grow sore and abraded. The sky outside grows dark. Eventually, I have two boxes of bricks, and five or six full sets with instructions. I turn off the light and go downstairs.

I sit in the kitchen with my phone. There's no one to save me from myself. I cut up an apple and wash the knife under the tap. I can't even lose myself in crap on the internet, because it turns out someone has decided to put the doom into doomscrolling. The post is public.

WHICH SISTER @*Leoniesangel* • 10h
@RosalieK-L When are you going to come clean with all the people you've been lying to?

WHICH SISTER @*Leoniesangel* • 7h
When are you going to tell the truth?

WHICH SISTER @*Leoniesangel* • 2h
Did you love her?

WHICH SISTER @*Leoniesangel* • 2h
Do you miss her?

WHICH SISTER @*Leoniesangel* • 18m
@RosalieK-L you're next

Oh, God. I lower the phone, press a trembling hand to my lip. Did I love her? There's a knife missing from the knife block. Third from the left.

Shivers overtake me. *You're next.*

I try desperately not to remember what Josh said, but I can't block it out. *They never caught Woźniak.* I suddenly don't want to be in the kitchen, where the multitude of windows looks out over the deserted grounds. I snatch up my phone and my computer, the iPod, the two canisters of film, and go upstairs.

Leonie's dress has fallen off its hanger. It's on the floor, crumpled, shimmering black. I move tremulously to pick it up.

Something's wrong.

The fabric's slashed, hanging in ruined shreds. I choke back a sound that I don't recognise. It slips through my hands, pools at my feet; I stumble a step backwards . . .

There's somebody here.

"No," I whisper.

No. The alarm was set. There's no one here. Only me. *Only me.*

I think, for a moment, of fleeing. Of getting back in the car and driving . . . where? To Palace Gardens? To Dell? To my father's apartment?

Like I said, no one's going to save me.

When are you going to tell the truth?

The truth. Bile has risen in my throat. I scrunch my fingernails into my palms. The whole truth. *Nothing but the truth.*

There's a screwdriver in the utility cupboard. I turn all the lights on, so that I can be sure. That I'm not back in the nightmare. The place that's always waiting . . .

What's happening to me?

"Please," I choke. "*Please*. Make it stop . . ."

The silence hurts my head. Leonie is still watching me from the stairs, her gaze boring into my skull. I clamp my hands over my ears and sink to sit on the bottom step.

It can't be. It's not possible.

Mary, Mary, quite contrary . . .

But if it's not . . . ?

If it's not, then there's someone else here. In the house. In the shadows. There has been all along, and no one will believe me. I can't run. There's nowhere to go. I can only hide. Hide. Keep the lights on. Stay quiet.

Ready or not, here I come . . .

I can lock myself in. I unscrew the cloakroom bolt first, then the bathroom, and take them to my room. My bedroom door is hard and old, resistant to my efforts, but I don't stop. Not until my trembling arms ache and my palm blisters, and the screws bite deep into the wood.

Then I bolt the door, sit in the middle of my bed and try not to think of Kasper Miller, while the pool of lamplight burns around me like a ring of fire to ward off whatever presence, real or imagined, creeps beyond.

CHAPTER 20

"Rosalie."

He's there, on the doorstep. His hand is raised to knock. I see him take a step back, surprised by my premature appearance. I hope he doesn't think I was waiting. I wasn't waiting, not really.

Except I've been waiting all night. Startling at every sound: the stifled creak of a door, a stranger with a knife . . . I've prayed, for hours, for the dawn to come, for the safety of his pickup pulling to a halt on the gravel.

And now?

"Hi," I say lightly. As if I can fix everything by carrying on pretending. "You're bright and early."

Does he know? Can he tell? That I've lost my mind; I must have. He regards me for a beat.

"Haven't got enough hours in this week. Guess that's what I get for taking a day off."

"Oh." I smile. I can't help it. Despite my shaking hands and the pervasive nausea of exhaustion. His voice, his steady gaze, in the straightforward morning light, is like coming up for air.

"It's only Tuesday. I guess there's still time. Did you . . ." I chew my lip. "Did you do anything nice with your day off?"

There are cameras, CCTV, razor wire. The only person who has been in the house is me. I must know that, deep down. If I accept it, it doesn't have to destroy me. I could talk to Sandeep. Tell the truth. *The whole truth?*

"Oh, you know." Kasper shrugs. He doesn't smile. But something lightens in his eyes, a shimmer of the colours in the grey. "Sea views, breakdown recovery. I actually came to see if I could borrow your car key. Figured I should sort out your space saver in case you have . . ." He pauses. "Any more bad luck with your tyres."

Sea views. For a moment I'm frozen, the recollection fresh in my mind. Shabby props and canvas prints.

"Sure," I manage. But my throat has constricted. Sea views. Antonio DiPaci . . . I know what I need to do.

I duck inside to find the key. Kasper's eyes scour my face as I pass it to him, but he doesn't say anything. What was it Josh said? Hard to read. And yet I'm increasingly sure that Kasper Miller can read me like an open book.

"Thank you," I add.

I don't watch him this time. I can't. It's a mistake, to want to. To want to look back, to tell him, to find out, if he knew, whether he . . .

No.

I grit my teeth and go inside to fetch the Lego.

* * *

I don't message Tony. I have the distinct suspicion that if I forewarn him of my intentions, he won't be at home. I wait for Kasper to pass back my car key, for him to pick up the boxes, the slightest flicker in his expression as he looks down at the toys. Then I pocket the films, stomach churning, and set out for Skegness.

The road outside Lawrence Photography is devoid of life. I wrap clammy fingers around the film canisters. The blackouts aren't down. Perhaps Tony is out? I stand on the doorstep for a long time before I knock.

I see him through the window, and he sees me. We both realise in the same instant that he can't pretend not to be there. He opens the door.

"If it's about the biography—"

"It's not about the biography." I stop short of putting my foot in the door. I open my hand. "It's about these."

I see Tony's gaze travel downward. His eyes darken. He steps back.

"You'd better come in."

I do as he says. The soft boxes are off. The white screen has been replaced with a grey one, the colour of Kasper Miller's eyes.

"You could take them to Boots," he says flatly. "Why me?"

"You know why." My voice is less steady than I want it to be. "Because they're hers. You said you develop the ones that matter."

I see him swallow.

"Leave them with me. I'll see what I can do."

"No." I get it out before I can lose my conviction. "Yes. But no. First, I need to know—"

"Who doesn't?" he cuts across me, acerbic.

"Why do you have pictures of her?"

"So that people like you can jump to the wrong conclusions." His eyes seem to bore into me. The door to the back room is closed. He sees me looking and strides the length of the studio to open it.

"There you go. You want to see? Go on in. Some of my best work." Tony waves his hand at the walls. Walls hung, floor-to-ceiling, with canvases. I stumble inside and come to an uncomfortable halt, my eyes poring over the pictures. Faces, some of them familiar. Films. Catwalks. *Cannes?* I frown. He ushers me further in.

"Look. Why not? At the greatness I achieved. Him? He's dead. Drug overdose. And her, there, eating disorder. She has never recovered. And this . . . here, most famous of all, huh?" He gestures. "Maybe *you* would like to have them? Or your mother? As a reminder of what good it did for her? No? I didn't think so. So nobody, ever, will look at them again. Except me."

Her bright eyes gaze down at me in triplicate. I've never seen these pictures. They must pre-date L'Église Rose. Her hair is braided round her head, her freckled face still holding a mischievous, childish charm that was gone by the days of *Contraire*. She's pouting but she's laughing; he's caught it in some way I can't explain. Her essence. I realise my fingernails are digging into my palms. The rest of the room is dull, dark by comparison, three weighty shelves of books narrowing it to barely more than a corridor with a staircase at one side. There's a single armchair by a mantlepiece over an electric fire, a drop-leaf table. At the far end, a cork-panelled arch leads into a tiny kitchen with a cold, damp lean-to conservatory. In the bramble-ridden rhomboid of back garden beyond there's a rotting maroon hatchback with grass growing out of its wheel arches and no glass in its windows.

"Does Lara know about these?" Tony jerks his head at the films. "I guess you talked to her?"

I assess him, the crease in his brow. I shake my head.

"No. She doesn't know."

He pauses. "Does anyone know?"

There's a sudden glint in his eyes. I hesitate.

"No."

The silence stretches into an abyss between us.

"So. When they're ready . . . I call you?" Tony holds out his hand. I can hear the blood rushing in my ears. With a feeling of inexorability, I drop the canisters onto his palm.

"Yes. Please."

"Not Lara? Her agent?"

I frown. "No. Just me."

He nods.

"Okay." He starts back towards the studio, and I follow, unable to stop my eyes from travelling again over the thread-bare furniture and the hipflask on the table.

"Did she . . ." I falter. "Did Leonie ever talk to you?"

"She talked to me about photography." Tony holds open the door. I step back into the studio.

"But what else? About life? People . . . ?"

"What question are you asking, Rosalie?" He turns the canisters between his fingers. He's not looking at me.

"Did she ever talk to you about Krzysztof Woźniak?"

Tony lowers the canisters.

"I'll tell you the same as I told the detectives, the investigators . . . your mother. I never once heard that name before people came asking about him."

"Would she have told *you* if she was going to run away?"

"Why would she tell *me*?"

"You were a mentor . . . a . . . friend?"

"Not as far as your book is concerned."

"Then how do I tell the truth? I'll be lying by omission."

"That's your problem, not mine. I don't think Lara needs the royalties, huh? So I guess you can figure that out in your own time. I have a client at ten."

He's walking me towards the door. I shoot one last glance at the props and screens. There's something. Something else. A question that I can't frame. I have a brief and frantic urge to snatch the films back from him, but it's too late, he's pocketed them and I'm already in the street.

I don't drive back to Shellingsby. I walk into the town centre instead, in search of a dress and shoes for the literary lunch. Finding either takes longer than I anticipated. But it's a relief to be away from Hailbury. In the dreary safety of the seafront, my head seems clearer.

I walk with her music playing in my ears, navigating the scroll wheel of the iPod with my thumbs. Whatever's going on, in my own head or otherwise, I'm not going to let it scare me off. Not just as I'm starting to get to know her. Because I *am* starting to know her. I *do* know her favourite songs, her hobby, what made her tick. I've seen the laughter in her eyes, the girl who didn't want to be a model or an actress, who took photos in secret. The girl who spent her nights listening to songs about becoming somebody else. About faking it. About running away.

I'm not going to run away.

There's an eeriness as I corner back into Tony's road. The street is graveyard empty and Lawrence Photography's black-outs are closed. I go to unlock my car, then realise I must not have locked it. I get inside with a shudder, and freeze.

The glovebox isn't properly shut.

For long seconds all I can do is stare at it, a chill creeping over me. I didn't open it. I reach, trance-like, to touch the latch, and it falls wide open with a crash.

"Ohh!"

A hiss of air escapes my lips. There's a knife inside. A kitchen knife with a wooden handle — the knife block, third from the left . . .

The car was unlocked . . .

I turn in panic, fingernails clawing the upholstery.

They're in the car . . .

They're not. The back seat is empty. No one is in the car. No one was at Hailbury. No one was swinging on the swing.

I feel distinctly sick. I climb out, open the doors one at a time to check. The boot. The back seat. No one.

I'm going to write her story. I've got to. Before I go insane.

The sky over Hailbury is pregnant with clouds. I take my laptop to her room and sit at her desk keeping the swing in the periphery of my vision as I type. When Tony gives me her pictures, then I really will know her like no one else did. Won't I?

I work for hours, revelling in the give and patter of the keys under my fingers. After a while the silence starts to hurt my ears, and I turn on her CD player. The cleaners don't seem to have come. I pull my legs up to my chest and type past my knees, listening to the enraged crescendo of the wind outside. The laptop screen flickers and the CD skips. I glance around, uncomfortable.

I get to my feet and walk to the window. The driveway is empty. There's nobody there. Not even Kasper Miller with his cynicism and his unsmiled smiles. I pick up the flower from the carpet and turn it in my fingers. Where did it come from? Did I dislodge it from her wardrobe when I took the dress? Are there more? I click open the latch.

The music stops so suddenly that it makes me jump. The laptop has dimmed. Over the howl of the wind, the hushed swish of the CD free-spinning to a halt sends a prickle along the length of my spine. I shut the wardrobe.

It's a power cut. The laptop is running on its battery. I click the switch for the ceiling light, just to make sure. The wind sobs again around the corner of the house. I turn off the CD player at the wall and bolt for my room.

The still air smells of emulsion; the comforting, child-hood smell is gone. I unload my shopping, sitting on the unmade bed to try on my shoes. The table lamp turns itself back on without warning as I pull the labels off the soles and teeter in front of the mirror.

When are you going to come clean with all the people you've been lying to?

It's small, too small to notice at a glance. There, on the dressing table. I see it out of the corner of my eye. Lego.

For a moment I don't understand. Lego, four figures: two parents, two girls. The perfect family.

Except it isn't.

Why won't you leave me alone?

I can't . . .

I stumble out of the shoes. Put out a hand to save myself.

The second girl is lying down, gazing blankly at the ceiling, painted eyes and red, red mouth . . .

"No . . ." I rasp. "I didn't . . ."

I grab the drawer, and the figures all fall over. I jerk it open, gasping. The broken edges of the melamine stare up at me. The little girl in her bonnet, surrounded by scuffed-off flowers.

Sorry. I'm sorry . . .

I reel backwards a step. She's white, sweating, blinking fast. The black circles in the middle of her eyes are so wide you can hardly see the green.

No. I press my hand to the bridge of my nose and hold my eyes shut. *No.* I feel for the foot of the bed, to ground myself, the smooth turned shape of the pine, but my hand finds plastic and carbon-fibre instead. I snatch up the laptop.

Did you love her?

Oh, God. A lie by omission. What if it's *all* a lie?

I won't. I can't. I sweep the Lego into the bin, open the computer screen with trembling hands. I can't do it. The story has taken its own course and I can't control it. I can't let it carry on like this. The folder is open, waiting. I highlight it, hit delete, then open the recycle bin. *Are you sure?*

Am I sure? Suddenly I think it might be the only thing I *am* sure of. And with one press, it's gone. Just like her. There should be an answer, some residual trace, but no one will ever find it. No one will ever know.

Will they?

I fling the iPod into the drawer, earbuds and all. If only there was a key that I could throw away. But life doesn't seem to work like that.

Perhaps it would, if I were to leave; if I were to go back to Palace Gardens and the white wardrobes and transcribe what Stefan and my mother want me to put into words. I could abandon Hailbury to be the keeper of its own secrets.

I can't. I retreat to the unmade bed, huddle with the blankets around my knees. I can't go back to Palace Gardens.

After half an hour, my pulse slows. The Lego is gone — like the bowl, and the dress, and the memory. I make myself get up and get changed. My squash racquet is in the hall with the flowers, so many flowers; I pull them out of the vase and put them in the kitchen bin. My phone lights up.

ARMSBY & WOLDS SQUASH GROUP
Paul: *No club night tonight. Leisure centre power out.*

I lower the racquet to the table. Am I destined just to quietly lose my mind, here, alone, with Vesna's ghost trying to console me with kysil and sweet cheese cookies?

ARMSBY & WOLDS SQUASH GROUP
Stu: *Social? Room 42 on mkt square still on. Drinks at 7?*

I leave the racquet in the kitchen and go to get changed back out of my kit, teeth chattering. The notifications come thick and fast until I lose track of the various expressions of assent, timings, plans for food. Eventually I stop looking.

I don't want to lose my mind.

* * *

Room 42 is heaving. Apparently word has got around that Harriet's power is still on. I search the bistro's crowded tables. My new shoes are uncomfortable, and my phone has no signal. I weave unsteadily along the length of the bar, trying to get it to connect to the Wi-Fi. I can't see anyone I recognise. I can't even see a free table. I head towards the door, waiting for WhatsApp to catch up, but it's still connecting. This was probably a mistake.

I put out a hand to push the door, and stumble, off balance. Strong hands wrap around my forearms. It's already open. I glance up from the phone, colour rushing to my cheeks.

"Sor . . ."

But it's not a stranger who's come to my rescue in the doorway. And this time, it's not Joshua London, either. Shock jolts through me as his touch registers.

"Kasper." His name slips from my lips. I'm not sure I've ever said it out loud before. For a lingering moment, he doesn't let go. Then I right myself, cheeks flaming, and he lowers his hands.

"Rosalie." He's not wearing his work clothes. Or his squash kit. He's wearing dark-blue jeans and a slim-fit T-shirt the same deep grey as his eyes. Out of place, out of context, there's something understated about his confidence. He knows he looks good, and he doesn't care.

"You're going." It's as opaque as ever. As much an observation as a question.

I nod in reply. "I guess plans must have changed." I shrug. "There's no one else here."

Kasper eyes the bustle.

"There's a sofa free. We could wait. See if anyone shows." He shrugs, too. But his gaze rests on me. I can feel it, acutely. Every second of his scrutiny.

If he knew. If I told him . . .

The breathlessness hurts, the flutter in my chest, when somewhere beyond Harriet's walls the memories circle like vultures, waiting to lay me bare.

"Okay," I say.

The sofa in the window is only recently vacated and still warm from being sat on. I don't mention the fact that there clearly isn't enough space for anyone to join us. Neither does he. There's low-level late nineties pop playing over the speakers, something about heartache and mistakes. Kasper doesn't sit down.

"Drink?" He gestures.

"Lime and soda please."

He nods. Disappears. I've never seen him in Harriet's. I'm disorientated, my grip unsteady as I unbuckle the ankle straps of my shoes to restore the circulation to my feet. The warmth and light of the bistro are somehow dreamlike; I look up every time the bell on the door chimes as if reality might stride in to reclaim me. It's got dark outside. No one else has come.

"Thanks for the toys. Yvan was over the moon." He's back, lowering my drink to the coffee table. He stands a bottle beside his empty glass. He either doesn't drink or he's driving too; the beer is alcohol-free.

"The Nintendo was a hit. I'm impressed it still works. I think I had the same one when I was ten."

"That's Hailbury for you." I don't want to think about Hailbury. "I'm glad it made him happy."

Happy. Is that what it is, this feeling? Because the lurch in my stomach every time I look at him feels almost like pain. His elbows are on his knees, like yesterday on the bench, but closer. And I suddenly don't know what game we're playing. He pours the drink slowly. The split on his knuckle is starting to heal. There's a steadiness in his eyes, an intensity that's impossible to escape.

"Are you enjoying the home improvements? The colour suited you."

I blush. He's teasing. Serious, edgy Kasper Miller is teasing. I reach to rub an imagined paint splatter from my cheek.

I know I should lie. He can't find out; I don't want him to. I want to carry on skirting the abyss, in a world where we play squash and collect seashells on the brown sand.

But I can't. I can't lie to him. Because Hailbury is waiting for both of us, and someone knows the truth.

"Actually, not as much as I hoped." There's a tremor in my voice that I can't quite repress. "I thought it would make it less creepy, but . . ." I exhale. "Yeah. Do you need your ladder back?"

"I can collect it tomorrow." He pauses. "You find the house creepy?"

"I can't fathom that anyone wouldn't."

He sighs. "Jeanette's house was just sad."

"Jeanette . . . your stepmother?"

"Yeah."

I think he's going to elucidate, but he doesn't.

"You were close?"

"I'm not sure I've ever been close to anyone, Rosalie." His stare is very direct. "But I owe her everything I am. She gave me the world, despite everything."

Everything? I almost ask. But he's looked away, out of the window, and I'm not quite brave enough.

The darkness outside seems to have intensified, the rolling clouds interrupted by a few raw patches of night sky where the wind has ripped holes in them. There's a plane tracking across one of the gaps, a rhythmic flash of light between the few faint, apprehensive stars.

No one's going to save me. I remind myself of that. Not even Kasper Miller. No matter how desperately I want to imagine otherwise. I curl tight in the corner of the sofa. The bistro's bustle has become more of a hum around us, appetites satisfied, conversation ticking over. After a while, Kasper goes for more drinks, and I glance at my phone. The Wi-Fi is working now. I have fifteen new notifications.

T-W *@triggerwarning* • 3h
Rosalie. Please DM me. We need to talk.

A little choked-off sound escapes my throat. How many more? *Did you love her? Do you miss her?*

"Are you okay?" He's back. I let out my breath and flick the app closed.

"Oh. I'm fine. . ." I'll delete it. All of it, every message, every social media account I've ever held. "The others went to the Otter because Harriet had no tables." I show him the group chat instead.

"You want to go?" His eyebrows lift, and the lurch in my chest is at odds with everything I know, everything I think I know. I shake my head. And I think I see a smile tug at his mouth before he can conceal it.

We fall into silence. I don't let myself look back. At what I thought I saw, reflected in his eyes. At the way Harriet's gaze followed him from the bar to the place we're sitting. I don't know how long it lasts. Long enough that we finish the second round of drinks. The tea light in the middle of the table flickers valiantly from a residual few millimetres of molten wax.

"We should get another drink." Kasper's soft voice startles me. "Before Harriet kicks us out. Are you hungry?"

I shake my head. Harriet stopped serving food a long time ago. The specials board is face down. It's half past ten. We're almost out of time.

"No, thanks. I'll get this one."

"No. It's okay." Kasper picks up the glasses. He goes to the other end of the bar this time, orders from someone who isn't Harriet. I can't help wondering whether he noticed, too.

"Boarding school." He puts down the drinks and sinks back in the sofa. "That sounds like hell on earth."

I give him a wry look. "You've clearly never experienced living with my mother."

"No."

"You went to secondary in Armsby?"

He nods.

"Not Queen Victoria?"

He shakes his head.

"Do people recognise you a lot?" he asks. His question takes me by surprise.

"They didn't until I came back here."

"Do you regret it?"

"Huh?"

Something of my momentary panic must show in my face, because I see him frown.

"Coming back."

"Oh." I take a slow breath. I look at the little crease between his lowered brows, the hard set of his jaw, the tension of the inked skin over his upper arm as he reaches to pick up his drink, and I try desperately to fight back the other reality, the one that's waiting for me inside Hailbury's doors.

"No," I say. And, despite everything — whether or not being at Hailbury will destroy me — it's the truth.

He doesn't reply. We finish our drinks as Harriet calls last orders. Across the square, the church bells are chiming quarter to the hour and the contents of the litter bin have blown into the bus stop, circling in excited uproar. A few heavy drops of rain spatter the glass. If the wind was enraged before, then now it's bereft, wailing inconsolably around the shops and buildings. An inverted umbrella scurries past, crashing into bollards and parked cars before it comes to rest temporarily against a kerb. I put on my shoes. Kasper clears the glasses.

"Will you be okay getting home?" He holds open the door. Harriet's sign is squealing in protest as we step out into a barrage of wind.

"Yeah." I force a smile. "I'll be fine."

Will I?

He walks me to my car. The swings in the playground are swinging in wild abandon, and the creak of the chains sends a chill down my spine as I get in. He crosses to the footpath and waits for me to start the engine before he finally turns away.

My eyes burn with tiredness as I navigate the tight bends. Hail and rain pummel the windscreen; I can barely see to put the code into the gates. I park under the shelter of the fountain, more by habit than good sense.

Will I?

I have to survive another night at Hailbury. Another night with the whispers growing louder, another night counting down the seconds with the covers pulled over my head, praying that whatever is beyond my circle of lamplight doesn't get to me before the morning does . . .

I throw my blazer over my shoulders and jog for the steps. The dread is swelling in my abdomen as I halt at the bottom and feel for my key. I don't want to go inside. To be swallowed up by her secrets. My secrets.

The gravel is littered with twigs and bits of shattered branches. The trees are groaning their dissent, and the wind isn't listening; it's ripping at them, forcing its way between them until they bend to breaking point. A shudder runs through me. I open the door.

There's a brief let-up in the rain, like a pause for breath. I withdraw my key from the lock with fingers that aren't quite steady.

There's something else on the gravel, beyond the sticks and debris. Drawing closer, I hear it corner . . .

The pickup growls into sight, wood snapping under its tyres. The beam of the headlights swings wide over the fountain, illuminating the limestone ghostly white. It stops, and so do I; so does everything, except the roaring of the blood in my ears.

He followed me?

The truck door slams. I descend the top step and pause, my hair whipping across my face. I push it back with a hand that's somehow hesitant, somehow thrown off course by his careful approach across the Cotswold stone. He stops at the bottom of the steps.

"You left it in the truck. I thought you might need it."

There are stinging raindrops flying at our faces. Kasper lets the yoga mat drop from his shoulder, its strap blowing wildly in a gust that ricochets around the corner of the house. He mounts the step to pass it to me, his sudden proximity blocking out the wind. I let go of my hair.

"Right," I whisper.

Two days ago. I left it in the truck two days ago. It's almost midnight; in a few hours he'll be back here to work. He said so himself.

"Thanks."

"Any time." Kasper's voice is very soft. I see him take a breath, as if he's going to say something else, but he doesn't. There's aching resolve in the grit of his teeth. But there's something else altogether in the lift of his hand, the half-step closer that means I have to tip my head to look up at him; the momentary flicker of his gaze to my lips. A swell of anticipation paralyses me, huger and more imminent than Hailbury's darkness. I can't even breathe out.

He steps back. "Goodnight."

That word again. I try to reciprocate, but it won't come. There's too much in the way. Words, thoughts, a conflicted bottleneck of terror and emotion.

"How long are we going to keep this up?" I ask.

The silence is absolute. Even the wind has dropped. Something in his gaze softens. But the set of his jaw doesn't.

"I don't know what you're talking about, Rosalie," he says at last.

I inhale.

"O . . . Okay."

I manage, somehow, to nod. To keep my chin high, even as his words bury themselves in my chest. I turn away before he can see the scorch of tears. The door has blown open, sending rain spatters across the marble. I make myself release my lip from my teeth, and I wait for his boots to strike the gravel before I go inside.

I close the door. Kick off my shoes and wilt against the frame, the ache in my feet nothing against the one in my chest. For a moment I'm motionless, listening to his receding footfalls on the gravel, the growl of the pickup engine, almost immediately swallowed by the intermittent lash of the rain and hail against the windows. The pounding of my heartbeat.

I drop the yoga mat and lay the blazer on the hall stand, overwhelmed by a compulsion to run and shut all the blinds, so that the wild black night can't see in. With the lights on, I'm in sharp relief to anyone outside, and suddenly I'm afraid.

Of what? The creak of a hinge? A child's swing? #*leoniesroom*? Myself?

I choke back my own stupidity. But the fact remains that Hailbury was a lot less frightening before the doors started opening.

The fist against the Farrow & Ball is forceful, a knock that jars the wood. Adrenaline surges in my veins. If I was thinking straight, I wouldn't answer. But I'm not thinking straight. I haven't thought straight in days.

I release the latch.

Kasper's eyes are thundercloud dark. His hair is damp, rain flecking his T-shirt and running over his arms. He doesn't speak, or even miss a beat. He strides forwards instead, and his fingers wind into my hair. Then his lips crush mine.

We stumble out of the gale into sudden, ringing silence. There's no word of explanation. We both already know. He fills every one of my senses, woodsmoke, pine, the delicious unfamiliarity of his tongue in my mouth; I reach for him, clutch at his T-shirt as he kicks the door shut and lifts me in his arms.

My back collides with the banister post, and only then he breaks off. The intensity of his expression makes me catch my breath, a half-frown that reminds me, inexplicably, of the small boy in the cloakroom. I hold his face between my hands, study his grey eyes, his mouth, the unsteady rise and fall of his breathing. Can he see the desperation? The fear? How I need him so badly that it aches? My lips find his and he takes them hungrily, oblivious to her watching eyes: Leonie, the shade I will never outrun. The stairwell is in semi-darkness; I feel myself curl into him, and how it forces a little rush of breath between his teeth.

"Rosy." His voice is laboured, uneven. His hands move over me unchecked. He's revised his answer, and I retract the question. There's no one here to call us out on our misjudgement. Only her, in all her silence.

The lamp on my dressing table casts our shadows long. The bedroom curtains are open, a frame of tree silhouettes like ghosts ravaged by the gale, their limbs waving wildly in a warning that neither of us heeds. His hands are calloused, his fingers gentle as he slides down the straps of my cami, sending a swathe of goosebumps over my arms. I slip my hands beneath his T-shirt, hear his intake of breath. He helps me pull it off, leaving me lightheaded with need. I can't tear my gaze away from him. Dark ink, the ripple of muscle under bare skin. He dispenses with the cami; his hands resume their course over my hips, my waist, teasing the button of my jeans undone, travelling to the small of my back, pulling me into him.

He doesn't speak. Not with words. Only with his silence. I've never wanted, like this. Never felt, the way I feel his fingers on my skin. He reaches to brush back the hair from my face.

"I . . ." There's an edge to his voice, a darkening. "I'm not the person you think I am, Rosalie."

He hasn't moved. His fingertips are paused at my temple. His eyes search mine, shadowed with foreboding. And with something else, something undeniable and raw, whose pull is much stronger than the whisper of warning in his words.

I suck in a ragged breath. "I . . . I don't have to think anything."

He shakes his head.

"Kasper . . ." I rasp.

He lays me down, jeans and bedcovers kicked aside, legs entangled; I curl my fingers through his hair and his kiss is slow and certain. I touch his frown, the tension of his trembling arms.

"You can't ever have imagined that I didn't want you." His words are growled through his teeth as if he wants to keep them in but can't. As if it's forbidden.

But it's not forbidden. Why would it be?

"Rosalie . . ."

It's there in his voice. The foreboding, the uncertainty, the sweetness. The wary child, the man at a distance. The one I wasn't meant to want. His eyes are locked on mine: every colour, between the shades of grey. Every colour, vulnerable and dark and sure. And I hear the air rush, jagged, between my lips, and the labour of his breathing . . .

And that is where I'll fade to black. Like Lara Lee Knight's BAFTA-winning performance; the gentle dimming of the silver screen leaving only shadows and inference. There need be no more. Silence, serious and intense. Maybe a whispered voice, a cry escaping just-parted lips. And, as a change in the wind drives a fresh assault of rain against the glass, the last shreds of before are gone. The table lamp flickers. It flares first, then dies, and we plunge into darkness.

CHAPTER 21

Kacper

It would be so much easier to hate her. So much safer. I know I shouldn't have let this happen. I shouldn't have come here. Tonight. Ever.

The power is out. The wind is howling, rattling the windows, and it's too late, on every count. Sweat is standing out on my skin. Her fingers are still twisted in my hair; I reach behind me to pry them gently free. Does she have any idea? Can't she see what this is? How it's going to end? She must realise. We can't get away from it.

"Rosalie," I say, and my voice is rougher than I intend. It's so dark. The lights haven't come back on. Maybe the mains fuse has tripped. Or maybe there are power lines down, in which case God knows how long it'll be off. She looks up, and the words abandon me.

"What's the matter?" she asks. There's a waver in her question that isn't quite disguised. I feel her shift, glance around at the darkness. It hasn't passed me by that she's put two bolts on the inside of her bedroom door. Why would she need to bolt her door?

"I don't like you being here. It's too isolated. You're alone." I reach to brush back her hair. I can feel her breathing. She's so close. Painfully perfect.

"It's the middle of the night and you just opened the door when I knocked. I could literally have been anybody. How can I know you're safe?"

"The razor wire isn't enough?" Her response is soft, teasing, but not convincing.

"No," I whisper. Enough? Enough to keep people out? Enough to protect her? I look back at the bolts. To protect her from who? What? From the truth? It's going to rear its head eventually. What the fuck am I doing? What am I even thinking?

"Then stay." Her voice is barely audible. "Stay with me?"

Stay. I can't. Not with anyone. Especially not her. But I will, I already know that, too. I trace a thumb along her cheekbone. Josh fucking London is never going to touch her again. I slide my arms around her and press my lips to her hair, and she nestles her head into my shoulder. Suddenly, I can't breathe at all. Suddenly, I realise that she doesn't know; she *actually* doesn't know. Yesterday when she asked the question — "Are your parents still local?" — she wasn't testing the waters. The truth about me has never even crossed her mind.

There's an unbearable ache in my chest.

"Kacper?"

Everybody else knows. I can't lie to her. I swallow.

"If you want me to." I search her eyes in the darkness. "I'll stay if you want me to."

She glances up through the unruly fall of her hair.

"You can't ever have imagined that I didn't," she retorts, and the gibe is wry and soft on her lips. Her fingers rest against my breastbone. I catch her hand. But we're so far past the line I drew that I don't even know where it used to be. And I want more; I want to rescue her, the girl from the school gates. To break her out of this house, these walls, the shadow of Leonie Knight-Langton. The problem is, I've lived in the shadow of

Leonie Knight-Langton for twenty years, too. And as far as I can see, there is no way out.

"I can't sleep in the dark, anyway." She says it flippantly, but there's a wobble in her voice that catches me. I frown and reach for my jeans, find my phone and flick on the torch. The blue-white light spills over us.

"You don't like the dark?"

I remember Sunday night, the dusk, her silhouette in my headlights. She didn't look afraid. She never looks afraid. Except . . .

Except it was there in her eyes on the doorstep this morning. As though she hadn't slept at all.

"It's hard to explain. The issue's more . . . the sleep."

"You're afraid to go to sleep?"

"Just in case you needed convincing that I'm out of my mind." She shrugs, drops her gaze. And I find my fingers under her chin, lifting gently so that she has to look at me.

"You don't need to convince me of anything, Rosalie."

She takes a little breath. I give in and run my thumb across her lips. It's too late. Too late to walk away. Even if her name alone pretty much guarantees that I'm ruined. The certainty is a rush, a hit of adrenaline that tightens every muscle in my body. This house, these walls. Whatever it is that's wrong, whatever it is that's haunting her, nothing and no one is going to get near her. Not tonight.

Not ever again.

I roll onto my side and pull her close.

And for the first time in my life, I understand. I understand why Jeanette hid the passport under her bed for twenty years. She did it because there was no choice. *Shouldn't* and *can't* were never a choice.

* * *

It's daylight when I wake. The table lamp is on, and my phone is face down, completely dead. I'm alone, disorientated by the stream of sun through the open curtains. I get out of bed and retrieve my jeans.

She's not here. Her clothes from last night are draped over the chair. The room smells of emulsion and faintly of coffee. My stepladder is beside the window.

I pull on my jeans and pause, swamped by an uncertainty that I've never felt in my life. I've never done this, a morning after — I've only ever been the first to leave — and it's paralysing. My gaze travels over the room, the four-poster, the closed laptop on the dressing table. The bin has fallen over and I stoop to right it; its contents have cascaded onto the carpet. Tissues. A scattering of broken glass and . . . Lego? I pick it up. Four figures, like the ones in the sets she gave to Yvan.

I frown.

The clink of crockery echoes distantly as I go downstairs. She's in the huge kitchen, flitting between the cupboards and an aged fridge. I watch as she takes the percolator off the Aga and sets it down on the worktop. Even after last night, I still can't tear my eyes away from her. She's drowned in a woollen jumper several sizes too big, black leggings. Her hair is wet from showering, bundled up carelessly, and she's wearing her glasses again. They don't seem to fit right either; I watch her push them up her nose, a frown of concentration between her brows as she pours two cups from the percolator, the tendons in her wrist standing out under the weight of the pot.

The clock reads seven forty. I don't know how long she's been up. She glances up as I approach.

"Hey." Her voice is breathy, a little unsure. "I was just making coffee."

She turns, and the movement almost puts her in my arms, warm and slight. Half of my anxieties melt. The rest expand, squeezing the air from my lungs. Escaped tendrils of damp hair cling to her neck and the white triangle of her shoulder exposed by the oversized jumper. I can't help myself. I trace them with my finger, pull her into me and press my lips to her hair.

"Smells good," I murmur. I hear the catch in her breath.

"I wasn't expecting you 'til eight," she teases.

"For some reason I didn't have you down as an early riser," I say. She ducks away to retrieve the coffee and presses a cup into my hands.

"I like the mornings," she breathes.

The mornings, when it gets light. I look down at her bare feet on the tiles, at the prominent bones of her ankles and the varnish on her toenails, and think about the table lamp burning in the sunrise.

"Usually I do some yoga." She sidesteps to pick up her mug. "Until the last couple of days, anyway. Someone took my mat."

She's teasing again. I catch the glimmer of it in her eyes. She's hard to get the measure of; one moment it's ferocity and wit and unreturnable drop shots, the next it's a terrifying vulnerability that she's trying to brush off with coffee and deflection.

"Guess I'd better make a start." I put down my cup. I shoot a glance at the shed and the raspberry canes, and see consternation flicker for a moment across her face before she figures out that I'm teasing, too.

"Fuck," I exhale. "Don't look at me like that." I wind her hair around my fingers. She lets out a little breath, and I don't mean to, but I kiss her.

I have no idea what I plan to do next. Apart from denial: avoiding every whisper of her past and the God-forsaken book she's writing. The thought of her going through all the head-lines and pictures makes me feel sick. I want to get her away from Hailbury, from all of it, but how? We can hardly go elsewhere. We can't exactly stroll back into the bistro, Jesus Christ. And Jeanette's . . . how can I take her to Jeanette's?

What I should do is get out while I still can. Give Nathan Langton my notice. Not come back.

Outside, the sky is clear and bright. The grass is wet. It was Rosalie's idea to walk. She twines her fingers blithely through mine, and I stride beside her trying to ignore the crushing feeling in my chest.

The storm's done a lot of damage. There's debris everywhere, branches and twigs scattered over the lawns. One of the beeches has lost a bough. It's lucky it wasn't over the drive; it would easily have written off a car. Instead, it's gouged a muddy hole in the grass and flattened a swathe of the juniper. Rosalie stops, a tiny frown on her forehead as I go to examine the tree. When I turn back, she's trailing her fingers through the wet juniper, pausing to look at something, the frown deepening into a dark furrow between her brows. Leaves. A stem winding its way out—

"Rosalie, don't touch that!"

She jumps. I'm not close enough to snatch away her hand, but I don't need to. She pulls away like she's been burnt.

"Belladonna." I realise how sharp I must have sounded. Her eyes are wide with alarm. "Deadly nightshade. I thought I'd got rid of it all, but it keeps coming back."

She doesn't reply. She's staring at me, white-faced. But she doesn't seem to see me. She's focussed somewhere else altogether, a thousand miles in the distance.

I try not to feel the prickle along the back of my neck. She's breathing fast. I'm suddenly not sure if I should touch her, like someone who's been woken from sleepwalking.

"Rosy . . . are you okay?"

She blinks. Then she takes a step away.

"I . . ." Her eyes meet mine and they're strangely shadowed. Like Hailbury and its untold secrets have caught her up, and are trying to suck her in.

Her voice is a whisper.

"I'm not sure."

CHAPTER 22

Rosalie

The word "stay" slipped from my lips, and he has. Here, at Hailbury, the one place I never imagined I would find happiness.

He disappears for half an hour most mornings, comes back for coffee before he starts work. He's spent every day in the grounds. And instead of writing, I've learnt more botanical names than I imagined knowing in a lifetime; I've walked for miles amongst the apple blossom and primroses and fading narcissi with my fingers twined through his. I've spent four days in his company, five nights in his arms. And in the slow burn of the lamplight I've learnt about intimacy. About desire. About being whole.

There's a nagging awareness in my mind that he must have had work to do elsewhere. When I've asked, he's brushed it off, quiet amusement — and something else, something I can't quite put a name to — playing in his serious eyes. I haven't pressed for an answer. I don't want one. With him here, the shadows have receded. I've put Leonie's dress back in my wardrobe and the knife in the knife block, and despite the stems of nightshade that he pulled out from between the

213

spikes of juniper, the only secret that matters anymore is the one we share — bright-eyed and hungry — in the silent hours before dawn.

It's occurred to me more than once that I'd tell him. If he asked, I wouldn't lie.

I abandoned Shavasana to make coffee this morning when I heard the pickup come back. I thought I heard the car door slam as the aroma swelled from the percolator, but he never materialised.

I leave the cups steaming on the side. Kasper isn't in the hallway, and neither are his boots. I unlatch the door almost without thinking, with nothing more than thundercloud kisses playing on my mind.

Then I stop.

Peonies are scattered across the step. Pastel-pink and cream: an abandoned battlefield of severed blooms and spilled water. My sleeves are wet. I glance over my shoulder at the piano, unnerved. The vase is gone.

I'd tell him. I could tell him. About the messages. About the flowers, and the mirror and the knife . . .

And the berries? I curl my bare toes against the tiles. The front of my hoody is damp. I pull it off over my head. Squeeze my eyes closed and open them again. The peonies are still there.

I gather them up before anyone can see, picking up the heads of the flowers, sweeping together the stems. I take them to the kitchen bin but they stare up at me from amongst the packets and coffee grounds. I tie off the black bag by its handles, leaving the coffee untouched.

The orangery is warm. My hands have almost stopped shaking by the time I cross the travertine tiles. Kasper is half in and half out of the louvred cupboard and the cover is off the pool. There's a tropical plant between the sun loungers, huge waxy leaves that dip as I touch them, and I fight away a sudden unwelcome image of my sister sprawled across the damp cushions, trailing her fingers in the water. I push my hands into the pockets of my shorts.

"Rosalie."

I jump. He's turned. His mouth is serious, but his eyes are smiling.

"I didn't realise you'd finished." He shuts the door. "Thought I'd get a head start on a couple of jobs."

It's Sunday. I narrow my eyes at him. The smile escapes to pull at the corner of his lips.

"Do you fancy a swim?"

"Not unless you've turned the thermostat up." I try for flippant, but my voice doesn't sound even. He moves towards me, and I let out my breath as his arms close around me to pull me close.

Suddenly, I don't care about the peonies. I slide my fingers through his hair and grip it tight. His breathing is heavy, his hands hard around my waist, but his kiss is as light and gentle as the whispering vines that tap the glass roof above our heads. When I open my eyes, all I see is the dance of the colours in the grey.

"What?" I breathe.

He shakes his head. "Nothing."

He hasn't let go.

"*What?*" I repeat.

And then my feet leave the floor.

"*Kasper!*" I gasp. Water explodes in my ears. I kick for the surface, and I hear him plunge beside me, a rush of bubbles racing past my face. I erupt, spluttering. He surfaces a second later. My cami is stuck to my skin.

"*You* . . ." I'm speechless, still gasping, shaking back my sodden hair from my eyes. Kasper pulls off his wet T-shirt and throws it onto the side. Then his arms slide around me.

"How is it?" He manages a straight face. "Is twenty-eight too cool?"

He ducks my splash. I launch myself at him, and he grabs my arms and pulls me with him, kicking his legs to keep us afloat. I lock my arms around his neck. Then his mouth takes mine, chlorine-tasting and careful, and his hands are on me and there's a look in his eyes that might break my heart: serious clouds that have broken to let through the sun, playful and wistful and young.

I'm out of my depth. Treading water, a tangle of wet denim and bare skin. I trace the patterns that the sunlight makes on his chest, the playing shadows of the leaves. He draws me back into the shallows.

"Rosy." His voice is very quiet. I reach to touch his lips and he catches my hand and holds it there. There's a question that he isn't asking. About nightshade and school photographs. *If he asked, I wouldn't lie.*

"I . . ." There's an answer that I don't know how to give. I look at his hand. At the rivulets of water running down his wrist, like rain in a storm.

"I remembered you," I whisper. "I didn't think I could remember anything. But I remembered *you*."

Conflict flickers in his face.

"Yeah." For a split second, he studies me. Somehow, the clouds have grown darker. Shivers overtake me. The pool has turned cold.

"Kasper?" I look for the sun, but it's gone, blotted abruptly out.

He lowers our hands.

"Yeah. But what you don't remember can't hurt you."

* * *

The church in Summercliffe was full. I sat in the transept, pretending to help Yvan with jigsaw puzzles while Kasper translated for Iryna and went with her to the altar rail for communion. The silent prayer on my lips wasn't the same one that everyone else was murmuring.

We walked to the beach afterwards, shivering in the bitter wind. The tide is on its way in now, waves tumbling gradually closer to our feet. Yvan is collecting shells, a bucket swinging from his hand, and Kasper watches him like a hawk. I try to pretend I haven't noticed, because there's something unspoken and harrowing in it — *to lose a parent* — and the realisation aches in a way that I can't explain.

I walk behind with Iryna, listening to the babble of unfamiliar words that flows from Yvan's lips. After a while he offloads his bucket and runs ahead.

"Yvan . . ." Kasper's voice carries on the breeze. He swings his rucksack from his shoulder. Tosses out a ball and kicks it in one fluid move. Yvan darts for it, leaving a trail of gleaming footprints in the wet sand, and belts it back. There's a little smile on Iryna's lips and an indiscernible sadness in her eyes.

"How old is Yvan?" I speak into my phone, and she pauses to look at the translation. She holds up seven fingers.

"Seven." I nod. There's a momentary silence. She pulls out her phone and types.

Elena, his mother, trains to be a surgeon. My daughter. She remains in Ukraine after her husband is killed.

I nod again. I already knew, but the written words are somehow bleaker. The football hits the surface of the sea with a thwack. Kasper jogs into the tide.

"I'm sorry," I say. It doesn't seem to be enough. There are no words that ever could be.

"Do you know where she is? Do you hear from her?"

It takes a second for the words to appear. Shards of sunlight are breaking through the clouds. Iryna squints at the screen as she types.

She is in Bakhmut.

Oh. I gaze at the translation. It occurs to me suddenly how insignificant my problems are, shredded black silk and dead flowers.

"Was your home in Bakhmut?" I ask, and regret it before it even translates. *Was. Is?* I frown at the screen.

She types, for a long time, her brow creased in consternation. The words aren't right; she deletes them, tries again, more times than I can count. I watch the translation morph slowly into a paragraph.

My home was Lviv. I raised my daughter there. She is married there and Yvan also is born in Lviv. Two years Elena went with Yvan and Andriy to Bakhmut to live. After my husband's death, I went also to their apartment in Bakhmut.

A story? I'm holding my breath, aching with the realisation of where it leads.

A year later the war began. Andriy is shot and killed. There is no end in sight to this horror. We pray for opportunity to be safe for Yvan. I drive with him to Lviv. Elena will not come. She tells me she only will stay behind because her skills are needed at the hospital. But even in Lviv they shoot. There is no safe place from shelling. I took Yvan by train into Poland.

"You're incredibly brave." I'm blinking hard. My voice is choked, and the phone doesn't hear me; nothing translates. "Your daughter is incredibly brave."

Still nothing. I type it instead, but the signal has dropped and the app isn't working; a blue wheel spins in indefinite circles. Iryna shakes her head. I give up.

"I'm so sorry," I whisper again. Iryna gives a little shrug. A shrewd, sad smile. We both look ahead at where Yvan has scrambled up a bank of sand to balance along the top through the tufts of marram grass, his feet crumbling the edge like a cliff. Kasper scoops up the ball and tucks it under his arm. I watch him follow, walking heel to toe, like Yvan, along the low precipice, his eyes fixed on the horizon. On the ferries that sail out of Hull.

It's starting to spit with rain. I zip up my coat and dash the droplets from my eyes. *Atropa belladonna.* I stare at his silhouette, his long, athletic strides. Did I know . . . ? Could I have . . . ?

"Hile . . . Hayel-bury . . ."

Iryna's voice makes me jump. I freeze. She's stopped, a pace away.

"*What*?" The word slips my guard, a breath, no more.

"You . . . ." Her eyes are on mine. "You house."

"I . . . ?" My voice isn't working. "Hailbury?"

She nods.

"Hayelbury. You house."

"Hailbury. Yes," I croak. "Yes, I live at Hailbury. Sort of. I—"

Ahead of us, Yvan has started to run, his shadow flitting across the dunes. Iryna watches him go. Her phone is still in her hand, its screen spotted with rain. She seems to be waiting. I can't quite make myself move. I stare at her face, at her lips, as if I might have imagined the word coming from them. There's a sudden chill in the air.

Iryna holds out the phone.

"Vesna."

The sand seems to have dropped away from under my feet. I gaze, dumbfounded at the age-faded photo: a cardigan, curls of black-brown hair. *Curd pancakes . . . ironed school uniforms.*

Iryna's voice is soft, barely a whisper. Her hand hovers an inch from my arm, as if she wants to touch me but can't quite make herself.

"Long time. Vesna."

Vesna? I look up. Try desperately to fight away the chill, but it won't go.

"You know Vesna."

CHAPTER 23

My sleeves were wet. I look up at the house, at the crenulations and the creeper. The water had run up my arms. There's no trace of flowers on the step, not even a stray petal, but how would I have wet my sleeves from a vase of flowers anyway?

It wouldn't wash away. My fingers weren't working; the water was too cold.

Somebody knows.

I hug myself. I don't want to go inside. Not without him. He dropped me back at Hailbury on his way to football, my hair still damp with sea spray, my mind racing with Iryna's words. It can't be a coincidence.

There's an explanation to everything; I know that. I steel myself and unlock the door. Leonie is looking at me over the banister, scepticism in her glowing green stare.

"It's none of your business," I tell her. But her gaze only seems to intensify.

"Tell me, then." I glare back. "Tell me what the *fuck* is going on."

There's sand in my shoes. I tip it out on the doormat.

I fetch my wet laundry and take it to the orangery to air. The floor is still drying in patches from this morning. *What you don't remember can't hurt you.*

But what if it can?

I sent the draft to myself. It's there, safe in my emails. The knowledge has loomed large, in the unseen pre-dawn hours, as I've paced Hailbury's corridors alone. Hailbury. I never thought it would turn out to be my nemesis.

I wrap my arms around my chest, thinking about school uniforms and gingham dresses. Vesna, fastening clothes on the line outside, her mouth full of pegs. Vesna, who grew up in Lviv, who went to college with Iryna, who studied nursing, qualified and worked with her, who helped to deliver her daughter. Vesna, who moved to the UK in 1995 to work for a family while she learnt English. Who never went back. It was Vesna that helped Iryna and Yvan to escape from Ukraine. Vesna, who looked for a sponsor close to where she lived in Summercliffe, and found them Kasper.

Vesna, who — then — must have been here, or somewhere close by, all this time.

But now she's gone. The reunion never happened; Iryna hasn't heard from her since March.

And I haven't heard from her since 2003. Why did she never contact me?

I have a sickening feeling that I know the answer.

I still need to get rid of the bowl. I haven't done it, just like I haven't read the notifications on my phone, or deleted my social media accounts. I go upstairs to fetch my laptop, take it to the kitchen and set it up on the table. I restore the draft from my emails, like I must have known all along that I would. Then I sit very still and wait for the ghosts that I've spent too long trying to banish.

I write about kysil, and sweet cheese cookies. About Leonie reciting Shakespeare, her hair fanning around her as she twirls on the spot, scorn falling from her lips in iambic pentameter. About hide and seek, and collecting shells from the wet brown sand, and feeding the ducks on the millpond. About riding boots and arguments heard through the floor. I type furiously, but as I do the feeling only grows. The nauseating certainty.

What am I going to tell Tabitha? It's the literary lunch on Wednesday. I'm hoping, from the fact that I haven't had any phone calls or worried messages, that she hasn't been keeping too close tabs on my social media. And what about Stefan?

I pause my typing and listen to the silence. To the ping of another notification on my phone in the hall. How long is a football practice? I wish with every fibre of my being that Kasper was back. I slide the laptop into my bag and go in search of my phone. The silence in the hall is even worse. Now that I've let her in, there's no escaping her. Everywhere I go, she seems to follow: my sister, swanning between the sun loungers, raiding the fridge, pirouetting and pouting in front of the hallstand mirror.

I can't do it. I can't stand her eyes on me.

I flee for my car and drive to Armsby. It doesn't occur to me until the bell chimes on Harriet's door that I haven't been back since Tuesday, the night of the squash social. I try to slip inconspicuously inside, but the bistro is empty and there's nowhere to hide.

I sit down at my usual table and offload my bag. Forty-six notifications. *@justiceforleonie @Leoniesangel @triggerwarning — Rosalie, please message me back.* I'm not sure what's worse, facing them or Harriet.

The most recent is a picture. I'm mentioned. *#leoniesroom.* Her bed, made up, the covers crisp and smooth.

WHICH SISTER @*Leoniesangel* • 2h
@RosalieK-L make your bed and lie in it.

There's a video underneath. A blurry five-second clip, looped, of someone lying in Shavasana. I stare, sick, at the mat. But it's dark red — not mine.

How's your Sanskrit @RosalieK-L? You'd make a beautiful शव:

222

I can't keep looking. There's a tingling in my fingers and my lips. Razor wire. I make myself breathe out. CCTV.

"Rosalie!"

I almost drop the phone.

"What time d'you call this? When I've barely seen you inside of t'week?" Harriet hands me a latte and a slice of lemon drizzle that I haven't ordered. "I was about to close up!"

She plops down on the end of the sofa beside me, balancing her own cup on her knee, and I try desperately not to think about alcohol-free beer and dark-blue jeans.

"Are you still on for Tuesday?"

Tuesday. Tuesday? Squash? I look up in confusion. No. Not squash. Skeg Vegas. *Girls' night out.* She messaged me earlier in the week, and I forgot about it.

"Oh . . ." I flounder, fork to cake. "Yeah. Sure."

"How're things?"

"Yeah. Okay." I take a scalding sip of coffee and don't quite meet her eye.

There's a loaded silence. I shave off another forkful of cake. Harriet adjusts her grip on her mug.

"You din't see Kasper at Hailbury this morning, did you? I know he sometimes puts in some weekend hours. Only I've been trying to call him since last night and I couln't get hold of him. It's not like him. I haven't been able to track him down for days."

"Uh . . ." I try to think fast, but I'm a terrible liar. "Not that I . . ."

Harriet lowers her cup to the table.

"Rosy, tell me . . ." Something has sparked in her eyes at my reticence. She's seen two twos and she's making four. I pretend not to have noticed.

"Tell me you didn't go home with him on Tuesday night?"

I tighten my hands around the cup and stare at the cake crumbs, as if an alternative answer might reveal itself there. I didn't, technically. I try to make myself say it, but I can't. I can feel her dark gaze locked on my face.

"You slept with Kasper."

"Uh . . ." I press the cup to my chin, attempting desperately to think of a way out.

"Oh my God. You actually did. Not Josh London. *Kasper*."

"I . . ."

"Oh. My. God." There's a rising note in her voice. Dawning realisation. "That's where he's been. This week . . . last night . . . He was with *you*?"

Family, of sorts. I study the tabletop, eyes watering. There's no point in trying to pretend. Harriet gets to her feet. She walks to the door and flips the sign to closed. Then she comes back. She doesn't sit down. Her voice is uncharacteristically quiet.

"Have you even thought about what you're doing? How this is going t' look, for both of you?"

What? I glance up. She's deadly serious.

"What do you mean?" I'm flushed. Defensive? I can't discern anger from trepidation. "How *does* it look?"

"*Really*?" Her eyebrows arch. There's no dodging her scepticism.

"You're Rosalie Knight-Langton. Everyone around here knows more about you than you do. It'll be everywhere by tomorrow. Have you thought about how your parents are going t' see it? Or t' press?" She sits down heavily on the sofa arm. "Christ, Rosalie. It'll certainly stir opinion. And it's not going t' take long before it makes it into t' media, is it? Unless you both plan never to set foot outside of Hailbury again. Have you thought what kind of reaction *that's* going t' provoke?"

My parents? The media? Sweat has broken on my top lip. What is she talking about? Visions of messages dance through my head. Of profile shots. Of Shavasana. Corpse pose. I'm not in any doubt as to the translation of शव:

"I don't understand. The media doesn't care about me. Even if . . ." I'm blushing, furiously. "It's nobody's business. I'm not my mother. My mother has nothing to do with it."

224

"Nothing to do with . . ." Harriet's mouth hangs slightly open. She seems to be searching for the right words. "You're kidding, right?"

"What?"

"You . . . you and Kasper haven't talked about this?"

"About . . . about *what*?" There's a disproportionate feeling of unease in my gut. Faint nausea.

Harriet buries her forehead in her hand.

"About Leonie," she breathes at last.

It's not faint nausea. It's immediate and swelling.

"*What*?"

"I think you'd better talk to Kasper." She gets to her feet. "Not me."

Leonie. What would Kasper know about Leonie? He has nothing to do with Leonie. Harriet holds out her hand for my cup and I relinquish it tremblingly. Does he? How could he? He was nine or ten . . . he wouldn't have known her, couldn't have known her. He'd have told me, if he did.

Wouldn't he?

Except he did know something. It was in his eyes and his silence, right back at the start. *What you don't remember can't hurt you.*

Talk about nowhere to hide. There's nowhere to run anymore, either. Not even the bistro is safe. My head is starting to throb as I make my excuses and stumble into the spitting rain, the door jangling closed behind me. *You'd better talk to Kasper.* About what?

About the bowl in my dressing-table drawer?

About Leonie?

* * *

Hailbury's driveway is deserted. I slip inside. I don't want to ask. I don't want to know; I don't want anyone to know. There's a strange taste in my mouth, a cloying smell in my nostrils as I drag myself up the stairs, trying not to look at her face. Her wide, accusatory gaze.

Sorry, I'm sorry . . .

My father's study is cool. I put my laptop on the desk and bang the window shut, shivering. Fiction. It would be so much safer to write fiction. My thoughts stray to Antonio DiPaci and the films he hasn't developed. Back to the picture on Iryna's phone, of Vesna, all those years ago.

Before.

I open Facebook on my phone. I don't even know what to search for. I don't know Vesna's second name. I falter. Iryna. She'd been messaging Iryna.

But I don't know Iryna's second name, either. Kasper would know. I could just wait and ask him. Unless . . .

Kasper Miller. I type it in, but there are only four hits and none of them are him.

With the window shut, the air seems thick. The smell in my nostrils is growing stronger. I lower the phone. A hot, chemical scent hits the back of my throat, more imminent and inescapable than the silence. I jolt to my feet.

I stumble to the study door and shove it open, the screech of warning piercing my brain. An alarm.

Shit . . . *shit.* I snatch up the phone, my laptop. A fire alarm. There's smoke in the hall, filtering up the stairs, hanging and undeniable. It's squeezing around the utility-room door, reaching wispy tendrils towards the piano. The stench is acrid. By the time I'm across the hall I'm coughing. I burst out through the front door, choking and nauseated . . .

"Rosy—"

I almost drop the laptop. Josh London's hand shoots out to catch it.

His nose wrinkles and his eyes widen.

"Holy shit, Rosy!" He grabs my arms, pulls me down the steps, away from the door. I'm gasping, insensible.

"Fire service." He's somehow already got his phone to his ear.

"Hailbury House, Shellingsby St Mary. House fire. Yes. Christ, I don't know. There's smoke. Quite a lot. Yes . . . no . . . okay . . ."

I can smell it from outside now, too. The gravel is sharp, biting into my bare feet. I limp backwards as Josh's voice echoes in the periphery of my awareness, trying to think. Iryna. Vesna . . . *We need to talk . . . When are you going to tell the truth @RosalieK-L?*

"Rosy?"

I start. The pickup has pulled up without me even hearing it.

Kasper jumps out, boots crunching the limestone. There's a look of incredulity on his face. His eyes fall on Josh London. On the phone. On the thin faint curls of smoke spiralling their way out into the spring air.

"I—" I start.

"*Jesus fucking Christ.*" He snatches open the pickup door and grabs an extinguisher from under the seat. "Where's it coming from?"

"The utility," I gasp. There are sirens in the distance. "Kasper—"

But he's already jogging across the gravel, T-shirt pulled over his mouth. Josh takes a step after him, alarmed.

"Mate, I wouldn't—"

But he's gone, invisible in the gathering darkness. A new kind of fear grips my gut. I run across the stones. The sirens are drawing closer. Beside me, Josh is staring, open-mouthed, at the doorway.

"*Fuck,*" he mutters.

I don't know how long we're there; time seems nonsensical. I stare, too, until my heart gets the better of my head and launches me towards the door.

It swings wide before I get there. Slams. Kasper's chest is heaving. He wipes the sweat from his face with his arm, smearing the soot.

"Fucking dryer," he pants.

I gape at him. I don't know if I'm livid or relieved. A half-sob threatens in my throat as I stumble up the last step. He reeks of smoke, his clothes, his hair; his arms are streaked with smut. I reach for him and then realise that he's looking past me at Josh, and the swerving thunder of the fire engine that's just cornered the last stretch of Hailbury's drive.

"I think it's out. I pulled the plug. But there's smoke everywhere." For a lingering second, he looks back at me.

"They'll need to get in and look. You'd probably better call your father."

I nod, speechless. He starts down the steps. The firefighters are disembarking; one of them meets him on the gravel and I see Kasper gesture back towards the house. The sound of their voices fades in and out. There's a buzzing in my ears as they go inside, a confusion of boots, helmets, masks.

"Rosy." Josh's hand brushes my shoulder. "Bloody hell. Are you alright?"

"Uh . . ." I look down at my bare feet. "Yeah. I think so."

"Wow. Fuck. I'd messaged you. I only dropped by because I'd got some bits in the car from Jericho for you. Things from that Easter, Leonie, I . . . *Fuck*. What *happened*?"

"I have no idea." I'm shivering. My voice is a croak. "Kasper said it was the dryer."

The dryer. But I didn't *use* the dryer.

"Bloody hell," he repeats. "And you were alone in the house? *Jesus.* Thank God you realised."

There's a momentary silence.

"What can . . . what can I do?" Josh rubs his forehead. "How can I help? Seriously, Rosy. Do you think they'll let you back in? There must be smoke damage. Did it get upstairs? Do you need somewhere to go?"

"No. She doesn't."

My stomach contracts.

There's a pause, a tightening in the air. Kasper's grey gaze is like cold steel.

"It's covered. Thank you." He alights the steps. His jaw is clenched, and the ferocity in it makes my heart race. I can feel the tension in his folded arms even at half a pace away. Josh steps back.

"Oh . . . right. Sure." He nods, pauses. "Good."

His eyes travel briefly between us. Then he exhales.

"That was quite a risk to take, Miller. Nicely done."

He extends his hand. For a beat, Kasper doesn't move. My breath seems to have caught in my throat. The abhorrence in his eyes is undisguised.

"Thanks." His voice is clipped. He steps around Josh's offered hand, towards the door. I frown.

"Rosalie, the fire officer said it's okay to retrieve some things now, if you need to."

There's a painful silence. Josh lowers his hand.

"I'll make a move, then."

I nod.

"Give me a shout if you need anything, Rosy. I'll take those bits back to Jericho. Let me know when you've got ten minutes to come and take a look. You're welcome any time. You know where I am."

"Thanks, Josh."

"I hope you're okay. Make sure you take it easy this evening. Literally, anything you need, call me."

"I will."

It isn't until the Tesla pulls away that I realise how much I'm shaking. Kasper is waiting by the door. He watches the car, too, as it manoeuvres around the fire engine and disappears along the drive. It's not until the sound of the tyres has receded into the distance that he looks back. Back at my bare feet and helpless shivers.

"Rosalie . . ." It's a breath, between his gritted teeth, visceral and stifled. Then his lips are against my hair, and his hands are wrapped around my upper arms, clutching tight. I bury my face in his chest.

"You were inside." His voice is grim.

I nod, wordless. I feel the shudder of his breath.

"This fucking place."

I look up. His jaw is still clenched. His face is filthy. I try desperately to swallow the sudden threat of tears, the lingering terror dispersing like smoke in an April breeze. The dryer.

It was just the dryer. I remind myself of Joy's notebook. Of things that definitely are, and things that definitely aren't. Things I know. Things I think I know.

"I meant what I said," he says, and his voice hasn't lost its edge. "About you being here. You can't stay here tonight."

"No," I manage.

"Get some things." Kasper takes a step back, although he doesn't release my arms. His gaze searches mine. I accede with a tremulous nod.

We go into the hall together. He stops to talk to one of the firefighters, and I find myself ascending the stairs alone. I can feel her watching me, my sister. Emerald eyes wide, all-seeing, all-judging.

"I'm not crazy," I tell her, a whisper.

I don't listen for a reply.

By the time I go back down, Kasper's on the phone. I cross the hall on tiptoe, like a child.

"It was out before it spread. Minor smoke damage. Yeah, they said it's okay to go in. I've taken some photos. The dryer, yeah. Yeah, it was. Yeah, the electricity and gas are off until they come out to check it. Yeah, yeah. Outside, yeah. She's okay. Yes. No. I think she's arranged somewhere. Sure. Do you want to speak to her?"

My father? There's the oddest feeling in the pit of my stomach. I elect to pretend I haven't heard.

"Okay, Mr Langton. I'll ask her before I leave. Yes. I can sort that. The cleaners . . . Uh-huh. Okay. Thank you. Thanks. Sure. Will do. Bye."

I slip outside. The pickup is unlocked. I go and sit in the passenger seat, staring at the chaos of rubble sacks and cable ties in the footwell until he gets in beside me and shuts the door. He takes a breath as if he's going to say something, but doesn't. I wet my lips.

"My clothes were in the dryer?" I don't quite look at him.

I can sense him hesitate. "Yeah."

I can't reply. I nod, instead. He's frowning.

"Rosy?"

"Nothing." I curl my fingernails into the leather seat. *I'm not crazy.*

"Have you got what you need?"

I let out my breath. "Yeah."

"Your father called. He got an alert when the alarms went off."

"Oh." I pull out my phone. Four missed calls. I flick it to airplane mode and shove it back into my pocket. "What did he say? Did he—"

"He wanted me to check you'd sorted out accommodation for tonight. And he said to make sure you left me the key when you go back to London tomorrow."

His eyebrows have lifted. I chew my lip.

"I said I'd ask you to call him." Kasper turns the key in the ignition. But his eyes haven't left my face.

"Right," I whisper.

We pull away. There are bluebells emerging on the periphery of the driveway, breaking through in rebellious clumps under the trees. We turn left out of the drive, towards the village. There are bluebells in the churchyard too, and an early scattering of forget-me-nots. I've never really thought about the irony of the name before. I want to forget it all. Every last little thing. Forgetting was the one thing I used to be good at.

We turn along a cut-through, onto a lane with a bus stop and unspoilt views of fields and woods. Kasper stops the engine.

"It's not very big." His voice is difficult to read. "It's definitely not Hailbury."

I bite my lip. "It sounds perfect."

There's a garden path with an arch and a gate, purple buds opening against the white pebble-dashed walls. Flowers and herbs spill from stone-edged borders, an overflow of colour. Beside the front door, there's a post driven into the earth. *For Sale.*

The hallway is cool and dim, with smooth oak boards. There aren't two straight lines in sight; none of the doors are level and Kasper has to duck his head to pass through the one at the other side of the hall. The kitchen would have been tiny before it was extended; now its low beams give way to an airy high ceiling with a rooflight, a swathe of conservatory doors. I'm thrown by the smell of emulsion, the remnants of masking tape on the skirting boards, the memory of a stepladder. The dark-blue kitchen units look brand new. There's a kitchen island, its stone worktop covered with paperwork, a floor lamp and a sofa in front of a wood burner, strewn carelessly with blankets.

"Here." Kasper moves to pick one up, and I realise that my teeth are chattering. He drapes it over my shoulders. I sit down on the sofa, taking a few steadying breaths.

"This is where you grew up?" I remember what he said, about the house being sad. About his stepmother.

"Yeah." He nods. He doesn't quite make eye contact. "I've done it up a bit, since she died."

I look around. Outside, the cottage garden is walled in stone, a breathtaking canvas of herbs and flowers illuminated in pinkish hues by the setting sun. It's got later than I'd realised.

"It's beautiful."

"Spoken by the girl who grew up at Hailbury," he points out, wryly.

"Hailbury's not beautiful." I feel my expression darken. "It's . . ."

I look down at the blanket, trying to fight away the chill. Cold water. An explanation, to everything.

". . . Never mind."

"I need to go and shower." Kasper hasn't moved. "Will you be—"

"I'm fine."

He falters. "What he said, about you going to London . . ."

232

"I'm not planning to." I meet his eyes. Grey clouds, no sun. Kasper nods. He doesn't quite smile. But there's a softening in his gaze, something like relief.

"I won't be long."

He disappears, and I curl my knees under me, wrapping myself in the blanket.

What am I going to do?

I didn't use the dryer. Did I? I'm sure. So, so sure. Just like I'm sure that I don't remember. I don't remember Leonie. I don't know what happened to her, no one does. I didn't break the mirror. Or take the knife . . .

"Oh, God." I grip my hair with both hands, try not to look beyond the reflections on the windows. "*Oh, God.*"

But if I didn't, who did?

And why are they coming after me?

When are you going to come clean with all the people you've been lying to?

I have to breathe. I let go of my hair. I just have to breathe. I'm not at Hailbury now.

There's a sound close at hand. A thud, a jolt of motion. I shrink against the cushions. *Breathe . . .*

The cat jumps onto the other end of the sofa and regards me with piteous amber eyes. It's quite possibly the biggest cat I've ever seen, tabby ginger; I hold out a tremulous hand and it comes closer, starting to purr.

"Hey, big guy." My voice sounds shaky. There's something grounding, reassuring, in its harsh rattle of contentment, the kneading of its paws in the blanket. I rub the top of its head.

"I'm sorry, have I stolen your seat?"

The purring intensifies, and it settles itself down beside my feet, extending its neck in bliss as I scratch under its chin. My shivers begin to subside. The kitchen grows darker and I search out a switch for the floor lamp. Its glow falls over the sofa and the cat gets up, nudging its way under my arm onto the blanket, a warm heavy bulk of crooning fur.

"Sorry." Kasper's voice startles me. He's in the doorway. "He's a bit needy. Throw him off if you don't want him."

The cat looks up disdainfully, as if it's understood. Then it circles back and butts its head against my chin. I smile, despite myself. Kasper smiles too, although he still doesn't come any closer.

"What's his name?"

"Ginger Tom."

"That's original," I tease.

Kasper shrugs. There's a little curve of amusement at the corner of his lips.

"Legacy," he says. "I couldn't bring myself to call him Boris."

He goes to one of the cupboards, gets out a foil sachet and the cat pricks its ears. It jumps down with a thud and runs to wind around his legs. I slide to my feet and the blanket falls to the floor. It's almost completely dark now. I can see myself reflected in the window as I move to look outside. I see his reflection cross the floor behind me.

There's an intensity in his stare, a protectiveness that hurts my heart. I turn. He draws me close.

"Are you okay?"

Two of his fingers wind a lock of my hair, so gentle that I can't think at all. *You'd better talk to Kasper.*

"I . . ." I glance down at the front of his T-shirt. The rise and fall of his chest. Back up at his storm-cloud eyes.

"Yes," I whisper. "I am now."

He glances down too. And everything shifts. Everything that should matter doesn't matter. Not anymore. Forget-me-nots, *what you can't remember.* I breathe him in. Let my touch stray over his cheek, the slight roughness of his jaw. His lips take mine. He doesn't look away.

The stairs are twisting and narrow. My clothes smell faintly of smoke. His thumb and his index finger can encircle my wrist entirely; the covers on the bed are white and the walls are midnight blue. He's already turned on a lamp — because

I can't sleep in the dark — it burns like a beacon on the bed-side table, spilling incandescent over sheets and skin, pooling in the crisp cool pillows with his fingertips and the tangles of my hair. I'm aching, every part of me. Trembling with need, as he lifts my hips and peels off my leggings. As he tugs my top gently over my head and his hands slip behind my back. I trace my fingers over the tense, rigid skin of his abdomen, reach for his jeans. His eyes search mine, a smouldering conflict of desire and disbelief. And something else. Something that terrifies me.

He hesitates.

"What?" I whisper. "What is it?"

"I thought it would feel wrong, you being here." His breathing is ragged, uneven. His eyes are still locked on mine. "But—"

"Why would it feel wrong?"

"*Rosalie.*" His voice is raw.

He buries one hand in my hair and tips my face to his, his mouth capturing mine, absorbing my cries with his kiss. I feel my lips shape his name, and I don't know if it's a plea or a promise. All that's left is rain on juniper, sweat on skin, dark ink and breaking cloud. And I'd give anything. I'd forget forever, if I could keep this. Only this. The jagged whisper of his want. Sweetly shadowed bliss. Our downfall.

But what if I can't?

I need to tell him. I need to tell him about the bowl. About Hailbury.

About Leonie.

CHAPTER 24

Kacper

It's too late to calculate risks. I wake up every morning, and I'm terrified. So is she. She won't admit it, and I can't bring myself to question it. I don't want to ask, because I don't want either of us to start having to answer questions.

What choice did I have but to bring her here? Against my every instinct. And yet . . .

I stoop to pour biscuits into Tom's bowl. The cat turns his back, ignoring me. I've been in his bad books since the night I didn't come back from Hailbury.

Rosalie is asleep. At Hailbury, she seemed not to sleep. Or she would, so early that I'd lie and watch her for hours and then wake at three or four a.m. to find her gone. By dawn, she was always up, pacing the rooms like a tiger in a cage, or standing in the conservatory, gazing at the garden. But this morning the sun rose over her silent and flushed and she didn't stir when I stroked back the hair from her forehead, so I left her sleeping. I've been trying to ignore work, but I can't avoid it forever.

I leave a pack of coffee on the side by the machine, think briefly of writing a note about breakfast cereal and work, then decide not to. I message her instead. I can come back. I'm only going to be two doors down the road.

On every other count, I wish it wasn't Stapleford Lodge today. I almost didn't take the job at all; the sight of the Blakemans' old gates makes me grit my teeth. I press the buzzer. I've already deferred from last week; I can't again.

The driveway at the side of the house hasn't changed since the days I got familiar with it as a kid, mostly face down on the tarmac. Once or twice they pinned me against the garage doors; the outbuildings are just out of sight of the road. There were only a few times when I was unwitting enough to end up on the wrong side of these gates. I got wise quickly.

I don't know when it went on the market, or how much it sold for. I never saw a sign. The new owner has a big job on his hands. The garage and sheds are untouched and full to the brim with junk; before his first stroke, Richard Blakeman used to like to tinker with old cars. There's apparently even a disused inspection pit under one of them. I don't fancy the building regs associated with sorting that out.

Zach Blakeman runs his father's old business now, a car recovery company based in Hull. Marcus joined the marines in his early twenties. Richard Blakeman had his third stroke a few months ago and has been hospitalised ever since; I don't even know if he's still alive. Maybe that's why the house was sold. Maybe it's why Marcus is back. Rumour has it the marines chucked him out for assaulting someone.

"Hi. Hi . . ." The guy who answers isn't familiar. "You're here for the garden? Jamie said you were coming. Sorry, I'm mid-conference call."

I follow him through the gates. There's a new extension round the back, a gleaming expanse of still-stickered bi-fold doors. "Feel free to bring your van round. I'll leave the gate open."

"Sure."

My gaze travels over the outbuildings. There are still *Get Brexit Done* signs in the shed windows, which pisses me off, mostly because they remind me of Little Lord London and his damn suit jacket around her shoulders. I make an effort not to grit my teeth. He's always polite these days, on the unfortunate occasions that our paths cross. I think I'd find it easier if he wasn't. *Does she need somewhere to go?* Over my dead fucking body.

"I'll only be clearing today, anyway. Maybe we can recap the rest of the plan later." I eye the jungle of brambles and emerging nettles, self-set elder and buddleia and broken paving. There are bits of rusting metal everywhere. More pieces of cars, probably. I don't remember the place being such a tip as a kid.

"Do you want the scrap weighing in?"

"Oh . . . er . . . yeah, why not? Cheers. Actually, I'd better get back in. Meeting . . ."

"No problem."

I set to work. If it wasn't for the high hedges, I'd be able to see Jeanette's garden wall from here. Not Jeanette's much longer, or mine. There have already been a couple of offers. I was supposed to call the estate agent back yesterday. I didn't.

Because somehow, I've lost clarity. Plans and figures have been replaced by pictures that never belonged. Her bare feet on Jeanette's kitchen floorboards, her fingertips on the smooth worn line in the banister, the flow of her copper hair in the lamplight. Brief, unlikely glimpses of a future that I can't even let myself consider. It can never be. I know that. I've held whole conversations in my head with Jeanette where I try to convince one or other of us that this could turn out okay. I never win.

I exhale and search out my phone. Rosalie hasn't replied to my message. I have a missed call and a text from Harriet. I ignore them and turn my attention to the brambles.

It takes most of the morning to de-veg. When I've finished, the mess is even worse than I'd anticipated. I'm going to need a skip. There's scrap buried all over, and random patches of dumped concrete and broken slabs dotted here, there and everywhere. I order the skip first, then call Yarrops for some topsoil, pacing the length of the garage wall to the sound of their hold music and kicking at the concrete with the steel toe of my boot. There's a lone rosemary bush behind the garage, struggling for life; I move to examine it, and something catches my eye in one of the filmy windows.

I backtrack to look more closely, an odd feeling in my chest. It's a flashlight. I come to a stop by the window. The bastards must have stolen it from Jeanette. It's so familiar that the memory hurts; I can picture it hanging in her grip by its plastic handle down at the stables on a winter night, when it was already dark by the time she went to lock up. She let me carry it once or twice, back in the days when we didn't really know each other, and I'd stumble warily over the frozen mud, with Tata whistling cheerful tunes beside me. I press my face closer to the window but it's too dirty to see through properly, dusty and choked with cobwebs.

I wonder if she knew. The old anger runs hot in my blood as I stare at the filth and chaos. Jeanette *did* know. She knew for years what I was to them, by proxy. And there was nothing she could do about it. It had never occurred to me that she was a target, too.

Fuck them. They're gone. I back away, hanging up on Yarrops. It's lunchtime and no one is answering. It's going to be cathartic, watching these buildings get bulldozed.

I knock on the bi-fold doors to tell the guy I'm leaving and warn him about the skip. He gives me a thumbs up from behind his screen, and I walk back to Jeanette's with an unsettled feeling in my stomach.

It's weird, remembering that the cottage isn't empty. Opening the door, knowing that she's inside. I pull it closed behind me.

"Oh . . ." Rosalie appears in the hallway, mug in hand. "Hi."

Her voice is soft, husky. She's wearing one of my T-shirts over her leggings, and it drowns her, the hem falling almost to her knees. Her hair's thrown into a messy knot, wisps of it escaping at the nape of her neck and around her face. I feel the breath leave my body.

"I got your message. My reply wouldn't send. I'm sorry." She turns her eyes upwards. I put down my keys on the table.

"It's okay," I hear myself say. But I'm distracted by the T-shirt, by the colour that's crept into her cheeks. By the thought of her in my bed.

Screw skips and topsoil. Screw the Blakemans' garden, and the fact that someone's going to need to meet the electrician at Hailbury in half an hour. I stand still for a moment, tortured by the knowledge of the missed calls on my phone, and the framed picture that I put away last night, tucking it into Jeanette's bedside drawer.

"How was your morning?" She's biting her lip, and it kills me. She pads across the floor to put her cup on the table and slips her arms around my waist, under my gilet. I swallow.

"It was okay."

"Ow . . . Jesus!" She withdraws, reaches a tentative hand into my pocket and pulls out my multitool. She wields it doubtfully. The bottle opener has half unfolded. It must have caught her through the lining.

"Are you okay?" I ask. I can't quite keep the amusement out of my voice at the look on her face.

"Do you . . . *always* keep a uh . . . a . . . *this* in your pocket?"

"It's a multitool." She's standing so close that I have to look down at her. I'm acutely aware of her every movement. "And only when I'm working."

"Are you working now?" She snaps it shut. Runs a finger along the closed edge of the knife blade instead, her other hand resting against the front of my T-shirt. I take a slow breath in.

"I'm done for now." I catch her wrist, wrest the multitool gently from her grip and twist the safety lock over the blade. The idea of it on her fingertips makes me feel queasy. I drop it back into my pocket.

Then her palms are on my shoulders, and I shrug out of the gilet, the folded knife hitting the floorboards with a crack. She reaches her mouth for mine, and despite every remaining shred of good sense I close my arms around her and draw her onto her tiptoes. I press her into me, the T-shirt gathering under my hands. Somewhere on the floor my phone starts to ring. We both ignore it.

I pull her into the kitchen. Her laptop's cast to one side on the floor beside the sofa. Seeing it sends an unwelcome jolt through me, and I look deliberately away from the tight ranks of typed words, before the reality can set back in, like I know it should.

"Kacper . . ." she murmurs.

I kiss her. Hard. Harder than I mean to, desperation taking root in my gut. I know why Harriet's trying to call me. We sit down with a bump and Rosalie murmurs something incoherent, her hands on my belt buckle, a flush of pink in her cheeks. A little gasp slips her guard as I grab her hips and turn us both over, breathing hard.

My phone pings a message in the hall. I try to block it out. But it's there, with Jeanette's imaginary counter arguments, and my father's picture in the bedside drawer.

I know what I'm going to have to do.

* * *

Yvan runs through the kitchen to let himself out the back door almost as soon as we've delivered him through the front one. The sun through the windows of the bungalow is dazzling. Iryna stoops to hug him, and he ducks away and throws his second-hand school sweatshirt in a heap on the floor.

Iryna had to go to the job centre, so today I did the school run. Until two months ago, it wasn't something that featured in a list of things I ever saw myself doing. Luckily, the electrician was done at Hailbury by three. The fuse box was fried and he had to replace it. The power's back on, although the gas isn't yet.

I watch Rosalie follow Yvan into the tiny garden. She didn't speak a word at the school gates. I wondered what memories it stirred for her. Then again, she doesn't remember. I think of her words in the pool at Hailbury, and the irony stings. She remembered me. Except she didn't, did she? Because if she did, she wouldn't be here.

She insisted on buying Yvan a gift, two plastic tennis racquets and a ball, and she's showing him how to play, hitting it off the back wall and sprinting across the lawn to return it. I watch them for a long time, too long, running the words through my head in every combination, my fists ground into the kitchen worktop.

"Kacper."

I start.

"Dlaczego milczysz?" *Why are you silent?* Iryna moves beside me. "Coś cię niepokoi?" *Is something bothering you?*

I seem to have an inability to get things past her, like Jeanette. I swallow. Evening birdsong is filtering through the door with Yvan's yells of triumph and the soft thwack of the ball on the bricks. Rosalie has ditched her boots and is barefoot on the grass.

I shake my head. "Nic mi nie jest." *I'm fine.*

She nods once, not fooled, and goes to get plates out for tea. I watch Rosalie dive for a backhand, knocking the ball gently so that Yvan can hit it back. She's scooped her hair into a high ponytail that flies like a banner in the breeze. Inexplicably, it seems to hurt to breathe. I force myself to exhale, to fold my hands back into my pockets, away from Iryna's shrewd dark eyes.

The grass is getting long. I need to bring the mower, next time I come. I turn my back on the window and find myself looking at Lego sets instead. Iryna is ladling soup into bowls. I pace to the living room, cursing myself under my breath. Outside, Yvan's shriek of exultation carries on the wind, followed almost immediately by a wail of dissent as Iryna calls him in for tea. When I go back, Iryna is shepherding him towards the sink.

"Zostaniesz?" *You'll stay?* She gestures at the food. Rosalie is in the doorway, two spots of colour burning in her cheeks.

I shake my head. "Sorry. Przepraszam. Not tonight."

Rosalie glances at Iryna, at the meal. At me.

"Thank you." She turns to Iryna, brandishing her phone in gesture. "I'll message you."

Iryna nods.

My phone is in the truck, on silent. I press my lips together, waiting for Rosalie to fasten her boots. I let her lead the way outside, which is a mistake, because all I can look at as we walk to the truck is her, the way her hooded cardigan slips down her slender shoulders, the way she bites her lower lip as she glances back at me and sees my eyes on her.

She showers when we get back and dries her hair at Jeanette's dressing table, and I watch her from the doorway, even though I know I shouldn't. Even though I know letting her set foot in that room is wrong.

It's dark by the time we go downstairs. The reflection of the lights in the empty glasses on the table makes me think of Harriet's. I have four more missed calls on my phone. I frown at the screen, trying to swallow my bitterness.

"Kacper."

I spin. There's a tremor in Rosalie's voice that makes my blood run cold. I drop the phone, face down. Her chin is high, the cuffs of her cardigan screwed into her hands. She gulps a breath like there isn't enough air in the room. Like she's drowning.

"I need to talk to you."

"Rosy, I—"

She's stopped, a pace away. I remind myself that she doesn't know. That Harriet didn't tell her. But even as I frame the words, we're hurtling towards destruction, like a train on a broken track.

"Rosy, I have to tell you something first."

A frown of uncertainty flits across her forehead.

"I can't . . ." It takes all of my effort not to grit my teeth. "I can't lie to you. When I said I'm not the person you think I am . . . I . . ."

I don't know how to carry on. The realisation is crushing the breath from my lungs. She's staring at me, confusion still creasing between her brows. She's so beautiful that it hurts. The words hurt. It hurts to say them.

"I'm not. My name's not Kacper Miller. Jeanette Miller was my stepmother. I changed my name to hers when I went to secondary school.

"My real name's Kacper Woźniak. I don't speak Ukrainian, Rosy. I speak Polish."

A flicker of recognition. Her frown intensifies. She doesn't comprehend. Or she doesn't want to.

"Krzysztof Woźniak was my father."

CHAPTER 25

Rosalie

There's a place. It's there, between asleep and awake, always waiting. It won't be revoked or dismissed. It can't be filled. There's no one there. No one to save you. No strong hands to turn you around in the doorway and pull you back.

Some monsters are real. And they're not the ones you think. They're not the faces in the photos, filed in the police reports, littering the headlines. They're closer than that. They're inside. Where what you can't remember can definitely still hurt you.

It's dawn at Hailbury. There's no heating; the gas is still off. The smell of smoke lingers in the hall, even though the cleaners have scrubbed away the evidence and someone has taken away the blinds and curtains to launder.

The evidence. It's been here, all along. In my room. On my screen, staring out of the Wiki page, *Knight-Langton Abduction*. And in my hand . . .

In my hand is a broken bowl, a faded bonnet, a scratched dress. It fell on the floor, on the bathroom tiles. It was wet from washing. I tried to wash it away: the evidence.

There can't be two realities. I know that. They can't exist side by side.

So what can I believe? We've both lived our lives as somebody else. We can't change what's underneath. It can never go away no matter how hard we try to pretend to forget.

I remembered you. Kacper Woźniak. The boy in the cloakroom, serious and silent.

I scrub the tears from my cheeks, but new ones replace them. They won't stop coming. Where do we go from here? It shouldn't matter but it does. *I can't lie to you.* But he did. A lie by omission.

The driveway is empty. He hasn't come after me. He watched me go, quiet and motionless, as though he'd already accepted that the conclusion was foregone. I wanted to say something — anything — but I couldn't. I collected my laptop, my phone, my boots. We stood in the hallway and faced each other, and the answer wouldn't come. The one that told him to take it back. To unsay it. To lie to me forever, because I didn't want to know. Because I . . .

Because I'd give anything?

I walked away. Out into the road. Ten minutes from Hailbury, two minutes from where the stables used to be. Where Leonie Knight-Langton got into Krzysztof Woźniak's car, never to be seen again.

Except . . .

My lungs seem to have forgotten how to breathe. I gulp, trying desperately to fill them. I get to my feet, press the two halves together, *Mary, Mary, quite contrary.*

No. I snatch it up. Some things aren't meant to be found. The radiator is cold. I shove the bowl back where it came from, melamine grating on metal. Never to be seen again.

I go to the bathroom and run a bath. Thankfully the immersion heater doesn't need gas. I slide into the foam and wrap my arms around my legs.

Tuesday. I'm supposed to be meeting Harriet tonight. Tomorrow I've got to be in London for the literary lunch.

What am I doing? A savage sob rises in my throat, another, an onslaught, until I can't choke them back. I press my forehead to my knees. What the fuck am I doing?

"What do you want from me?" I turn on her, trying to blink away the water, the tears, her face. Leonie. She's there, perched on the chaise beside the broken mirror, watching me, one long leg folded over the other.

"Why do you always fuck everything up for me? What are you trying to tell me?"

I blink again and she fragments into history. Cracked melamine. I pull out the plug.

I can't do this. I rub myself dry. Panic is taking hold, squeezing my chest. I pull on my clothes and pack a bag: the uncomfortable shoes, the Skegness dress. I've destroyed him. I've destroyed him, and yet all along I've known there's another truth, a worse one, one that changes everything . . .

I stand in the window, teeth chattering. He hasn't come. He isn't going to. I pick up my phone and dial.

"Rosy."

My hands are shaking. I feel sick to the stomach.

"Josh."

"Rosy, hi! Is . . . what's . . . is everything alright?"

I dash away the fresh wave of tears. Shit. It's six fifty in the morning. I've woken him up. He's groggy, confused.

"Everything's . . . everything's fine."

A pause. I remember that it's me that needs to speak.

"I . . ." There's a tremor in my voice. "I was wondering if . . . if today was a good day to look at those things."

Another brief silence. He thinks I'm crazy. I shut my eyes, trying not to remember the clothes in the dryer.

"I just . . . just need to talk," I whisper. "Away from Hailbury. I just need to talk. If that's okay."

"Of course it's okay." There's something sharp in Josh's voice. Beyond the puzzlement. "Rosy, has something happened?"

"No." My throat is trying to choke off my words. I need to hang up. "No, nothing. I'll . . . I'll come in a bit. I mean . . . later. . ."

247

"You know the address? Don't use the postcode. It takes you to the wrong place. It's off Sheepfold Lane, you'll see the drive. Come as soon as you need to."

"Thanks, Josh." I push a trembling hand through my wet hair. I end the call and pace the length of the landing, contemplate the fountain with no water, the perennials that have started to erupt in a variegated blush of colour at its foot. There's a stab of pain in my chest.

I go to my father's study. The laptop is open. I stare at what I've written for nearly an hour. Vesna. What about Vesna? Vesna was there. In the attic bedroom, she had the flu . . .

Kacper Miller. I open Facebook and type it again. But this time I spell it right. And this time, he's there. Seeing his face makes the pain redouble, and I screw my fingers into the leather-topped desk. I work backwards. Armsby & the Wolds Hosting Page. *Ирина Черныш*; I recognise Iryna's photo. Sweat stings my upper lip. I copy her name into the search box, and the page narrows instantly to just a few posts: ones that she's in.

It's there at the bottom. January 2023. *Seeking help for Ukrainian family.* She's tagged by the author: Vesna Mihaylova.

Do I really want to do this? I hesitate with the cursor over her name. Do I really want to have this question answered? After all these years? There's a reason she hasn't contacted me. There's a reason she's disappeared. I hug my arms around my chest.

Do I have a choice?

I send the message and close the app without waiting for a reply.

I'm frozen to the bone. But as I descend the steps into Hailbury's drive with the church bells tolling nine, the morning is warm. There are birds in the trees singing fantasies of summer; my car is hot inside. I warm my hands on the steering wheel. Jericho. Josh has sent me a screenshot of the map.

The road towards Armsby is deserted. I take the bends slowly, unusually aware of my own fallibility. Sheepfold Lane is a single-track road, cutting up through woodlands, *Private*

Property. Jericho's grounds? The tarmac driveway is long and straight and lined with birch trees with mesh guards; deer wander, unconcerned, over the acre or two of parkland leading up to the house. I was expecting the seat of the Lord of Armsby to be ancient, but it's not; it must have been built in the eighties or nineties, a vast crisp-cornered mansion with windows that glitter in the sun. The tarmac gives way to yellow gravel, another fountain, seven or eight garages with wooden doors. There's a Maserati parked by the steps and the Tesla is around the corner beside a Range Rover with a stove-in front end that strongly conjures his recollections over dinner of teenagers and parties, the day they crashed the Land Rover into the ditch in the grounds.

I climb out of the car, unsure whether to knock or to call. I don't have to decide, because he appears instead and comes to greet me.

"Rosy." Josh's eyes do a quick scan of my face, puffy and red despite my best efforts with a cool flannel and a concealer. "It's good to see you. Come on, why don't we sit outside? It's a gorgeous morning."

He ushers me through a gate, his hand an inch or two behind my shoulders. I try to remember what he does, aside from fine dining and golf. Something in political circles. I actually have no idea.

We pass through a tunnel of grapevines and emerge onto a patio. There's a broad striped lawn beyond, a timber-clad pool house and a glimpse of tennis courts. A patio table with eight chairs bears croissants and plates and a discarded newspaper; the hum of a hot tub fills my ears with white noise.

"Here." He pulls out two of the chairs. "Let me get you a drink. In the nicest possible way, you look shattered."

I nod dumbly and sit down. Josh vanishes, and I stare at the back page of the newspaper, football and Formula One. He reappears a couple of minutes later with a mug. Sugary tea. The very British answer to a crisis. I sip it and try not to shudder.

249

"Croissant?" He pushes the plate towards me.

"No, thanks."

"How's the fire damage?" Josh's brow creases with concern as he takes the seat beside me. "Was it bad? Are you back in?"

"Oh. Yes." I swallow. "I am. It . . . wasn't bad."

The silence is tangible. I study my tea.

"You wanted to talk?" he says at last.

"I . . . Yeah. I mean, actually, I . . ." I exhale. "Do you remember the au pair?"

"Oh." He's taken aback. "Christ, maybe." He screws up his face. "Dominique or something, wasn't it? French?"

"Something like that, I think." I chew my lip.

"I always figured that's why Leonie was so good at it." He shrugs. "I was bloody useless."

"Did *she* talk to you? Leonie?"

"Well, yeah." He frowns, puzzled. "We were a tight group. We talked all the time."

"No, I mean . . . Did she *talk* to you? Tell you secrets?"

"Oh." He picks up a croissant and toys with it. "She used to. Once."

"Once?"

"Before things got . . . complicated. Being fifteen is fucking complicated." He puts the croissant down. "Honestly, Rosy? It's like you said. I was completely in love with her. And she wasn't interested, not like that. She was my best friend. I thought I was . . . we might . . . but she wasn't . . ." He shrugs again. He's still looking at the croissant, not at me. He picks up the newspaper and rolls it into a tube.

"I still couldn't stop myself wanting to spend time with her, though. Guess I hoped she'd change her mind. She was seeing someone. Someone older, I think. I kept hanging around, waiting for it to fall apart so I could be there, so that she might notice me . . ."

He glances back up. For a second too long, our eyes meet. And I think of suit jackets and white fairy lights, and look quickly back at the table.

"Do you . . . Do you think she's dead?" I blurt.

Josh's mouth opens. He shuts it. The newspaper unrolls in his hands, a soft swish as he lets go.

"I don't want to answer that question," he says quietly. "Because I want to carry on believing that she isn't."

"What would be worse?" I persist. "If he took her alive, and no one ever knew what happened? Or if she'd been dead all along?"

"Rosy . . ." A look of consternation has crossed Josh's forehead. Of unease. "What—"

My phone starts to ring, cutting him off. I fumble for it in my pocket, a leap of some wild, unnamed emotion in my chest. *Kacper?*

No.

"Tabitha," I gulp. "Hi. How are you?"

"Rosalie. I'm glad you're there." The line is crackly. She doesn't answer my question. "Can you talk?"

"Sure." Talk, now? For some reason, my palms are sweating. We're meeting tomorrow for dinner.

"Great." Is it my imagination, or does she sound curter than normal? "Good. I didn't want to spring it on you tomorrow. I thought it would be better if I called now."

Spring it on me? I stand up. My brain seems to be working in slow motion. What?

"I've just got off the phone with Stefan and Alison. The biography's off."

"What?"

"I'm really sorry, Rosalie. I know it's been difficult. But, as Alison said, it hasn't been very forthcoming, and . . ."

"Actually, I—"

". . . and frankly, your credibility to write it has just taken a nosedive."

"*What?*"

"Your mother's decided it would be better to use a ghost-writer. Someone objective."

"My *mother* decided this? Now?"

"You must realise that it just wouldn't be received the same way now. Your perspective on the whole thing will be in question. Can you imagine the scrutiny you'd be under?"

"You . . . I . . . You mean . . ." Nausea, comprehension, are mingling their way upwards from the depths of my abdomen.

"I *mean* that yes, it's only social media, but it reaches a lot of people. Exactly the kind of people who would have bought into the biography. You've got ten thousand followers, Rosalie, who now don't trust your motives. It's not a risk worth taking for any of us. Like I said, I'm sorry. Once you're back in London we can chat about it, about where to go next."

Only social media. I barely hear the rest of the sentence. Harriet's voice rings in my ears. *It's not going to take long.* I feel slightly sick. I sink into the chair, lower the phone, oblivious to Tabitha's voice still spilling from the speaker, and hang up. Achingly slowly, I open the app. Sixteen hundred notifications. *Sixteen hundred?* I gaze stupidly at the tiny bell. I'm trending.

@RosalieK-L #*leonieknightlangton* #*leoniedisappearance* #*knightlangtonabduction* #*leoniesroom* #*Woźniak*

I don't even want to see. The top thread loads slowly. The phone feels clammy in my hand. An image, not quite in focus, taken through glass. I grip the edge of the table.

We're captured in profile. Wet hair, sodden jeans, water beading on skin. His hands are on my waist, my lips on his bare chest. His face is turned, in full view of the shot: Kacper Woźniak, his jaw clenched defiantly, his eyes dark. The blurred reproduction of a different face, one that I've known for twenty years . . . and I didn't see, couldn't see — how could I?

LKL<3 @*justiceforleonie* • 2h
Time the world sees what's going on at Hailbury. Some serious research for @LaraLee's bio by @

RosalieK-L. Doesn't look like garden maintenance?
#Woźniak #leonieknightlangton #leoniesroom

LKL<3 *@justiceforleonie* • 2h
Like father . . . like son. . . So where did he take
her, @RosalieK-L? *#Woźniak #leonieknightlangton*
#leoniesroom

I feel myself recoil.

"Rosy." Josh has got to his feet. He's standing behind my
shoulder, voice tinged with concern.

"Is everything alr— *Christ*. What the fuck is this?"

His gaze has fallen on the phone. He takes it from my
hand, and I don't stop him.

"Jesus Christ. *What?* Where did they get this? Who posts
this kind of utter . . ."

Then he pauses.

"Is this for real?"

Oh, God. The paving slabs move in a haze. I stare at
them fixedly.

"Never mind." Josh shakes his head. "It doesn't even
matter. This is fucking appalling."

He passes me back the phone.

"In fact, you know what? Good for you. Good for him.
It makes more sense of the whole burning building thing,
anyway, and why he looked so ready to punch me outside
Chez Marques.

"And as for this." Josh reaches decisively to turn off the
screen of my phone. "Report it. Then forget about it. It's
fucking bullshit. As if either of you hasn't had enough of that
already. They're trolls, Rosy. They have nothing better to do
with their sad lives. Don't let it get to you."

The anger in his tone takes me aback. I look up. Josh
shakes his head.

"Frankly, selfishly, I wish it didn't have to be him."
There's something meaningful in the way his eyes fix mine.
"I'm sure you know that. But what right does anyone have to

judge you? Like he can change what his father did or didn't do? Like he could have done anything about it? He was a kid, for fuck's sake. I know I hold no standing with him. I can't blame him for that. He and I were never going to get past it, and neither of us can change it. But he's done nothing wrong. He's worked his whole life to overcome the hand he was dealt, and come to that, so have you. It's about time you both got a shot at being happy. I can't even . . . I can't *fathom* that some-one would insinuate something so sick."

I remember Chez Marques. The spurned handshake in the driveway at Hailbury. I'm lost. My frown is making my head ache.

"Get past what?" I whisper. In my mind, the animosity was mutual. It had never once occurred to me that it only went one way. "Why does he dislike you so much?"

Dislike. It isn't even the right word. It was abhorrence, outright mistrust: anger — accusation even — in Kacper's eyes. The memory still makes my gut constrict.

"*Why?*" Josh's eyebrows shoot upwards. "Are you serious?"

Something cold closes around my heart. A seeping sense of déjà vu. How is it that, once again, I don't know? What, clearly, everybody else knows? He's gazing at me in consternation.

"What?" I exhale.

"You genuinely don't know, do you?"

"Know *what*?"

"It was me, Rosalie. It was my statement that put Leonie in his father's car. I was the witness."

I can't react. I'm not sure I can even move. My head is pounding.

"I was cycling home. I saw Leonie getting in his car. I didn't even know if I should come forward. It was her choice. She chose to get in that car. He didn't make her."

I slide my phone into my pocket. I can hear my own breathing, deep and slightly uneven. How *didn't* I know for all this time? But Kacper knew.

She got in the car under her own volition. *By her own free will.* It was a headline. *Leonie lead in Rzeszów.* I'm waiting for the

254

pieces to fall into place, but the picture is all wrong. Sweat is stinging my upper lip. Josh has started to pace.

"I worried about it." He glances back, gauging my reaction. "I worried about it for a long time. For years and years. I worried about what I'd done. What I'd told them. What if I'd got it wrong? It could have been anything, couldn't it? Maybe she wasn't meant to be out. Maybe he was just giving her a lift home? Fuck knows. I see it in my nightmares. What if he had nothing to do with what happened to her . . . and because of me, because of what I said . . ."

He trails off.

"I know it's nothing compared to what you or Kacper went through. But it was a lot for a kid to carry around."

There's something obstructing my throat. I try to swallow past it.

"If he'd taken her home, why would he have disappeared?"

Josh shakes his head. "I don't know."

He sits down heavily in one of the chairs. For a moment we're both silent.

I focus on my breath, on drawing it in through my nose and out between my teeth. She got in that car. She got in Krzysztof Woźniak's car, on 28 April 2003, never to be seen again. Didn't she? He didn't give her a lift home. She never went back to Hailbury. She didn't sit at her desk, picking at a bowl of fruit and yoghurt, her long hair cascading over the back of the chair; *Piss off, Rosalie.*

Did she?

It could have been anything, couldn't it . . . ?

The tingling from my fingers has progressed upwards to my wrists; numbness is spreading around my lips. The buzzing in my ears has become a high-pitched sound, like the shrill of a fire alarm.

"Rosy, are you okay?" Josh is on his feet again, and this time he's right beside me. "We shouldn't have talked about this, I'm sorry. Christ, you look dreadful . . ."

"I'm okay." I don't sound okay. I screw my hands into my pockets to try and stop them shaking. Everything is shaking.

What can I tell him? The truth? What happens then? Who next? My parents? The police? *Kacper*? I think I might vomit. Or do I lie? *By omission.*

"I'm okay." I produce my phone, unsteady. I unlock it and open the app, scroll to the pictures. *Make your bed. And lie in it.*

"I . . . I just . . . don't know what to think anymore. And I don't know what to do about this. About Hailbury." I pass him the phone. "Someone's . . . I mean, I don't know if . . ."

"*What*? Shit." He looks up sharply. "Rosy—"

"They're old, though." There's a shrill note in my voice. I'm not sure who I'm trying to persuade. "Urban explorers — the photos have been on the internet for ages. It's like you said, they're just trolls, right? It doesn't matter."

"Rosy . . ." He scrolls down, down. Back up, frown deepening. "No. This . . . this needs to go to the police. This is fucking . . . I don't know. I don't even *know* what it is. Is this the pool at Hailbury? You and Miller?"

He's suddenly grim. So unlike his usual blazers and blasé charm that I can't make myself respond.

"How would someone have got this? They would have to have been in the grounds. You need to go to the police. Has your dad properly background-checked everyone who's working there?"

Has my father background-checked everyone? There's no point in stating the obvious, that there's no way he ever background-checked Kacper Miller. That the gate codes and alarm codes have been the same for twenty-five years. I swallow.

"Yeah. No, you're right." I stop short of snatching back the phone. "You're right. I'm going back to my father's today. I'll talk to him."

"You're not leaving?"

"No. No, it's just for a couple of days. I'm speaking at a . . . at an event."

Why, then, am I suddenly not sure? Haunted by grey eyes, faded anger, sweat on skin. I blink hard.

"Actually, I probably ought to make a move." My voice is still threatening to betray me. "The . . . it's . . . long drive . . ."

Josh insists on seeing me out. I buckle my seat belt with fumbling fingers, and he raises a hand in a not-entirely-easy wave. I drive at a snail's pace along the tarmac drive, the shapes of the deer blurring in front of my eyes. There's a passing place in the woods, and I pull up, branches scraping the passenger windows. I turn off the engine and sit absolutely still, staring at the shadows and the dappled patterns of the sun through the budding leaves.

It doesn't add up. The pieces of other people's stories, the fragments of my sister's timeline: they don't add up. My own memories don't add up. Joy, the others, the therapists and counsellors that I've seen for as long as I *can* remember. The melamine bowl.

I take out my phone to message Harriet. *So sorry, I'm going to have to bail on Skeg Vegas.* There are more notifications, new notifications, even in the three or four minutes since I left Jericho. The taste of sweet tea seems to have curdled in my throat.

#rosaliesroom

It's another photo of Hailbury. Of Shaker panelling and walls freshly painted pale grey. Of a white four-poster with voile curtains and fairy lights. There's a DM, too.

I'm not going to panic. I wipe the sweat away from my top lip with icy fingers. I'm not going to . . .

WHICH SISTER

The message is a video. I know I don't have to click on it. I don't have to play it.

But I do.

It's a knife. A knife from the block on the granite kitchen worktop, third from the left. Beyond it is a blur of movement, marble floors, oak stairs, carpet. The black dress, lifted on its hanger, held up in the air by the window, *#rosaliesroom*. The blade slashes through the fabric, again, again, and I drop the phone into the footwell.

You need to go to the police.

But I won't go to the police. I can't go to the police.

Did you love her?

Do you miss her?

Did I—

No. *No.* It can't have been me. It just can't. The mirror, the glass, the knife. The clothes in the dryer . . . *things I know, things I think I know.* I was in that picture. I can't have taken it. Whoever took it was in the grounds.

But who can have been in Hailbury aside from me?

Who could possibly know?

Who am I kidding? It's like Harriet said. Everyone around here knows more about me than I do. The whole of Lincolnshire knows I'm here.

And what I did?

I slide my laptop out of my bag. I'm not crazy. It's not in my mind. There's material proof. Someone's watching me. Someone else has found out the truth.

I open the screen. My own story: second by second, word by word. The relentless teasing. The resentment. I wished to God that she didn't exist. And then, one day, she didn't.

I'm going to have to finish writing it. There's no one else to confide in. No one else to tell. I did want to. I wanted to tell him, Kacper Miller. But it's too late now.

I angle the screen, and I start to type.

I write about earth and wet juniper. About Vesna having the flu. About picking berries, one at a time, a damp paper towel and the sound they made as they rolled into the bowl — *how does your garden grow?* About a blanket of yoghurt, a spoon. About the skip of a CD player, a fallen flower, the black circles in the middle of her eyes so wide that you could hardly see the green.

I remember. I promised myself I wouldn't, but I do. And now that the doors are open, there's no shutting them.

I remember the day I poisoned my sister.

CHAPTER 26

Nathan Langton lives in a three-bed penthouse with a twenty-four-hour concierge in a gated development opposite Wimbledon Common. He walks five miles every morning, commutes into the City once a week and, other than that, he very rarely leaves. He even more rarely has visitors.

I don't have a key or a code. I have sweating fingers, sunglasses over my red eyes, and he doesn't recognise me — his own daughter — when I press the buzzer.

I wonder who it was that invented the lie. Which of them it was that sent Vesna away when they couldn't deter me from going back, how much they paid her to leave Summercliffe, after all those years of keeping silent.

I'm too unsteady to take the stairs, dizzied by the growing certainty that the last twenty years haven't been real at all. My mother's an actress. Isn't it her job to lie to the world? The concierge watches me astutely, perhaps concerned that I'm going to vomit in the lift. I press the button and stand back.

My father is in the upper lobby. He takes my bag and shows me inside; he's saying something, but I can't process what. I gulp lungfuls of the air-conditioning and stare at the pallor of my hands against the dark tiles.

He wasn't expecting me. I didn't call him, didn't message. I haven't been to his apartment for over a year. When he gave Kacper the instruction that I was to return to London, he thought it would be to my own flat. The one I haven't told him I'm subletting.

". . . you. Rosy . . . ?"

He's stopped in the middle of the hall, my holdall at his feet. No one would recognise him anymore as the Nathan Langton of the nineties and noughties. He looks like a recluse, not a banker, with a five o'clock shadow and coffee stains on his Airlie sweater.

"Why?" I blurt. "Why did you lie?"

He's blank. Stunned.

"You lied to everyone!" My voice sounds like my mother's, shrill and unexpected. "When were you going to tell me? How many more people would you have paid off, shut up, got rid of—"

"*Rosalie?*" He says it so sharply that I flinch. He's never called me Rosalie. I was Little Rosy. The wrong daughter. The one they didn't want.

"I . . ." I take another gulp of air. Why can't I breathe?

"I killed her," I whisper. "I poisoned Leonie . . ."

"Give me that." He swipes my phone from my hand. "In here, and sit down."

The dining room is very dark for a room with so much natural light. The dining chairs are grey velour, hollowed cubes like padded cells. My father takes off his glasses. He lays my phone on the tabletop and pushes it towards me. His fingers are shaking.

"Put your code in."

I stare, vacant.

"*Rosy,*" he snaps. I don't know this version. I only know the stuttering, emasculated man who pays cleaners to lay out hairgrips and scrub away evidence.

I lay my thumb on the touch ID. The screen brightens. A red bench, beach huts. The concierge might have been right; I am going to vomit. I press my hand to my mouth.

He finds the number, dials on FaceTime. Stands the phone on its side, reflecting back the anthracite lustre. It rings, rings . . .

"Rosalie, darling—"

"Lara."

"Nathan . . . *What?*" Her face appears suddenly, a flicker of light and fury. She's in a car; there's a bluster of noise and a blur of movement past the windows.

"She remembers, Lara." His voice is flat, hard.

A sound. A breath. My mother doesn't use expletives.

"What have you told her?"

"Nothing. I called you. I didn't think you'd appreciate me waiting for legal mediation."

"*Nathan—*"

"No. I told you she was too unstable to go back to Hailbury. I told you. But you always know bloody best, don't you? You *always* come first! She should have been nowhere *near* this. Nowhere near your bloody 'biography' or your self-serving—"

"How dare—"

"*NO!*" he roars, and I cringe upright in my seat. I've never once heard him shout. Saliva is flying from his lips. "Not again, Lara! I'm not losing a second daughter to your ceaseless bloody narcissism . . ."

"We're not having this conversation now. I'm—"

"Mum." I leap to my feet. The padded chair teeters and doesn't quite fall.

They both stop. My knuckles are white on the edge of the table.

"I've only come for the truth. It's over. Tell me. The world was going to find out eventually."

The silence yawns open between us. Me, my father, the phone. Lara Lee Knight.

"Rosalie," she manages. "No. You don't know what you're—"

"Why? Why did you ask me to write it? Why *me?* Did you know I'd find out? Is that what you wanted?"

I let go of the table. And suddenly, I'm shouting too.

"Why didn't you just tell me and get it done with? Well . . . guess what. I remember! I remember that I poisoned her! Why don't we call the press, and get it over!"

My father has sunk backwards in his chair. His hand is pressed to the bridge of his nose.

"Which one of you is going to tell me? Which one of you is actually going to say it?"

"Rosy . . ." He lowers his hand. "You didn't . . . She isn't—"

"Yes," Lara Lee Knight cuts him off. "Yes, Rosalie." Her voice is clipped. "You poisoned your sister with belladonna. But it happened six months before she disappeared. Leonie was only hospitalised for two nights. She made a full recovery."

It doesn't seem to be able to penetrate my awareness. *Mary, Mary* . . . The rhyme is repeating itself in my head.

"She was okay. But you—"

"But you weren't," my father interrupts her. My father, the one of us who was supposed to have lost his mind. "You needed help. We tried to look after you at home. But you wouldn't eat, wouldn't speak, we had no choice."

No choice. I close my eyes and remember. Leaves, like fluttering blood. Someone packing a car. Winding the tough, woody stems around my fingers with Jessica poking out from the top of my bag. Virginia creeper wouldn't have been red in spring.

"I was . . ." I sit back down. The chair feels insubstantial underneath me. "You sent me away . . ."

"You were admitted for your own safety, Rosy. They kept you in for eight weeks. Even when they let you home, the au pair, Vesna, supervised you twenty-four seven. You had a one-on-one at school. You can understand why we didn't want it made public. When she . . . When Leonie vanished . . ."

The room swirls. Eight weeks. Six months.

"I didn't kill her." Coolness floods my body.

She didn't die. She vanished. She got in Kacper's father's car . . . I want it to be relief, but it isn't, because all that comes in place of the terror is the image of his face. The anguish in his eyes; *I'm not the person you think I am.*

"No." My father's voice is quiet. The pause is aching. My mother shifts at the other end of the phone, a pixellated movement and an exchange of voices. And it occurs to me that she already knows about the picture. About Kacper.

"Stay where you are, Rosalie. I'm on my way."

She rounds back on my father. "Make sure she stays until I get there. She's not working on the biography now. She's finished with Hailbury."

On her way? I gaze in horror at the phone. The rush of scenery past the window beside her is making me feel carsick. To the airport? She's flying back.

"I'm not staying." My voice trembles.

"Rosy," my father starts.

"I presume, given the obvious security risk, that you've sacked your groundsman, Nathan?"

He's adrift. I can tell from the way his hand moves from his nasal bridge to hover at his chin. The telltale sign that Lara Lee Knight has outmanoeuvred him. *She* knows. He doesn't.

"I'm sorry," he says at last. He sounds suddenly exhausted. "I actually don't have any idea what you're talking about, Lara."

There's a glint of triumph in her eyes. Even as the scenery blurs and the video fragments, I can see it. She's won. She's revelling in her superior knowledge, in the fact that its very existence has already crushed me into silence. Her secrets are safe: her not-so-perfect family will remain securely under wraps.

"Perhaps you and Rosalie can discuss it?" There's a screech of brakes. She glances over her shoulder.

"Rosalie, while you're waiting, delete your social media accounts. Things don't need to get any further out of hand. And for the love of God, make sure you're not pregnant."

And then she's gone. The call ends, leaving us both staring speechless at the phone. I snatch it up and stumble to my feet, reeling from her parting shot.

"*Rosy.*" The edge hasn't faded from my father's voice.

"I can't talk about this right now."

"You're not . . . ?"

"No," I cut across him.

He's back to the bridge of his nose. Pinching it between his finger and thumb.

"What was she talking about, Rosy?"

I'm as far as the door, and the tears that have been threatening for the last eight hours are in burning imminence.

"Not now," I rasp.

"*What was she talking about?*" The crack of his hand on the table makes me leap and turn back. He doesn't have social media. The only news he reads is the *Financial Times*.

"Dad, I can't—"

"Do I need to ring Miller? Or am I going to find out he has a reason not to pick up?"

"You've never met him." I turn back. "Have you? You've never even set eyes on him. You wouldn't have a clue." The sobs are breaching my defences. "You don't have a clue who he is, so why the fuck should it matter?"

"*Rosalie . . .*" His voice is dangerously low.

"Y-y-you know what? Go f-figure it out for yourself. I'm s-sure it'll be e-everywhere by tomorrow."

I thrust open the door. He doesn't follow. I don't know where I think I'm going to go. The dining-room door shuts behind me. The open-plan lounge and kitchen with its two-million-pound view are awash with light. I falter on the threshold. I could leave, walk out. He wouldn't even know. If my mother thinks I'm going to wait here while she flies back from Cannes to chastise me, she's wrong. My phone battery is almost flat. Last-minute hotel rooms . . . I scroll numbly, looking for something I can afford.

"Give me the key."

I jump.

"Now."

My father's phone is in his hand. Who did he call? Kacper? Stefan? Nobody. The browser is open, the screen brightly backlit.

264

"Did you know?"

I stare at him. "No." My voice sounds strangled. "How could I have—"

"So you've ended it?"

I can't answer. Another sob gains momentum. Another. I screw my fingernails into my palms.

"Tell me you've ended it."

"I . . ."

"He lied to you. He lied to me. He can change his name, but he can't change what he is. He's no better than his scum-of-the-earth father, and he knows it."

"Don't . . . even . . ." I wheel around, fury cold in my chest. The tears are fierce and fast. Tears of outrage. For myself, for the boy in the cloakroom. "How *dare* you talk about lies? *You* lied to me. You *both* lied to me for twenty years! *He* didn't lie to me. He wouldn't. He's . . . I . . ."

I what?

I blunder past him. Out. My father follows me into the hall.

"You sublet your flat."

How does he know?

"Where are you going? You're not going back to Hailbury." He reaches me in a stride. "Give me the key. Your mother's right. You're staying here. This is done."

"No." I face him, unflinching. "It's not. It's not done. It's a world away from done."

Nathan Langton's lips are pressed together so hard that the skin around his mouth has turned white.

"The key," he reiterates. "Or I'll have the locks changed."

A bitter laugh escapes me. "No, you won't."

He grits his teeth. We're at stalemate.

"I'll do what it takes," he breathes at last. "I'll do whatever it takes to keep him away from you, Rosy. You're my daughter. I'm not losing you to . . . to *him*. To that bastard's family."

I stare at him. Doesn't he realise? Doesn't he realise it's too late? It's too late to pretend that *I'm* the one he doesn't want to lose. Years too late.

I pick up my holdall. Pass him the key. For a moment he doesn't move. Then he steps aside to let me through, shoulders sagging.

"Rosy—"

"Goodbye, Dad."

There's already a lift waiting in the upper lobby. I don't look back as the doors slide closed, don't let my bravado crumble until the first jolt of movement. Then I slide my pounding head against the cold metal wall.

I didn't kill her.

Then who did? *Krzysztof Woźniak.* The lift doors chime open. The foyer is empty. The concierge is gone.

My footsteps echo. Falter.

There's a black SUV on the other side of the glass. At first, it doesn't register. Then the split-second snatch of traffic noise breaks in with the inexorable movement of the rotating door, and suddenly she's in front of me.

"Rosalie."

I feel myself take a step away.

She's fully made-up, high-heeled and immaculate. Here, not in Cannes.

My mother.

"I . . ." I'm gaping, speechless. She leans in to embrace me, and a chill runs down my spine. I can't look away from her eyes. Her pale, bright eyes and the make-up that doesn't quite hide the creases that have appeared at their corners.

Here. Why is she here?

"I think we need to talk, don't we, darling?"

"No," I breathe.

"Let's not dance around it, sweetheart. I assume Tabitha called you earlier? It was an indiscretion. I understand." She reaches out a hand for my shoulder. Her fingernails are the colour of blood. Or berry juice.

I recoil. "I didn't know you . . . thought you were—"

"Oh, darling." She cuts me off mid-sentence. "No — I couldn't exactly stay in Cannes, could I? I flew back the second that Stefan called me. I've already had a word with him about damage control. Come on."

Sweat has broken on my palms. *Come on?* Where? I feel my eyes travel to the waiting driver in the SUV; the private-hire plates and tinted windows. To my sister, climbing into a man's car, by her own choice . . .

Damage control?

I stumble another step backwards.

"No." I shake my head. "Thanks. I—"

"Now, Rosalie." There's steel in her voice. The strike of her stilettos echoes off the walls. Where's the concierge? There's something cold in my chest, something that makes me feel suddenly sick to the stomach. It's fear. I'm afraid.

Of my own mother . . . ?

"No," I rasp. "No. There's nothing else to talk about. I don't want to tal—"

She tilts her head, locks me in her stare, and to anyone at a distance, it would be earnest: a mother entreating her daughter to come home. Her fingers wrap around my wrist. Just hard enough to hurt.

"Rosalie, sweetheart." She speaks between her teeth. "Get in the car."

CHAPTER 27

Get in the car. The outside air hits my face in a blast. Her grip on my wrist has loosened now that there are passers-by, now that someone might see. I can taste bile in my throat. *An indiscretion.* The realisation chokes me. She doesn't care who's going to take the fall, as long as she can keep me under wraps.

The car door is open. I dig my heels into the granite pavement.

"No, thank you," I say.

And then I twist my arm free, and I bolt.

I unlock my own car from across the car park. Fling my bag into the passenger seat and drive away without looking back to see if she's followed. In the mirror I see the bright LED glare of reversing lights. I pull out into the traffic.

I don't know where to go. I'm still expected at the literary lunch tomorrow. I can't go to my flat.

I navigate to Crouch End anyway, too confused to think it through. I leave the car in my old space. The new tenant doesn't drive.

It's a fifteen-minute walk to the tube, and every passing SUV makes my stomach lurch. It's a relief to plunge below ground, to turn off my phone and slump in the seat of a pre-rush-hour train with the rails screeching their hundred-decibel protest.

A budget room costs me most of £200, and the view from the window is of a brick wall. I lie on the bed with the curtains shut and listen to the trains in and out of King's Cross until darkness falls. Eventually I must sleep, because I wake fully clothed and disorientated at four a.m., and drink a glass of warm water from the bathroom tap. I don't dare turn on my phone, so I open my laptop and stare at the story without an ending.

I didn't kill her. She didn't die.

The breakfast buffet opens at six thirty. The literary lunch isn't until half twelve. There are no Coco Pops so I sprinkle an over-generous serving of sugar over my Rice Krispies and get my money's worth out of the refill coffee.

I sit for a long time at the white-clothed table, thinking of Room 42, lattes, door chimes. Dark denim and candle flames reflected in glass. There are freesheet tabloids in a rack by the coffee machines. I pick one up and flick through it with a sense of impending doom. My phone buzzes the second I turn it back on. I ignore it, until I see Harriet's name pop up on the home screen.

Where are you?

Why does she want to know? It won't be about Skeg Vegas. The tabloids are the same in Lincolnshire. I toy with the phone.

I'm in London

Are you coming back?

I don't know

You're running away from this? After everything?

There's a pain in the middle of my chest. I don't reply. The backlight dims, but her message is still there. Staring back at me. My fingers tremble as I type.

Not my choice

It is your choice.

I glare at the phone. How is it my choice? How would it ever have been my choice? I look back at the newspaper. Page six. It was a gut punch, even though I knew it was a possibility. My mother might have faded from A-list to C-plus at best, but Leonie never stopped being famous. And now I'm stamped indelibly on top of her with the doppelganger of her presumed killer looking over my shoulder and his hands around my waist, and all I can think is not that I don't want this, but that I want to go back. To his hands on my waist. To feeling like I felt in that picture.

He won't want me back. Trust me.

That's a load of shit, Rosalie. Have you asked him?

What do I think I'm doing?

I dash the tears angrily from my eyes and take the paper back to my room. I have to check out by eleven. I put on the dress, a blazer, the uncomfortable shoes; tame my hair with curling irons and go to sit in the tube station instead, buffeted by the preceding draughts of the trains.

Asked him what? Where his father is? Where my sister is? Why he didn't tell me the truth at the beginning?

Thanks to Jeanette, he managed to live twenty years without once being in the spotlight. He's built

himself a business and a life. And he's risked all
of that, for you. Don't sell him short.

I watch people come and go. There are newspapers here,
too. Folded on the bench. Sprawled in a mess of broken pages
and blowing along the platform. The twenty-sixth of April.
Two days before the twenty-year anniversary. I couldn't have
timed it better, could I? *It'll be everywhere by tomorrow.*

Shit. I glance around the platform. Are people looking at
me? Everyone in the country knew Leonie's face. Everyone.
And now . . .

I can't do this.

"Shit," I mumble. "Shit." I snatch up my bag.

"*Shit.*"

Everywhere. Including Rains College, where I'm about to
stand up and talk about dystopia — or more likely field fifteen
minutes of questions about a biography that's just been cancelled. I'm trembling from head to foot. I'll have to say I'm sick,
no matter how transparent that excuse is. It's that or career sui-
cide. And Tabitha, what about Tabitha? I half run out of the station, the weight of the holdall dragging on my shoulder, take the
stairs instead of the packed escalator, dizzy and gasping. What
about her? She has to protect her interests. It's probably better if
we don't meet tonight. And if my mother has spoken to her . . .

I swipe out through the barriers, stand in the chaos of
commuters and search through my emails for a number for
Rains College. I can't find one. I send an email instead, mark
it as urgent, turn my phone to silent and collapse against the
wall. I email Tabitha too, even though I have her number and
we're normally on WhatsApp terms, harbouring a vague hope
that it will stay lost in her inbox until it's too late.

I can't stomach the idea of going back into the
Underground so, at the risk of my overdraft, I hail a cab to
Crouch End. There's a newspaper on the front seat. I pretend
to be in a call so that I don't have to speak to the driver, slip
off my shoes and search out my ankle boots from my bag.

Don't sell him short.

I close my eyes, but I can't fight the images away. *I'm not the person you think I am, Rosalie.* He did try. He tried to tell me at the beginning, and I didn't listen.

The journey seems to take forever. I jitter in my seat until we double park outside my flat. I don't spare it a second glance as the taxi pulls away. I unlock my car and shove my possessions into the passenger seat, key Shellingsby St Mary into the satnav, kill the radio and set off in silence.

I don't know what to think anymore.

Because I do remember Hailbury. I know the chapters of its disaster. And someone has to write an ending. Someone has to find one.

I drive without intermission, without a plan. I don't even have a key. The back roads seem narrower than ever, the verges greener overnight, overflowing with cow parsley and ambitious dandelions. The hills and woods have bloomed voluptuous green, and navy clouds threaten rain on the horizon. The monstrous shrubs of the drive open their arms in welcome, the Cotswold stone grumbling reluctant assent under my tyres. I'm not going to be able to get in. The adrenaline is a headrush as I swing around the last corner and stop in front of the house, the breath stuck in my chest.

KMM Ltd. I climb out of the car and clutch at the door. He's here somewhere — in the grounds, the trees; the truck's unlocked, his keys are in the ignition. I can hear the rev and rip of a chainsaw.

For the briefest moment, I finger the screen of my phone. Then I push it into my pocket and cross the gravel. I plunge through the stone arch, wet grass streaking my boots. Raspberry canes, blackcurrant bushes, the smell of herbs. The chainsaw has stopped. The shed door is ajar.

The heavens open.

CHAPTER 28

Kacper

She's gone. I wondered if it was only a rumour, until I arrived and saw for myself. The house is deserted, and there was nothing left in the hall except the flowers. I didn't go upstairs. The alarm was set. I reset it and locked the door. I probably won't be back. I'm surprised that Nathan Langton hasn't already called to sack me.

The cottage is cold and empty. Even Tom is ignoring me. I cleared the Blakemans' garden yesterday, then drove Harriet's old car to Summercliffe for Iryna, and spent the afternoon organising her insurance. I went out of my way to avoid Hailbury, even passing the gates. But by this morning, I had to know.

And now that I do?

There's no satisfaction in the smell of the soil today. The budding colour of the gardens seems pointless. In reality, it always was pointless, when no one else was ever going to see it.

Until her. Until she was there, on the doorstep. In the hall. Trailing her fingers through the juniper. Asking me names and facts and reciting them back like a child on a field

273

trip, the blood blanching from her bottom lip as she pulled it between her teeth. There *was* a point when she was here, when I knew that the garden would be the first thing she saw every day as the sun rose on her in the conservatory window.

I've tried not to torture myself. I don't know what I thought she'd do — cry, rage? I didn't expect her to go without a single word.

I fetch my chainsaw and ear defenders from the pickup. I need to saw and move the beech branch. Because Langton hasn't called, and it's damaging the lawn. I ought to get a tree surgeon. Although I guess by tomorrow it won't be my problem.

I've seen Harriet's messages. Something about a picture, the internet, the *Wolds Post*. I haven't clicked the link. I don't really want to know. It makes no odds now, anyway.

There's an empty feeling in my chest as I start cutting, drowning out my thoughts with the noise. I try to remind myself that I knew better.

I work up a sweat moving and stacking the logs. A week ago, I would have chopped kindling and filled the basket in the lounge. But no one's going to light a fire at Hailbury now, and Nathan Langton's logs will most likely rot like the rest of his estate.

One or two sizeable raindrops hit my face. I pause, glance up at the clouds. It looks like a passing storm. I take the chainsaw and head for the shed.

The downpour hits the trees with a roar, hail rebounding off the shed roof. I take off my gloves, breathing in a few slow breaths of the newly fresh air. What am I doing here? There's nothing to stop me ending this sorry fucking mess myself, pre-empting Langton and giving him my notice.

The problem is, I don't want to. A stupid, unreasonable part of me wants to cling to those few ill-fated days when I pretended she could be mine.

The rain shows no sign of easing up. I top up the chainsaw from the jerry can. The shed door bangs behind me, taken by the wind.

I turn.

But it hasn't closed. It's opened.

She's standing so still that for a split second, I think I've imagined her. I lower the can to my feet. The sleeves of her blazer are folded back, revealing her slender wrists. Her hair is wet, strands of it sticking to her face, and I think suddenly of the orangery and have to swallow a few times to fight the memory away.

Gone. She was gone.

Under the blazer she's wearing a tea dress, meant for somewhere else. A function, a meeting: somewhere that she isn't. There's cut grass sticking to her boots and a ladder in her tights. The jolt of pain and want cripples me with confusion. It's still pelting with rain. I take a hasty step back, so that there's space for her to get inside.

"Rosy?"

She takes a little breath, scattering the raindrops from her lips. She doesn't speak. There's rainwater dripping from her hair onto her face. I want to wipe it away.

"I thought you'd gone back. To your flat. Your parents."

I brush her wet hair from her cheek, reach to tuck it behind her ear. She doesn't stop me. A lunch. The recollection reaches me dully. There was a lunch she didn't want to go to . . .

"Jesus, Rosalie." I bury my face in her hair, let my lips stray briefly to her neck, feel her inhale. The mix of hope and desire is heady and intense. I try to fight it away; she still hasn't spoken, not a single word. I don't know whether I can face what she's really come here to say.

"I did," she whispers.

Her hands are against my chest. I'm frozen. I don't know what I'm supposed to do.

"He took the key. My father. I can't get in."

Her father. So she did go to her parents . . . Has she come to collect her things? I clench my teeth so hard it hurts.

"Why are you here?" I manage at last.

"Because I . . ."

Her head snaps up. She looks suddenly on the verge of tears. There's a crack in her voice that destroys me.

"Because I had to see you. Because, when I'm near you, I can't think. I feel like I can't breathe. But I . . . I don't even know if that's okay anymore. And I'm scared that it's not, that it's not okay, and it's going to break one of us."

"Rosy," I exhale.

The rain has stopped. I can't keep the bitterness out of my voice.

"You know who I am, Rosalie. That's not going to change."

"No." There's a scowl on her lips, fierce and trembling. And the tears, fuck, the tears shudder in her lashes and drip down her cheeks with the rain. And she was right, it's going to break one of us.

"No. *You* didn't take her. You were nothing to do with what happened to her."

The pain in my chest is unbearable. "Neither was he."

"You truly believe that."

"Yes."

"It doesn't matter," she breathes. "Don't you see? It doesn't matter to me, even if he did. That I—"

I can't bear it.

"Stop." I press my thumb to her lips.

I can't curb it any longer. I pull her into me, the soft printed fabric of her dress gathering under my hands. I actually don't care who might see anymore. If the fucking paparazzi have followed her to Hailbury. I don't give a shit. A stack of bamboo canes clatters and falls, rolling in chaos around our feet. Her mouth is compliant, hungry. I grasp her damp hair.

"Please," she rasps.

And I'm gone. I'm done. I'm done with this place. I'm done with burying the truth.

The grounds are sodden: the grass, the raspberry canes, the privet. The windscreen of the pickup is beaded with rain.

She hesitates on the gravel, and I take her hand and lead her away from Hailbury. I drive us back to Jeanette's with the sun breaking through the clouds. I shut the door and lock it, and Rosalie turns, the tears streaming over her cheeks. And something takes root inside me; certainty, anger that I can't even justify. I wonder what they said, Langton and her mother. What they told her, to crush her so efficiently.

We go upstairs and sit on the edge of the bed, and I hold her, feeling the sobs shake her from head to foot. They seem to last forever; I don't know how to make them stop. Eventually she turns her face against me. I can feel her tears soaking into my T-shirt.

"*Rosy.*" My voice is a growl.

"I thought . . ." Her face is still hidden. "I thought I did it."

What?

For a second, I can't make out what she's saying.

"I thought I killed her. I poisoned her. They lied to me, they tried to hide it . . . That's why I can't remember. Because they sent me away."

What? I press my lips to her hair. *Poisoned.* For a split second I think of her fingers wound through the Atropa belladonna.

"I was . . . unstable. They sent me away because I was unstable."

Leonie. Her words are garbled and difficult to make sense of. She's talking about Leonie.

"And I . . . I *did.* I tried. I . . . I *hated* her. I was seven, and I tried to poison her."

Fucking hell.

"But she didn't die. She didn't. *She didn't.*"

"Rosalie." I pull her into me. I want to make it stop. I've got to make it stop. "Rosalie . . ."

"I remember doing it." Her shoulders are shuddering. "I found the bowl. I . . . I didn't know what to do. I . . ."

She turns her face upwards to look at me, haunted shadows, salt-tracked tears. If she believed she did it . . . then she believed *he* didn't. The realisation is like being hit by a truck.

"Don't you see?" I breathe. "It doesn't matter to me. Even if you did. I don't care."

Her eyes are wide. Uncomprehending. At my words — her own words, thrown back at her. There's a snag in her breath. At last I feel her body loosen, and her trembling fingers weave through mine.

"I thought I'd lost my mind," she whispers. "I was so afraid."

Afraid. The dark, the torchlight, the locks on the door . . . Jesus Christ.

"No . . ." I exhale. "Rosy."

She'd lost her mind? Or I've lost mine?

"I'm sorry," she murmurs.

"No. Listen to me, Rosy. Don't you understand? Nothing you can tell me would ever—"

I grit my teeth and bite it back. I think of Jeanette and the passport. Of the girl at the school gates, her eyes swimming with tears. It can't be too late. *To break her out.* Out of the shadow of Leonie Knight-Langton. I let her pull me to lie beside her, watching the spill of her hair, damp and dark, against the white pillows. I'm dazed, like the kid stumbling back from the Blakemans' house, without enough words to explain what happened. Punch drunk.

"You can be anything." I don't know where the words are coming from. A memory, a vapour trail in a blue sky. "Anything in the world. She doesn't define you. Leonie doesn't define you."

The tears have run backwards, into her ears, her hair.

"Whatever happened to her, it's not on you. You don't have to go back to Hailbury. You don't *have* to remember."

We're beyond risk, beyond self-preservation. What's left? There's nothing I wouldn't gamble. Her body curls into me, her fingertips finding their way under my T-shirt.

"And, for the record, you're not the only one who can't see straight, Rosalie."

I don't even recognise my own voice; it's rough, barely audible, as I help her lift off my T-shirt. As I hitch up her dress, and she clutches at my hair to pull my face to hers. As she whispers my name.

And for the first time, it really hits me. That she knows. She knows my name, *my* truth, the one I've tried for so long to leave behind. It was only ever going to be her. I've known that for a long time. Since that first day on the doorstep. Longer, somehow.

CHAPTER 29

Rosalie

There's no table lamp burning. We've watched the darkness fall. The curtains are still open, and the last brooding shapes of the clouds linger, swollen and waiting, on the horizon. Kacper's arm is around me, tight and a little too tense, and his chest is warm, and his breathing still slightly unsteady.

There are questions that we're going to have to answer, or at least ask. What next? Where do we go from here . . . what path do we tread, between the truths that we've each grown up with?

I turn my head. My voice sounds husky.

"I didn't expect you to be at Hailbury."

"No." He shifts onto his side. "Neither did I."

"He hasn't sacked you?" I bite down on my lip without meaning to and he reaches to stop me.

"I guess that pleasure's yet to come."

I frown. It's nine p.m. and, for all my father's talk of changing the locks, there's been no call. Unless . . .

Unless he's coming to do it in person. The thought makes me queasy.

"The picture's everywhere."

"So Harriet told me."

"The internet, the tabloids, I . . . I don't even know how . . ."

"I guess how's pretty irrelevant." There's a wry twist to his lips, brief and painful.

I think of Harriet's message. Twenty years without once being in the spotlight. How can I say it? That someone must have been in the grounds? That there's more; that it's not just one photo, one post, it's a dozen, and they're still there, waiting for me in the ether. Waiting for one of us to set a foot wrong.

Trolls, *just trolls.*

I breathe out.

"Tell me about him," I whisper. I roll onto my side, to face him. "Tell me about your father."

I feel him stiffen.

"You already know."

"No," I breathe. "I don't."

There's a flicker in his expression. Something I still can't read.

"He didn't do it," he says.

"How can you be sure?"

"Because he was my father. Because I know. I knew him. He didn't take her." His eyes are dark and his jaw is clenched.

"He came here to build us a better future. He worked every hour of every day, on the farms, at the livery yard — that's where he met Jeanette. He was so determined to do well for us. He tried only to speak to me in English once we were here. He wanted me to learn.

"But more than that . . . more than that, he taught me about patience, Rosalie. About kindness. About turning the other cheek. About justice — that life can be fucking hard, that there'd always be people who tried to knock you back, but you could be better than them if you did what was right. There's no way, *no way,* he ever hurt anyone. He didn't take Leonie."

"Ohh." I pull the covers around me. The edge in his voice isn't anger, it's certainty. Certainty that bleeds from his every tensed muscle, from every fleck of colour in the grey of his gaze, despite every piece of evidence from the last two decades.

"Then . . . where did he go?"

"I don't know." Kacper's teeth are gritted. "I don't know."

Something is uncurling deep inside me. The knot that has been tied tight for days, weeks. Years? There's an answer, a truth, and we both need it. *Leonie*. She's tied into everything we are, and it's time to tease her out.

"You were living here? *He* was living here?"

"With Jeanette." He nods tersely.

"What did Jeanette say happened?"

Kacper draws his breath between his teeth.

"He came home. He put me to bed. He said he was join-ing the search, and he went out, and she never saw him again."

I close my eyes, overrun by the images: torches in the dark, a kiss goodnight.

I open them again. "You can see why that would look bad for him."

Kacper rolls over and swings his legs out of bed. He pulls on his work trousers and clicks on the light. I blink against it, taken by surprise.

"That postcard." He turns back. "The one of your bench, that you never showed anyone. This is mine. This is my memory."

He stands up, jerks open the drawer of the bedside table and pulls something out. Tissues. Sellotape. A small, tightly wrapped parcel. He hands it to me. I stare at it.

"What . . . is it?" I glance at his face, uncertain. I peel back the tape. Black faded plastic, metal, grubby and ingrained with dirt. I'm not sure I understand, and yet . . .

"It's his car key."

"It . . ." Comprehension washes through me. She got in his car. A nationwide search . . . but the keys are here?

"He could have had another set?" I can't drag my eyes away from the scuffed oval badge, the remnants of dirt in the embossing. Kacper has taken something else out of the drawer — black leather, crested with silver. He holds it out.

"This is his passport."

I take it, hands trembling, and open the cover. I look at the picture, the one burnt onto my subconscious. Something shifts. Realisation, dizzying and almost impossible to grasp. Interpol. A lead in Rzeszów.

"Did . . ." My voice is barely audible. "Did anyone . . . *know* this?"

"Jeanette knew."

"Why wouldn't she have told someone?"

I raise my eyes to his. Kacper doesn't look away.

"I don't know. Unless . . . unless she thought he might need it." He sits back down on the bed. "If she'd given it to the police they might have kept it, and then she wouldn't have had it if he came back."

There's a pause. His eyes are still on mine, watching me absorb what he's saying.

"She would have protected him?"

"She knew he was innocent. She knew that no one would believe her. And she loved him. She loved him until she died."

And she'd have given anything. My throat is aching. *Anything in the world.* I look around at the four walls, the midnight blue. The painting of a jet plane propped on the bedside table. I think of the boy with grey eyes, standing in the corner as they unpacked his lunchbox, *turning the other cheek.* I think of a braid of hair, a teenager who didn't want to be a model, about rolls of film. About an au pair sworn to secrecy, a photographer with sea views and barely a penny left to his name.

"How did you . . ." The ache in my throat is unbearable. "How did you *live*, with . . ." I slip free of the covers to go to him, my fingers still clenched around the keys. "With *this*? With what everyone said he did? When you knew . . . ?"

The wry smile is back. Agonising and bitter.

"I found ways to survive," he says.

"But—"

"I was never going to change what people believed, Rosalie. I was always going to take the fallout. Jeanette couldn't stop it. I couldn't stop it. That's why I took her name, not because I wanted to pretend, or because I thought he was guilty, but because I had to survive. There were other kids, kids who knew her, kids who would have killed me, given half the chance. I learnt how to protect myself."

I look down. At hard muscle, dark ink. Up, at the memories that flit over his face. And I realise. It's not about Lara Lee Knight. It never was. It's not about audiences or sales. It's about a teenager on the wrong side of the camera and a man who was condemned, and the fact that no one knows the truth and no one's even trying to find out anymore.

"They must have missed something. At Hailbury." I lay down the car key. "There must be something else. An answer to what happened."

"I've spent twenty years telling myself that." Kacper's lips press together, the cynical ghost of a smile. Abandoned rage, discarded expectations. "Wasn't that why you came here in the first place?" His voice is painfully quiet. "Isn't that what you were really looking for?"

I can't quite frame a response. Like the stained glass, the tint of colour. He can see right through me. He has done all along.

We need to go back. Before my father changes the locks. We need to go back to Hailbury.

* * *

Beyond Armsby the hills plateau into expansive flat fields of still-green corn and heavily perfumed, dazzling yellow rapeseed. The houses are sparse, the signboards and Summercliffe's peripheral scattering of chalets and campsites holding their breath for summer. Yvan has a fever and Iryna needs someone to translate. Kacper is driving to meet them at the health centre.

"What was Little Lord London doing at Hailbury, any-way?" Kacper's voice is concertedly casual. I glance up.

"Oh." I frown. "He came to drop off some stuff, to do with Leonie."

"Right." He studies my face. Then he looks back out of the windscreen.

"She was his best friend." I'm not quite sure why I need to qualify it.

"Yeah."

"I . . ." I glance sideways at him. "I know. About him, that it was him that witnessed her getting in the car. He told me."

For a moment, Kacper doesn't reply. His knuckles are white on the gearstick.

"I know it doesn't make it any better. But . . . he's con-sumed with guilt about it, the implications of what he thought he saw. I think he wants to put it right."

"And he told you this over the veal and truffle." He's not looking at me.

I bite my lip.

"Not exactly. No. I . . ."

He shakes his head.

"Kacper." I reach to touch his arm. It's rigid. He changes gear and moves his hand to the wheel, and we turn down a side road, lurching over the speed bumps.

"He isn't . . . You have every reason to despise him, I get that. But he's scared he got it wrong, that what he said is the reason they didn't find her. I think maybe he needs answers as much as we do."

We draw to a halt. The car park is busy, the tiny health centre a bustle of people, wheelchairs, prams.

"Yeah." Kacper's eyes have narrowed. The reflection of the sun is in his face, and I can't quite read him.

There's a flash of silver, a door opening a few cars along. Kacper releases the door of the truck and jumps down without

285

another word. I watch as Iryna climbs out of a dented silver hatchback and stoops to help Yvan out of the back. I wait in the pickup. Kacper accompanies them inside.

Twenty years is a long time. If Vesna knew everything, why has she never got in touch? Even if my parents warned her off, there would be no reason for her to stay away anymore. But she hasn't responded to my friend request and there's no reply to my message. I type another one with unsteady fingers.

I know about the poisoning. My parents told me. It doesn't have to be kept secret. I know you looked after me. I'd like to talk, if you feel like you can. Rosalie.

I'm tormented by the idea that she's just around the corner. I've read her posts: she was looking for a host in Summercliffe so that Iryna would be close to her. But she disappeared at the mention of my name?

It's almost an hour before Iryna and Kacper reappear. He's holding Yvan's hand. Iryna unlocks the car — Harriet's old car; I remember him mentioning that he was sorting out the insurance. Kacper straps Yvan in and pauses to say something. A second later, he opens the pickup door.

"Tonsillitis." He swings himself inside and fastens his seat belt. "He's got some antibiotics. Iryna said she wanted to show you some things at the bungalow, if we've got time? I know you wanted to get to Hailbury."

I'm not sure that he wants to go to Hailbury. It's there, in his eyes. There have been a lot of truths in the last twenty-four hours. He doesn't know about Vesna.

"Actually, yes." I clear my throat. "It'd be good to see Iryna."

His brows lift, quizzical.

"She had a friend who lived round here." I'm not really sure how to explain. "You might have spoken with her online."

"Vesna?" He glances over at me as he starts the engine.

"Mm. Yes. Well . . ." I scuff the toe of my boot in the footwell. "I'm not sure . . . I think I might know her. But we're struggling to track her down."

"Yeah." A frown flickers on his forehead. "I haven't heard from her since February. I spoke to her on the phone — she helped me do all the visa paperwork. I thought she'd be around to help Iryna once they got here. I invited her to come to the airport to meet them, but she never got back to me."

"Mmm." I examine the lock screen of my phone. There's no reply. Only an unopened message from my father. *Where are you?*

"I think that's what Iryna thought, too." Something uneasy is nagging at the back of my mind. Something about the timings, and how they're a little too perfect.

The inside of the bungalow is in semi-darkness. Yvan clambers onto the sofa and hugs a duvet around his knees, cartoons flickering from the television. Iryna goes through to the kitchen. I hear a running tap and the switch of the kettle. Kacper crouches down beside the sofa and says something in Polish. Yvan half turns his head, a smudge of tousled hair and shadows. There's a fierce pout on his lips, and it occurs to me for the first time just how much anger there is in his eyes. I see him shake his head. Kacper pauses. He shifts his weight forwards and whispers something else, and Yvan releases his knees and regards him doubtfully.

"Rosalie." Iryna's voice startles me. "Tea? You would like?"

Her English is stumbling, a gap between each word as she tests the pronunciation.

"Oh, yes please. Let me help you." I follow her to the kitchen. Has she found something out? Maybe Vesna has contacted her? The smell of baking stops me in my tracks.

Iryna drops teabags into three mugs. There's a battered envelope on the worktop beside her, stamped in currency I don't recognise. She slides it towards me; her eyes glitter on mine for a moment, before she turns back to pour the water into the cups.

"Elena send. From Ukraine."

"Elena is okay?" The momentousness isn't lost on me. "She's well? Safe?"

Iryna's lips press together. She gives a nod, a shrug that doesn't need translation. Who knows? She was safe when she posted it. Now . . . ? I glance in the direction of the living room. Iryna stirs the tea and gestures to the table. I sit down.

The envelope is already unsealed. I slide out its contents. Documents, papers, mostly handwritten, the characters unfamiliar. Some must be official; there are stamps and dotted lines. Others are letters, scribed on small sheets of patterned notepaper. There are photos, too, a few faded Polaroids. Young women: her and Vesna.

Iryna sits down beside me and speaks into her phone. I wait for the app to translate.

I will make interpretation of documents from Vesna.

I nod. She's speaking again.

Here is all correspondence since she left Ukraine. At the beginning, every few weeks. Then nothing, for many years, until the war.

"Is there an address?" I flick through the pages. There is, on some of the notepaper. But it's old. There's no need to translate my question; the first line is Hailbury.

Help me to understand, where is she? How I can find her?

If only I knew. I falter, my thumb between the pages. What can I do? What *do* I know? There must be something. The two of them were youthful, glamorous, with their bright red lipstick and sparkling eyes. Before tragedies, life choices, wars, everything else that went so badly wrong. Now here we are, in the dim light of a borrowed kitchen, each on our own broken path and without answers, any of us.

Iryna takes a tea towel off the plate of sweet cheese cookies and loads them onto a tray with the drinks. I follow her to the sitting room. The duvet is on the floor, and Kacper is on the sofa with Yvan huddled under his left arm and a controller in his right hand. Yvan is clutching his with both, his attention fixed on the screen, his shoulders finally relaxed and his bare feet tucked under him. He edges closer, even as I watch. *To lose a parent and leave everything behind . . .*

The scalding tea only just makes it past the obstruction in my throat. I wonder when the anger fades. How long it takes for the pain to get buried. *I'm not sure I've ever been close to anyone, Rosalie.*

I perch on the arm of the sofa. Iryna passes me the plate of cookies, and I take one and hold it, inhaling its scent and thinking of medicine and ribbed cardigans. I'm not sure how long I sit, lost in thought. It's the sudden flick of light to dark that brings me back, and I look up to see that Kacper has turned off the TV.

Yvan is asleep, his small body lost in the crook of Kacper's arm, his head flopped against the back of the sofa, cheeks flushed. Kacper eases the controller from the child's half-curled fingers, and there's something fleeting in his expression, something so heart-rending in its context that I have to look away. He lowers Yvan gently, picks up the duvet from the floor and tucks it over him, then rises to his feet. Iryna says something as she gathers together the teacups, and I see him nod.

"We should go." He turns to me. "If you're ready?"

"Yeah." I let my fingers skim the back of his hand, the faint pink scar on his knuckle, and I feel him inhale. Iryna's eyes are on us.

"Thank you," she says softly.

I pause. I'm not sure that she's addressing Kacper. My thoughts dwell for a moment more on the pictures in the battered brown envelope. She moves to embrace me, and I fold the cookie in my hand.

* * *

The drive back to Shellingsby is fraught with tractors and caravans, and largely silent. I think about Iryna's pictures. But what about *Leonie's* pictures? She took her films to Antonio. He developed them. And then what? There *are* no pictures. I went through every box. I would have found them. They weren't in the briefcase. They're not at Palace Gardens. And I've heard no single word from Antonio DiPaci.

I take one last look at my phone. Nothing. I switch it off. My parents can't call it if it's turned off. The tone of my father's last message suggested that he knew full well I wasn't in Palace Gardens.

Kacper lets us in and unsets the alarm, and the silence of Hailbury's hall echoes around us. I can sense his tension as we climb the stairs. He carries the boxes down from the attic two at a time, and I unpack them in my father's study, stacking and sorting their contents on the desk. There's nothing I haven't already seen. L'Église Rose and the agency portfolio. Numberless exercise books, school projects, end-of-year reports. Mementos from theatre trips, trinkets and wedding favours.

"What kind of answer are you looking for?"

I glance up. Kacper's stare is very direct.

"I . . ." I falter under his scrutiny. "I don't know."

"You don't have to do this." There's a grim set to his lips. "Not for my sake, you know that?"

Whatever it takes, to keep him away from you . . .

I shake my head.

"No," I breathe. "But I do for mine. *I* need to know."

"Okay." There's still a crease between his brows. "What next?"

The landing floorboards creak under our feet. Her door is closed, and I falter, as usual, with my fingers on the latch. He watches, raw-gazed, as I tiptoe across her floor. I see him take it all in: the bed, the cushions and throws, the swing. I don't touch the swing.

There are more books and binders under her bed. Crates, stashed in the bottom of her wardrobe. It's already almost four p.m., and my stomach is growling as I turn them out, filtering through English essays, science coursework, a script scribbled on in scathing pencil: *Katherina* and *Petruchio*, the *Taming of the Shrew*.

"There should be photos." I sit heavily on the edge of her bed. Kacper pauses a moment then sits too, his gaze playing on the doll.

"She was learning photography. She was taking films to the photographer who did her modelling portfolio, in secret.

290

He developed them, critiqued them. I met him. He has a studio in Skegness. Those pictures must *be* somewhere."

"The police would have found them, surely? They'd have had the place apart. They must have copies of everything."

"No. They can't have. No one knew about it."

"Have you asked your parents?"

I chew my lip. Somehow, I don't want my mother to know about the rolls of film. Not yet. She can't have known about Leonie and her tutelage from DiPaci; she wouldn't have wanted me to interview Tony if she'd thought he'd disclose something she'd kept quiet.

"No. But I'm certain the police didn't find everything. *I* found stuff. Her iPod, undeveloped films, in a briefcase downstairs. So they didn't look everywhere. They can't have done."

So what am I missing? My stomach growls again as I get to my feet. Her notebooks are on the desk, the academic diary.

"Do you have any food in this house?" Kacper stands up too. "If we're staying to do this?"

"Oh." I hadn't thought about it. Eating. Staying. "Pasta, maybe?"

His eyebrows flicker.

"I'll go to the Co-op."

He disappears, leaving me in silence. I repack the crates, pausing to flick through the clothes in the wardrobe. Blazers, jodhpurs, school uniforms: grey tartan, navy and blue. Flared jeans, miniskirts, indecently short shorts. And dresses, a whole rail of dresses. I didn't find flowers in any of the crates.

I move back to the diary on the desk. A girl who didn't want to be a model or an actress, smart, headstrong; a girl who spoke French to piss people off, who could argue you round in a circle. I flip it open.

u got a bf then?
No.
at the yard?
No.
Liar

Wot r u thinking? Ur mum will freak out
my mum won't know if no one tells her
fuck off leo she'll kill u
just because someone's older than me doesn't mean I can't be
in love with them

"Rosy."

I jump. The book bangs shut on my fingers.

"I bought food. You need to eat." Kacper is in the doorway, arms folded.

For the strangest split second, something jerks in my memory. I freeze.

"Rosy?" He moves inside, unusually hesitant. I drop the diary.

"*Fuck*," I whisper.

I know where the photos are. All this time, I've known, and no one else did. Not my parents, not the police. Not even Vesna?

Her green eyes are hot, the blood in her lips is bright, bright red.
Fuck! You freak! Get out—

"The windowsill."

"What?"

"The window." I fall over my feet, rending the voile curtain. "She was in the window, here, right here. I came in and I caught her . . . she was mad because I saw. She was moving it. The windowsill. She was hiding something."

I fumble with the sill. It's heavy, awkward. Too big to lift more than one end. If you didn't know it moved . . .

"Kacper," I breathe.

He catches it before it crushes my fingers.

"Dry lining," he exclaims under his breath. "They dry-lined the external walls."

I can't reply. I'm staring into the darkness of the cavity. She dropped it all: paper, mostly. It's there, where she'd been trying to hide it. Lined notepaper, dog-eared A4, envelopes and pieces of card. A ribbon-bound book, covered with cobwebs.

I can only just get my hand into the space. The book is slim and there's barely any purchase for my fingertips. The pages are full of dust. I drop it on the floor and reach back in to scoop together the unbound paper. I fall to my knees on the carpet.

Kacper lowers the sill.

"That's . . ."

"It's got to be." My mouth is dry. I flip the book open. Photos, still glossy beneath the dust. Of scattered shells, of fronds of Virginia creeper. Of two teenage boys arm-wrestling across a table: the heir apparent of the Lord of Armsby and a bare-chested friend, their eyes and smiles captured in ageless sepia. Of beer cans and Babycham bottles like skittles. Of a small child standing in a garden, skinny-limbed and bushy-haired, her fists clenched, her back to the camera, and a woman in a brown dress watching her from a distance. There's a name on the inside cover. *Leo Langton.* I frown.

"These are letters." I pick up the envelopes. Two of them are still sealed. I run my fingers over the writing on the front of the top one. *To T.*

"Is this a railcard?" Kacper has crouched beside me to retrieve something. A flimsy plastic wallet: the top card is a photo ID; her name, her picture. The next card down is a receipt.

"It was the twenty-eighth of April, wasn't it?" There's an odd note in his voice. "That she disappeared?"

He's drawn out the receipt. It's printed like a ticket, striped white and orange. £25.69 26-04-03. There's nothing else in the holder.

"She bought tickets, to somewhere."

I don't really hear. My eyes are on the second envelope. Its flap is still stuck down; I imagine her running her tongue along the glue, moisture glistening on her red, red lips.

to Rosy

My name is in her handwriting, faded purple gel pen. My ears are ringing. I should open it. It's to me. I falter with my fingers under the seal. She listened to songs about running away. Wrote letters and bought train tickets. She cut her hair.

I can't make myself do it. I can't break the seal.

I pick up the other envelope instead. There are probably laws against this. I should put on gloves and drop it into a sandwich bag, take it to the police and wait for them to precis me the contents. I peel back the flap.

> *I love you. I'm going to write it, so you know. I don't give a shit what they say. We'll be together, I know it in my heart. All the BS they give me about priorities and opportunities, they wouldn't know love if it smacked them round the face.*
>
> *I don't care if people think it's wrong. You've taught me more than they ever could. You've loved me more than they ever did.*
>
> *I know we can make it work. I won't give up if you won't. Wherever you end up, I'll find you, ok?*

There's a photo tucked between the pages, printed four times over, not one of hers or DiPaci's. It's come from a pho-tobooth, the kind that does passport shots. Leonie's hair is almost invisible in a low ponytail; she's wearing a beanie hat and there's a silver stud in the tragus of her ear and a camera hung on a strap around her neck. Her smile is impish, hol-lowing out her cheeks; her face is thinner than in the L'Église shoot — she's lost weight she didn't have to lose — her shoulders are frail and bony in an oversized hoody that makes her look boyish. The arm slung around them is tanned and ringed with a half-dozen bracelets. There's a star tattooed on the inside of the wrist, a glittering stud in the girl's protruding tongue. Blue eyes, sandy hair. I think about the confidante in the homework diary, but the fit of the pieces is tenuous. Did she tell her what she was about to do?

Her camera isn't here. It isn't at Palace Gardens. There was no camera in the briefcase. Where would it be, apart from on a strap around her neck, on a train, to a destination that no one ever found out?

Wherever you end up, I'll find you.

Someone knew. It's a credit card receipt.

My hands are shaking. I hold her up to look at her afresh. Did she? Could it be . . . is there even the slightest possibility? That Krzysztof Woźniak was innocent. That Leonie Knight-Langton was never snatched. Never taken.

That she made a choice, *by her own free will*.

And that somewhere, *somewhere*, there's a woman who used to be my sister?

CHAPTER 30

We didn't stay at Hailbury. Perhaps I knew better than to test myself. The peonies on the hallstand stood glorious and intact as we locked the doors behind us and drove back to the cottage, where the purple flowers blossom against the white render, where there aren't unsolved mysteries buried in the walls. Where, strangely, I can sleep without the light on.

I woke not long after sunrise; we drank coffee together in front of the wood burner and set off in the early light to walk — here, to the woods — where the soft, golden morning sun accumulates in drifts in the clearings and drips between the leaves. The world's not up yet, just us; the only sound is the birdsong.

I let my hands trail through the dewy foliage. If there used to be a path, there isn't now, just overgrown runs of meadow grass and a hundred thousand bluebells, their violet glow lifting, incandescent, from the leaflitter.

"I didn't even know this place was here." My voice is lost to the whispering trees. Kacper has fallen behind, and I turn back to look at him. He seems to personify this place, the silent dance of warm sunlight from behind the clouds, the effervescent hints of colour in the shadows. He catches me up and I wind my fingers through his.

"I used to play here." He shrugs. "I'd bike here. For hours on end, as a kid."

It doesn't look passable by bike. I glance around at the uneven ground and tangling plants. We've almost reached a clearing. He lets go of my hand to stride through the undergrowth, balancing over the ridges and mounds in the earth.

"I spent hours digging it out, making ramps, jumps. It was a safe place back then. No one else came here."

"Safe." I frown. "From the other kids?"

"From the world." He gives a wry smile. He doesn't elaborate. I pick my way through the nettles to join him, lost in the smell of wild garlic. I look down at the mounds and hollows, imagining a spade, a bike, a boy, alone.

"Did you believe he'd come back?" I pick a dandelion to examine it, the perfection of its seedhead, the trembling fragile stalks. Kacper takes the bullet without flinching.

"I wrote him letters."

Letters.

"He never read them. I kept them for years."

Twenty years. I feel for the envelope in my pocket. The indentation of the purple gel pen.

"You should read it."

I glance up. How does he know?

"I don't know if I want to."

"No," he concedes softly. "But you still should."

Should I? I swallow. Really? *Did you love her . . . Do you miss her?*

"Why didn't you go to the police after Jeanette died?" I counter. "With his keys, his passport?"

"Because it wouldn't have changed anything. No one's looking anymore. It's too late to clear his name."

"What if it's not?" I take a step back so that I can face him properly. I've already spilled my secrets, mangled and broken, for whatever they're worth. But his are tightly bound, inked in tense and unforgiving black, and behind them the gaze of the small boy, like Yvan's, is still wary and dark. He doesn't look away.

"What if her letter tells you where to find her?"

"It won't," I whisper. But I can't help but finger the paper. I realise he's waiting for me to explain.

"She despised me." I don't know why it hurts so much to say it. "Ridiculed me. I was nothing to her."

"It doesn't look like nothing." His downward glance is pointed.

"The best it would be is good riddance."

"What if it's not?" His eyebrows lift.

We've tied at ten all, and I don't know whose serve it is. I draw the envelope out, into plain sight, slide one finger under the flap. Twenty years, today. The glue is old and brittle.

to Rosy

> *I'm glad you're home, little owl.*
> *I made Jessica some new clothes while you were gone.*
> *Vesna helped me. I hope you like them.*

I'm paused, the wind tugging at the paper. *Jessica's spare outfit, hand-stitched by someone once.* My heart is beating hard.

> *I've missed you. Crazy, huh? My freaky little sister. Don't ever stop being freaky. Don't let them change you. Don't let them try to fix you. Stay wild. Dance in your welly boots, cut your hair. Be what you want. Tell them you won't. Show them you can. Say no. Say yes. Be brave, be afraid, be fearless, be strong. Be you. Make your own map and don't let anyone take it away, Rosy-Roo.*
>
> *It was my fault, what happened to you. I realise that; I'm not stupid. I guess I wanted to say I'm sorry. I'd probably have tried to kill me too.*
>
> *I'm not sure yet when I'll give you this. Whether I will at all. Maybe tomorrow, not tonight. Maybe next year. Maybe when you're 17, or 27, maybe by then you'll have forgiven me. We'll fly to Paris, and dance, and cut our hair, and all of this will be a funny story. I hope so.*

I put some books on your shelf. If you want someone to read them to you, come find me. I'm pretty good at telling stories.

Leo

xxx

She put some books on my shelf? There's a hollow feeling in my chest. But I was nothing to her . . . I fold the note over and over on itself, a rectangular wad of paper that I cradle in my hand, confusion knotting in my abdomen.

Books, read by torchlight. The curtains pulled around the four-poster, the two of us in darkness besides the twinkle of the tiny bulbs, like stars in the canopy over our heads. *Anne of Green Gables, Pollyanna, Matilda, The Secret Garden.*

"I'm not sure it was good riddance," Kacper says quietly.

My pulse is thumping wildly. There's no date on the note. No dates on any of it.

"I'm not sure it was goodbye."

* * *

"You have reached . . . *Tabitha Anderson* . . . I'm sorry I can't take your call right n—"

I hang up and toss the phone onto the kitchen side with a crack that echoes around the walls of Hailbury's kitchen.

All those years, with no idea.

I make a fresh percolator and put it on the hob, although I'm already buzzing, my mind in a hundred places at once. Leonie's photo album is on the table, along with the notes and letters. Kacper has gone outside to work; we walked here hand in hand, *an indiscretion*, in stubborn disregard of onlookers and social media slurs.

I wasn't guilty. It wasn't my fault. It's like a fog has lifted, the weight that crushed me from the moment I stepped back through Hailbury's door. I might not remember, but I don't have to lose my mind.

She left some books on my bookshelf.

She was running away. And she has a story that needs telling. Like Harriet said, if anyone's going to tell it, it should be me . . .

I move to spread out the papers and pictures, to photograph them with my phone, and flip open my laptop. I've got an inbox full of revisions and missed extended deadlines. At some point, I'm going to have to stop ignoring it all, and start working on some better excuses, ones that don't involve any questions about *#leonieshouse*.

I collect two clean cups from the draining board and glance out of the window, searching the borders and the raspberry canes, but he isn't there.

I scan back over the paper. The loose dog-eared sheets weren't letters. They were mostly quotes, song lyrics: little snatches that, however I combine them, don't seem to make any sense. *To T.* My eyes are drawn back to the envelope. T?

I sit down on one of the stools, the prattle and bubble of the percolator filling my ears, and open Google. He was famous, once. There are a few old profile shots, on Wiki and a couple of photography websites. I was right; Antonio DiPaci was good-looking in his youth, tall and dark with piercing heart-throb eyes. Strong jaw, black hair clipper-faded short and sharp . . .

I stop scrolling suddenly. I open Krzysztof Woźniak's Wikipedia page in a new window, *Knight-Langton Abduction*, my hand cold on the trackpad.

They wouldn't have been so different in age: four or five years. Not so different in build or colouring, not through a car window from a distance. Leonie vanished and Antonio DiPaci said his bit and quietly faded from view. *He can change his name but he can't change what he is.*

If she ran away, what was she running from? Or, more to the point . . . who would she have run *to*?

The crash of the front door startles me from my thoughts. I hear Kacper's boots on the marble. He comes to a halt in the doorway.

I slide to my feet.

For a moment he doesn't move. His phone is in his hand and his knuckles are white. There's a jolt of dread in my abdomen.

"What's happened?" My breath leaves me in a rush. "Oh God, what—"

"The hospital's been hit." He's still motionless. "In Bakhmut."

To start with, I don't process what he's saying. It seems to hit my awareness and bounce off.

"Elena was at work."

"No," I whisper. In an instant, I've forgotten Antonio DiPaci.

Kacper doesn't reply. My eyes have filled with tears of realisation.

"Oh, God. Iryna." I sit down heavily on the stool. "Yvan . . . ?"

"He doesn't know."

Finally he moves. Crosses the floor, every muscle in his body tight, and reaches past me to close the window on the laptop and open a different one. A news page, updated this morning: the colours of devastation, stretchers, flames.

"Fucking hell," he whispers.

I have to look away; I can't bear it.

"Has Iryna seen this? Have you spoken to her? Has she heard if—"

"She can't get hold of anyone."

"Oh . . ." I inhale.

"We should . . . I should go to Summercliffe. She's beside herself." Kacper shuts the laptop. "Fuck, I need to do *some*-thing." Suddenly, he's moving.

I hang back, uncertain.

"I don't want to make things worse. Maybe I should stay here." It seems like trespassing, somehow, imposing myself on another catastrophe, when it's already my fault that Vesna isn't here to support them. I catch sight of his expression. "Or at yours."

Kacper pauses. I see him swallow. He pulls a key from his pocket and folds my hand around it.

"Not here." His voice isn't quite even. For a lingering moment his fingers grip mine. And then he turns to go, and I follow him to the hall, and watch him drive away.

I stand at the foot of the stairs, conflicted and cold even though outside the April sunshine has grown warm. *Elena.* There's nothing I can do. Nothing that could ever start to make this better.

Unless maybe, just maybe . . .

I go back to the kitchen. One message, and it's not from Vesna. T-W @*triggerwarning*. I make myself remember what Josh said: *They're trolls, Rosy, don't let it get to you.* I delete it without reading it, and block the account.

I open Facebook instead, backtracking via the Armsby refugee hosting page to find Vesna's profile. Vesna Mihaylova. There isn't much information about her, not that's visible anyway, no marital status or recent posts. But there is an employer. *Senior staff nurse — stroke unit* at *NHS*. And the name of the hospital.

I snatch my purse from the hallstand, threading the key to the cottage onto my keyring.

* * *

There's a car on fire on the Humber Bridge and the traffic is queued for miles. The journey takes much longer than the supposed hour and a half, and by the time I get to the hospital, it's almost noon. I ask at the front desk for the stroke unit and follow the directions with growing trepidation until I find myself stood outside a set of double doors.

There's a buzzer to press. I search desperately for the words I rehearsed in the car. The door opens before I'm ready and a man comes out, fumbling with his pocket. He almost walks into me. I take a hasty step back.

"Sorry." He glances up at the last second, then double takes, the colour draining from his cheeks. The door bangs shut.

I stare back. "It's o—" I start.

But he's gone, his steps brisk on the polished floor.

What?

I wrap my arms around my chest. It's a hospital. God knows what he was walking away from, on the other side of those doors.

I move back to the buzzer, trying to remember my story. I grit my teeth. This isn't for me. This is for Iryna. I waver with my finger over the button.

"Excuse me, please."

There's someone behind me. I'm in the way of the door swipe.

"Sorry." I stumble aside and realise in the same instant that she's in a uniform. She swipes her badge. Adrenaline spikes in my bloodstream.

"Actually," I blurt, "could you help me?"

She turns back. I can see her ID: *Kim Wallace, Sister, Stroke Unit.* I pull myself up straight.

"I uh . . . I'm looking for my friend. Vesna Mihaylova."

Silence. It echoes between us, expectant and oddly tense.

"I'm . . . I'm really worried about her. She was supposed to be meeting me, and she never showed. I know she works here, I just wondered if . . ." I'm running out of momentum. "Wondered if you know if . . . if she's at work? My name's Rosy. She um . . . she's a really close family friend."

Seemingly, the sleep deprivation and stress play to my favour. Kim looks at my haggard face and steps back from the door.

"She's not here." Her voice holds sympathy. A hint of concern? I fold my hands behind my back.

"She left at the end of January. She'd decided to move further down the coast, a little town near Skegness, although she was still coming back to do a few bank shifts while she applied for jobs closer to home. But we haven't seen her for weeks."

"Oh." I stare over her shoulder at the doors: Vesna's life after Hailbury. I wonder whether she still wore cardigans, whether she brought cookies to work. They haven't seen her for weeks? I can feel my fingernails biting into my palms. Something's off. I don't know why I'm suddenly so sure, but I am. Why would she have stopped turning up to work? Maybe she left Summercliffe when she found out I was coming. Maybe the move down the coast was less appealing when she realised I'd be ten minutes away, digging up lies and unhappy memories at Hailbury. But this place is nothing to do with me, and it's miles from Hailbury.

"I hope everything's okay." Kim fingers her badge. It's clear she has to go. I nod.

"So do I." My throat feels suddenly tight.

Kim swipes her card again.

"Was it Rosy, you said?"

"Yeah."

"If she does book any more shifts, I'll let her know you came. I hope you find her."

"Thanks," I whisper.

It's a dead end. I navigate the corridors to the exit, trying not to think about explosions and falling rubble as the hospital bustle swells around me. I tap my card at the parking meter and get in the car. Vesna can't just have vanished. People don't vanish. Apart from Leonie Knight-Langton.

And Krzysztof Woźniak.

I inch my way back towards the tolls, gazing at the view from the bridge. From high above, the water in the estuary looks deceptively peaceful. I think of Kacper, and the ferries crawling along the horizon, then the traffic starts to move and I'm swept along in the outside lane until I'm off the bridge and lost in the three lanes of motorway.

My phone pings as I finally pull up to put the code into Hailbury's gates. I left all of Leonie's things in the kitchen. I snatch it up, guilty. I told him I'd go back to the cottage, not here.

But it isn't from him.

It's another DM. Another video.

The world is suddenly ringing in my ears.

Trolls. Just trolls.

I was in the photo from the orangery. Someone had to be in the grounds to take it. Someone who wasn't me. Someone who took a knife from the knife block, third from the left . . .

"Oh, God." I choke.

I should delete it. Block it. I know I should.

But I don't.

At first there's only darkness. Then light flashes across the screen. The room is bright, sunshine reflecting off the pale grey walls and the Shaker panelling, the unmade white bedclothes. A gloved hand. It holds something up, bringing it close to the camera: a glossy auburn head, a pink chiffon dress. The fabric arms of Leonie's doll hang flaccid. There's something on its skirts, red and sticky, and a twist in the chain around its neck. The video jerks, blurs, cuts out and back in. And then the camera is lifted high into the air, watching at an awkward angle as the gloved fingers fasten the chain around the top rail of the four-poster. Watching the doll fall, limp and staring, to swing gently to and fro in its noose, the sun shining through the bloodstains in the chiffon.

You're next.

CHAPTER 31

Kacper

Yvan's not stupid. Kids know. I knew, a long time before Jeanette would ever talk about it. He can see straight past Iryna's resolute smile. When I arrived, he was eating borscht from a bowl in silence whilst she clattered around the kitchen cupboards with her phone in her hand.

I brought him out. It seemed like the best thing to do. The sun is warm on the five-a-side pitch behind the children's playground. His fever is better, although his feet seem to drag on the worn-through astroturf. He kicks the ball half-heartedly and it crashes into the fence with a jangle of chain-link.

Iryna hasn't told him. She's not going to tell him. I sent him to the garden to get his football, and we had a brief but heated conversation in the hall. She doesn't want to tell him until she knows for sure.

Jeanette wasn't going to tell me until she knew, either. But she never knew — no one ever knew for sure. I think about Garden Gate, hiding behind the compost sacks, all the things I heard that I wasn't meant to. What if Elena's never found? It's more than a possibility.

I jog for the ball and kick it back to him. He stops it with his feet and picks it up, his eyes scanning over me, dark eyes like Iryna's: shrewd, bitter brown.

I gesture towards the goal, *do you want to shoot or keep?* I'm never sure how much of my Polish he understands. Some days, I think it's everything. He'll reply to me, a smart answer, and it's a struggle to keep a straight face. Others? He was only five when they moved east from Lviv, and it's not his first language. I just can't tell.

Yvan looks at me and shakes his head.

"Okay." I nod.

He retreats to the fence, watchful and scowling, still holding the ball, and I pretend to look at my phone, not him. Rosalie hasn't messaged, and I'm not sure that's a good sign. I hope she isn't still at Hailbury. I should have asked her to come. It bothers me that there's something she's still not saying, something I can't add up. I grit my teeth, and then release them again, aware of Yvan a few paces away. I'd almost be relieved if Langton did sack me and change the locks.

The clash of the chain-link makes me jump. I lower the phone. The ball rolls back across the astroturf into Yvan's feet. He kicks it again, viciously, and it hits the fence with a clatter that echoes around the deserted playground. Again, so hard I think he might trip, the fence reverberating along its length. Again . . .

"Yvan," I say softly.

Again. More violently, closer range; his small shoulders are braced, he's breathing fast.

"Yvan." I move gently toward him. He spins.

The wild swing of his fist takes me completely by surprise; it hits me in the ribs, winding me. I catch it on instinct; he lashes out with the other instead, his scream of rage shrill.

Then his feet strike me hard in the shins; he wrenches away and flies at me, raining punches against my chest, and, for a moment, I don't know what to do except let him. I catch his wrists. And suddenly he's sobbing, trying to jerk them free, and I'm afraid I'll hurt him, but I'm more afraid of releasing my grip, that he might run, light-footed and fast, that he'll dart between the bollards and the beach huts and I'll lose him altogether.

"*Nie!*" He gets one hand free. Punches again. And this time his voice cracks, and the words flow uninhibited, a mash of Polish and Ukrainian that shouldn't be intelligible, except it is, because it's there in his eyes, every word of it, and it doesn't need translation. *I hate you. Let go of me. I hate you! You're not my tato!*

I do what he says. I let go. I stand still, and his fists beat against me once, twice more, and then his face is buried against my abdomen and his screams fade into hiccups that seem to tug their way from deep inside him. I don't move. For long, painful seconds, I'm back in the school office with a washing-up bowl in my hands and vomit on my second-hand shoes.

"No," I say at last. "*Nie jestem.*"

I kneel down. I don't know how to hold him. I don't even know if I should. He's right. Who am I? I'm not his father. I'm nobody. Just a bearer of bad news. I think of Jeanette, and hesitantly I reach out and rub his back. After a beat, he hides his face in my shoulder, and we stand like that for a long time, neither of us saying anything else, until at last the hiccups ease into little unsteady breaths, and he picks up his ball and I offer him my hand, and we make for the gate together, his fingers wrapped tightly around mine.

We go to the beachfront restaurant. The tables and chairs date from my childhood, plastic seats and steel posts bolted to the floor. The menu is basic, easy to translate, and I let him pick whatever he wants. He orders chips and chocolate ice cream, and we sit in the window with his tattered football between our feet. He chews a couple of chips and moves onto the ice cream, savouring every spoonful. He scrapes out the sundae glass, and I push him my full one across the table. He takes it, still wary, and I wait for him to finish before I go and pay.

Outside the late afternoon sun is bright, but the wind off the sea is very fresh. I take his ball and help him into his coat. It's too big for him — one of the hand-me-downs from Harriet — he's either small for seven, or Rohan is tall. I pause as the sudden thought occurs to me. I'm sure when Harriet first found out about him and Iryna that Sandeep mentioned something about Médecins Sans Frontières. Yvan climbs over the seawall, and I follow him onto the sand. Perhaps there *could* be a way to find Elena. Or to confirm the worst, if it has to be the worst. At least he wouldn't have to live his whole life not knowing.

He picks up a stick from the shingle and drags it behind him, drawing a track that I follow with my feet as I debate whether to text Harriet now or call Sandeep later. I've been avoiding Harriet. I should see what news there is from Iryna first.

We walk until we reach the dunes on the North Prom, and Yvan goes to dig in the spiky grass with his stick. I sit down on the sand and look out across the waves. After a while he sits down too, edging closer to me for shelter from the wind.

"Promy." I point. *Ferries.*

"Poromy." His echo is a surprise. He looks up at me, eyes questioning.

"Mój tata i ja popłynęliśmy promem." *My tata and I took the ferry.* I swallow. I haven't said that name out loud since the day Jeanette died.

I'm not sure if he understands. For some reason, I think of Rosalie on the bench, the held-back tears, the ache that resounded in my chest. I felt like she knew, which was stupid, because she didn't have the faintest fucking clue about me. But for a few lingering minutes, it was a shared space. The bench, the ferries. The memories that neither of us have let ourselves own.

Even though it's nearly May, the beach is cold, and I realise Yvan's starting to shiver. It occurs to me that maybe it's his fever. We've been out all afternoon, and I haven't heard anything from Iryna. I get to my feet. He takes my hand, and we battle the wind back the way we came, descending past the empty paddling pool and the playground. There's a shiny Maserati in the beach car park, at odds with the shabby railings and disused ticket machines. Yvan tries to tug me closer to look, and I resolutely keep my distance, guiding him around the graffitied back of the railway station instead. There's only one train a day from Summercliffe-on-Sea. It literally is a dead end.

"Miller!"

I come to a halt. It takes all of my self-control not to curl my hands into fists.

"Hey, Miller! Sorry." Josh London jogs the last ten metres to catch us up. His eyes fall briefly on Yvan. "Sorry, I didn't mean to catch you at a bad time. I . . ."

He tails off. I can count on one hand the number of times Josh London has voluntarily spoken to me, and not one of them has ever been an apology. I hold Yvan's hand tighter than I really need to and draw in a deep breath through my teeth.

"Actually, I need to talk to you." His eyes scan from Yvan to our surroundings, the empty pavement, the litter blowing across the playground. "Have you got five minutes?"

Have I got five minutes? For him? He's got to be joking. I can feel the real answer manifesting itself in my expression. I haven't got five fucking seconds for him, and he knows it. How did he know where to find me?

"I need to get Yvan home," I say.

"Two minutes, then." Josh doesn't take the hint. "In there?" He jerks his head at the playground. "Maybe . . . he—"

"Yvan."

"Maybe Yvan wants to play?"

"What's this about?" I cut to it. Enough dancing around whatever it is he's cornered me for. The sooner we're out of here, the better.

"I . . . Look. We need to talk about Rosalie."

I feel myself stiffen. I release Yvan's hand and lower the ball to the pavement.

"What about her?" It's an effort to keep my voice even.

"I don't know if . . ." He glances at Yvan's suspicious frown. "I'm not sure it's the right—"

"He doesn't understand anything you're saying." I push my hands into my pockets, so that neither of them can see how close I am to losing it. *Get out of my way, scumbag.* It's a bit of a change of tune.

"What is it that you want to say?"

"I'm worried."

"Worried. About what, exactly?" I take my hands out of my pockets and fold my arms across my chest. Gone are the days of him and Zach Blakeman stood head and shoulders above me. We're eye to eye, and there's a gravity in his expression that I don't remember.

"Look." He lets out a heavy breath. "I'm not asking you to like me, or even to trust me. Just . . . Just hear me out."

"I'm all ears." It's more biting than I intend. Yvan has wandered in the direction of the swings. I watch him push open the metal gate.

"Someone's stalking her."

My gaze snaps back.

"*What* did you say?"

"Someone's stalking her, Miller." Josh shoots another look at Yvan, as if to check he's out of earshot. "There's someone — someone messed up — who won't leave her alone. They seem to know a lot. Too much. Exactly where she is and what she's doing. I thought you needed to know."

"What . . ." I suck in a sharp breath. I can hear my voice trembling. "What are you talking about?"

"She mentioned something a few days ago. I was worried — I told her she should go to the police, and I'm guessing she didn't. I thought she might listen to you. Have you seen the posts?"

"What?"

"Online."

I shake my head. I don't do social media. I have no desire to scroll through other people's sugar-coated existences; apart from signing up to the hosting scheme, I've only ever very occasionally used it for the business, and I haven't logged in since Iryna arrived in March.

"There are pictures. Someone's been in the grounds at Hailbury. They've . . . Look." He reaches into his jacket for his phone. "Look, I'll be level with you. I didn't want her to like you any more than you wanted her near me. But I think we'd better put our differences aside. I don't think she's safe. Here . . ."

He hands me the phone and I take it. He's already opened the app. The page has her profile shot at the top, the same one that appears under her name on her column. @RosalieK-L. I scan down it, and every muscle in my body tightens.

What the fuck? I stare at the picture, wordless, shaking with rage: the orangery, the pool, the outline of her body only partially obscured by the stream of sunshine.

"It's not just that." Josh's voice is low, grim. "That fire. How sure are we that it was an accident?"

How sure? I can't tear my eyes away from the phone. Her voice is in my head: *My clothes were in the dryer?* Flat roofs, skylights . . . She's put locks on her bedroom door. The blood is racing in my ears. I think of her walking in the grass verge, her silhouette in my headlights.

I turn off the screen and pass it back to him. I've seen enough.

"Someone slashed her tyre," I say between my teeth. The silence rings around us, broken only by the slow squeal of the chains on the swing. Someone who knew exactly where she was and what she was doing . . .

I grip my hair with one hand, on the cusp of pulling out my own phone and calling her, here and now. If she's still at fucking Hailbury . . .

I let out my breath. Yvan has got off the swing and is opening the gate.

"She told you this?" I look back at London's face, and I hear the rawness in my own words. He shakes his head.

"She wasn't going to. She got a call from someone, I overheard it."

"I've got to go." I pick up the ball. I can hear my own breathing, heavy and laboured. Yvan is approaching across the tarmac. For a split second, Josh London's eyes meet mine.

"I tried, Miller. But she won't listen to me."

I can't reply. The rage, the loathing, are burning in the base of my lungs. I don't want to trust him. I don't want to owe him for this. But the creep of comprehension chills me to the bone. He knew, and I didn't. He's right — she's not safe. Yvan slips his hand back into mine and it's ice cold. I turn on my heel and start to walk, keeping him close against me, until we're away from the chain-link and the Maserati, and out of sight.

* * *

The bungalow is unnaturally tidy and freezing cold. I turn on the gas heater in the sitting room. Iryna's bedroom door is shut. I can hear her on the phone. I put on the TV so that Yvan can't hear what she's saying, find the antibiotics in the fridge, and measure out the dose onto a spoon. Yvan accepts it without protest, then gags, and I run him a glass of water to take away the taste. We sit at the kitchen table, and I let him flick through the pictures on my phone, the sounds of the TV spilling from the lounge as I stare for long minutes at the tablecloth.

I've been trying not to think about it. About the fact that what she's dug out of the walls at Hailbury could prove what I've been sure of for twenty years. There didn't seem any point in raising my hopes when it wouldn't make a difference now anyway; Jeanette's dead and the reality is, if he didn't take

Leonie, then he either must be too, or he didn't want us to find him.

Or both.

But it's not about him anymore. Is it? It's not even about Leonie. I grind my nails into the edges of my chair. A week ago, I could have called Langton. Got more cameras installed, a better alarm. That's not exactly an option now.

I stand up. I need to go back. But Iryna's still on the phone, and Yvan's upturned face is pale and tearstained. *Fuck*. I push my hand back through my hair and start to pace. I don't know what to do. I promised myself I'd stay away from this, right from the beginning. That I'd keep away from her, from history. Now I'm up to my neck. And she's in over her head.

Jesus Christ. I exhale forcefully. It's getting late. The sun has moved around the house and Yvan is visibly drooping. There's buckwheat in the fridge, and I heat it up with some milk. We sit in front of subtitled cartoons, and I keep half an ear on Iryna's bedroom door, the other on my phone.

"Kacper." When Iryna appears she's red-eyed and exhausted. "Przepraszam. Wybacz mi." *Forgive me.*

I can't ask, not in front of Yvan. Her expression gives nothing away. She sends him to get into his pyjamas, and he rematerialises before I have time to frame the question. Out of nowhere, he wraps his arms around my waist. There's a thick feeling in my throat that I can't clear, even as I walk to the truck, and see the light cut off as Iryna draws the curtains.

I drive home, although instinct almost sends me straight to Hailbury. Rosalie's car is on the street outside the cottage, and the surprise and relief hit me like a breaking wave. I unlock the door. The lamp's on in the hall and there's a spill of light from the kitchen, but she isn't there. I walk through to the sitting room. She slides to her feet as I come in. The room's in semi-darkness.

"How's Iryna?" She speaks before I can.

"About as expected." I watch her cross the floor. Her feet are bare and the short legs of her jeans graze her ankle bones.

She's put on a woollen sweater, the one she was wearing the day that she arrived at Hailbury.

"Yvan?" she whispers.

"He knows." I shrug. "She hasn't told him, but he knows."

Rosalie nods. "Kids are like that." She sucks her lip between her teeth and I have an overwhelming urge to take her cheek in my hand and stop her, but I don't.

"Yeah."

I study her face. *@RosalieK-L.*

Someone's stalking her, Miller.

"Are *you* okay?" She slips her arms around my waist.

I feel myself tense.

"You said there was a picture on the internet. You didn't tell me that you were getting threats."

She freezes. We're both rigid. Immobilised.

"They're not really threats," she mumbles at last. "Just a couple of posts online. It's nothing, I—"

"Show me."

Rosalie swallows and draws out her phone.

"Show me," I repeat. She unlocks it and hands it over.

"It's nothing," she insists. But her gaze is on the floor. "It's just some asshole being creepy."

I scroll down the page. There are a lot more posts than I'd expected. *Did you love her? Do you miss her? #leoniesroom,* more photos. *#rosaliesroom.*

My finger falters to a halt on the touchscreen. There are private messages, too. I open the inbox. One is from this afternoon. It's a video. I tap.

"Rosy . . ." I can hear the blackness in my own voice.

I hold it up, where she can see it. My arm is rigid, the phone trembling in my outstretched hand. *There's someone — someone messed up — who won't leave her alone.*

"I . . ." She takes a sharp breath, closes her eyes. When she opens them again, they're wide and dark with dread. She moves away, out of my grip.

"I thought it was me, but it wasn't. They were . . ." Her hands are shaking more than mine are. Her voice is small. "They were in the house, Kacper," she whispers.

I suddenly think I might vomit. The video is playing on a loop. I watch it again, again, even though I don't want to. A doll with red cheeks, dark-copper hair: the chain, the drop, the rail of the four-poster, affirming everything he said in brutal clarity. Someone's stalking her. They were in the house. I clench my fist around the phone, bile rising in my throat.

I tried, Miller, but she won't listen to me.

"You're not going back there." I'm breathing hard.

"You sound like my father." There's a defiant tremor in her lips, but the fear in her eyes is real.

"Then your father's right. He needs to change the locks. The sooner the fucking better. Fuck, I'll happily arrange it myself."

"You can't." The pout on her lips is more than I can bear.

"I can. We'll access the CCTV and go to the police."

"You don't understand . . . I can't, I won't. She was my sister. *I've* got to do this. Don't you see?"

"No." I say it more forcefully than I mean to. Rosalie spins back, dashing the back of her hand across her eyes.

"No, I don't." I go to her, catch her hand in mine. Pull her into me and hold her tight. "You haven't got to. You don't have anything to prove."

"There's everything to prove," she says fiercely.

The twilight has dwindled. The road outside is too dark to make out. I don't want to argue with her. She's right — there is. There's everything to prove. I just don't want her to be the one to prove it. I don't want there to be pictures. I don't want there to be someone else thinking about her in the fading light. Imagining her. Watching her. Waiting . . .

I shudder.

"Kacper," she murmurs. She's soft and slight in my arms, and my whole body aches. The feeling of her against me is a distraction and an affirmation all at once. Leonie's gone.

My father's gone. But she's not. She's here. I exhale. She half turns to rest her cheek on my chest, and for a long time I don't move.

There's a chill on the landing when we go upstairs, a darkness that doesn't belong to the cottage, and I can't get rid of it, even with the light on. She undresses and slips between the covers, and I lie down beside her.

If I was a better person, I'd make her leave. I'd call Langton. Something — anything. I'd get her away from here.

Instead, I pull her close. And I press my lips against her hair, fix my eyes on the shadows, and think about a doll, defiled and bloodied, with a noose around its neck.

CHAPTER 32

Rosalie

The grass in the park is wet. There are initials scratched in the wrought-iron bandstand rails; an exhausted mother is rocking a buggy back and forth. It seemed safer not to be alone.

Kacper left at seven. I barely managed to convince him not to cancel another day's work and drive me straight to the police station. He wants me to go to the police, just like Josh. But what would I say? That someone's been trolling me online? Leaving threats in a house that I'm little short of breaking and entering? That I've been concealing evidence about my sister's twenty-year-old cold case, and my parents covered up the fact I tried to murder her?

We compromised on calling 101, even though I couldn't help remembering the car that wasn't in the ditch, and how well *that* conversation went. He sent me a message at half eight to check I'd called. I haven't.

I drove to Hailbury myself after he went to work, waited in the drive until I saw the cleaners arrive. It took most of my courage to follow them in, to go to my room instead of fleeing like I did yesterday. I unwound the chain from around the doll's neck and wrapped her in a Tesco bag. Then I stood in the utility room, and stared in gathering realisation at the burnt-out cupboard: at the brand-new fuse box and the melted black box that the electrician cut out from beside it. I don't think Kacper is going to be able to access the CCTV. I don't think anyone is.

The church bells in Armsby are chiming nine. I didn't reply to his message. I stopped short of throwing the doll in the wheelie bin; I put her in the boot of my car instead and drove away, like I was dumping a body. He read my silence and sent another one to ask where I was. He's coming to find me; the pickup has just pulled up in the car park. I watch him get out, a frown lingering between his brows, before he catches sight of me and starts across the grass.

The coffee I've bought is still steaming, in two paper cups from the van in the car park, not from Harriet's. There are Coronation flags fluttering from the bandstand. His eyes don't leave me once. Kacper takes both cups from my hand and stands them on the rail.

"Why aren't you taking this seriously?" There's reproach in his tone. But there's something more in his eyes: intensity, a darkening of anxiety that makes it strangely difficult to breathe.

"I am."

"Then why—"

"I can't tell them half the truth. I can't take this to them and not tell them about the rest. The photography, the train ticket . . ."

"Then tell them," he says fiercely. "Just tell them."

"And the passport?" I raise my eyes and see his jaw clench tight. For a moment neither of us moves. He's rigid, unspeaking. I slide my arms around his waist and he flinches.

"I can't," I breathe. "Don't you see?"

"Rosalie." His teeth are gritted.

"I'm sorry."

Slowly, Kacper shakes his head. His fingers span the small of my back.

"I don't think I've ever known anyone so stubborn." His mouth moves against my temple.

"I think you mean single-minded," I whisper.

"Whatever you have to call it. I can't let you destroy yourself." His hands have closed around my upper arms. I shiver.

"I used to be quite risk averse, before I came back here."

"If you won't listen to me, then at least wait for me?" He releases my arms. His hands travel over my jeans instead, light and careful. At first I don't realise what he's doing. His fingers slip into my pocket.

"Don't go there without me." He draws out Hailbury's door key and folds it into his fist. His eyes lock mine. "Please? Not anymore."

How does he know?

I don't look away. Can't. What choice is there? I want to kiss him. To scream at him. To snatch ineffectually at his closed fingers and let him overpower me. Kacper reaches around me for the cups of coffee and presses one into my not-quite-steady hands.

"I have to be in Louth for ten," he says. "You could come."

He already knows I won't come. It's there, in the level grey. I press my cup to my lips.

"I said I'd meet Iryna."

"At Harriet's?" His eyes don't leave me.

"Yeah."

"She's meeting Sandeep?"

I nod. "Before his afternoon surgery. I said I'd keep an eye on Yvan. He's not at school. They've got an inset day."

Kacper breathes out slowly.

"I'll be finished by three. When I get back . . ." He breaks off. I'm not sure if it's a promise or a warning, as he tips my face to his. As his lips take mine, gentle and incendiary.

I don't mention the CCTV. I walk to Harriet's still reeling from his kiss. I haven't seen Harriet since our messages in the tube. Yvan is in the window, his fingers making smudges on the glass. I can't help pondering that Kacper didn't want to

320

come here. That he suggested the park, not the bistro, despite the fact he knew Iryna and Yvan would be here. It must have been him that knew about Sandeep's contact at MSF in the first place. I push open the door.

There are four or five tables occupied, and Harriet is busy behind the bar. I intended to tell Iryna about the hospital and the trip across the Humber, but she's in a conference call on a laptop, and Sandeep is sat beside her, his tie tucked through his shirt buttons, his face grave. The memory of our conversation in the surgery is an unwelcome jolt that makes me backtrack hastily to find Yvan instead.

Harriet has set out a plate of cake and fresh fruit, which he's eyeing suspiciously as he sidesteps around the window ledge. I sit down on the sofa. He doesn't come any nearer, so I unpack my offering of brand-new boxed Lego beside the plate and start building the spaceship myself. I manage to assemble most of it without reference to the instructions, then flounder with the final touches.

"Rosalie."

I put down the Lego. Harriet has come to a halt behind me. I can't tell if the pause is awkward.

"I'm glad you came," she ventures at last.

I let myself glance up.

"Me too," I say.

There's a momentary silence. Then she perches on the chair arm.

"I think you needed t'put back boosters on first." She picks up the Lego. "This bit's upside down."

I smile.

Harriet smiles back. "Kacper's still avoiding me, then?"

"I think he's avoiding everyone," I mutter.

"Can't really blame him." She reattaches the boosters and holds the toy out to Yvan. He shakes his head at her, and she lays it back on the table. "How's Hailbury?"

I falter, glance outside at the bunting and Union Jacks, and try not to shiver. She misreads my hesitation.

"You're not staying at Hailbury." Her smile is knowing.

"No." It's not a lie. I glance over at Sandeep and Iryna. I can't tell what language Iryna is speaking, or whether Yvan can hear what she's saying. Her eyes are rimmed red. Yvan has sidled in beside Harriet's legs to pick up the toy, uttering little sound effects as he flies it along the window ledge. The door jangles open, and for a moment I half expect to see Joshua London. But it isn't him, and Harriet gets to her feet and makes her way back to the bar. I watch Yvan position his miniature figure inside the cockpit, closing the plastic window with a snap.

Josh. Josh saw Leonie get in a car. *Somebody's* car.

I need to know what he remembers.

He may not realise it — and Kacper may not want to — but he's the one other person who might be able to make sense of everything. Her best friend. He's there, in her photos. He was part of the story, the one that I'm going to persuade Tabitha I should really have been writing all along.

I type him a message, still half-watching Yvan over my phone. When I look up, the conference call has ended. Sandeep shuts the laptop and comes to say a measured hello whilst Iryna superficially admires the Lego. Harriet brings Yvan a carton of juice as Iryna types to me on her phone: Sandeep's contact has a friend in Bakhmut. Tonight, Yvan will play with Sandeep's children so that she and Sandeep can make some more calls. I nod my understanding. It doesn't seem the right time to tell her what I know about Vesna.

I wait until Sandeep has accompanied her and Yvan to their car, and then I get up to leave. For the first time, Josh London hasn't replied.

I drive to Summercliffe. There's a car park near the sea-front, mostly empty. A red-brick building with a timetable and the characteristic overhang of a station platform; I hadn't realised Summercliffe has a station. I slip Leonie's letter inside the photo album, tuck it under my arm and ascend onto the promenade, struggling to get my bearings. I try to conjure the soft rap of Kacper's boots and the jerk of his head, *this way*. I can't remember if he said North or South Prom, but South feels right, so I go with it. It feels further, alone, through the windswept dunes, than it did with his long strides next to mine, the forbidden proximity of his fingers.

There's no one on the bench when I get there, and I sit down, surprised by the intensity of the sun. I look down at my hands, at the book of pictures, at the skinny, bushy-haired child in the photo. A child who wouldn't speak, wouldn't eat, who filled her pockets with seashells: tiny ones, no bigger than her little fingernail. The girl who took that photo was fourteen years old. She walked on the brown sand in her bare feet. She was good at reading stories. And somebody bought her train tickets; somebody picked her up, in their car, in Shellingsby, to take her . . . where? To a train? Here? To the old-fashioned peeling-painted canopy of an end-of-the-line station? Or somewhere else altogether?

I turn the page. There's a thrill of goosebumps along the back of my neck, like someone's there. But no one's there; it's just the wind in the dunes. I scan over the photos, heart thumping. Maybe the messages *are* threats; maybe I should be terrified, maybe I really *shouldn't* go back to the house.

Or maybe, just maybe, someone is trying to warn me off in the only way they know. There has never been a broken window or a forced entry. The alarm has never gone off. My father left the locks unchanged and the codes the same for twenty-five years so that if she ever came back, she would be able to get in.

Is it too much to imagine . . .

"Rosy."

I leap almost off the bench. The album falls from my lap, its pages splaying on the sandy concrete.

"Christ, I'm sorry." Josh drops to his knees to pick it up. "I didn't mean to frighten you. I messaged you. I thought you must have seen it and that's why you were here."

His eyes fall for a moment on the pages. Beer and Babycham. I see him swallow. He passes it back without comment as I slide to my feet.

Here? My face must betray my puzzlement.

"I was on the golf course when I got your message. Bloody awful signal, maybe my reply didn't send. I suggested we meet at the seafront. I wanted to show you somewhere . . . fuck, this whole conversation's backwards now." He pushes his Ray-Bans back through his hair. "Shall we sit, or walk? I could do with starting at the beginning. And you said there was something you wanted to ask?"

"Oh. Yeah." I did say that. But in person, the question seems much less askable. I wet my lips. "It can wait. You go first."

"Sure." He pauses. "Shall we?"

He gestures at the promenade. I dust the sand from my clothes.

"Can I carry anything?" Josh glances at the photo album.

"Oh, uh, I'm okay. Thanks."

"I bumped into Kacper, actually." Josh pushes his hands into his pockets. His eyes dwell on the album for a second more. "By the playground, with the little boy. Yvan? I wasn't sure . . . Is he . . . ?"

"He's from Ukraine. Him and his grandmother."

"I'd heard a rumour. Miller's hosting them? He keeps things quiet. I wanted to know if I could help."

I look up at his earnestness, the untidy fold-back of his expensive shirtsleeves.

"Seems like the least I can do." He shrugs. "Is there anything they need?"

"I don't know, specifically. They . . . Actually, Yvan's mum is missing. And his dad was killed. I'm not sure there's anything anyone can do."

"Oh, God," Josh exhales. "*Killed?*"

"In Bakhmut."

"Jesus Christ . . ." Josh tails off. It turns out I'm not the only one who has no idea what to say.

I let my eyes wander over the deserted beach and empty promenade. For a warm May day, the place is oddly desolate. There's an aching silence.

"Do they come up to the beach?" Josh's question takes me by surprise.

"The beach?"

"The little boy and his granny."

"Oh . . . yeah. Yvan likes it. It seems to take his mind off things."

"Yeah." Josh nods. "Yeah, I get that."

"Is it always this quiet here?"

"Pretty much, this far out of town. Place is full of pensioners, not many people make it out here on foot. The mobility scooters don't tend to do well on that last set of steps."

I can't help but smile. "It's pretty, don't get me wrong."

Josh smiles too. "Mm. We spent a lot of time up here as teenagers."

"You and Leonie?"

"And Zachary. One or two of the others. Actually, that's sort of what I wanted to show you. When I saw Kacper with his little Ukrainian boy, I had an idea. I didn't know if it would be any good to them . . . but, I've got a hut, up here on the South Prom. Not far from the edge of the golf course. I appreciate it's a long walk, and it must need some work — I haven't been in it for years — but I'm still paying the licence, and if they wanted to use it, it would be . . . well, it would be great for it to have a new lease of life."

I think of the dim light of the bungalow, the heavy feeling of loss that somehow lingers in the borrowed furniture.

"That's . . ." I don't know what to say. "That's amazing. Thank you. I'll ask Iryna. I think . . . I think they'd love that."

"It's nothing. For everything they've been through, it's not much, but if it'll help, then they can use it as much as they want. You can see what you think — it's not much further up here."

He nods ahead, to where a cluster of huts huddle together on a terrace with wooden rails, and a distinct lack of bunting. They're all shuttered, and have been for a long time, hinges and padlocks rusted, peaked asbestos roofs discoloured and dark, lichenified like Hailbury's ageing statues. There are weeds growing between the concrete slabs as Josh leads the way onto the terrace and fights with the padlock of the middle hut.

"Dad bought it when we started at Queen Victoria." He wins the fight with the padlock and starts a new one with the bar across the front of the shutters. It gives suddenly, and he stumbles.

"We came here a lot, as kids. Leonie and me, and the others. They were good times. Campfires, underage beer." He grins sheepishly. "But it stopped being cool to her eventually. When she was off to London or Paris or Italy at the weekends."

I look back at the beach. The patch of sand in front of the terrace is sheltered on both sides by dunes, a smooth hollow filled with sunshine.

"Then, after. . ." There's a waver in Josh's expression. "I just couldn't bring myself to come back, really. And I'm too sentimental to bloody sell it. So there you go. Here it is."

I stand back as he pulls open the shutters. It isn't picturesque, but it's peaceful, shady and dry, despite the musty smell of disuse that hovers heavy, like at Hailbury. The floor is wooden and sandy; the walls are clad in pine boards that feel as though they should have faded but have been in darkness for so long that they're unchanged. There's a bench with a cushioned seat, a kitchenette with a gas ring, a folding table and deck chairs stacked against the wall. A lot of cobwebs. Josh brushes them aside with his arm, shoes crunching. He pauses, and something in his expression sends a shiver through me; he's staring in silence, uncharacteristically still. I can't tell if he's looking at me, or through me.

The chime of a bike-bell on the prom seems to jolt him back to life. He glances around at the four walls.

"Sorry." He clears his throat. There are wooden double doors in the back wall too, and he moves to try the different keys.

"Christ, I've forgotten which one even unlocks this. Here. Oops. Aha."

He throws them open, letting in a stream of late spring sunshine. We look out onto a patch of uneven paving, fenced-off and empty. Beyond it, a bank of sand and scrub slopes steeply down to what looks like it was once another car park, its surface broken and riddled with weeds. There's an old, graffitied shipping container with a boarded-up window, professing to sell coffee and bacon rolls, and at the far end of the overgrown concrete there's a building with steel sheets over its windows and a rotting sand-blasted sign: *The King Edward Arms*.

"That's the nature reserve." Josh points to our left instead, where a dusty track separates the deteriorating concrete from an expanse of reeds. "Salt marshes. Lots of rare species, apparently. I think they've opened a visitors' centre at the other end, up near Charnsby Point, for birdwatchers. And the golf course isn't far, up there."

I can't really see what he's pointing at. There doesn't seem to be any civilisation for miles. Gulls and seabirds swoop low over the rippling reeds. There's a tang of stale salt and mud on the air, but a brisk breeze blowing between the beach huts. With the front and back doors open, the hut is transformed, full of rippling light. I imagine buckets of shells, spades and sandcastles, a football. Iryna obsessively brushing the floor and Yvan playing in the dunes.

"I think they'd love it here," I tell him.

"Ask them." He shrugs. "Bring them. Like I said, they're welcome. It would be great for someone to make use of it."

"What do you remember about the car?" I ask, while he's still looking the other way.

Josh turns back.

"The . . ."

"The car. The one that Leonie got in."

"Rosy," he starts. Then stops. There's a lingering silence. He squares his shoulders.

"I remember everything about it, actually. Except the reg plates, I wasn't close enough to see them properly, but they started with an L. It was dark red. It had a bumper sticker. It pulled up with its wheels on the kerb. I've dreamt about it for twenty years."

"Could you see anyone inside it?" I whisper.

"Rosy." There's a note of foreboding in his voice. "What—"

"It doesn't matter." I shake my head. Look out at the salt marsh, at a hovering bird, trembling on a swell of wind.

"Did *you* know about her photography?"

"Photography?" he asks softly. "You mean photography, or modelling? Everyone knew about her modelling. But she did have a camera. She pretty much always had it with her. She'd snap anything."

"I've looked for it everywhere. But I can't find it."

"What, the camera?" There's the tiniest flicker of a frown on Josh's forehead. "Don't your parents have it?"

"Did you know she was meeting up with someone about it?"

He narrows his eyes. "Meeting someone?"

"The photographer who took those pictures for L'Église. My parents didn't know."

There's a loaded pause. Josh studies me, eyes sharp.

"She was meeting up with her photographer? Without anyone knowing?"

There's a flash of something across his face, a reaction, an emotion that isn't quite disguised.

"How did you . . . How did you find out?"

"He lives in Skegness."

"In Skeg . . . hang on. What?"

"I met him. My mother wanted me to interview him. She had no idea. He changed his name, Tony Lawrence, Antonio DiPaci. He's the same person. He told me about how they used to meet up; Leonie would send him films to develop. I wondered whether you knew."

It goes without saying that he didn't. Josh breathes out hard. He rubs his chin, and I see his hand drift to his phone.

I can't help noticing as he pulls it out that there are messages on his home screen from Kacper Miller. I try not to look like I've seen. Why would Kacper be messaging him?

"Is that what this is?" Josh reaches for the book, and I let him take it. He's turned off the screen of the phone; I can't see what they said. "Her photos?"

"Some of them," I concede.

It's there again, in his face. A twist of memory. Something sharper. Pain? He takes the book inside, and I hover in the doorway as he flaps the cover open.

"That's Zach." A breath of reluctant laughter falls from his lips. "And me. And this is . . . this is you?"

I curl my toes inside my pumps. I don't look at the album, or at his face.

"This is crazy," he says. I watch him turn the pages, slowly, almost reverently. "I . . . I had no idea . . ."

His hand has drifted to his mouth, curling into a fist against his lips. White knuckles that betray his composure.

"God . . ."

I see him swallow.

"God, Rosy, I miss her."

The heavy feeling of loss. I look at him, and I realise it's everywhere, not just at the bungalow. At Kacper's cottage, *alone in the world at twenty-two*. At Hailbury. Here.

"I know," I exhale. "Me too."

* * *

I walk back to my car with my headphones in my ears and her songs streaming on my phone. Songs about faking it. Songs about running away. There's a recovery truck parked on the slipway and a group of teenagers in the playground, drinking alcopops in the noon sun and passing round a vape. It's got hot. By the time I approach the beach car park I'm sticky all over. I stop in the shade of the station canopy to take out my water bottle, swigging from it with an odd feeling of unease.

I pull out the headphones, but there's nothing to hear. Just the distant repartee of the kids in the park and the suck of the rising tide at the sand. I struggle out of my cardigan, wipe the sweat from my top lip. Through the barb-topped bars of the station fence, I can see the tracks, riddled with litter and purple-flowered plants that grow from the ballast. The timetable has one arrival and one departure a day. If you leave, you can't come back.

The chill recurs, rippling my arms and the back of my neck. I glance around at the one or two other cars.

My phone chimes. I start, and my bottle hits the tarmac with a crack.

A message.

The bottle has broken. Water is bleeding around my feet from the fractured plastic. I stoop to pick it up.

It's a text message, not a DM. I've deleted my social media accounts, created a new email address, a new Rosalie K-L. I open it.

Your pictures are ready. Can you collect?

Antonio DiPaci. *Tony Lawrence*. As if he's read my mind. As if he saw us there, in the shadows of the desolate beach hut, the skinny-limbed child and the heir apparent, staring at our own histories. Can I collect? The chill has spread from my arms to my insides. A ripple of apprehension and urgency.

Yes.

Today?

I stare at the screen. At my thumbs on the letters.
Someone knew. Someone who had a credit card in 2003.

Yes.

330

CHAPTER 33

You've taught me more than they ever could.

My keys are in the ignition. I turn them with shaking fingers. The heat inside the car is stifling. *Have you ever been to Skeg?* More than once. Skegness has a station, too.

All the streets are busy with parked cars and draped with Coronation flags, even Antonio DiPaci's, despite its underlying drear. I have to leave my car a good half mile away and walk, my pulse bounding in my throat as I approach the filmy windows and closed blackouts. There's a broken pane of glass in the front door. I falter on the step, overcome with shivers.

So when they're ready . . . I call you? Not Lara? Her agent?

No. Just me.

I raise my fist to knock. The door opens. He doesn't speak. Neither do I. I follow him inside. The soft boxes are on and the computer is off. The desk is in darkness. I trail to a halt.

"What . . . ?" I whisper.

"We need to talk."

Tony gestures at the desk. He pushes a computer chair at me, and I catch it. I can't quite bring myself to sit. He's still standing. In my pocket, my phone starts to ring, vibrating rhythmically. Tony's eyebrows lift. I flick the phone to silent.

"You need to answer it?"

I shake my head.

"I'll call them back."

"It wouldn't be Lara? Her investigator? Her new ghost-writer?" His stare is piercing. "Would it?"

Somehow, I still can't move.

"How do you know—"

"You told them about Leo and her photographs?"

"No."

"Perhaps you should have told *someone* where you are." He takes a sudden step towards me. I freeze, my fingernails digging into the back of the chair.

"Perhaps you shouldn't have come alone?" he suggests. His voice is so soft it's barely audible; my eyes fix his face, heart-throb eyes, strong jaw . . .

"Perhaps we have not been honest with each other, Rosalie."

The phone is ringing again. Pulsing insistently against my leg.

"*Where's my sister*?" I breathe.

Silence. Except the phone; it pauses and starts again. Buzzing, buzzing, it won't stop . . .

"You should get that," Tony observes.

I'm suddenly afraid to take it out. I slip it from my pocket. *Kacper*. I press to end the call, feeling Tony's eyes on me as I type.

I can't pick up. I'm in Skeg. I'll explain in a bit.

"Tell him where you are. Give my name. Why not? That will be safer for both of us, Rosalie. We are both good at protecting ourselves, are we not?"

"*What*?" At last, I find my voice. I let go of the chair and face him. "What are you talking about?"

"Whatever your speculation, I don't know the answer to your question. I don't know where she is. But you were right, she did talk to me. She did tell me. She wanted me to drive her to Sheffield, two days before she went missing. And I refused.

She tried to negotiate — a lift to Lincoln, or here, to Skegness, instead. Still, I refused. It was my mistake. I protected myself, and not her. Just as your parents protected you."

"Wait. You mean—"

"Institutionalised, hey? Leo was heartbroken. She blamed herself."

"I don't understand," I whisper. "She told you?"

"She told *us*," he corrects me.

"Who?"

"These are the photos that Leonie took." He reaches the desk in a single stride and slides an envelope along it; A4, *fragile, do not bend*. I hesitate.

"Go ahead."

It isn't sealed. The prints inside are glossier than the ones in the album, newer, untouched, and there are negatives folded in a white paper pocket behind them. I draw them out. Tony flicks on the lights.

The girl with blue eyes looks back at me, the girl from the photo booth. She's in the countryside; there's a glow in her cheeks and an unbridled joy in her smile. Behind her, a horse is cantering. I still don't really understand. I take out the next one. Phoenix, the palomino showjumper, caught mid-toss of his head; it must have been spring, judging by the blossom on the soft-focus trees.

The next one. The seafront at Summercliffe-on-Sea, an arty, edgy black-and-white shot with brooding clouds and angry water. The next, a fire on a beach, a crowd of blurred-out faces, two boys in the forefront, in the dark, with hand-rolled cigarettes in their mouths and bottles at their feet — they're in focus when everyone else isn't — the heir apparent and the boy from the arm-wrestle. His face strikes a sudden chord of familiarity.

The next two or three were snapped at a party; a mass of people, dancing, close-crushed. A refracted disco light in a smoky room. A spilled bottle of red drink on the floor, like blood.

And then it's the blue-eyed girl again, sat side-saddle on a magnificent black horse with a tightly braided mane, her dusty-blonde hair blowing behind her. This time she's looking straight into the camera, unsmiling and beautiful.

"Who is she?"

Tony doesn't reply. There are two left. Taken in the mirror. A boyish Leonie, her long hair scooped in a tight ponytail, a ring through her tragus, the camera artfully obscuring her face other than the pout of her red, red mouth. Leonie, writing backwards on the mirror with crimson lipstick: *destiny? not anymore*

I lower them uncertainly to the desk. Antonio DiPaci is watching me. Destiny? I frown.

"There's something more you need to see." He still doesn't answer my question. "Those were Leonie's pictures. These . . ." He produces a ribbon-bound book from under the desk. "These are the shots she and I did during her Easter break, before she disappeared."

The pause is tangible. I look down at the satin card, the pristine paper.

"I didn't know there was another shoot."

"No one knew there was another shoot." Tony puts out a hand to lean heavily on the desk. "No one but the three of us."

"Three . . ." I turn over the cover, not quite grasping. Three. The setting is familiar. The apple crates. The curiosities.

"You were *here*?"

"This was my mother's house." Tony's voice is flat, hard to read. "Where I grew up. This was where my work started."

"You were in Skegness when Leonie disappeared."

"No," he says sharply. "No. I was in London. I had been in Skegness. I spent Easter in Skegness at Leo's request. To do these. Probably the best photos I have ever taken. The best art I ever created. And nobody has ever seen them. Not even her. I was too late."

Too late. I gaze at them, at the two of them, my sister and her blue-eyed stranger. At the truth unravelling itself across the silk paper.

The photos are a different calibre to Leonie's pictures. Hers were snaps, unrefined visions. These are something else. Even the word art doesn't quite do them justice. They're paintings in higher definition than the human eye. They're momentary masterpieces, angled creations of darkness and light, of essence and emotion. Of interlinked arms, hands on protruding hips, lips on skin. White long-sleeved T-shirts and dark-blue ripped jeans. I suck in a sharp breath.

They're sensual, beautiful, exuding intimacy without a millimetre of indecency. Rebellion without a hint of wrong. They're kissing, for the camera, fingers entwined in flowing tresses, tender-eyed tension, parted lips. Leonie, with her new edgy look; piercings, smoky eyes. Leonie, her fingers curled through the handle of the scissors as she hacks off her braid, her bright green gaze locked on the lens, loose strands unwinding, massacred, at her feet. *destiny? not anymore*

I've come to a dead stop.

"You see now why I kept these hidden? I wished to God I'd never taken them. How would it have looked for me? When these materialised, when people came asking questions? I would have been incriminated without a second thought.

"Leo wanted them to be public. She wanted them to be controversial. We argued about it . . . and then she was gone."

"Who . . . *is* this? Who was she?" I can't drag my eyes from the last picture. From the waterfall of dusty-blonde hair contrasting with Leonie's hacked-back brown. From the happiness shining, vulnerable and unguarded, in my sister's eyes. From the gentleness in the entangled fingers, the brush of lips against a glowing cheek. My eyes are burning and my throat is thick. I try to swallow it and fail; it wells, unfettered, to the surface, and I scrub my eyes with the heel of my hand.

I won't give up if you won't. Wherever you end up, I'll find you, ok?

Antonio DiPaci lets out a slow breath. He seems to deflate, as he does. Shrinking, sinking into the shadows, the faded curiosities and the apple crates. I notice for the first time the hipflask beside the computer.

"Tessa Whittaker. Tess." He's turned away. Something seems to have fallen from him, some weight that hasn't so much lifted as shifted, and now he's lost his anchor.

"Where is she?"

"I don't know."

"She was local?"

"Local to Leonie, yes."

"What happened to her?"

"I said." He wheels around suddenly. "I don't *know*."

Tessa Whittaker. I dash the tears viciously from my face.

"Why should I believe you? You lied about Leonie. How should I know you're not lying about *her*, too?"

"Her family moved her away that Easter. The day after we finished the shoot."

"Where?"

"Somewhere . . ." He breathes out heavily. "Somewhere near Sheffield."

I stare at him. All I can do is stare.

Train tickets. She wanted him to drive her. He refused.

Which means . . .

Tony starts violently at the rap on the door. I drop the book onto the desk, a tang of fear in my mouth. For long moments, Tony doesn't move. He doesn't go to answer it. The knock comes again, louder, an insistent hammering. He picks up the flask from the desk and unscrews the lid with unsteady fingers. I watch him throw back a mouthful before he turns, his feet soundless on the floor as he strides to the door and tugs it open.

"We are closed," he mutters.

"Where's Rosalie? Is she here?"

My heart lurches at the sound of the voice. *Kacper*.

"Where is she?"

"It depends who is asking, *Woźniak*."

I snatch my breath. There's a lingering silence. For a stomach-dropping moment, I remember the caption on the picture from the orangery.

He's grim, conflicted, a flash of warning in his charcoal gaze as Tony steps back to let him in.

"Rosy," he breathes. "What're you . . . ?"

I go to him. His grip moves up my arms, before he reins it back with evident effort.

"What . . ." It's a grimace more than a word. "What were you *thinking*?"

"He developed the pictures. Leonie's pictures."

"And you didn't . . ." He breathes out, hard. "Never mind."

Antonio DiPaci's eyes are on us.

"You thought, perhaps, that I would put her into my car and drive away never to be heard from again?" His bushy eyebrows have lifted; there's a note of undisguised bitterness in his voice. I feel Kacper bristle.

"We are done here, Rosalie," Tony says flatly.

"Tessa Whittaker," I start. "You said—"

"Thank you for your time in coming." He punches the button on the remote and the blackouts creep up the windows, letting the rays of sunshine flood the desk. I squint.

"But . . ." I'm clutching at straws. "Don't you think she should have them? The pictures? Isn't that what Leonie wou—"

"Take them." The bitterness escapes, unconcealed, in his laugh.

I pick up the book, fingers trembling.

"Take them." Tony shakes his head. Then he turns away, his broad shoulders sagging in silhouette against the window as he unscrews the lid from his flask. "Better if you have them. Better that I never set eyes on them again."

"Do you think she did?" I ask suddenly.

Tony spins. "Did what?"

"Run away."

"She was young. She was in love." His eyes flicker from me to Kacper's undisguisedly clenched fists.

"I think she tried," he says.

* * *

337

Tessa Whittaker.

I pace from one end of the cottage to the other, weighing up the phone in my hand.

Tessa Whittaker: T-W@*triggerwarning*. She was trying to contact me. She has been for weeks. I unlock my phone for the hundredth time and stare at the faded colours of the postcard. I deleted my account, created a new one: ROSY@*thelittlesister*. I can't see her messages anymore.

Maybe Antonio DiPaci is telling the truth when he says he doesn't know what happened to her. I'm not really sure who to go to for the truth. But I might know how to find her.

My heart beats a drumroll in my chest as I open the app.

I walk to the extension and stand by the doors. It's half past five. The garden looks like Eden in the dawn light, out of reach on the other side of the glass.

Sure enough, her handle brings up her profile: T-W@ *triggerwarning*. I compose a DM and read it back to myself over and over again, until my palms are sweating and I've memorised every word. Then I press send.

I sit on the edge of the sofa. No one's going to reply at quarter to six in the morning. I try to think of a distraction: the deadlines I've missed, the work I could be doing instead of sitting and staring. But every fibre of me is taut, pent up. I go to the hall. I need to get out. To clear my head, in the fresh air where the birdsong will drive away the silence.

I change into my shorts and hoody. The memory of Hailbury's perimeter and the crashing footfalls behind me in the trees should put me off, but it doesn't. I summon wild, heart-pounding imaginings instead: of turning back instead of running. Of catching a glimpse of who was there, an arc of fanned-out chocolate hair . . .

She was young. She was in love . . .

I was right. Kacper couldn't access the CCTV. The DVR is fire-damaged, the data irretrievable. I stoop to lace up my trainers, and take the keys from the hook beside the front door. Upstairs, the floorboards creak.

"Rosy."

He appears before I'm quite prepared. His jeans were pulled on in a rush, his chest is bare, arms folded and tense.

"I'm just . . . going for a quick run." It sounds less than sensible even as I say it. I slip the key into my pocket and we both look down.

"It's five to six."

"Yeah."

We stand a pace apart. His silence speaks a thousand words. Words about murdered dolls and death threats. I swallow.

"I need to get out," I mumble. "I need to, I just—"

Kacper moves to block my path. His hands around my wrists are gently firm.

"Listen to me," he breathes. "Please. I don't think it's a good idea."

"Come with me, then."

"Rosalie." His voice is grim.

"Or squash?" I can hear my own desperation. "We didn't go last night."

I can sense the upward flicker of his brows.

"It's not even morning. The leisure centre doesn't open until half six."

"Please? It won't be far off?"

I can see the frustration that glances across his face, the tiniest shake of his head. I want to drive away the clouds from his eyes, but I don't know how. He goes to get changed, and I turn the phone over and over in my hands.

The leisure centre car park is empty. We park right by the doors. There are two hardcore swimmers doing lengths in the pool, a lone devotee in the gym. The squash courts are in semi-darkness. Kacper flicks the light switch and waits for me to unzip my racquet case.

"Do you want to take first serve?"

"No," I whisper. "We can spin."

He wins. I watch him serve, watch the breath he sucks between his teeth. He hits hard; the crack of the ball echoes around us like a gunshot. I stumble.

Kacper serves again. This time I slice it back and we rally. He takes a second point and I realise I'm already out of breath.

Another serve. The force through his racquet is unrestrained, his whole arm rigid. I chase down the shot, flick the ball low into the front right. He dives in, I sidestep for a return that never comes, and we crash into each other a metre in front of the wall.

Kacper's racquet clatters to the floor.

And then I'm between his arms, my heels against the tin. My back hits the wall.

"What the fuck are we doing here?" he pants.

I drop my racquet. His expression is darkness manifest.

"You're beating me at squash," I retort. But my response is breathy. Suddenly unsure.

"No," he growls. "Fuck this. Fuck this, Rosalie. I can't. I can't *do* this anymore."

Something cold penetrates my chest. Something worse than the fear of Hailbury and its shadows. I glance up at his face. The rise and fall of his chest is laboured, forceful.

"I don't know how to keep you safe anymore."

"You don't have to."

"Don't you get it?" His jaw clenches, unclenches, the muscles working furiously. "How can you still not get it?"

His hands close around my upper arms, his forehead close to mine. I can taste the sweat on my lips, the desperation in his words.

"You're driving me out of my *mind.*"

"I—"

"It could have been him, Rosalie! The photographer. It could have been him, and you just walked in."

"But it wasn't."

"You don't even know that."

"Why would he have lied?"

"*Rosalie* . . ."

I reach my mouth for his. I press a kiss to his lips and feel him inhale and move against me.

Then he baulks, breaks away. He snatches his racquet from the floor.

"It's time to go," he says.

I pick up my racquet, too, and the ball from the floor. I watch him turn, his fist clenched around the grip so hard that his knuckles are white. My heart is pounding in my chest.

I smack the ball with all the force I can muster, a clean forehand, not even a proper serve. Kacper spins. For a fraction of a second, I think it's going to hit him. Then he leaps backwards, takes the backhand from shoulder-height. I hit a forehand drive and he curses and returns again, a conflict of expressions crossing his face.

I don't know how long it lasts. I'm gasping, incoherent; he's breathless, sweating, his T-shirt plastered to his skin. I don't even know who wins. The ball goes out of play, and I slump against the glass. Kacper presses his hands to his knees. Somewhere in the corridor behind us, his phone is ringing, the gentle ricochet of an alarm clock that echoes in the emptiness, and I realise it's his alarm for work.

It's hot in the pickup, suffocating. Kacper winds down the windows as we set off, both of us winded and silent.

He opens the cottage's gate instead of the front door, and I collapse, hot and exhausted, on the grass. The sun is just warming the borders, awakening the colours. Behind us, a sea of forget-me-nots spills from a bank of wildflowers. He sits down beside me with his arm around his knees.

"I'm sorry," I whisper.

"This is fucked up." His voice is raw, broken. "It's too fucked up. Whatever happened to her, to my father . . . it's not worth this. They're gone. You're not. Jesus Christ, Rosalie, I thought . . ." He lets go of his knees, turns to face me. "When I got your message, when I realised where you'd gone, I thought—"

"I know." The rush of the breeze through the leaves almost swallows my confession. "I did, too, for a moment."

My hair has blown across my face. I reach to push it back, but he gets there first, curling it around his fingers.

"She was your sister, I get that, but—"

"But what if she's still out there?" I blurt. It sounds stupid, out loud. Worthy of my father. Like I think I can exonerate myself, both of us, all of us.

"And even if she's not . . . I . . ." I falter. "I want to tell the truth. My whole life has just been a cover-up. It's down to me to write her story. To tell people who she actually was."

His mouth has set tight. And for a second, I'm not looking at Kacper Miller. I'm looking at the skinny boy in the cloakroom, quiet and motionless in the face of his tormentors. Suddenly my heart is hurting.

"You're putting yourself at risk." His fingers are tight in my hair, almost too tight. "I know I said you could be anything . . . but don't. Please, just . . . *don't*. It was bad enough when you were in London, when I thought you'd left. And the worst thing was . . ."

He releases me suddenly.

"The worst thing was, I knew I should let you. I still know it. That I should let you go, fuck I should *make* you go, because at least you'd be safe."

"No," I breathe. "I wouldn't. I told you, I—"

"But you're going to write the book, and then you will? You'll go back."

I glance up, thrown.

"I . . ." It emerges as a croak. "I don't know, I . . . guess I always thought I would. "

"If . . ." He pauses. And the set of his jaw pulls me up short. "If I said I don't want you to, would that change anything?"

The pain in my throat is unbearable. Does he really not already know?

"It would change everything," I whisper.

"Then I don't want you to."

"Ohh." I hear the air rush between my lips.

And then we're lying in the grass, a sea of forget-me-nots bluer than the May sky, and at last his lips find mine. There's a fresh breeze through the leaves, a ripple through the plants and petals that close ranks to guard our Eden. To keep us from the world.

I have no other words. No other answer. None that he can't read, like the true colours behind the stained glass. The urgency swells between us, an advancing tide, until the first wave breaks, the desperate crash of mouths, the tug of hungry hands on clothes, the sweet engulfing surge of touch obliterating everything else: the fear, the loss. Other people's stories.

He kisses me again. And his arms are trembling, and the urgency in his restraint might break my heart.

It would change everything.

CHAPTER 34

Tess Whittaker lives near a place called Sutton-in-Ashfield. She runs a riding school. We exchanged numbers last night and she sent me her address. I didn't ask her where my sister is. I didn't ask her how they've kept it a secret for all this time. I didn't ask her if she knew who was trying to scare me away from Hailbury.

Because Leonie loved me. She put story books on my shelves and she read to me by torchlight. She told me to be fearless, so why would she try to scare me away?

I fasten the chain around my neck. The locket feels heavy, weighted down by the memories that were never made. I stare at my reflection.

destiny? not anymore.

The floor in the upstairs of the cottage is uneven: sloping wooden boards that creak as I cross them and descend the stairs.

What if she was, what if she is . . . after everything? What if she *is*?

And if she is, who are we now? Are we still sisters? Would she hold me? Would I sob . . . *sorry, I'm sorry?* Would she tell me — now I'm twenty-seven — would we talk about Paris and cutting our hair? Would I forgive her?

Kacper is pacing the length of the kitchen counter. He looks up as I come in, pushing his hands into his pockets. It's an attempt at nonchalance that neither of us is buying. Because from the age of sixteen, Tess Whittaker worked as a stable hand for Jeanette Miller. Tess Whittaker knew his father.

"Shall we?" he says. I nod. I slip my hand into his pocket, too, and he holds it tight.

He drives and I open my laptop on my knees, nauseated by the twists and undulations in the rural roads, and type an email to Tabitha: an outline, the opening three chapters, like I've stepped back in time to the days of stamped self-addressed envelopes. Except now everything's at stake. If she agrees to this — this tangle of truths, this carefully worded dance around my mother's lawyers — we're both crazy.

We stop at Lincoln for fuel and petrol-station coffee, followed by a brief respite of dual carriageway. I close my emails and try to piece together my overdue Coronation-week commentary about the cost of bunting and strawberry Pimm's versus mortgages. But my mind is elsewhere, and the dual carriageway doesn't last, and after a few minutes I succumb to the scenery and carsickness and stare out of the window instead.

The sky darkens as we head west, through mining towns with wheels and towers, pebbledash and pregnant clouds. Trees queue on the hillsides, crowding slowly into forests, vast dark swathes of pine and older thickets of oak and ash that bring to mind feathered hats and archers. Wind turbines in a valley ahead circle their blades into our path, slicing the expectant air in lethargic, relentless rhythm, until the road drops and we pass between them. I slide my computer into my satchel. Amidst the industrial units and warehouses of another exhausted pit town, I can't help wondering how easy it would be to hide in plain sight. To become somebody else.

We skim the outskirts of the town and emerge back into patchwork fields and copses, a decadent equestrian landscape that contrasts with the smoke-stained semis and council houses. We turn onto a track at the edge of a village, a muddy dead-end driveway to three attached cottages. The last one has a vast garden and a block-paved patio. We pull to a halt.

More than one person lives here. There are two cars outside. A horsebox, two upturned pairs of women's boots on the stand beside the door. There's a house number, a picture of a phoenix on the gatepost.

I realise my hands are shaking.

I get down from the truck to knock. Kacper is close beside me. His hope for this is not the same as mine.

There's an eruption of barking, the skitter of claws and the thump of tails. A firm voice, a dash of legs. The door opens.

The woman who answers has ashy-blonde hair pulled into a ponytail, a warm, slightly weather-beaten face. Her eyes are vivid blue. We regard each other for a moment without any words at all. Her gaze travels to Kacper.

"Come in, please," she says. "Don't worry about your shoes. Are you okay with dogs? I can shut them in the utility."

Before there's a real chance to answer, they swarm around us, three hunting dogs with bright eyes and long swishing tails.

"Yeah," I manage. "No worries."

"Come through." She gestures into the kitchen. There's a table with a fruit bowl in front of the doors onto the patio, its block-paving almost invisible beneath plant pots, furniture, dog toys.

"I'm Tee. Tess." Her eyes are on my face. "You're Rosalie." It isn't a question. "And . . ." She looks again at Kacper. A long, penetrating look. He doesn't flinch.

"Kacper," he provides impassively. His grip on me hasn't loosened. I duck free of it to take a seat at the table.

"Can I get either of you a drink?"

"Tea, please. Milk, no sugar."

"No, thanks."

I glance up at him. His face still isn't giving anything away. Tess goes to put the kettle on.

"How was your drive?"

"It was fine, thanks." I glance around at the warm, untidy kitchen. "The roads are definitely better this side of Lincoln."

Tess pauses.

"You came from Hailbury."

"From Shellingsby."

She nods. I watch her stir the tea. There's a little black star on the inside of her wrist. She carries the tea over.

"Help yourselves to biscuits. You met Tony DiPaci, then?" She sits down in the seat opposite me. "I wasn't even sure that he was still alive."

Her observation is unnerving. Why wouldn't he be? I take a digestive, frowning.

"I never heard a word from him." She pauses, then qualifies her statement. "Since the day I left his studio twenty years ago."

I. I study her face. Not *we.* *She* never heard a word from him. And what about Leonie? The elephant in the room is growing larger and larger. Where is she? Is she going to walk in, a wordless surprise, her green eyes wide and innocent, a banished Disney princess? The house is silent, aside from the excited patter and snuffle of the dogs running back and forth along the hall.

"Did anyone know?" I lay down my cup on the table. "Did anyone know about you and Leonie? Did anyone come to ask you? You were . . . friends."

Tess laughs softly.

"Officially?" She shakes her head. "Officially, I was questioned once. Unofficially, people definitely snooped around for a lot longer than that. And officially, yes, we were friends. Unofficially . . ."

". . . she was seeing someone at the stables," I whisper.

"Yes." Tess's pause is heavy. There are a thousand words behind it. She closes her eyes. When she opens them again, she's not looking at me. "Yes. She was seeing me."

She was questioned once. But no one else knew, because my parents didn't want them to. Because the photos in the media were Leonie Knight-Langton with her glossy hair and her movie-star smile, not sharp-edged Leo with the girl she fell in love with. Once again, my parents lived the lie: the perfect family, no nonconformity. I'm suddenly not hungry. I put down the biscuit.

"I saw the photos. The ones that Tony took. I—" I touch the strap of my satchel. The weight of the book inside it lays heavy against my legs. Beside me, Kacper is unmoving. Listening, without a word. His fingers grip the edges of his seat.

"There was a lot of trouble. Behind closed doors." Tess has put down her cup, too. I see her gaze drift to Kacper again, astute.

"When her — your — parents found out, they would have had me in court. She was fourteen. I was eighteen. It was illegal for me to love her. But it wasn't like that. Nothing ever . . . It wasn't. They didn't understand. Leo was beautiful. Sassy, clever . . . uncontainable. In her head, she was so much older than fourteen. We talked for hours and hours. It was never anything more than a kiss."

I look at the faint creases around Tess's eyes, the fullness of her lips, remembering the waterfall of dusty blonde, the shining happiness, the entangled fingers. She's wrong. It was so, so much more than a kiss.

"My parents moved me away. The twenty-fourth of April 2003. My dad took a transfer to Sheffield because he knew I couldn't afford to do anything except go with them. We were heartbroken. Leo was heartbroken. I have never forgiven our parents for what happened to her."

I meet her gaze across the table. Her parents. My parents. The ones that made the decisions on everyone else's behalf.

"Leo wanted to run away. I told her that she couldn't come to me because people would find her. I promised her I'd wait for her. And I did." She swallows. "I waited for ten years."

Ten years. I swallow too. Look at the bi-fold doors, the garden. Two pairs of boots . . .

348

Tess shrugs, gestures around her.

"I actually thought she just didn't want to be found. For years . . . I don't know, I . . . I suppose I always thought one day she might get in touch. Even when I first met Carly, I still couldn't stop looking back. Wondering . . ."

"You're telling us you don't know where she went?" Kacper breaks in suddenly. "When you were probably the one person she would have told?"

Tess Whittaker looks back at him with fiery-bright blue eyes.

"She got in a man's car," she says.

Deadlock. They gaze at each other across the table. Kacper's brows flicker a fraction downwards. Tess's lift. There's silence.

"So I've heard," he replies levelly.

Tess doesn't lower her brows. She addresses me, but she's still looking at him.

"I had no reason to doubt that she did, Rosalie. No one could seem to figure out why she'd have got in a car with Tofs. But it was obvious to me. Tofs would have done anything for anyone. He wouldn't have said no, if she'd asked him. If he'd thought she needed help."

Kacper's teeth are gritted.

Tess holds the gaze squarely. "And he most certainly would never have taken Leo anywhere against her will."

"But you didn't tell anybody that." Kacper's voice is a growl. I want to touch him, but he's still gripping the chair, his knuckles white, arms rigid.

"How could I? I thought I knew where she was trying to go. I believed, for days, that she'd turn up on my doorstep. If she *had* . . ." She trails off.

"The train tickets," I exhale. "She'd got train tickets."

"Vesna bought them for her. You must remember her. She was your au pair. She bought them so Leo could come to Sheffield on her birthday. I'd got us tickets to a matinee at the Crucible. She wanted to come on the twenty-eighth instead and sleep over, but Vesna said no, she couldn't cover for her overnight. Leo was going to stay on the number six after it stopped at Queen Victoria on the Tuesday morning, get the train from Summercliffe at ten. She would have been home by evening — hell, I even had cash for the taxi fare to get her back from Skeg. No one would have needed to know, and if they found out, it would only have been a slapped wrist or a grounding — it was worth the risk.

"Vesna called me on the Monday night. We both thought she'd just been defiant — Leo was like that — that she was already on the train somewhere, and she'd pitch up at some stupid time of night. I waited . . ."

There's a break in her voice that takes me off guard. A wobble, a memory, unrepressed and excruciating.

"I waited on Sheffield station for most of the night. She never came."

One of the dogs has slunk between the table legs to rest its head against her. Tess fondles its ears, and I see the muscles tighten in her throat. Kacper gets suddenly to his feet.

"I need to take a call," he says. "Excuse me."

I watch him cross the floor, phone in hand. I'm not even sure that it rang, but the screen is backlit. The dog lifts its head at the bang of the door. I look back at Tess.

"Carly?" I ask at last. Not because I really need to know, but because the silence is suddenly too empty and the air seems to ache with it.

"We got married in 2014." Tess smiles, although the ache doesn't seem to have receded.

"Does she . . ."

"We talk about Leo often." Tess strokes the dog's head. "If that's what you're asking. She was a huge part of my life. Carly gets that. She's important to both of us, in a silly way; it doesn't make a great deal of sense, I know. But love rarely does."

I can't think of a reply. I look at the tangle of weeds outside the glass doors, the forget-me-nots fighting their way through the grass stems. My drink has gone cold. I hug my arms around my chest.

350

"He's Tofs' kid?"

Tess's voice startles me. I glance back.

"Kacper."

I nod.

She leans her elbows on the table to regard me. "He knows something."

"I'm sorry?" I look up sharply. "What?"

"He knows something. It's in his eyes. You can't tell me you don't see it." She raises her eyebrows at me. "You and he are . . . ? Right?"

"I . . ."

"Fuck." Suddenly her face has lit up. Laughter pulls at her lips. "Your parents must *really* love that. Seriously. Rosalie, you've made my year."

And I realise, out of nowhere, that I like her. Even if I've only known her for half an hour. Her frankness, her sharp eyes, the unrefined edges of her humour, shining not-quite-censored from the tiny dimples in her cheeks. She despises my parents. Against all odds, I find myself smiling too.

Tess shakes her head. "He reminds me of Tofs. Just . . . darker. Angrier."

"It's hardly surprising," I point out softly. "Is it?"

"Christ." She's still shaking her head. "No. My oldest is nine. I can't even comprehend."

She has kids. It hadn't occurred to me. I scan the room anew, for photos, clues, and they're everywhere. The matted hairbrush on the end of the kitchen counter. The jar of colouring pens on the windowsill. The jumble of paper stuck with magnets in layers over the front of the fridge: gymnastics certificates, a colour-coded timetable, a drawing of a horse. Two girls; they're in a frame beside the phone.

"Olivia." She's seen me looking. "And . . ."

She pauses. I glance back at her. Something in her gaze has shifted.

"And?" I think I already know what she's going to say.

"And Leonie."

For some reason, there's an obstruction in my throat. A welling of emotion that I've never felt, in all the years that she's been gone. My sister. Who, it turns out, I didn't know at all.

* * *

She twirls on the spot: so fast that her hair fans out, chocolate silk, licking at the air like flames. But her face is thin, and her cheeks are gaunt; there's the glitter of a stud in her nose, a ring through her tragus, and the strap of a camera around her neck, hanging empty . . .

"I'm not the person you think I am, Rosalie . . ."

* * *

I start upright. Rain is striking the single glazing. Beside me, Kacper stirs, and I hold myself still, hugging my arms around my chest to control my shivers in an effort not to wake him.

"Rosy?"

He isn't asleep. His voice is husky with tiredness; there's a new scruff of stubble on his jaw, dark rings under his eyes. I lie back down. But my teeth won't stop chattering. The sheets feel damp against my skin.

"I'm okay," I breathe.

"I know." He doesn't believe me. He shifts to surround me. It's dark outside the curtains but there's a bird already singing, a robin or a thrush.

"I was wrong," he whispers at last, and there's something in the way he says it that makes my blood run cold.

"What?"

"About you going back to your flat. I'm not sure you were safe there at all."

"*What?*"

"If she tried to run away, why did she fail?" His eyes are locked on mine.

Why did she fail? I'm motionless, sick to the stomach. I want to pretend that I don't know what he's saying. But I do. *Rosalie, sweetheart. Get in the car.* His eyes are bleak.

"When will you go to the police?"

He sounds exhausted. Defeated. I think about the doll, the messages, the SUV. About Tess Whittaker, waiting at Sheffield station until the early hours of the morning.

"Not yet."

"You think you can find her."

I hesitate.

"I don't know." There's a crack in the curtains; I get up and open them to stare outside at the sunrise bleeding onto the grass. When I turn back, he's watching me. Grey clouds and foreboding.

"Maybe."

* * *

A fire on a beach, blurred-out faces. Two boys, cigarettes, bottles, the heir, the ever-present friend. Leo, Josh and Zachary. A refracted disco light, a smoky room. On closer inspection, there are banners, black and pink balloons, posters of movie ratings: *15*. It was almost her birthday. They had a party . . . It's not Hailbury — Jericho, perhaps? The rooms are vast and the lights are low. Josh would know the answer. I text him to ask. She cut her hair. She was going to the Crucible to watch a play.

The glut of information was too much. Vesna. The train tickets. I still feel nauseated. Even typing it out doesn't help. The words in black and white are more confusing. I thought I'd find her, but I didn't.

I shiver and glance outside at the market square. Harriet isn't here. The man with the beard is behind the bar, and there are no cakes, only croissants. I forgot my laptop charger. There were ghosts at the cottage this morning. A small boy with a lunch box. A fierce-jawed man with a buzzcut and a torch, going out in the dark to look. I couldn't bear it.

Kacper was still hollow-eyed and sleep-deprived when he left for work, explaining something about topsoil and a house down the road. He's been on and off the phone since yesterday; I've caught snatches of his conversations, mutterings about Hailbury, skylights and data recovery that he hasn't elucidated on. The one person who doesn't seem to have called him is Nathan Langton.

I steel myself. My father's number rings out when I dial. When he calls back the vibration of the phone on the tabletop makes me jump.

"Dad."

"Rosy."

The line buzzes with static. Neither of us speaks.

"Rosy?"

"I thought I'd better let you know I'm—"

"I know where you are."

"I'm not at Hailbury."

"I know. You and Miller might not pick up, Rosy, but the cleaners do."

The cleaners. I rub my head.

"You haven't sacked him. You haven't even spoken to him. Why?" It's not the question I meant to ask, but it's there: *I'll do whatever it takes to keep him away from you.* My father pauses. I can sense his fingers on the bridge of his nose. My phone buzzes a notification mid-call.

"Because . . ." Another pause. We're both hanging on what hasn't been said. "Because unlike your mother, I've learnt from my mistakes."

His mistakes? I stand up and stare at the tabletop. At Tess Whittaker's face looking up from the pile of photographs. *I have never forgiven our parents for what happened to her.*

"Krzysztof Woźniak didn't take Leonie," I mumble. The static fills my ears.

"I hope you know what you're doing, Rosy."

"I do." And I'm not the only one who does. I chew my lip. Another buzz. Someone else is trying to get hold of me.

"I've got to go." My laptop dies, the screen turning black. I shut the lid. My hands are shaking. Too much caffeine, not enough food. "I'll call you, sometime."

354

"*Rosy* . . ." There's an ominous note to the word.

"What?"

"Don't trust everything he says to you. I've made my own mistakes. But maybe . . . maybe so did your sister."

"No," I breathe. "Her only mistake was trusting that anyone cared about her happiness. I'm not going to make that one."

"Ro—"

"Bye, Dad."

I end the call. The texts are from Tess. I sit back down on the edge of my seat to read them. She's gone to see Tony, after all this time. Will I be at Hailbury this afternoon if she comes over afterwards?

I left her the book of the Easter shoot. I felt like it was hers to keep, not mine. There's a letter at Hailbury that belongs to her, too. She at least needs to read it.

I pack up the laptop and go outside. There was no space in the car park; the recreation ground is full of marquees and market stalls. More bunting, miles and miles of bunting, fluttering like trapped butterflies. I start back towards the side road where I left my car, typing a reply to Tess.

"*Uff.*" All of the air seems to leave my body. I've walked into someone, the jolt of contact knocking me backwards. "Oh God, I'm so sorr— Stefan?"

What?

A thrill of fear runs the length of my spine.

"Rosalie?" His eyes dart in all directions. "It *is* you!"

He leans forwards to embrace me, and I take a step away, the feeling of ill ease stealing outwards to my extremities. Stefan. In *Armsby*? I haven't seen him, other than on Zoom, in years. He's thinner than I remember and his tie is out of place in the rural sunshine.

"I was about to message you, darling." He recovers his cool. "I'm staying in a little hotel, just up the way."

"Why?" I blurt.

For a second, he seems thrown by the question.

"Oh, you know, clarifying a few things for Lara. The biography's in full flight — oh, sorry. . ." He breaks off, as if judging my expression. There's no apology in his tone. Clarifying things for my mother. My mother has had no interest in Hailbury for over a decade. There's a tingling in my lips. I stare at him, lightheaded. She sent him?

"Oh, it's not a problem." My voice is shaking. "I've ended up quite busy, anyway."

"Yes, of course. If we're honest, darling, that's why I was going to ring you. I gave Tabitha a call, but she was very vague about your new project."

He pauses, lets his words sink in. My project? I'm motionless. Cold. *I'm not sure you were safe there at all . . .*

"I don't—"

"I thought it might be useful if we could have a little catch-up in person, Rosalie. Perhaps a sit-down together at Hailbury?"

Hailbury? All I can think of is the note of premonition in Kacper's voice, the dawn chorus spilling over the windowsill. I swallow.

"I don't have a key," I say.

"Oh, Lara seemed to think you must do. Or perhaps the groundsman does?"

"This conversation is over."

"Aren't you just *so* much like your mother?" Stefan gives a little laugh, and the gall of it makes me want to smack him. "That little fiasco's the other thing she wants us to chat about, actually."

If there wasn't a car coming, I'd step into the road to get past him, but I'm trapped. Stefan leans in to peck the air either side of my cheek.

"Anyway. Better dash. Perhaps we can lunch? Just drop me a message when you know your movements."

"Will do." I grit my teeth. "I can send you my father's lawyer's number if you want? In case you need anything from Hailbury?"

He doesn't take the bait. I seize the opportunity to jog across the road and duck into the pharmacy.

No wonder Vesna has made herself untraceable. Her life must have been misery if my mother found out she'd defied her to help Leonie.

My mother. She knows — she must do — that I've got too close to the truth. Stefan's in Armsby. Could she really have sent him to follow me? I'm shaking from top to toe. Does she know I met Tess? Why hasn't she confronted me herself? I can't let myself think it. What Kacper was suggesting can't be possible. That she was somehow involved. That she knows more than she's ever told . . .

I pretend to look at hair dye and sunglasses for ten minutes, to be sure Stefan is gone. When the coast is clear, I drive to the cottage. The key to Hailbury is on the hall table with Kacper's wallet. He's two doors down the road; he didn't take it with him. I slide it off its ring and pocket it. He wants me to be careful. But I won't be alone. I'll be safe enough meeting Tess.

I walk, retracing my sister's steps. The ones from the bus stop to Hailbury's drive. The ones she didn't take on 28 April 2003 because she got into a man's car.

The driveway seems longer than ever, closed over like a tunnel with new summer foliage. The shadows move in patterns at my feet. I look to the razor wire for reassurance and pause at the fountain, shivering afresh. The windows are blank and waiting, the blinds like half-closed eyelids regarding me against the glare of a cloudy white sky. It's later in the day than I'd realised; the cleaners are already gone.

I unlock the door and unset the alarm with a disturbing feeling of finality. Why would it be the last time? I rub my bare arms; the house is much cooler than the spring air outside. It can't be long until Tess gets here. It seems unlikely she'd spend much time in Skegness. That's if Tony opened the door to her at all.

I go to my room. The hairs on the back of my neck are stood on end. I open the wardrobe. The dress is still there, slashed into shreds. I pull it out.

#rosaliesroom

I sit down at the dressing table. My laptop is dead. I can't write.

I get up again and take the books from the bookcase: *The Secret Garden, Anne of Green Gables, Matilda, Pollyanna.* I stand on a stool to untangle the fairy lights and wind them around the pine rails. I draw the voile curtains like a shroud, a shimmering mist of bygone sanctuary; there was no danger in the world I knew.

No danger. I open the first chapter, the paper trembling in my fingers.

THERE IS NO ONE LEFT.

I swallow and start to read. About an unwanted, fretful child and the ayah who didn't come. A little girl making heaps of earth and paths for a garden, hibiscus flowers.

> *Mistress Mary, quite contrary,*
> *How does your garden grow?*
> *With silver bells, and cockle shells,*
> *And marigolds all in a row . . .*

On the dressing table, my phone is ringing. Ringing and ringing, like it did in Antonio DiPaci's studio, as if by its frantic repetition it might rouse me from my stupor.

I slide to my feet. I don't have a photo of Tess. It's just her name in white pulsating on the screen. I swipe to pick up.

"Hello?" I whisper.

"Rosalie?" Tessa Whittaker's voice is sharp with panic. "Rosalie?"

Dread grips my stomach. I put out a hand to steady myself and the dress slips from its hanger and falls to the floor, a soft swish: a pool of black.

"Rosalie, Tony's dead."

CHAPTER 35

Kacper

The key's not here.

I went to Garden Gate. I hadn't been there in seven years. I couldn't get my head straight.

Even shifting twenty tonnes of topsoil wasn't enough. And I needed plants, so I drove there, covered in dirt, pre-occupied by thoughts of Jeanette's garden, the Myosotis, the colour of Rosalie's hair against the short grass. I wandered the aisles of alpines and inadequately watered herbaceous perennials without a clue what I was doing, until I realised I hadn't got my wallet anyway.

I almost drove back to the cottage. I should have gone back. Then I would have realised she wasn't there. But I drove to Summercliffe instead, with the mountain bike I'd bought for Yvan's birthday. And a helmet, because Jeanette's voice never strays far from my mind.

They were at the beach hut with Little Lord Do-Gooder London. I didn't stay long. I borrowed the key from Iryna and dropped the bike in the shed at the bungalow while they were still busy sweeping floorboards and arranging patio furniture.

The hut's a dilapidated place. It's too far out of town really, with the vandalised King Edward Arms and the salt marsh as a backdrop, and a pig-headed part of me actually hoped Iryna wouldn't like it just because I didn't want something else to owe London for.

I don't want him to be right, about any of it. But he *is* right, there has to be something. No one makes a hole that size in the sidewall of a car tyre without knowing it. The fire was too much to be a coincidence, right underneath where Langton kept the DVR for the CCTV; I've sent the box off to a data-recovery company, but no one is optimistic. And something else is nagging at me, something about those pictures — the ones the photographer gave her — and no matter how many hours I lie awake, trying to pin it down, I can't work out what it is.

Fuck.

I screw my hand into my hair. Her car's still here. It was here before I left for the garden centre; it hadn't even occurred to me that *she* wasn't. Not until I came home and opened the door, and the emptiness hit me like a fist.

Her phone's going straight to voicemail. I try to fight the wave of fear as I lock the door and jump back into the truck. That doll . . . Someone was in the house, there's no two ways about it. She said it herself. Why the fuck would she go back?

It's not possible to drive fast through Shellingsby. I have to pull to a halt close against the church wall to let a tractor through, cursing it under my breath, and there's a recovery truck almost blocking Armsby Road. I skid to a stop at Hailbury's gates, punch in the code and swing onto the drive.

The gravel's empty. I don't know what I was expecting. I jump down and start for the porch, then realise I'll either have to knock or go round the back. I still have keys for the orangery and the sheds. I jog around the side of the house. The wisteria is in flower, obscuring the camera again. I let myself in and come to a dead stop at the poolside.

There's something in the water. Floating, just below the surface.

"Rosy . . ."

I hear my own gasps as if from miles away.

But it's not. I press my hands to my knees. Jesus Christ. The hit of adrenaline is racing through me. It's not. It's fabric, clothes: a vest top, half afloat, a pair of leggings that have sunk, distorted, to the bottom. What did I even . . .

Her clothes. They're hers.

"Rosalie?" I push through the door into the corridor, the utility, the taste of ash in my mouth. There's a gap under the charred cupboards where the dryer used to be, a bubbled scorch mark that hasn't washed off the plaster.

"Rosy?" The hallway is empty. Leonie Knight-Langton's bright green eyes stare down at me from the stairwell.

"Shit," I breathe. "Shit."

Which room? Leonie's door is closed. Hers is open. I push it, my pulse crashing in my ears.

"Rosy!"

She's huddled by the desk. T-shirt tucked into her jeans, bare arms wrapped tight around her knees. Her phone is at her feet; a crumpled heap of black fabric is spreading around her like a bloodstain. She raises her eyes as the door swings wide.

"He's dead."

"*What?*" I stare at her, incapable of logical thought.

"Dead. He's dead. She found him when she got there. She—"

"Who?" The fear in her eyes has sent a ripple of dread through me.

"Tony. Tony's dead." She stumbles upright, her feet slipping on the fabric: a dress, it's a dress, the one she was wearing the night she and London were at Chez Marques.

"He's . . . he's . . . Tess found him. Oh God." She's clutching at something. A book. And I'm still just staring, unable to make sense of what she's telling me. Unable to make sense of the chain that glitters around her neck, rose-gold against porcelain skin, like the doll . . .

"At the bottom of his stairs, his dark room, the cellar. He-he . . ."

The Secret Garden. I pull it from her hands. Lay it down on the desk.

"It's okay," I exhale, even though it's not. The photographer. Shit. *What?* I draw her close to me, cradling her head against my chest. "It's okay."

But it isn't.

Her teeth are chattering. I stare over the top of her head at the carpet in the doorway. There's a scattering of sawdust on the floor.

Sawdust?

I let go of her. There are holes, from the screws. Twelve holes. Two bolts.

Except the bolts aren't there.

There are no bolts on the inside of the door.

"Rosalie," I choke. "We've got to go. Right now."

CHAPTER 36

Rosalie

Happy Birthday to you . . .

I turn sideways, trying to stop hearing. Trying to stop seeing.

Number 15s and black balloons. People, singing.

Happy Birthday to you . . .

A party, smoke, lights . . .

Happy Birthday Le-O-nie . . .

No. I screw my eyes tight shut. Open them again. A dream. I know it's a dream, precipitated by yesterday afternoon at the bungalow, the cream-filled cake, the fruit, the streamers, the gaudy paper cups and napkins. I was there but I wasn't; I couldn't drag my mind from the darkness of the police station, from the helpless disintegration of my story under scrutiny, when I had no messages to show anyone because I'd deleted my social media accounts. From the unconvinced face of the officer looking at a dirty child's doll, and the pictures of the bolts on the outside of my bedroom door and a twenty-five-year-old tumble dryer. From the fact that Antonio DiPaci was found at the foot of his cellar stairs reeking of whisky, with an empty hip flask and catastrophic head injuries and they're not looking for anyone else in connection with the death.

Happy Birthday, dear Yvan . . .

He didn't understand the singing. He stood in the corner, hair tousled, eyes suspicious, with his hands balled into fists while Iryna carried the cake and Harriet carried the tune, her two boys presenting him with gifts and cards that he didn't open. He didn't move until the singing had finished and the candles had burnt too low to be left, so Iryna blew them out; until the cake was cut up and distributed, and Kacper stole in with a quiet word while everyone else was eating, and they both went outside into the garden, instead.

I watched from the window. The grasp of a small hand in a strong one, the latch on the shed, the blue ribbons on the bike, battered by the pouring rain. The fleeting flash of disbelief and excitement that transformed Yvan's face back into childhood, where it belonged. The way he grabbed the handlebars, and Kacper wrapped a steadying hand around the saddle, something indescribable in the wry smile that escaped to play on his lips, something that ached deep in my chest, so that when they came back in, waterlogged and whispering, I was still blinking too hard.

The moment fled. The cake was too rich for me to eat. We drove back to the cottage and I caught Kacper checking that the windows were all locked before we went to bed.

I couldn't sleep. I turned on all the lights downstairs and I set up my laptop in the sitting room, where there were curtains to draw so that no one could see in, and I wrote it. All of it. Hide and seek, belladonna, the homework diary, Jessica's clothes. *The Secret Garden* and *Pollyanna*, the fairy lights on the bed, the girls on horses, the first kiss, and the last. The perfect family. The perfect lie. All of it, except the end.

Because there still isn't an end.

It's gone midday. Kacper came to find me at six, made coffee and took the laptop. And he read it — all of it. The boy in the cloakroom, the red Virginia creeper, the bench by the sea. The girl who hated her sister, who wished to God she didn't exist, until one day . . .

I don't know what time I fell asleep. I wasn't even wakened by the church bells. The sky has cleared and the sun is streaming brightly through the kitchen windows. Kacper is looking at the pictures on my phone: Leonie's album, Tony's last shoot — I photographed all of them before I gave the book to Tess.

Is there an ending? Antonio DiPaci is dead. No one else knew where Leonie was going. Did they? No one except Vesna.

I haul myself to sit. My neck and my head are aching. Kacper is frowning at the pictures, running a hand backwards through his hair over and over again, as if somehow he can't see what he thinks he should see. He glances up as I slide from the sofa, and briefly his gaze softens. Then he gets up, the darkness re-establishing itself abruptly in his face.

"I've got to go out," he says. The suddenness of it catches me off guard. "To Lorraine's," he clarifies. "Jeanette's sister-in-law. Near Summercliffe. I . . ." He's frowning. "I won't be long. A couple of hours. I have to find something."

"Okay." I nod. His eyes are on me. I realise my lip is between my teeth and I make myself release it. I slip my arms around his waist.

"I didn't want to go while you were sleeping." His fingers skim my cheek.

"It's fine." I'm not sure that's the truth, but it's what he needs to hear; I can see the tension radiating from him. "I'm good, here. I'm just going to do some editing. Maybe cook something for later. I've got yoga at seven."

"I'll be back. I'll take you."

"It's okay, I can—"

"No." His lips have pressed tightly together. "I'll go with you and I'll wait outside. I'll be back."

I nod. He breaks away, goes to get his keys. Car keys, house keys, Hailbury's keys. They're in his fist as he turns back. I reach to brush a kiss across his lips, and for a second he's immobilised, taken by surprise, and his eyes and his mouth linger on mine. Neither of us says another word.

I watch him go. Then I lock the door behind him and go back to my phone. Leonie looks out at me: choppy, cropped hair, feisty and fearless, scissors still in hand.

I have an unread message from Iryna. A copy-and-paste, questionably translated in Google.

> *The lady at English lesson she is familiar with the picture of Vesna. She remembers where she is living in a place the cross road in summer cliff.*

I sit down at the table. The crossroad? My laptop's still open. I type it into maps, but there's no Crossroad or Cross Road in Summercliffe.

My sister has been missing for twenty years. I type the message and then delete it. Then I type it again. *I think Vesna knew where she went.*

Why do I think that? Why do I feel almost sure that I *know* it?

I switch from maps to the search engine. Crossroad.

The Crossroads Guest House Summercliffe-on-Sea.

I freeze.

Iryna hasn't replied. She's typing. The phone trembles in my hand.

> *Yes. ((((She wrote to me one letter before we completed the visa application which I did not understand well to translate. And now I must show you.*

A letter. Another letter? I wet my lips.

> *I found the address. It's a guest house.*

I copy the postcode for her, screenshot the map and send it to her. A second later she replies. It's a scanned-in letter, but the text is in Ukrainian. Her message flicks up underneath.

I will try to translate for you later, when Yvan sleeps. Now I will find the house for guests.

I let out my breath. It's warm in the kitchen. I'm sticky, dishevelled, still in last night's clothes: my leggings, Kacper's T-shirt, pulled on in the small sleepless hours. I leave the phone on the side and go upstairs to wash and tie up my hair, to change into my yoga clothes in front of the mirror. *You look a lot like her.* My big, beautiful, stolen sister.

Nothing like her. *I'm nothing like her.*

Something shifts, downstairs in the hall.

I stand immobilised.

A scratching. A mournful wail . . .

I blunder downstairs, then come to a halt, feeling like a fool for the aftertaste of fright that's still in my mouth.

The cat is digging forlornly at the foot of the front door. I unlock it, jerk it open and he skitters out as if I've offended him. Then he pauses on the step to sniff something.

A gift bag. I swallow, trying to ignore the rush of blood in my ears. Pearlescent paper, pastel colours. Tom rubs his face against it, bending the paper.

I pick it up. It's not sealed or addressed. The inside is filled with shredded tissue paper. The cat darts down the garden path. There's no one in sight.

Maybe it's for Yvan. A birthday present. It can't have been there long, or Kacper would have found it. I steel myself and feel inside, for a card, for a . . .

Bottle. A water bottle. I take it out, my hands starting to shake. Brand new, identical to the one that I broke in Summercliffe. I reach backwards blindly for the door. There's something else in the bag too, smaller and heavier. A box, satin cardboard and embossed rose-gold print, still wrapped in cellophane, the weight of another bottle inside it. Déjà Vu — by L'Église Rose.

367

I choke, almost slam my fingers in the door as I fumble to close and deadlock it. The bag falls on the floor, a snowstorm of tissue paper around my feet. I can hear my breathing, rapid, ineffective. The bolts. The bolts were on the wrong side of my door. Someone moved them. Someone was at Hailbury. And they were in Summercliffe.

And now . . . now they're here.

I back against the telephone table, where I'm out of sight of the window. They know I'm here.

One . . . two . . .

The edge of the wood bites into my back.

Three . . . four . . .

My phone is in the kitchen; I can hear it buzzing on the worktop where I left it. In full view of the glass doors.

Ready or not, here I come . . .

"Oh God," I whisper. I squeeze my eyes closed.

They know I'm here.

The doors and windows are locked. I need to be rational. The gate into the garden is locked, too; I saw Kacper draw the bolts. No one can get in. I need to get to my phone.

I tiptoe into the kitchen, not letting my eyes stray to the glass, snatch up the phone and the laptop and take them back to the semi-dark sitting room. He won't be long. A couple of hours.

And Iryna's gone to the guest house.

And Antonio DiPaci's dead.

I press a trembling hand to my forehead. Pain is throbbing behind my eyes. I need water but I'm not brave enough to go back to the kitchen. I clutch the laptop to my chest and slide down to sit on the floor, curling myself into a ball around it. My phone buzzes. A message. Iryna.

No, Kacper.

He's still at Lorraine's; it's taking longer than he thought. He doesn't think I should be alone.

I exhale, reading, re-reading, lightheaded with relief. Harriet's going to pick me up. She'll take me back to hers. He'll explain the rest when he gets there.

There are a thousand replies at my fingertips. The rest of *what*? What's taking longer? *What did you remember*? There was someone on the doorstep . . . Please come back.

I don't type any of them.

Okay. I hit send and press the phone against my mouth, trying to still the shaking.

Twenty minutes pass. The cat lets itself back in through the cat flap in the kitchen; the bang of the magnetic catch makes me jerk upright. He purrs into the sitting room, nuzzles his way between my arms and my knees, dislodging the laptop. My phone lights up. Harriet. *I'm outside.*

I pull myself to my feet. My legs prickle with pins and needles. A car door slams. The cat scarpers.

A knock.

"Rosy?" Harriet's voice is right outside the front door. I limp to the hall and push my feet into my shoes.

"Coming!" I aim for light, but it's shrill, artificial.

"What's goin' on?" She's in the doorway as I wrestle it open. Behind her there's an estate car parked outside the gate, a chaos of children crammed in the back on booster seats. I see Yvan's face pressed up against the window, looking out.

"Nothing," I lie. She raises her eyebrows at me.

"Why doesn't Kacper want you t'be left on your own?"

"I . . ." I'm all out of lies. "I'm not completely sure."

"You'd best tell me later." She looks unusually grim. "Come on. I told the kids we'd go to the Coronation thing on the school field in Rollingford."

"I've got yoga at seven, not far from there." I pick up my mat from the hall table, trying to feign normality. "I can probably walk round, after."

She waits for me to lock the front door. Her eyes linger on the key in my quaking hand.

"Rosalie . . ." she starts again.

"I didn't know you had Yvan with you." I dodge the oncoming question.

"I wasn't expecting to. Iryna left him with us. She came to see Sandeep, about Elena, and she had to go on somewhere else. It seemed urgent. She asked if I could watch him. Here." Harriet opens the passenger door, and I climb into a pile of sunhats and picnic blankets. "It's a good thing I've got seven seats."

She glances back at the melee of children. At Yvan's solemn face, still pressed against the glass. *Urgent.* I chew my lip. Iryna's gone to find the B&B. I fold my hands in my lap.

The school field is secluded, tucked out of the way behind high hedges and a green mesh fence. The air smells of barbecue and the sky threatens rain. Harriet spreads the picnic blanket on the grass. There's a bouncy castle and a jazz band playing. The boys run off to bounce. I watch as Yvan kicks off his shoes and socks and wavers on the crash mat.

"What's Kacper doing at Mum's?" Harriet's eyes are fixed on the bouncing, not on me.

"He said he needed to find something."

Harriet frowns. "Something of Jeanette's?"

I shrug.

"Is this something to do with your book?"

I feel her sideways glance. I keep my eyes fixed on the grass.

"There've been a couple of . . . incidents. I think he's worried someone's been breaking into Hailbury."

"What—"

There's a howl from the bouncy castle. Harriet gets to her feet. I'm saved by catastrophe. She returns with a hiccupping Rory on her hip. Rohan and Yvan are still bouncing. I drift closer to watch them. Kacper should be here soon. Perhaps even Iryna. The babble of assembled people feels comforting. An ice cream van has parked in the school playground, and I help Harriet herd the children to it and choose ice creams, furnishing Yvan with a cone and a flake. Unexpectedly, his hand slips into mine as we walk back between the picnic rugs and deck chairs, and I hold it tightly, wondering what news Sandeep had for Iryna.

The afternoon sun loses its edge, and by six the sky is clouding over. The Pimm's and strawberries sell out, and the ice cream van moves on. The band keeps playing, like the quartet on the *Titanic*, as the bunting and the blankets flap in wild and noisy disarray. It starts to spit with rain, and I roll up the rug as Harriet shepherds the children into the car. Iryna hasn't come.

Neither has Kacper. The realisation unsettles me more than it ought to.

I can see the church hall from where we're parked, so I fob Harriet off with promises of a phone call later, and retrieve my yoga mat from her car. I text Kacper as I walk: *I've gone straight to yoga, I'll meet you there.* Harriet gives a light toot on the horn as she passes me, and I watch Yvan's face pressed against the glass as they disappear out of view.

* * *

One, two . . .

Why was Stefan in Armsby?

Three . . . four . . .

Did Tess Whittaker know more than she was telling me?

Five . . .

Shavasana. I try to clear my mind.

Ready or not, here I come . . .

"And when you're ready, rolling onto your side and coming up to sit. And we'll finish with hands together. Namaste . . ."

Murmurings of thanks, see you next week. A smattering of small talk. I make my way outside.

The car park is full of cars, windscreen wipers, slamming doors. It must have been too full for the pickup. I walk out into the street, but there's no one there. The rain is getting harder. I wait by the gateway as everyone else leaves, as the instructor closes up the hall and gets into her car. She drives past me without looking up, and I realise suddenly that everyone has gone.

There is no one left.

The street is very quiet. Just the fall of the rain on the tarmac, the flutter of the residual red, white and blue flags tugging at their bindings in the wind. I try his phone, but it goes straight to voicemail.

He sent me a message. 18:56, before yoga. I fumble to open it, my fingers sliding in the rain on the touchscreen. But it's just a picture. No words. Two kids on donkeys and a blue car.

What?

I stare at it, starting to shiver. A blue car. Someone is sat on the bonnet, a boy. No, a girl. A girl with short hair. Leonie.

There's another blast of rain against my face, a warning shot, as I dial him again, once, twice, three times. *You have reached . . . Kacper Miller . . .*

Where is he? Something cold grips my gut. I scour the street again. Maybe he's called Harriet. I dial her instead, pacing back and forth as it rings.

"Hey up, Rosy."

"Have you seen Kacper?" Shivers overtake me. "I was expecting him to pick me up."

"Oh . . ." The background is noisy: kids, shouting. Someone's crying over the clash of crockery and the blare of a TV. "No. Is everything okay? He sent me a photo earlier, just after we got back. I'll forward it to you. I called Mum to check he'd got your message, but he'd left ages ago."

"Left?"

Ages ago? I swallow.

"Sandeep's just gone to the shop. Yvan's still here; we weren't expecting an extra mouth for tea. He'll be back in ten, fifteen minutes. Do you need picking up?"

"No." I glance along the street, sweat breaking on my palms. "No, it's alright, I'll walk round to yours. I think I know the way."

"Okay." She doesn't sound convinced. "I'll leave the door on the catch. I'll see you in five, unless he comes to get you first."

"Thanks," I breathe.

He'd already left Lorraine's. I'm not sure why I suddenly feel so sick. Leonie, a blue car. The rain is torrential now, plastering my hair to my head. The street is deserted; I'm completely on my own and I've never felt so exposed. Déjà vu. I wipe the rain off the phone and swipe back to his number.

You have reached . . . Kacper Miller.

"Shit." I clench my hand around it.

It buzzes.

Thank God.

But it's not him. It's Iryna.

Vesna has a rental room at the house. But she is not here ((since several weeks. She informed the owner that she will drive to Hailbury House and she did not return to her room.

Vesna. What? Vesna came to Hailbury? I'm convulsed with shivers.

Iryna is still at the guest house. Which means if Kacper went to the bungalow there wouldn't have been anyone there. I type frantically.

Where's Kacper?
Is he with you? Do you know where he is?

He isn't here. He isn't with Harriet. And he's not with Iryna. Fear has worked its way up from my gut to close around my throat. He said he'd be back and he isn't.

He found something out.

Harriet has forwarded the picture. It's the same one. The same one. He remembered something. He knows something. And now . . .

Tears are stinging my eyes. I can't panic. I can't. Who else? I clutch at the phone. *Josh.* He'd been messaging Josh.

Rain is pouring over my face, driving my hair into my eyes. I can barely hear him answer.

"Rosy?"

Blustering, crackling. His voice is indistinct.

"Rosy, is that you?"

"Josh." Relief crashes over me. "Thank God."

"Rosy, what is it? I can hardly hear you. Are you okay?"

"Oh God, I don't . . . Can you . . . Have you heard from Kacper?"

"*What*?" The line is breaking up. "What did you say?"

"Kacper," I gasp. "Something's happened. He's not here. I can't get hold of him. I—"

"Where are you?"

"At yoga. The church hall. Rollingford. There's no one here. Oh, God, Josh. I think something's happened to Kacper."

CHAPTER 37

Kacper

Just gone two. I look out at the churning waves as I turn onto the coast road. I shouldn't have left Rosalie at the cottage. I should have brought her with me.

But I wasn't sure. I need to be sure.

I don't know why the picture stuck in my mind. The more I looked at it, at the teenager with short hair, the glittering nose stud, the impish smile, the more certain I was that I'd seen her before. Somewhere she didn't belong.

Charnsby Sands is only five miles out of Summercliffe. It's small, a string of pre-fab houses and a cluster of cul-de-sacs just along the coast.

I feel sick at myself for even thinking it, but as the hours have passed and the shock has worn off, I've started to feel relieved that the photographer is dead. The parents are fucked up, there's no doubt about it. But Antonio DiPaci . . . I saw his eyes on her in the studio. And those pictures were fucking wrong — whichever way you look at it. As I sat at the table this morning and watched her sleep, it seemed to me that if he's drunk himself into oblivion then perhaps it's no more than he deserved. Perhaps it's some kind of justice.

Perhaps, with him gone, she could be safe.

There must be proof. I just don't understand how it fits together. Why her parents didn't tell the truth. How Tess was involved. If it wasn't my father's car Leonie got into, then whose was it?

The pictures. It all comes back to the pictures.

Except . . .

I pull up outside Lorraine's bungalow. The block-paved driveway is riddled with weeds, and I feel briefly guilty that since dumping Jeanette's affairs on her I've never really come back. I could at least offer my help. The truth is, I've never really felt like her family. Harriet's, maybe, just about. But Lorraine . . . what am I to her? A stray, taken in by her brother's widow.

I knock on the front door. Eventually she appears, drying her hands on a tea towel. We exchange niceties on the doorstep and she ushers me in.

"Tea?" she asks, and I shake my head.

"No, thanks."

I think of Rosalie in the hall at Hailbury, the oversized mug and the cardigan sliding off her narrow shoulders. Lorraine gestures me through.

"I pulled out t'boxes from t'outhouse." She shows me into the cramped kitchen. "But t'others are in't loft. I'm afraid you'll have to fetch t'ladder, if what you want's not in these."

I nod. It isn't; I can already tell. God only knows how I'm going to find the right one. The picture wasn't in an album. It was in a stack of paperwork with a couple of others, things that seemed to bear no relation to each other.

"I'll get the ladder. Where is it?"

"Just out back. Help yourself, love. Are you sure I can't get you a drink?"

"I'm okay. Thanks."

The loft hatch is in the hall, and the ceiling's so low I could probably get up without the ladder, but I fetch it anyway. The roof space is warm and airless, and I'm sweating within minutes even after taking off my gilet. There's no light, so I rig up my phone as a torch and contemplate the boxes with despair. I'd forgotten just how much stuff I moved from Jeanette's. This is going to take forever.

The phone vibrates itself over, landing with a thud in the dust. I pick it up. Harriet — she's taking the boys to the Coronation picnic in Rollingford, do Rosy and I want to come?

I'm at Lorraine's, I type, then pause. Actually . . .

> *Can you pick Rosalie up, and make sure she's not on her own?*

It's a few moments before Harriet replies.

What's going on?

I can almost hear her suspicion.

> *Please. It's important. I'll explain later.*

OK . . .

I message Rosy and stand the torch back up.

I search box by box. There was so much, after Jeanette died: tonnes of paperwork from Garden Gate, legal stuff, tax. Boxes of old clothes, though a quick glance rules those out. It takes all afternoon; it's gone six by the time I slice through the tape on the second-to-last box, damp with sweat and shaking with frustration. I need to go back. I promised I'd be back.

I fold the multitool away in my gilet pocket, and pause. It's this one.

I exhale a slow breath and wipe the sweat from my eyes. I recognise the top stack of papers. They're written in Jeanette's loopy handwriting, mostly illegible. There's an account book, some typewritten documents, a whole ream of stuff about the sale of the livery yard.

The photos are underneath. I dump the documents to one side. Three of them. Seemingly random, meaningless. They can't even have been hers, because I don't recognise anybody in them. Or I didn't.

I do now.

I pull out the middle one and hold it up. Two little kids on donkeys, on the slipway up to the prom. I have no idea who they are. But behind them . . .

I realise I'm holding my breath.

Behind them, there's a blue car. It's not properly in focus. But the girl sat on the bonnet in her school blazer, bottle in hand, with short black-brown hair and a stud in her nose, is unmistakeably Leonie Knight-Langton.

And if she cut her hair in the Easter holiday, in the photographer's studio, but she disappeared on the first day of term . . . I swallow a couple of times in quick succession.

Then this is the day she disappeared.

And she's not with my father.

I jump back through the loft hatch so quickly that I nearly knock over the ladder. I hold the picture up, mind racing. My hands are shaking almost too much to get a steady shot of it with my phone. I send the photo to Harriet. *Do you recognise this car?*

I don't have time to repack the boxes. I garble some kind of apology at Lorraine about the state of the loft, rescue my gilet, wrestle the hatch closed and take the ladder back outside. It's spitting with rain. Lorraine sees me off from the doorstep as I jog to the truck with the picture shoved inside my gilet.

The blue car.

It was almost the last thing Jeanette said, before she died. *The blue car.*

I turn around in the drive and navigate my way back through the rabbit warren of cul-de-sacs, glancing down at the clock. Ten to seven already. Shit. I get stuck behind a cyclist, cursing out loud. We corner back towards the coast road, but the street is full of parked cars and there isn't room to get by. *Shit.*

The bike goes out round them, even though there's a van coming the other way, and it's as it skirts the last parked car that the driver's door opens. I hear the crunch, the clatter of the bike on the tarmac—

"*Christ!*" I kill the engine and fumble to open the door. "Jesus Christ!"

The van driver has stopped and jumped out too. The cyclist rolls over in the road, uttering a string of expletives. A woman leaps out of the car.

"Sorry! Oh my God. Oh my God, I'm so sorry."

But the sound seems to have tuned out.

All the breath has left my lungs. I'm staring at the tarmac, lights flashing in front of my eyes. *Sorry, Polack, mate, didn't see you there!* Bursting stars, dazzling sunshine, feet on the dashboard. A vulgar gesture out of the back screen . . . I blunder a step away.

A blue car.

Marcus Blakeman had a blue car.

My hands slide on the pickup door. There's a smattering of rain against the windscreen. The cyclist has got to his feet, someone has come out of one of the bungalows. I fumble my way back into the truck.

If this was those—

I just fell off my bike.

Silly, beautiful boy. What have I told you about helmets?

There's no room to get through. I reverse and find a place to turn around, detouring blindly towards the sea.

My phone vibrates on the passenger seat and I seize it in one hand and steer with the other. Rosy. *I've gone straight to yoga, I'll meet you there.*

Wind is buffeting the side of the truck as I finally turn onto the coast road. I can't type a reply. Instead, I forward her the photo, fingers trembling with adrenaline. Leonie was with Marcus Blakeman.

The sea defences and salt marshes pass in a blur. I cut inland, circumventing Summercliffe's residential streets. The wind seems to be getting stronger; there's another squall of rain. The road is suddenly devoid of traffic. On the seat beside me, the phone starts to ring.

"Rosy—" I snatch it up.

"Kacper, it's Josh."

What? I brake to a standstill and pull the truck up onto the verge.

"Mate, I'm really sorry, can you talk?"

Mate? I glare at the screen. I'm not your mate. Not even close.

"I'm driving." I grind my teeth together.

"Where are you? Can you get to Summercliffe? I was just leaving the golf course and I thought I saw your little Ukrainian boy. I think he was by himself."

Yvan? I switch the phone to speaker.

"What?"

"Are you close enough to get there? I don't think there was anyone with him. I tried not to lose sight of him, but—"

"He was alone? Are you sure? Where?"

"On the South Prom. Not far from the hut. He doesn't really know me; I thought I'd scare him to death if I went after him, and by the time I found somewhere to stop I'd lost him."

Fuck. I grip the wheel so hard my knuckles are white. Yvan. I should have put restrictors on the windows of the bungalow. It's after seven, past bedtime. Iryna can't even know he's out. She was meeting Sandeep today. *They've found something out about Elena . . .*

"I'll go." I can't even process it. Yvan. Rosalie, the yoga class. "I'm on my way."

I hang up, struggle out of my gilet and dial Iryna. It goes straight to voicemail. *Yvan.* If he's mad, upset . . . It's not safe. He's a kid. It'll soon be high tide and it's blowing a gale. I slam the truck into gear and swing a U-turn out onto the main road.

It's not lost on me that it had to be Josh London. Joshua fucking London. He always has to be the good guy. I try to breathe out slowly. Soon. Fuck yes, soon that's going to change. He'll at least have some questions to answer.

Because if Leonie was in Summercliffe with Marcus Blakeman on the day she disappeared, then Josh London lied about my father.

Summercliffe. I accelerate faster than is sensible around the bends. It takes five minutes to get there. I drive out of town and onto the track towards the salt marsh. The car park of the King Edward Arms is a wilderness of broken concrete and weeds, but the barrier's smashed and I can park right against the sandbank by the beach hut. The wind is howling around the container that used to be a coffee shack. I type a message to Iryna then drop the phone on the seat, eyes scouring the bank.

The back door of the hut is ajar.

"Yvan?" I leap down. I can hear the edge in my voice and I fight it back. I don't want to scare him.

"Yvan?" I address him in Polish. "Yvan, are you there?" I take the bank in a couple of strides, my feet sliding in the sand, and vault the low fence onto the uneven slabs.

"Yvan, it's me, Kacper. Are you there? Are you okay?"

I push the door.

"Yvan?"

There's no answer. It's dark. The front door is locked and the shutters are barred. There's a bucket on the floor and a scattering of seashells. He's not there. I go further in to make sure, shells crunching under my boots.

"Yvan?"

Nothing. I stand still. The sea is thrashing the seawall on the other side of the promenade. I can't hear anything else. The growl of an engine and the slam of a car door. If he's not here, where is he? He's been here, or Iryna has. He can't be far away. He must have been alone, not strong enough to open the padlock on the front. I push the bucket aside with my foot. Which way would he have gone? Jesus Christ. Sandeep's contact, Elena . . . It must be bad, and Iryna's told him, and—

And now it's getting cold and before long the sun will set, and he'll be lost. Even if someone tries to help him, he won't be able to understand what they're saying. He'll be terrified.

I have to look for him. I start back outside into the wind. No, I have to *find* him. And Rosalie, shit . . . what time is it? I feel for my phone. Glance up.

Stop dead.

"What . . ."

I stand for a moment in disbelief.

The pickup is gone. Rain is spattering the concrete. Over the roar of the wind a bird is singing from the reeds on the other side of the track.

"What the . . . *fuck* . . ."

Possibilities flash through my head. *How?* Someone's fucking jumped in it, in the seconds that I was inside? I left the keys in the ignition. Fucking *idiot*. I push my hand back through my hair, dumbfounded by my own stupidity. Who would even be out here? The wind is ripping through the scrub and buffeting channels through the reeds. I didn't hear anything. There was no one here . . .

I did. I heard the door, the engine.

I still can't quite believe it. I slide down the bank, sand pouring into my boots, and scan the car park again as if it might reappear, a trick of the light. The wind is howling across the salt marsh. I can hear the tide crashing over the seawall. Jesus *Christ*. I stride toward the graffitied container, gripping my hair with both hands to stop me punching something. *My fucking truck.*

Rosy. *Rosalie.* In forty minutes she'll finish yoga and she'll be stranded in Rollingford. I reach for my pocket, then remember dumping the phone on the seat.

Fucking *hell*.

I release my handful of hair.

The bird takes off. I hear its shrill of panic and the beat of wings. For a second, I don't process the rest. The crunch, close by, of feet on sandy concrete.

With a lurch of unease, I turn.

It's Marcus I see first. He's strolling towards me, the sleeves of his sports top rolled to his elbows. Then Zach skids down the bank, cutting off my escape. It dawns on me in slow motion, beyond the rage and disbelief. A cold, reluctant trickle of fear.

I hear myself swallow. My back is against the container. I stare at them, wordless, not quite ready to grasp what it means. That, after all this time, I've let this happen. I feel my hands curl into fists in readiness. Hear my breathing grow heavier.

The flashlight in the garage . . . the car.

I knew; I must have done. I've known, for twenty years. And now . . .

Zach Blakeman smiles.

"Alright, Woźniak?"

There's no chance to respond. The first blow is a low one, sending me reeling and winded before I can land a punch. The second pitches me back against the container. Marcus's face comes into grainy focus as I blink the blood from my eyes.

"Fuck you," I gasp.

My swing makes gratifying contact with his jaw. I pay for it immediately in kind. In my periphery, I'm vaguely aware of Zach. I half turn; his knee slams all of the air from my lungs and for a moment I'm staggering. I lunge for him. Get one hand around his throat and hit him with the other, with every ounce of strength I have left. With a rending of fabric, Marcus Blakeman pulls me off. Two blows in quick succession, and I'm barely on my feet. Everything is swimming. I need to stay off the floor. My mind is numb, struggling to process even the simplest thought. I need to stay off the floor or they'll kill me.

"Rosy . . ."

I barely know my own voice. There's blood in my mouth and running from my nose. I'm panting, choking. Spitting it into the dirt. *He's not here.* They are, but he's not. Josh London.

I knew.

I knew, and I didn't save her.

"Where is she? *Where's Rosalie?*"

CHAPTER 38

Rosalie

Rain, so much rain. I clutch the phone to my ear, teeth chattering. I'm disorientated by the silence, by the desertion. By the rain; everything looks so different in the ceaseless, merciless rain. Where is Kacper? Oh God, where is he?

Voices flash through my head.

If she tried to run away, why did she fail?

I've never forgiven our parents for what happened to her.

The groundsman . . .

An indiscretion . . .

"Stay on the phone. Stay on the phone and don't hang up." Josh's voice jerks me back. "I'm literally round the corner."

How much longer? My eyes scan the street again. How is there no one else here? *I don't think you should be alone.*

The Tesla corners silently into the road. I lower the phone. I see Josh catch sight of me, and the car pulls up at the kerb. I lurch for the door.

"Jesus, Rosy." His eyes are on my sodden clothes, my shaking hands. "What . . ."

I bang the door shut.

"Kacper," I choke. "He was supposed to come, but he didn't."

"I don't—"

"Someone was at Hailbury. Someone broke in. I thought, we . . . *Oh God.*"

I'm not making sense. The words garble together; Josh is staring at me, uncomprehending.

"I thought . . . I thought . . . but then, today . . . they. . . the cottage. And Kacper. Kacper went—"

"Hailbury?" Josh repeats, not quite grasping. "Someone broke into Hailbury?"

"Yes," I gasp. "No. I . . ."

"Miller went where? To Hailbury?"

"No. He went . . . he went to Lorraine's . . . but he's not there. It's been hours. He said he had to find something. I . . . *oh God.* Oh God, Josh. He'd realised something, about Leonie, his father . . . and now—"

"Wait." Josh's eyes are wide. "What? You're serious? You think . . . you think he could be in trouble?"

"I . . . I don't know."

"What's the last thing you heard from him?"

"He . . . he sent a picture." I pass him the phone. "He sent it to Harriet, too. It doesn't even make *sense.*"

Josh frowns at it.

"Okay," he breathes. "Okay, let's not panic. Can you track his phone on here?"

"No, I can't."

"Okay." He exhales again, slips the phone into his pocket. "Fuck . . . No, we can figure this out." He starts the car and the climate control purrs to life, warm air melting the condensation from the windows.

"Where are we going?" My teeth are chattering.

"Somewhere dry, where we can think. Then we'll try and retrace his movements. Where's the last place you know he was?"

"I don't know. Somewhere near Summercliffe . . . Lorraine. Jeanette's sister. Sister-in-law. Harriet's mum." I'm struggling to focus, clutching at the sides of my seat. Josh is driving too fast around the corners, not paying attention to the road. "I don't know exactly where."

We swerve onto a lane, jolting over the bumps. I'm carsick, momentarily disorientated, until we emerge onto familiar zig-zag bends, and I realise we've bypassed Shellingsby. He turns left without indicating, through the trees, and then Jericho's blundering deer emerge into view and the tyres fall almost silent on the last mile of tarmac. We crunch onto the gravel and come to a halt by the steps.

"Come on." He grimaces. I follow him up the steps as he opens the door to let us in.

"The kitchen's in here. You're bloody frozen. You need to get warm before we do anything else. Here." He pulls out a barstool and I perch, shivering, as he makes hot drinks and pushes one into my hand.

"The picture. Why did he send that picture?" I feel my pockets for my phone but can't find it. My clothes are dripping water onto the stool. Josh stands at a distance, cup in hand. I see his fingers clench and unclench on the handle.

"I . . . I'm not sure, Rosy." I can tell he's trying not to look agitated. It *did* make sense to him, and it's bad. I'm convulsing with shivers. I gulp the tea, trying desperately to get warm.

"You know," I whisper. My cup is unsteady in my hands. "Don't you? He's been messaging you. *You* understand the picture. He found something out, and now—"

"Rosy." He breaks across me, unusually firm. "Slow down. I only . . . it's only a guess. And we need to be rational. There's fuck all signal around Summercliffe, if that's where he is." He puts down his cup. "Look, you're wet through. I've got some stuff upstairs that might fit you — don't ask — but you can at least get dry. Then we'll drive there. Try and retrace his steps."

I nod, speechless. Josh is already past me; he barely pauses in the doorway.

"Two minutes," he tells me.

I swig another mouthful of overly sweet, milky tea and grip the kitchen counter with my free hand, watching the blood blanch from my knuckles. Only a guess. So why is he so worried? There's a sob of panic threatening in my chest. The shivering is exhausting. I jam my teeth together, trying to stop.

"Rosy."

He's back. His hand brushes my shoulder.

"I've got some things out in the guest room. Upstairs, third on the left. There's an en suite, if you need it. I'll try calling him again while you get changed."

I study his face. He's pulled together a semblance of calm, and it's oddly reassuring. Josh takes out his phone. I slide to my feet. I've left a puddle on the tiles. He's right — I'm so cold . . . I suppress another burst of shivers and climb the stairs, cradling my cup. I swallow the dregs of the tea and stand the empty cup on the end of the banister. Third on the left. I need to hurry. We need to go, and I don't even know an address.

Harriet would know. I search my sodden pockets again to no avail. My ears seem to be full of white noise. I turn the wrong way to start with. *Left*, third on the *left*. I turn back, counting out the doorways, suddenly disorientated. What's wrong with me?

I push open the door.

Some bits in the car from Jericho. . .

There's a strange ringing in my ears.

. . . things from that Easter, Leonie . . .

Leonie?

Josh has laid out the clothes on the bed. It's bare. No covers. No cushions or cascading throws. Just a fitted sheet. A pair of jodhpurs.

A school blazer.

Panic rises in my throat. I grip the door frame, but something seems to have happened to my body. My fingers slide, fade, dissolving into the wood. There's a leaden feeling in my legs, a slack warmth in my muscles. The room blurs. All that's in focus is the blazer. And a bottle, on the bedside table, Contraire — by L'Église Rose.

I stagger backwards, my pulse a slow-motion thud in my ears. The lights are all on.

"Steady, Rosy."

Joshua London replaces the empty cup on the banister with a click. I try to turn, a paroxysm of terror, but my body won't respond. His feet are soundless on the carpet.

"Easy." His whisper is against my ear.

Then one of his arms is around my chest, arresting my fall, and I hear the realisation choked off in my throat.

Leonie.

"This way. That's it."

Fifteen. *He was fifteen.*

"No . . ." It's blurred, thick. Nothing makes sense. A rush of nausea and bile. His voice, the throbbing silence, the blackness at the edges of my vision. The blood in her lips, so very red, as she reaches for me, her green eyes bright with despair. *Rosy!* She's screaming, trying to snatch me back. *Rosy . . .*

And then I'm forcing my eyes open again, forewarned by the flush of cold sweat, and I'm vomiting, helplessly, trapped in Shavasana, too weak and dizzy to do anything more than turn my head against the bedsheet. There's something plastic shoved under my chin, one of the rubble sacks from the foot-well of the pickup.

"What . . ." I slur. But my lips won't quite make the word. I'm on the bed, and my eyes won't focus, and her clothes are tangled under my feet.

It was me. I was the witness.

Gloved fingers jerk the bag away. Wipe my mouth. Stroke my face. I try to wrench aside but I can't. He's sitting beside me.

Her best friend . . .

The cup on the banister. He was checking I'd finished it. Comprehension dawns, a fresh wave of nausea and fear.

"What do you want?"

"Oh, Rosalie. You know what I want. I want to help you, remember?" The mattress dips under his weight. There are more on the floor. More bags. A cascade of plastic, cable ties. *Joshua London*. A sound I don't recognise escapes my throat. And then his fingers jam my jaw shut, holding it fast.

"I *know* where she is. I know where she is, and I can tell you exactly what happened to her. Don't you want to know?"

Oh God. I'm choking, his fingers digging deep into the soft flesh under my jaw. *Oh God.*

"I gave you so many chances. I was here, ready for you, all this time. Your secret would've been safe with me. We could have been the fairytale ending. A whirlwind romance . . . the Langton-London wedding . . ."

His other hand is at my throat.

"People don't say no to me, Rosalie." His index finger traces downwards, lifts her locket to toy with it. He leans close to whisper.

"You could have been everything *she* was meant to be."

I thrash my head. Try to move. To get away from his eyes, from the spearmint smog of his breath. But there's nowhere to go. He's everywhere I look, his grip squeezing my chin, clamping my mouth closed. I can barely swallow. My scream is drowned in my throat, gurgled and unintelligible.

"You thought you were losing your mind, didn't you? When I got into the house, messed with her things. I even spent a night in her bed." He laughs, under his breath. "Cutting up her dress — that was a nice touch, right? And the trolling . . . I thought it would be just enough to push you over the edge, to bring you running, and it almost did."

He's so close that I shudder.

"After all, how *could* anyone have been in the house? No one else had a key. Except her."

His lips don't quite touch my cheek.

"*She* had a key. It was in her blazer pocket."

He jerks my chin upwards so that our eyes meet. His lips are millimetres from mine.

"You really believed you killed her. Oh, and didn't you try, *little Rosy* . . ." His voice is soft. "Don't look like that. Of course I know. Your family were like my family. Remember? But you didn't do it. I did. And *I* remember every second. The look on her face . . ."

A stifled sound escapes me.

"She turned me down in front of a hundred people. That party was for her. She didn't even see. She didn't seem to understand. She didn't get to *do* that to me. . ."

He releases my chin suddenly.

"So I *made* her understand."

"*No* . . ." I struggle but my muscles are weak, sluggish. He catches my wrists and lowers them.

"Ssh, now, Rosy." He sits back, his weight trapping my legs. He's reaching for something.

"It won't wear off for a while. We can take our time. Don't you want the truth about her? That *is* what you wanted, isn't it? She was born to be in front of the camera. That's what they used to say, remember?"

In front of the camera. I can't grasp what he's talking about. My fingers scrabble the sheet. I can't get away. Can't comprehend . . . until he opens the case and pulls out the strap. Until he flips the cap off the lens.

"Is this what you were looking for?"

Embossed lettering, *Leonie K-L.* Her camera. *He has her camera.*

"Your friend Tony was so obliging. I had no idea if they'd even develop after all this time. I couldn't let him spoil the surprise though, could I?"

I'm watching myself from a thousand miles away. *Antonio DiPaci* . . . My mind can't piece it together. Everything is fragmented. Antonio DiPaci is dead. *I couldn't let him spoil the surprise.* My pictures. Leonie's pictures. I've got Leonie's pictures, they're at the cottage . . .

"I think they came out pretty well, huh?"

Josh's weight lifts abruptly. I scramble backwards into the headboard.

"No," I sob. "No . . ."

There's no choice but to see.

They're smudged with thumbprints. Not Leonie's photos. He casts them onto the bed, a handful of them, and my eyes are drawn to them even though I don't want to look, I don't want to know.

The floor of the beach hut, scattered with sand. Babycham, beer bottles, the boy from the arm-wrestle and the heir apparent. Another: a stubbed-out cigarette, black tape, school blazers strewn on sandy boards.

"What do you think?"

A third. *Leonie.* Contorted sideways, her wrists duct-taped behind her arched back, her shirt torn open. She's fighting, fighting with everything she's got . . .

A fourth—

"Did I get the light right? The composition?"

"Stop," I sob, retch. "*Stop . . .*"

Leonie, again, her head gripped between someone's hands so that she can't move, her mouth taped, her eyes wild with rage and terror.

I gag, heave. And then his hands are on me, dragging me down. His knees pin mine, his weight so brutally heavy that I feel like something's going to break. I gasp in pain.

"We took her for a little lesson. Marco was up for anything. He kept her still for me."

There were three of them. Blazers, on the floor. It hits me, a devastating, crashing wave. Three of them; she didn't stand a chance. She never stood a chance . . .

"Zach wasn't so sure. He almost bottled it." Josh smirks. "But by the time Marcus was done with her, fuck . . . there was no going back by then. He dared me to finish it off. I don't think he actually believed I'd do it."

His eyes travel over the pictures. His hand is at my neck, his fingers toying with the locket. With one sharp jerk, he pulls it off, snapping the chain.

"But it felt so good. So fucking good . . ." His thumb and index finger return to my throat, crushing my windpipe.

Panic jerks my limbs; I try frantically to swallow, to blink the darkness away, the images: *Leonie, again, defiled and limp, her green eyes glassy, the floor speckled with blood* . . .

He killed my sister. There's a rushing in my ears, senseless noise, and it's closing in. He killed my sister, and now . . .

Now?

No one knows I'm here. No one knows.

Krzysztof Woźniak. The pain is crippling. Saliva is pooling in my mouth. Antonio DiPaci. *Vesna*. The realisation is blinding.

"*Vesna* . . ." I splutter. Stars are bursting in front of my eyes. I claw at his forearm with both hands. But he's wearing long sleeves. He doesn't even flinch.

"Who? Oh. The au pair?"

He releases his grip. I gulp a stridulous breath.

"She phoned my father the night before you came back. She wanted to 'share her concerns', apparently. She tried to tell Lara. No one wanted to listen. Turns out . . ." He snorts. "Turns out she'd spotted Woźniak's car on the Blakemans' drive that night. What're the chances? She didn't put it all together, though. Not for all those years. Not until February, when Richard ended up on the stroke unit."

Saliva has run into my hair. I gulp desperately. The stroke unit . . .

"Zachary didn't recognise her. But she remembered him. She took a very interesting video without them realising. Sent it to Dad — she couldn't take it to the police — luckily. I'm fairly sure it's illegal to video your patients."

The stroke unit. The lightning bolt earths. *Zach almost bottled it* . . . The boy from the arm-wrestle. The man who walked into me in the stroke unit doorway when I was trying to track down Vesna.

"Fuck. You want to see?" Josh kneels back. A cry of pain forces itself between my lips. "Why the fuck not? He forwarded it."

He produces his phone. I snatch for it.

"Uh-uh . . . Easy, Rosy . . ." He lifts it out of reach. "No playing around. Not yet."

"*. . . this. Then . . . u . . . ear . . .*"

A crackle, distortion. A hiss of movement.

"*Of course I know what you did. He's been paying me for twenty years to keep quiet about it.*"

"*We can't sell it.*"

"*Unless you want to live the rest of your lives with that little gem under your inheritance, then you'll fucking have to. You break the car up, you fill that pit with concrete and you get the house on the bloody market, got it?*"

"She thought Dad might want to know someone was paying Richard Blakeman to keep quiet . . . What a discovery."

The smile hasn't faded from his lips.

"There aren't many people round here who can afford to pay for silence though are there, Rosy? Your parents . . . *My* parents . . . Your au pair didn't consider her options very carefully, did she? She mentioned she was planning a trip over to see you at Hailbury. And that would've fucked everything."

He turns off the phone. Tosses it onto the floor, out of reach.

"She was collateral damage. But you . . . you're so much more than collateral damage."

Josh's lips brush my hair.

"*So* much more."

Another shudder rips through me. *A nightmare . . .* a place between asleep and awake, paralysed and mute. Where you scream for help, and it's silent.

"You see, I had to share Leonie . . ."

He glances sideways. At the rubble sacks. The rope. *The rope.*

"But the Blakemans are a bit caught up tonight."

There's more. Duct tape, rolls of it. A box of nitrile gloves. Bolt cutters, from the pickup; they're all from the pickup. A phone, a car key, *a gilet* . . .

"What—" I sob. "What have you *done*?"

Tears of terror are squeezing themselves from the corners of my eyes.

"Oh, Rosy." He takes my chin in his hand. Inside the gloves, his hands are wet with sweat.

"Don't worry. They won't kill him. I need him."

Josh shifts his weight and the photos slide, a glossy cascade onto the carpet. He's reaching for something. The tape. I buck, try to kick. The tears run into my ears; I scream and for the first time the sound registers before he yanks the tape across my mouth, a rending of adhesive, the pluck of breaking fibres.

"You're right. It's all his. I found everything I needed in his truck. Going to look pretty bad for him when you're discovered in the back of it. And I bet they'll find him all over you, won't they?"

The breath. *Focus on the breath.* I try to tune him out, but I can't. *You'd make a beautiful corpse.*

"Like father, like son — it'll be like it's all come full circle . . ."

The gilet. It's a rush, a breaking wave. *Kacper's gilet.* The multitool is in the pocket. If I could reach . . .

"It's in the garage." Josh picks up the camera and toys with the strap. The first flash blinds me.

"So it turns out that Miller has his uses. Or should I say Woźniak?"

I force my eyes open against the light. The gilet's so close to the bed. So close, heaped against the bedside table . . .

I let myself go limp, let my arm fall to dangle uncomfortably over the side. Josh shifts and the flash goes off again. *Focus. Connect with the breath.* My fingertips are touching nylon and goose-down.

But it's too late. The camera drops on its strap. His fingers are feeling around the roll of tape for the end. My throat seems to have closed.

"Truck's got a tracker," I lie, wildly.

It's muffled, inaudible. Josh pauses.

"His pickup," I try again. Louder. The inside of my mouth is woolly and thick.

He rips back the tape.

"*What* did you say?"

"His truck's got a tracker," I gasp. "Kacper's truck has a tracker."

"Bullshit, Rosy." His voice is very soft. My lips are bleeding; I can taste it. He wipes them with his thumb. But his smirk isn't quite watertight. I see his gaze dart to the window.

He kneels back.

I can feel the stitching of the pocket. I can feel the stainless steel, cool and hard on my fingertips . . . closer, closer . . .

And then he's on top of me, and I fold my palm shut and bite back my scream. And the world is darkening at the edges, and I focus on the breath, *the breath*, and the notch in the edge of the blade, easing it outwards . . .

Her name is on my lips. The only thought that's left. *Leonie.*

Be afraid. Be fearless.

I thrust upwards. Shirtsleeve, skin. With a snarled profanity, Joshua London lets go.

And then I stab again, lower this time, burying the knife to its hilt in his thigh. And the last thing I see as I drag myself off the bed is the twist of rage in his face.

I land on all fours. Stagger to my feet. Grab the door to support me, the banister. The stairs are wide, echoing; I miss my footing and fall the last two, lurch across the hall. The catch, the lock: my fingers are too weak, slippery, slick with sweat. With blood.

Somehow, I get it open. The drive is empty except the Tesla. Jericho is miles from anywhere.

A flurry of raindrops. Gravel. I stumble, tasting vomit. My ears are ringing, sweat breaking cold on my top lip. Water is tumbling from the fountain, spilling into the pool at its base, deafening white noise. Garages. There are garages, seven or eight of them. Wooden doors. The end ones are pushed to, not shut. They won't close; whatever's inside is too long. I'm lightheaded with realisation: *it's in the garage.* The pickup. He meant the pickup.

Dusty metallic charcoal. I feel my way along the side to the driver's door. It's unlocked. The latch opens with a clunk.

The leather is warm, the air muted as I shut the door. The smell overpowers me, pine, woodsmoke . . . Kacper's house keys are in the cup holder.

But everything else is on the guest room floor.

"*Shit,*" I sob. "*Shit.*"

I fumble with the controls. There's a button for the locks. I find it and the indicator lights reflect off the brickwork, throwing the figure on Jericho's steps into sharp relief.

I was here, ready for you, all this time . . .

Fear pools in my gut. I jam my fingers down harder on the switch.

Please. Please, God.

Then, with a flash of orange lights that flare as they fade, Josh holds up the key.

CHAPTER 39

Kacper

"Otwórz oczy." *Open your eyes.*

She's speaking to me in Polish. I try to do what she says.

"Posłuchaj mnie." *Listen to me.* "Musisz otworzyć oczy." *You need to open your eyes.*

Her voice is in gentle harmony with the ringing in my ears. Has she always been here, waiting? Is Tata here, too? I didn't expect it would be so dark. That it would hurt so much. She's cradling my head in her hands, like a child. I find my fingers, screw them tight into my palms, struggle to force my eyes open.

"Gdzie . . ." My lips are dry, cracked. No sound seems to come out. "Gdzie jest Tata?"

I strain my eyes to see, but the pain resounds like a gunshot and I have to close them again.

"Musisz otworzyć oczy."

The voice grows sharper. More familiar. My eyelids jolt open. The ceiling moves in a haze.

"Zadzwoniłem po karetkę." *I've called an ambulance.*

Her face comes into focus suddenly. Not the face from Tata's photo, not the one I was expecting. I blink. Iryna. *Iryna?*

She's pale and grim; her phone is on the floor beside us. An ambulance. What?

"Rosalie . . ." I wrench upright.

Rosalie. The Blakemans. The blue car. . . Somehow I'm on my feet. I was too late.

"Ssh. Czekać." *Wait.* Iryna's hands reach for my shoulders. "Karetkę. Ssh."

"No." My voice cracks. "*No.* I can't wait for an ambulance. Rosalie. I've got to . . ." I thrust past her for the door. The door? Pine panelling, it's pitch black. I spin, disorientated.

"I've got to get to Jericho. Rosalie . . ." I'm barely coherent. I grip my hair, fighting the panic, tears. My head is splitting in two. I couldn't get to her in time. After everything, I wasn't there. "*Rosalie . . .*"

Iryna takes a step away. I see her gaze dart to the wall behind me then back to my face, sharp and urgent as I stumble to the door and try it. It's locked.

"*Rosalie.*" The urgency is in her voice, too.

Locked, but how could it be locked? I make to try again, but she grabs my wrist.

"Ssh."

For a second I don't understand.

"Oni są na zewnątrz." Iryna jerks her head. *They're outside.*

Outside. The car park. The King Edward Arms. The truck . . . Everything is confused. Iryna's fingers close momentarily around my arm.

"W samochodzie. Oni oglądają." *In a car. They're watching.*

I glance over her shoulder. The front door is ajar. She came in the front. And they're still at the back: Zach and Marcus. I reel another step away.

Josh London.

He made me come here. They could have killed me, but they didn't. He made sure I'd be here, that I wouldn't be able to get to her. That I'd know . . .

I feel the shudders rip through me.

"Vesna wiedział."

Iryna's voice startles me. She's moved towards the crack of light that's coming from the front doors. Her phone is in her hand and her eyes are on my face.

"Vesna wiedział." *Vesna knew.*

She tosses me something. I catch it, uncomprehending. Car keys.

"Będę odwróceniem uwagi. Szybko. Go to her. *Go.*"

I stare, not quite grasping. The keys are in my hand. Iryna's car keys. She opens the door and slips outside.

"*What?*" I whisper.

Outside . . .

The air hits my face, an assault of rain and wind as I stumble onto the terrace.

Iryna's already gone. I can see her between the huts. She climbs nimbly down the bank. Then she puts her phone to her ear and walks, brazen and unflinching, across the concrete towards the waiting car.

For a split second, I can't move. Everything is closing in. The sea is breaking over the seawall, salt spray lashing my face as I finally process what she said.

Będę odwróceniem uwagi.

I will be a distraction.

I hear the sudden screech of tyres. The clash of a horn. The slam of a car door—

And then I break into a run.

CHAPTER 40

Rosalie

Unlocked. I scramble backwards in the seat, gasping. He's unlocked the doors. I jam my fingers down on the button again. I can hear my breath in my throat. *It's all come full circle.*

There's no dividing wall between the garages. I can see into the next one and the next, a whole row of cars. The closest is dark blue or grey, not quite black; the nearside is smashed in and there are stickers in the rear screen: *Dogs die in hot cars, Give Blood, Slava Ukraini.* The ceaseless, jarring blast of a horn is ringing in my ears. *Collateral damage.*

Vesna.

"Oh God—" The realisation chokes off in my throat.

The garage doors swing fully open, a wave of fading, rain-soaked sunset. The key is still dangling from Josh's fingers as he approaches the driver's door. My clothes snag the hand-brake. The passenger door . . . If I can get to the door. . . I close my fingers around the handle. If I can just—

It's too close to the wall. Metal slams, grates against brick. Not enough. *It's not enough.*

There's a smile on his lips. His eyes lock mine through the window; I can see her reflection in them, screaming, fighting him off. But it's too late. She couldn't stop him. I can't stop him.

The blood has soaked a dark patch on his sleeve. Another on his chinos, spreading through the fibres of his pocket, reaching. Not enough, *he's still coming* . . .

His grip closes around the handle. The silence reaches fever pitch in my ears, deafening: the fade to black, dread-sick and still. The clunk of the latch.

She doesn't define you.

The seal of the door breaks, peels open . . .

Then it stops.

Still coming . . .

But he isn't. The door clicks closed.

Josh spins.

I hear, before I see. The crunch of tyres, skidding wheels, flying stones. The sound seems to fade in and out. Feet. Voices. I claw my way upright in the seat.

"What the fuck are *you* doing here?"

"Get the *fuck* away from her!"

And the whole world stops.

His voice. His voice, raw and raging. Breaking, tearing itself from his throat. And I can see him.

Kacper.

"I know what you did!" His chest: heaving, sobbing. The words cracking on his lips. "*I know what you did!* Get the *fuck* away!"

Blood, tracked and dried. Rain, filth. Fury: it's there, in his face. The crash is sickening. Bodies, metal; they collide by the front wing, grappling . . . And then his fingers are around the key, *the key*, and he prises it from Josh's hand . . .

And he swings—

Joshua London staggers sideways, the force of the punch sending him reeling. I watch in slow motion as he raises his head, blood running from his nose. And the chill in his eyes sends a bolt of terror down my spine. "You . . . *framed* . . . *my father* . . ."

Kacper lunges. His grip closes, white-knuckled at Josh's throat, pinning him against the bonnet. I see the tremor in his arms, the shudder of rage, the final split-second pause before Josh grabs back with his left hand and they teeter, off balance: a scuffle, a swing—

Josh punches low. A brutal, right-handed blow to the chest. Kacper flinches at the impact.

And then he lets go.

For a second it doesn't register.

I see him take a failed breath in. See the frown of realisation flicker across his face. Incomprehension. Dread.

The pickup key falls into the gravel.

Behind him the reflections on the bricks are blue, a fluorescent pulsation of light that splinters through every shadow except the one in his eyes. The one that's extinguished the colours in the grey.

You can be anything. Anything in the world.

Then he stumbles. His hands hit the bonnet first. His hip, his arm . . .

Joshua London flips the blade of the multitool closed.

I remembered you. Kacper Woźniak.

He twists as he falls. A final scuff of stones. Out of sight, out of reach. All that's left is the endless flash of light, sun breaking between clouds, forget-me-nots and soft green grass, the memory of the wind in the dunes, a haunting, reverberating sob of realisation and truth.

I didn't think I could remember anything. But I remembered you.

"No," I gasp. "*No!*"

And the sob is in my throat too, visceral and suffocating. I struggle for the door, spill out as it opens, legs buckling under me. There are more tyres on the gravel, cars, boots. It's too late. Full circle. Everything's fractured. Collapsing.

"Please . . ." It breaks from my lips, shuddering and uncontainable. "Please, no . . ."

Josh lowers his hand. He doesn't look round. He looks down, instead, unconcerned, vaguely repulsed. The tiniest sneer plays at the corner of his lips.

"Self-defence," he shrugs. "Scumbag."

He pushes him aside with his foot. Faded anger. Dark ink. Sweat on skin. And then he walks away, hands held up at his sides, a gesture of innocence towards the oncoming uniforms and jackets.

Innocence. The boy with grey eyes, turning the other cheek. *I was never going to change what people believed, Rosalie . . .* Kisses, chlorine-tasting and careful, the smile of the child, set free.

And as the clouds close over our heads, as the sun finally surrenders to the horizon, he's gone. Leaping down from the coat pegs. Turning away, hand thrust deep in the pocket of his shorts, lunchbox swinging; *I'm not sure I've ever been close to anyone.*

I fall to my knees.

I was wrong. Wrong to think there was an absolution. A place for us. Those stories weren't ours. They weren't mine to commit to paper; I could never have captured them with my words the way that Antonio DiPaci would have with his camera: happiness shining powerful and vulnerable, bitter-dark and perfect.

The picture has faded, left too long in the light. There's only the rain on the gravel, the give and patter of fingers on keys, the words that I thought would save us.

the end.

I won't write it. I can't.

Not for him.

So I'll let the gates creep closed instead, shutting off the shrubs and barring the beeches from the world. I'll let Hailbury have its secrets — I'll leave it to keep them — Du Maurier's ashes, blowing towards us with the salt-wind from the sea, the scattering of shells that break underfoot, the fluttering red leaves. I'll highlight, and I'll delete.

And perhaps . . .

Just perhaps . . .

I'll forget.

POSTSCRIPT

The stars shine no matter what. The ones in the raw night sky, between the ripped shreds of the clouds. The ones that glitter like treasure in the band of wet sand left by the tide, waiting to be scooped up, pocketed, carried away.

There are two girls playing. The oldest must be ten or thereabouts; her hair is long and wavy, stiffened by the salt and swept sideways by the wind. Her skin is tanned deep brown — from too many long summer days, not enough regard for the ministrations of her parents — the factor fifty has fallen by the wayside. She's standing tall on the dune, legs shiny and shingle-grimy, arms outstretched to receive the gifts and treasures: razor clams and crab claws, slimy seaweed pockets and tiny cowries, a starfish in a bucket clasped in chubby, sandy hands.

The smallest must be no more than three. Her hair is salt-stiff, too, and stuck in dreadlocks of mud and candyfloss, damp and happy as she relays her haul back and forth from the ocean.

I watch them for a long time, the exchanges that dart between them, exclamations of glee, encouragements and lisp-whispered confidences, until my heart hurts and the horizon beckons instead, and I turn my gaze on the sea.

I think of walking out into the waves, and the way the dust descended through the water, the flowers floating memorials on the tide.

I didn't forget.

The bench is unchanged. Still red, still rusty at the back. Warm from the sun. Once I couldn't remember. Now, I can't stop remembering. There's a ship, tracking along the line where the sky meets the sea. *Ferries, they sail out of Hull.* The bittersweet pull of a smile, neither wry nor hidden, the gentle blur of tears. I wrap my arms around my knees.

Do you need a minute?

The pain in my chest is unbearable. I screw my fingernails into the enamel. Try to breathe.

It's September now. The summer is almost gone. Lara Lee Knight's biography is on indefinite hold and *#rosaliesroom* has been taken away in boxes. I heard they brought it back, but I haven't been to look. They found Leonie's remains at the beach hut, under the uneven slabs. She never left. We never flew to Paris.

I've wondered, often, what's behind the gates now. Without anyone to make sure the shrubs are tamed and the bulbs are planted and the doors are painted. How long it takes for nature to begin to reclaim, for the lawns to become meadow grass, pastures grazed only by dappled deer that flit shy and transient like the fall of the light between the trees. What it's like, in the early morning, when no one else is up, and the only sound is the birdsong.

I start at the touch of a hand on my shoulder. Iryna's face is bronzed from summer, too, and the creases around her eyes have deepened. I didn't hear her footfalls. The clouds in the sky behind her are scudding and black, the colour of her clothes, outlining the beach huts with darkness.

I stand at her gesture. She doesn't speak. I nod in wordless reply. It's time to go. The tears in her eyes gleam bright, unshed. Her fingers tighten on the sleeve of my dress, crumpling the black polyester.

There are puddles along the bottom of the seawall. A boy, kicking a ball, a soft thwack as it lands in the water and splinters the surface. The trace of a breeze hurries the litter along the promenade as we walk in silence back towards the town. By the time we reach the slipway the sun has broken the clouds. We corner the railings, the wind chasing one last dalliance with the seaweed and sweet wrappers around our feet. For a moment, I can't see at all.

And then he steps forwards, out of the glare. The incarnation of every memory: discarded rage and abandoned expectations.

Of course I didn't forget.

Not a single, gut-wrenching moment. The police cars. Sandeep running across the gravel. Clothes cut through with rip-shears, blood, stones. The air ambulance that landed in the deer park.

He's waiting, keys in hand. I'm not sure who caught who looking. His eyes darken, every colour, between the shades of grey. I realise I'm holding my breath. Kacper pushes the key into his pocket.

"Are you ready?" he says at last, and his voice is soft and real.

I nod. "We need to go?"

"Yeah."

Salt spray, the suck of the sea. We could be the only two people left on earth. Iryna has drawn ahead, leaving us to our contemplation. I glance back out at the ship, and Kacper's gaze follows mine. We stand, disregarding our own instruction, fingers interwoven, words unsaid.

"Come on," he murmurs.

We catch Iryna up by the playground. The swings drift in the breeze. There's a train in the station, a noisy shudder of diesel smoke and the hiss of doors. I imagine Leonie embarking, a last look over her shoulder, teeth blanching the blood from her red, red lips, the determination shining from her eyes. *Wherever you end up, I'll find you, ok?*

It was Vesna's cremation this morning. We scattered her ashes in the sea. She had no family to come, only us: the people she'd tried to save. The car at Jericho was hers, the car from the ditch. The Blakemans run a car recovery business; they'd towed it out not long after I found it. Her body was hidden in bushes a short walk from the crash site. She'd been on her way to tell me the truth. The one that would have changed everything.

Harriet realised the danger, from the picture that Kacper sent. She remembered Marcus's car. Iryna phoned her as she climbed down the sandbank to buy Kacper's escape; Harriet heard everything down the phone: the scuffle, the shouting, and she called 999. The police arrived at Hailbury first, only to find there was no one there. Sandeep drove straight from Armsby and almost got to Jericho before them. Harriet had worked it out by then.

I gesture Iryna at the front seat of the truck, doggedly rejecting her protests, and climb into the back. We're short on time; it's going to be tight to make it back by three. I look at the bob of her sleek black hair as we accelerate out of town towards the downward roll of the hills. Without her, none of us would be here. By the time Marcus Blakeman realised what she was doing and drove his car at her, by the time Zach got out to chase Kacper down, they'd lost him. Unlike me, she even had the wherewithal to take the reg plates.

We walked in the woods last night. As the sun went down on the nettles and ferns and the ravaged earth, the scars still fresh and raw from where they exhumed Krzysztof Woźniak's body. He'd taken the flashlight, gone to join the search. We'll never know for sure which of the Blakemans killed him. He was found in the clearing, less than a hundred yards from where Kacper dug up the car key. And all I could think was that he'd been there, all that time. Watching over the lonely boy and his bike, building his ridges and jumps. *A safe place.*

We buried him in the churchyard in Shellingsby, beside Jeanette. Where the forget-me-nots grow.

* * *

Three thirty-five. We were late; the roads back from the airport were gridlocked. The green is empty. Everyone else is gone, the shouts ringing into the distance as I stride across the grass. There's a jet plane in the sky, a tiny speck, almost too high to make out. But it leaves a trail in its wake, a clean cut in the blue.

Someone has dropped a sweatshirt under the trees. I pause to pick it up from amongst the Colchicaceae and drape it over one of the empty bike racks. A few leaves are starting to fall, teased free by the gathering wind. I look back up.

He's standing at the school gate, sweatshirt tied around his waist, backpack on his back, his face up against the close mesh weave of the fence. His knees are bony beneath the hem of his shorts; he's grown taller over the summer. He's staring down at his second-hand shoes, scuffing his feet against the bottom of the fence. The last one, the very last, left far behind the fading echoes of laughter, conversation, *how was your day?* Pretending not to care that he's alone, that no one's come. Pretending that behind the scowl there aren't tears, waiting to spill.

I hang back, rest my hand on the bike rack. The metal is cool and hard and I curl my fingers against it.

The teacher touches his shoulder, and he looks up. She unlocks the gate.

Yvan stops dead. I see his mouth move.

"Mama? *Moja Mama?*"

There's a couple of seconds before the sound gets out. As the gate swings wide. As the backpack falls, forgotten, in the first drift of September leaves.

"Mama!"

I think of mountain bikes and helmets. Of a flashlight in the dark. A last kiss goodnight.

Elena is on her knees. Her arms close, folding tight, and her shoulders are racked with sobs. They're too far away for me to hear. Enclosed in a world that suddenly isn't mine, not anymore. I turn back towards the truck, watching the jet plane disappear into the glare.

It's gone, and the light is blinding.

Jeanette's voice is an echo, nothing more.

"*Beautiful boy*," she breathes.

THE END

THE JOFFE BOOKS STORY

We began in 2014 when Jasper agreed to publish his mum's much-rejected romance novel and it became a bestseller.

Since then we've grown into the largest independent publisher in the UK. We're extremely proud to publish some of the very best writers in the world, including Joy Ellis, Faith Martin, Caro Ramsay, Helen Forrester, Simon Brett and Robert Goddard. Everyone at Joffe Books loves reading and we never forget that it all begins with the magic of an author telling a story.

We are proud to publish talented first-time authors, as well as established writers whose books we love introducing to a new generation of readers.

We won Trade Publisher of the Year at the Independent Publishing Awards in 2023. We have been shortlisted for Independent Publisher of the Year at the British Book Awards for the last four years, and were shortlisted for the Diversity and Inclusivity Award at the 2022 Independent Publishing Awards. In 2023 we were shortlisted for Publisher of the Year at the RNA Industry Awards.

We built this company with your help, and we love to hear from you, so please email us about absolutely anything bookish at feedback@joffebooks.com

If you want to receive free books every Friday and hear about all our new releases, join our mailing list: www.joffebooks.com/contact

And when you tell your friends about us, just remember: it's pronounced Joffe as in coffee or toffee!